LORDS & LADIES
COLLECTION

*Two Glittering Regency
Love Affairs*

Miss Verey's Proposal
by Nicola Cornick

&

The Rebellious Debutante
by Meg Alexander

The Regency

LORDS & LADIES
COLLECTION

The Regency

LORDS & LADIES
COLLECTION

Nicola Cornick &
Meg Alexander

*M&B™ and M&B™ with the Rose Device
are trademarks of the publisher.
Harlequin Mills & Boon Limited, Eton House,
18-24 Paradise Road, Richmond, Surrey TW9 1SR*

First published in Great Britain in 2000 and 2002

THE REGENCY LORDS & LADIES COLLECTION
© Harlequin Books S.A. 2009

The publisher acknowledges the copyright holders of the
individual works as follows:

Miss Verey's Proposal © Nicola Cornick 2000
The Rebellious Debutante © Meg Alexander 2002

ISBN: 978 0 263 86721 3

052-0109

*Printed and bound in Spain
by Litografia Rosés S.A., Barcelona*

Miss Verey's Proposal
by
Nicola Cornick

Nicola Cornick is passionate about many things: her country cottage and its garden, her two small cats, her husband and her writing, though not necessarily in that order! She has always been fascinated by history, both as her chosen subject at university and subsequently as an engrossing hobby. She works as a university administrator and finds her writing the perfect antidote to the demands of life in a busy office.

Prologue

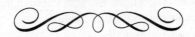

'Say you'll do it, Jane! Oh, please say you will!'

Miss Sophia Marchment leant forward, blue eyes pleading, golden ringlets a-tremble.

Jane Verey bit her lip, looking troubled. 'Oh, Sophy, I would truly love to, but—'

But the truth was that Miss Verey liked her food all too well and her friend was suggesting the unthinkable. Sophia's face fell a little.

'But, Jane, it is such an adventure! If you go to bed without supper and do not look behind you, you will dream of your future husband!' Sophia clapped her hands. 'Why, to my mind it is worth any amount of food!'

Jane thought longingly of the fresh loaf she had watched Cook bake only that day, the newly churned butter and the thick slices of ham that had been steeped in ale. Her mouth watered. No, it was impossible…

Sophia was pushing the book of legends towards her. The binding was coming loose and there was a dusty smell and crackling paper that implied great antiquity. Reluctantly, Jane peered at the faded words.

'...for if you go supperless to bed on St Agnes Eve and take care not to look behind, you will conjure dreams of your future husband...'

The bare branches of the oak outside Jane's window tapped impatiently on the glass. She jumped. Sophia was leaning forward, her golden curls gleaming in the candlelight.

'You see! Tonight is St Agnes Eve! Oh, Jane, do not condemn me to do this alone!'

Jane could foresee all manner of practical difficulties. How was one to close the bedroom door without looking behind? How was a dream to be interpreted if it contained not one man, but two—or even three? She was about to confront Sophia with these problems when her friend spoke again.

'Molly, the second parlourmaid, *swears* that it is true, Jane! Twice now she has tested the legend and on both occasions she dreamed of Gregory Pullman, the farrier, so she knows it must be true!'

Jane could not see the logic of this. The last time she had seen the farrier he had been attempting to tumble a maid behind the stables and the girl had certainly not been Molly.

'Does Gregory realise yet that he is to marry Molly?' she inquired practically. 'It might be twenty years or more before he grasps the truth, by which time she will have become a sour old maid! And is this not the same girl who washed her face in dew on a May morning, swearing it would make her beautiful, then caught the cowpox—?'

Sophia dismissed this with a wave of one white hand. 'Oh, Jane, how you do run on! It will do you no harm to miss your supper just this once.' Her blue eyes considered her friend's more-than-ample form.

'And you may dream of some desperately handsome man! Oh, please…'

Jane's stomach made a monstrous rumbling noise. To starve herself voluntarily seemed an intolerable thought, but Sophia was looking quite wretched.

'Oh, very well,' she capitulated reluctantly, reflecting that Sophia would never know if she got up in the middle of the night and went in search of some food.

Three hours later, Sophia had returned to Penistone Manor and Jane had trailed off to bed, looking very sorry for herself, but remembering not to look behind her.

'It's not natural, madam,' Cook complained to Lady Verey. 'A growing girl of fifteen should not be refusing her food like that! Why, she'll waste away!'

'Jane's growing in more than one direction!' Simon, her elder brother, said heartlessly but with some truth. 'She can live off her fat for a while!'

In the middle of the night Jane awoke, suffering from huge hunger pangs. The wind had increased whilst it was dark and small flurries of rain hit the glass in the windows. Disappointingly, Jane could not remember having a single dream, despite the fact that she had followed her instructions exactly. But perhaps, on a full stomach, she might have more success…

She slid out of bed, shivering in her thin cotton nightdress. She almost changed her mind when she thought of the warm, downy nest of sheets and blankets she had just left. The door creaked a little on its hinges as she started to open it and the dark passageway stretched away towards the top of the stairs. Jane had never been a superstitious child, but suddenly the old house of Ambergate and its shadowy corners seemed unfamiliar and unfriendly. Jane braced herself. She was about to push the door wide and take her courage in both hands when she heard a step at the top of the stairs.

A man was just turning the corner and coming down the corridor towards her. Jane shrank back with a gasp. The door was only open a crack, but through the narrow aperture she could see him clearly, for he carried a candle in one hand. She knew that she had never seen him before in her life, for she would most certainly have remembered. He could not be a servant and, for a moment, she wondered if he was in fact an apparition conjured up by a fevered mind that had been weakened by lack of food.

The first impression that Jane had was that he seemed very tall in the flickering candlelight and was clothed with an informality suitable only to his own dressing-room. His cravat hung loose and his white shirt was unbuttoned at the neck, revealing the strong brown column of his throat. His pantaloons clung to muscular thighs and the candlelight reflected on the mirror-polish of his Hessians. Jane caught her breath, staring in strange fascination. He was very dark, with silky black hair that seemed to gleam in the faint light. One dark lock fell across his forehead and he flicked it back with an impatient hand. His black brows were drawn together in a frown that made the saturnine face seem even more forbidding. Then those dark eyes turned thoughtfully towards Jane's door and she shrank back even further into the shadows, convinced that he had seen her. For a long moment he seemed to hesitate, staring directly at her door, before disappearing. There was no sound but for the soft click of a door closing further down the corridor.

Some ten minutes later, Jane found that she was able to move again and dived into the refuge of her bed, all pangs of hunger banished by fright. It was even longer before she was able to sleep, convinced that she had definitely seen an intruder or a ghost and reluctant to leave her room for help against either. Eventually she fell into an uneasy sleep and dreamed of the dark stranger who stalked the corridors of Ambergate.

When she woke in the morning, both her common sense and her appetite were restored.

'Why did you not tell me that we had a house guest, Mama?' she inquired, at breakfast, helping herself to two portions of kedgeree. 'I saw a gentleman in the corridor last night and was almost caught in my shift!'

Lady Verey exchanged a look with her husband, who cleared his throat but said nothing.

'We have no guests, my love,' Lady Verey said, giving her daughter a sweet smile. 'You must have been dreaming. And if you will eat cheese before you go to bed...'

'I had no supper last night and I did not dream it!' Jane declared stoutly, but she knew she was fighting a losing battle. Her mother's face wore the gentle but stubborn smile that meant that a topic was closed. Her father rustled his newspaper loudly.

'Always has her nose in a book,' he said shortly. 'Mistake. Shouldn't let the girl read. Stands to reason.'

Lady Verey turned her sweet smile on her spouse. 'Just so, my dear. Do you go into Penistone today? Perhaps Jane could accompany you—I have an errand for her with Mrs. Marchment…'

A meaningful glance passed between husband and wife. 'Simon is out riding already,' Lady Verey continued contentedly. 'He will be gone hours, I dare guess…'

Thus it was that neither Jane nor her brother saw the lone horseman who made his way down the lime avenue some two hours later. And though the servants talked amongst themselves, they all heeded Lady Verey's stricture that no one was to tell Jane or Simon of the visitor on pain of dismissal.

'What did you dream about, Jane?' Sophia demanded, when Lord Verey had conveyed her friend to the Manor in the gig. She did not wait for a reply. '*I* had the most extraordinary dream about a young man—he was *so* handsome, fair haired and blue eyed, and most dashing. I declare…' she clasped her hands together '…he *must* be my future husband!'

'I did not dream,' Jane said firmly. 'I had no dreams all night long.' She resolutely pushed away the image of the man she had seen in the corridor. She was certain that she had been awake when she first saw him; though she had dreamed of him later, surely that could not count. Sophia's face fell.

'No dreams? But, Jane, how dreadful! That must mean you are destined to be an old maid!'

Jane shrugged her plump shoulders, a mannerism that her mother deplored. 'I am persuaded that it would be better for me not to marry,' she said, her mouth full of Mrs. Marchment's cake and jam. 'I should not make anyone a conformable wife.'

Sophia was on the verge of loyally disagreeing when something stopped her. There was no doubt that Jane was the best friend ever, but she was not like anyone else.

'Perhaps you might meet a gentleman willing to overlook your odd ideas—' She broke off, blushing a little. 'Oh, Jane, I am certain that there must be a gentleman suitable for you!'

Jane did not bother to argue. She already understood that it would only make Sophia uncomfortable if she insisted on being different. Besides, her friend's next words summed up Jane's dilemma and there was no arguing with them.

'Oh, Jane,' Sophia said sadly, 'you have to marry! You must! For what else would you do?'

Chapter One

Four years later

It was late at night when Miss Jane Verey's laggardly suitor finally arrived at Ambergate. Dinner had been held for hours until Cook had complained bitterly that the sauce béarnaise had curdled and the pheasant compote had dried out and stuck to the serving dish. With a sigh and a glance at the clock, Lady Verey had had the food brought in and had eaten alone with her daughter, both of them uncomfortable in the unaccustomed finery donned especially for their visitor.

After dinner, they had sat for another hour in virtual silence, broken only by Lady Verey's plaintive cry of, 'But why does he not come? I am certain that he said the fifteenth! Perhaps he has had an accident on the road...'

Jane had fidgeted with her needlework, but had said nothing at all. There seemed to be little to say. After two months of vague promises and broken arrangements, Lord Philip Delahaye had still not honoured their agreement and met his chosen bride. He seemed a reluctant lover indeed, which sat ill with the information Jane had been given that the Delahaye match, as well as having her late father's blessing, was Lord Philip's most earnest desire.

Eventually, when Jane's yawns had become too pronounced to be ignored and the clock had chimed twelve, Lady Verey patted her daughter's cheek.

'You had best retire for the night, Jane. I shall wait up in case Lord Philip comes. Such disappointment is hard to bear, I know, but perhaps the morning will bring better news.'

Jane kissed her mother and went off to bed. She did not feel it necessary to explain that her disappointment amounted to very little at all. She had been persuaded to receive Lord Philip's addresses since it had been made very plain to her that they were now quite poor and that her father's dying wish was that her future be secured. Her brother Simon, the new Lord Verey, had been fighting with Wellington's armies and had not been heard of for a twelvemonth. Ambergate was falling about their ears and the servants stayed only out of loyalty. It was a melancholy picture.

It is not that I do not wish to marry, Jane thought, as she climbed the stairs in the candlelight, for I know I have very little choice. It is just that I imagined— hoped—that it might be so very different... And she thought of her henwitted friend Sophia Marchment, and could not help smiling. Sophia had imagined herself in love with no less than four young gentlemen in the last six months, but then she had remembered that none of them resembled the young man she had dreamed of so long ago on St Agnes Eve...

Jane had no illusions that her marriage would be

other than a business arrangement, a matter for sound common sense, and yet part of her wished for, if not a romantic passion, at least a mutual regard.

If I can just like him, she thought, then matters need not be so bad. And I hope that I *do* like him, for Mama can be most determined and I know that she means for the match to be made...

She stood before her bedroom mirror for a moment and wondered whether Lord Philip would like *her*. So familiar was she with her own features that Jane could scarcely see their charm. She decided that she looked rather like a cat, though admittedly a sleeker creature than the mangy tom that patrolled their stables. Her face had lost all its childhood fat and was now almost triangular, tapering from wide-set hazel eyes to a pointed little chin. Her mother was always telling her that she had the Verey nose, a delicate little projection that always looked weak on the face of Jane's male ancestors but suited her own proportions far better. The whole was framed by thick black hair as dark as night.

Jane sighed and started to undress for bed. She could see little to commend herself and did not rec-ognise her own intriguing mixture of innocence and allure. She donned her cotton nightdress hastily, for the spring evenings were still chilly and Ambergate had many draughts. Her best dress of slightly faded white silk was laid carefully aside, looking as forlorn as Jane felt.

It was five minutes after Jane had slipped into her bed that the front door bell pealed, harsh and loud in the night. It rang once, then several more times, with irritable repetition.

A loud male voice shouted, 'Deuce take it! Is the whole house asleep? Hello there! Wake up, I say!'

Jane slid out of bed and tiptoed along the corridor to the wide landing at the top of the stairs. She could see Bramson, the butler, hastily shrugging himself into his coat as he hurried to the door. The old man was almost visibly shaking at the shock of the sudden arrival and all the noise, and Jane could not but wish Lord Philip would leave the bell alone. The continuous jangling was giving her a headache.

Lady Verey herself now came running out of the parlour just as Bramson swung the door open. It was clear to Jane that her mother must have fallen asleep in front of the fire, for her coiffure had started to come down on one side and there was a vivid red mark on her cheek where it must have been pressed against the side of the chair. She had had no time to tidy herself and was straightening her dress with nervous fingers. Jane's heart went out to her as she saw the anxious look that creased Lady Verey's face. She was heartbreakingly eager for the visit to be a success.

'What the devil do you mean by keeping me standing out there in the cold!' The same loud, masculine voice demanded wrathfully, as Lord Philip stepped into the hall. 'You!' He pointed at Bramson. 'See to the stabling of my horses! They are worn to the bone by these devilish bad roads! And you...' he turned towards Lady Verey '...kindly take me to your mistress!'

With horror, Jane realised that he had mistaken her mother for the housekeeper. Fortunately, Lady Verey's good manners, if not Lord Philip's, were up to the occasion.

She dropped a slight curtsy.

'How do you do, sir. I am Clarissa Verey. I am sorry to hear you have had so poor a journey. Would you care for some refreshment before you retire?'

Jane waited to hear Lord Philip apologise for his late arrival, his poor manners or perhaps both. Instead, he looked down his nose as though he could not quite believe that the fright who was addressing him could really be the mistress of the house. He gave a slight bow. 'How do you do, ma'am. Some dinner would be excellent.'

'The servants are all abed,' Lady Verey said, colouring a little under Lord Philip's critical scrutiny. 'I hope a cold supper in your room will suit your lordship…'

Lord Philip gave a sigh. 'I suppose that will suffice! What extraordinary hours you do keep in the country, ma'am! Why, if this were London, we would only now be sitting down to our second course! Quite extraordinary!'

Jane shrank back into the shadows as her mother steered their guest towards the staircase, but she had ample chance to see Lord Philip's rather disparaging look as he took in the old-fashioned furnishings and the threadbare carpet. Something close to fury rose in her. She could see that Lady Verey was both offended and upset, but was bravely trying to maintain a flow of pleasantries as they mounted the stairs.

Lord Philip, however, was only concerned with the arrangements for his luggage and turned to shout over his shoulder at the footman, 'See to it that someone brings my bags up carefully, man! The last time I stayed in the country some dolt of a servant managed to ruin half my cravats with his man-handling!'

For a moment Jane indulged in the satisfying

thought of kicking Lord Philip's bags straight down the stairs, then she dived for her bedroom door as her mother ushered him down the corridor. She huddled under her covers, knees drawn up to her chin, and thought about what she had just seen and heard. How could this be her intended husband, this arrogant, boorish man who had made his contempt for country manners and country living so obvious in the space of only a few minutes? How could he humiliate his hostess so? His rudeness and scorn were not to be tolerated!

Her thoughts were distracted by the rattle of a tray and the chink of china. Lady Verey had sent hotfoot to the kitchens and even now she was labouring along the corridor, weighed down with food. Jane slipped out of bed again, opened her door a crack and pressed her ear to the gap. She heard the door of the green bedroom open and Lord Philip drawl in a tone very different from the one last used,

'Well, my pretty, what good fortune can have sent you to me?'

Jane pressed a hand to her mouth. Surely he could not be addressing Lady Verey! Then she realised that her mother must have left Lord Philip to the mercy of the servants and it was Betsey, the prettiest of the maids, who had run the errand. Betsey was giggling.

'I've brought your supper, sir!' There was a pertness in her tone that Jane had heard before when Betsey was flirting with the youngest footman, or Jack from the stables.

There was a crash and another giggle from the maid. 'Oh, sir! And you come a-courting here, as well! Whatever will Miss Verey say?'

'A pox on Miss Verey!' Jane heard Lord Philip say

lazily. 'What do I care for her? And a pox on this paltry dish! Here's one much more to my liking! You're a cosy armful—come and give me a kiss…'

The door swung closed. Jane, burning with a mixture of embarrassment and fury, slammed her own door, careless of the noise. How dared he! First to arrive so late that he missed dinner, then to scorn Lady Verey's hospitality and show his contempt for her home, and finally to seduce one of the maids before he was barely across the threshold! Jane knew that she would never accept Lord Philip now, even if he went down on bended knee.

Surely…*surely* Lady Verey would not insist on the match now… Jane shivered in the draught from the door. If only she could be that sure, but their situation was so perilous. With Simon missing, they had no one to protect them. The estate needed firm management and a great deal of hard work. Lord Verey's entire fortune was left to Simon, but for Lady Verey's widow's jointure and Jane's small dowry. It seemed inevitable that her mother would wish her to marry well and marry soon, perhaps so soon that she would be prepared to overlook Lord Philip's crass bad manners.

There was a crash in the corridor as Lord Philip ejected both the supper tray, contents scattered all over the floor, and a snivelling Betsey, who had evidently not received the reward she had expected for her services. Jane gritted her teeth as she heard the sobbing maid rush away downstairs. Enough was enough. She took a candle and crept through the adjoining door into the old nursery.

The nursery was cold and dark, the pale candle flame reflected in the window panes. Shivering, Jane tiptoed across to the huge Armada chest tucked into a corner, neglected for years since the Verey children had grown too old for dressing up. She dragged it out and threw back the lid. She was sure she remembered... Yes, there it was, the dress her governess, Miss Tring, had worn as the Wicked—and fat—Stepmother to Sophia's Cinderella. Sophia had made a lovely heroine, but Jane had preferred to play one of the Ugly Sisters, for she found the part more interesting. But Miss Tring's dress was perfect for her purpose. It had huge cushions sewn on the inside and had made her look outrageously obese. Then there were the little pads to fatten out the cheeks and the brown crayon for freckles. Jane gathered everything up into a hasty bundle and hurried back into her room. She had great deal to do before morning.

Lord Philip Delahaye was woken at some ungodly hour of the morning by a cock crowing outside his window. He groaned and turned over to bury his head in the pillow but the noise seemed to go on and on, skewering his brain. He vaguely remembered a pretty little maidservant and a large bottle of port... Groaning, he turned on to his back and flinched as the bedcurtains were flung wide and the light struck across his eyes.

'Good morning, my lord!' A voice trilled in his ear. 'Why, I declare you are quite a slug-a-bed! My mama said to let you sleep, but I declare you must be up and about and out riding with me before breakfast!'

Lord Philip opened his eyes very gingerly. Before him stood an apparition that seemed to have come straight from his feverish dreams. His incredulous gaze took in the mob-cap, perched on a frizz of black curls, the hugely fat figure and the mottled face. He goggled at her.

'Who the devil are you?'

'I am your affianced bride, my lord!' The apparition moved slightly so that the morning sun was directly behind her and gave a little simpering giggle. Lord Philip could see little more than a monstrous, dark shape menacing him from the side of the bed. He shrank back against the pillows.

'Beg you to retire, ma'am!' he stuttered. 'Whatever can your mama be thinking to allow you to visit a gentleman's chamber so early—'

'It is past six,' his future bride scolded, wagging a finger. 'What a shocking lazybones! Breakfast is served at seven and then we must be about to help with the milking and feed the pigs! This is a working farm, my lord, and there is much to be done!'

Lord Philip winced. The thought of breakfast brought on a rush of nausea and the sight of his bobbing, tittering bride made it much worse. He desperately tried to remember what his elder brother had told him about Miss Jane Verey. Alex had been very persuasive about the match, convincing him that it was the only way that he would have his debts paid and be given an increase in his allowance. Philip had reluctantly considered that a wife, provided that she was biddable and presentable, need not hamper his activities too much. Besides, the money had been the deciding factor.

He shuddered. He spent as little time as possible in the country and even its sporting pursuits did not interest him. He was a creature of the city, in thrall to the gaming tables and the clubs, shuddering at country taste and country manners. No wonder Alex had skated adroitly over the Vereys' situation! They were hardly in the first stare of fashion and he had known nothing of them before Miss Verey's name had been put forward as his potential bride. Now he could see why. Poor as church mice...working a farm to make ends meet...a shabby house, no food, a barely drinkable port... They evidently needed Alex's money as much as he did!

Miss Verey was hovering about his bed now, plumping his pillows, smoothing his sheets and all the while chattering on in a way that made his head ache abominably. Philip tried to concentrate on Alex's fortune and the improvements in his life when his brother deigned to grant him a small share in it. A wife could be *made* to look presentable, but he shuddered to think of the cruel amusement of the *ton* when he escorted Miss Verey to one of the exquisite Bond Street couturiers in the hope that they could work a miracle. Pride and appearance were everything in his circle. He would be a laughing-stock. He closed his eyes and concentrated hard on the money, but Miss Verey's chatter distracted him.

'Pray, ma'am, will you be quiet!' he snapped. 'All I require from you is that you summon my valet! Immediately!' Six in the morning—he knew that Gibson would be furious for, like his master, he was a late riser. Nevertheless, that could not be given consideration. Lord Philip knew that he simply had to get away from Ambergate.

Lady Verey did not wake until ten, for she had been exhausted by the events of the previous night and Jane had given the servants orders not to disturb her. The first thing she saw was her daughter, perched demurely on the end of her bed, face scrubbed and pale, black hair freshly washed and curling about her face.

'Lord Philip!' Lady Verey exclaimed, struggling upright. 'Have you seen to his lordship's requirements, Jane? He is most particular and I should not wish him to find fault with us—'

Jane came forward and patted her mother's hand. 'Do not distress yourself, Mama! I saw Lord Philip myself this morning—I went to his chamber to see that he had all that he needed—and alas, he told me that he must hurry back to London. He had some urgent and unexpected business, I understand.'

Lady Verey clapped her hand to her mouth in horror. 'Jane! You mean that he has left already?'

Jane nodded regretfully. 'I am sorry, Mama. He sent you his apologies and best wishes.'

'Did he say nothing of returning?' Lady Verey asked, clutching her head beneath its lacy bedcap. 'Surely he will be back with us soon?'

Jane shook her head. 'I fear he made no mention of it, Mama, and I did not wish to press him—'

'No, of course.' Lady Verey smiled distractedly at her daughter. 'Natural delicacy must prevent you from inquiring—' She broke off in exasperation. 'Oh, dear, this is so very unfortunate! What of the betrothal? He did not speak this morning? No, I can see that he would not have the time... Perhaps I should write... But if he did not seem anxious to return...'

Jane got up and made a business of brushing some imaginary dust from the skirts of her dress.

'I am persuaded that it would be best to let matters lie, Mama. I am sure that Lord Philip will come back to Ambergate if he wishes and that we should not importune him. As for the betrothal, well...' she tried to look suitably downcast '...we must bear the disappointment as well as we are able.'

'Yes, indeed!' Lady Verey took her wrap gratefully and slipped out of bed. 'What a sensible girl you are, Jane. Tell me, did you like Lord Philip?'

'I scarce had time to form an opinion, Mama,' Jane said carefully. 'His lordship is excessively handsome and seems most fashionable...'

Lady Verey's lips set in a thin line and for a moment her daughter thought that she was about to pass some criticism, but her innate courtesy triumphed over her feelings.

'Well, well, it is all most strange! He gave no indication of the business that had summoned him away so suddenly, I suppose? No, of course he would not. But perhaps he will return in his own good time...'

'Perhaps so, Mama,' Jane concurred. 'Perhaps so.'

Three weeks later, Simon Verey returned home.

'Is it not romantic, Jane?' Sophia Marchment exclaimed as the friends sat together in the parlour of the Manor. 'Your long-lost brother returned from the dead to save the estate from ruin! I declare you must be *aux anges*!'

Jane tried not to laugh. Sophia's flights of fancy were as extravagant as they were highly coloured, but she was the sweetest friend imaginable.

'I am very happy to have Simon back,' she agreed, 'for we were always close and to think him lost was a horrid thing! He has changed, Sophia, which I suppose is no surprise.' Jane wrinkled her brow. 'War has changed him. He seems older, not just in years but in attitude and experience.'

Sophia made a little noise of distress and took

Jane's hand in a comforting hold. 'Oh, Jane! Is he very sad?'

'Not precisely…' Jane smiled a little '…but he is serious and no madcap boy like he was before. He says he wishes to settle down! Imagine! He plans to go to London to find himself a suitable wife!'

Sophia coloured a little. She had been a little in love with Simon Verey for the last ten years.

Jane, realising she had been tactless, hurried on.

'Anyway, when Simon explained his plan to go up to Town, Mama decided that we should all go, for the Season. Apparently, Aunt Augusta Monckton has a house in Portman Square which she has offered to us and, although it is not the most fashionable of addresses, it is in a perfectly respectable area. Mama believes that we may afford it if we are careful and she is quite taken with the idea.'

'London!' Sophia breathed. 'Oh, Jane!' She looked round the manor parlour with its faded velvet and chintzes. 'The Season! Fashionable company! I declare you are the luckiest creature alive!'

Jane, reflecting how little she wished for her good fortune, gave her friend a smile. 'Well, it is not perfectly to my taste, for you know how I prefer the country, and I know you think me mad to do so! But what I really wished to ask was whether you would like to come with us? Mama thought it would be better fun for me if you were there and I should like it extremely—'

When Sophia had stopped screaming with excitement, had hugged her friend twice and had rushed off down the corridor to find the Squire and Mrs. Marchment, Jane sat back with a sigh.

She had spoken the truth when she said that she

was delighted to have her brother back, but his plans had taken her by surprise. She had expected him to want nothing but peace and rest after the privations and hardship of his life on campaign, but instead he had insisted on the entertainment and company of the capital. Lady Verey's enthusiastic acquiescence had made Jane's heart sink. She had not imagined that she would need to set foot in London.

She knew that her mother was thinking to bring her to Lord Philip's attention again in the hope that the Delahaye match might be saved, or, if that were not to be, that Jane might attract the interest of some other gentleman of means. Simon's return had staved off the most immediate threat of penury, of course, but she still had little alternative than to marry. She could not be a drain on her brother's limited resources indefinitely.

London. In view of the way she had disposed of Lord Philip, this was particularly awkward. Jane frowned. Her conscience had been troubling her, not about the way she had deceived Lord Philip by her appearance and behaviour, but over the necessity of omitting certain facts when she spoke of it to her mother.

For some reason, she had not anticipated ever having to see Lord Philip again and she was annoyed with herself for not considering the possibility. It would be very difficult to think up a convincing explanation for the sudden transformation in her appearance.

Of course, she might not even meet Lord Philip in London, but matters could become awkward if she did. Jane heaved another sigh. Thank goodness that no one else knew the embarrassing truth about Lord

Philip's foreshortened visit to Ambergate. It was not an episode of which she was proud but, given a little time, she was sure that she could come up with a plausible explanation for her behaviour.

The night watchman greeted the gentleman with the news that it wanted but ten minutes to two and the weather was fine. The butler at the house in Berkeley Square gave him the further intelligence that his brother was awaiting him in the library. Lord Philip Delahaye thanked both of them and tipped neither. The butler watched him go into the room and shook his head very slightly at the distinct unsteadiness of his lordship's gait.

The library was lit by the fire and one candle only. Lord Philip, coming to an abrupt halt just inside the door, said uncertainly, 'Alex?'

'Sit down, Philip.'

Alexander, Duke of Delahaye, spoke from the depths of the wing chair placed before the fire. He put his book to one side and got to his feet. 'A drink, little brother? Or have you already had enough for one evening?' There was the faintest, mocking undertone in his voice and, as always, it put Philip on the defensive.

'Devil take it, Alex, it's not even two o'clock yet! I'd only just got to Watiers as it was!'

'Not broached your third bottle yet? My apologies for finding you too soon,' his brother returned drily. 'Unfortunately, there was—is—a matter of some urgency I wished to discuss with you.'

There was silence. Philip watched a little sulkily as his brother crossed to the table and poured two glasses of brandy. He took one with a grudging word of thanks and sat down. Unlike the Duke, who was casually if elegantly attired, Lord Philip was in evening dress of a high dandyism. He felt rather than saw his brother's dark gaze skim him with thoughtful consideration and stiffened. Why was it, he wondered, that Alex could look so effortlessly elegant in his disarray whilst he had spent hours before a mirror and was still discontented with the result?

To make himself feel better he said spitefully, 'You look a little dishevelled, Alex. Been entertaining a lady?'

'No,' the Duke said indifferently. 'I have been waiting for you to come and explain to me why you are in Town rather than courting Miss Verey in Wiltshire.'

Lord Philip took a pull on his brandy. He felt he needed it. 'I did go to Wiltshire…'

'I know. And then you came back the following day. Why?'

There was nothing for it but the truth. 'The girl's a freak,' Lord Philip said viciously. 'A great, fat, whey-faced creature who can barely string two words together, and you and Lady Verey will not foist her on to me for the sake of any fortune! I'd rather starve!'

'And well you might.' There was still no inflection in Alex Delahaye's voice. The fire crackled. 'Have you forgotten that you'll not get another penny from me if you do not marry?'

'Marry, yes—but that?' Philip's eyes were wild. He slammed the glass down and the amber liquid jumped. 'Have you met Miss Verey, Alex? Do you really dislike me so much as to condemn me to that?'

Alex Delahaye raised his brows. 'I have not seen

her since she was fifteen and I'll allow she was a little on the plump side then—'

'Plump! Surely you mean monstrous fat! A great whale of a girl tricked out in pink satin!'

Alex winced. 'Must you always judge on appearance, Philip? I confess I have had no speech with her, but Verey assured me that she was of pleasant disposition and well to a pass—'

'Ha!'

'And that she was not unwilling to the match—'

'Maybe not, for what other chance will she get?' Philip drained the rest of his brandy in one gulp. 'No wonder she is not yet out! No wonder the Vereys had been hiding her away there in the country these years past! And now Lord Verey is dead and beyond retribution and I am promised to that fright!'

The Duke sighed with the first sign of irritation he had shown. 'As well he is dead, or you would be answering to him for your insults to his daughter! Philip, I will not carry on financing your escapades about town indefinitely. The alliance with Jane Verey is a sound one.'

'Oh, I know you want me to settle down.' Philip put his empty glass down with a sulky snap. All his remembered grievances were jostling in his mind, pushing forward, demanding to be heard.

'It is all very well for you to dictate to me, keeping me short of funds, making me beg to have my debts settled! You, with all the fortune and all the estates—'

'And all the responsibilities,' his brother finished, a little bitterly. 'Yes, it has been truly enjoyable for me, Philip, with five younger siblings to see settled creditably and three estates to return to profit! And then there have been fortune-hunting suitors to discourage on behalf of my sisters and the extorting landlords to deal with over breach of promise—'

'There was only one landlord,' Philip said crossly, 'and I never promised to marry his daughter!'

Alex did not trouble to reply. He stretched out his long legs towards the fire and sighed. His brother eyed him with disfavour.

'You have been married,' Philip said suddenly. 'How can you then condemn me to a loveless match?'

There was a sharp silence. 'I would have thought that my own experiences were the perfect example of the evils of a love match,' Alex said expressionlessly. 'I would spare you that, little brother.'

Philip said something very short and very rude. His brother only smiled.

'I sometimes find it difficult to believe you are only my senior by ten years,' Philip said, with a final vicious spurt of malice. 'You seem so very much older!'

Alex laughed. 'The weight of obligation!' he said lightly, but his eyes were cold.

'But devil take it, Alex, you like living like this! You choose it!' Philip reached for the brandy bottle, staring at his brother aggressively. 'You never go out, you never entertain... You cultivate your reputation as a recluse! And yet the toadies still try to tempt you with their daughters and their entertainments and their wine cellars!'

Alex shrugged, indifferent again. 'A Dukedom is perceived to be always in need of a Duchess,' he said. 'Unfortunately for the matchmakers, I am not in need of a wife! Which is where you enter the play, Philip!'

'Damned if I see why I should marry just to oblige you!' his brother said, aggrieved. 'I know Madeline played fast and loose, and after she died you wanted no more to do with women! But you hold the Dukedom—you provide the heir! Damnation take it, there are hundreds of women panting after you!'

Alex Delahaye stretched, crossing one ankle over the other. 'You're wasting your time, Philip! I hold the purse strings and I want you to marry! It's as simple as that. Now, you will renew your courtship of Miss Verey—'

'I can't do that!'

'Because of your aversion to her appearance? You will find that there is more to marriage than a pretty face,' his brother said coldly.

'It's not just that.' Philip's face was turned away, suddenly suffused with colour. 'I have told everyone—told the others how it was with her. I shall be a laughing-stock if I renew my suit!'

'The others? Whom?' Alex's voice cut like a whip.

'Ponsonby and Malters and Cheriton,' Philip muttered. 'It seemed a good joke—Verey tricking you into agreeing an alliance between the Delahayes and that pudding-faced wench! They found it amusing, at any event...'

'No doubt,' Alex said, with biting sarcasm. He got to his feet, towering over his brother's chair. 'Your drinking cronies have seldom been graced with wit and taste! Well, you must make your choice, Philip! Either you are a rich laughing-stock or you are a penniless one!'

Philip was out of his chair in a second, confronting his brother. Alex had moved away and stood before the fireplace, one arm resting idly on the mantelpiece. He was the taller, which gave him an immediate advantage, but for once Philip was too angry to care.

'Damn you for dictating my life,' he said, real hatred lighting his blue eyes. 'I wish you had died along with our parents!'

For a moment they stood as though frozen. Philip was the first to look away.

'I'm going,' he muttered, 'and do not think to try and pass off one of your candidates for matrimony on to me again! Damned if I'll ever marry, to oblige you or otherwise!'

'Damned if you don't,' Alex said expressionlessly, moving over to the fireplace and pulling the bell for the butler. 'Tredpole, my brother is just leaving. Be so good as to lock up after him. You may go to bed. I shall not need you again tonight.'

After the impassive Tredpole had shown Philip out, Alex resumed his seat but did not pick up the book that he had been reading. Instead, he sat staring into the dying embers of the fire.

Miss Jane Verey… She had been little more than a child when he had seen her at Ambergate, but she had seemed a pleasant and unaffected girl. Alex smiled a little as he remembered the first glimpse he had had of her, riding across the fields close to her home. She had had a good seat on the horse and was clearly enjoying both the fresh country air and the company of her brother, who rode alongside. She had seemed exactly the type of sensible girl who would best keep Philip's wilder excesses in check. Lord Verey had been flatteringly eager for the alliance, but they had agreed to wait a few years for Jane to reach her eighteenth year. All had seemed set fair.

Verey's death had thrown the plan slightly, but when the year of mourning had elapsed, Alex had been glad to find that the widow was still as receptive to the match. Philip had been giving increasing cause for concern over the years, with his deep play and unsuitable friends, and now that he had attained the age of four and twenty, Alex had decided it was high time that his brother settled down. Nor had Philip seemed particularly reluctant at first. Alex gave a rueful grimace. Money was the only currency that Philip understood and the inducements that he had offered alongside Miss Verey had obviously been attractive. More attractive than the girl herself, evidently!

Alex sighed. Perhaps he had been mistaken, in both Miss Verey and in the strength of Philip's feelings. It was not always easy to know what was best in the matter of his brother and sisters. There had been an ageing roué whom his sister Eliza had sworn was the love of her life. Alex had disapproved of the man but had not liked to oppose the match when he could see that his actions made Eliza so unhappy. Yet the very next season she had met a young baronet and was now happily married and living in Herefordshire. The other two girls were also married and the middle brother, George, was serving with Wellington's army. There was only Philip…

Alex strode over to the bureau beside the window. One of the desk drawers was half-open, a pile of papers almost spilling over the top. His expression hardened. Philip had been granted endless credit on the strength of the Delahaye fortune and now he was the one they were dunning for payment. He slammed the drawer closed, sending several of the bills tumbling onto the carpet. He would not stand for any more nonsense. The Verey match would be put forward once again and Philip forced to comply. Alex's jaw tightened. His brother's day of reckoning was approaching in more ways than one.

Chapter Two

'It's true, I'm afraid,' Lady Eleanor Fane said bluntly. 'It's the *on dit* all over Town, Alex, even eclipsing poor Maria Scrope's elopement with the footman! Everyone knows that Philip described Miss Jane Verey as an ugly, illiterate brood mare! Which,' Lady Eleanor added fairly, 'would be bad enough even without the rest!'

She removed her gloves, discarded her parasol and collapsed into an armchair with a heavy sigh.

Lady Eleanor, the Duke of Delahaye's aunt and godmother, was one of the few women allowed past the portals of Haye House. Impeccably connected and with a wide circle of friends, Lady Eleanor often acted as the Duke's eyes and ears in Society. And her intelligence system was faultless. Which was why Alex Delahaye did not interrupt, but simply waited for her to continue.

'Lady Verey has brought her daughter up to Town,' Lady Eleanor went on, reaching for the silver teapot and pouring herself a generous cup. 'Jane is not out yet—she makes her debut at Almack's next week. When I met Clarissa Verey in Bond Street she had not yet heard the rumours, but it can only be a matter of time before some spiteful scandalmonger stirs up trouble!' She watched Alex's face set in lines of deep displeasure. 'The girl is practically ruined before she starts! It was the utmost folly of Philip to speak as he did.'

'I know it.' Alex got up from the desk and strode across to the window, hands in his pockets. 'The foolish young cub! He could never resist bragging to his cronies. No doubt they all thought it a great jest, but if the Vereys hear of it—'

'If! When!' Lady Eleanor said energetically. 'The presence of Jane Verey in Town will stir the gossip to a positive maelstrom! Oh, Clarissa Verey glossed over Philip's desertion, claiming that the betrothal had been a mere suggestion rather than a definite match, but she will not be so kind when she hears what Philip has been saying about her daughter! And there is worse, Alex, far worse!'

Alex raised one black brow, a look of faint amusement on his face. 'What could possibly be worse?'

'Simon Verey has returned from the wars and is accompanying them to Town,' Lady Eleanor said, grimly. 'They are not without protection! If he should hear of the slur cast on his sister's name—'

'Scarcely her name,' Alex said mildly. 'Even Philip has not suggested Miss Verey is anything but virtuous!'

'Her intellect, her appearance!' Lady Eleanor amended crossly. 'Must you be so literal, Alexander? Simon—Lord Verey, I suppose we must now call him!—will hear some mention of it in the clubs and we will all be in the suds!'

'Very poetic, Aunt Eleanor!'

Lady Eleanor gave a snort of disgust. 'Upon my word, you are in an odd mood today, Alex! But I know that you have always rated Simon Verey most highly!'

'I have indeed—he is spoken of as a most intelligent and sound man!'

'But wait,' Lady Eleanor said impatiently, 'you have not heard the final piece of news!'

'I am all attention, ma'am,' her nephew murmured politely, betrayed only by the twinkle in his eye. Lady Eleanor let it pass in the interests of conveying her information.

'On the strength of our old friendship, Clarissa Verey invited me back to Portman Square,' she said. 'Well, of course, I could scarce decline, although I hoped she would not ask my advice on how to make her hideous daughter presentable. Don't smile at me, Alex, this is serious! Try to follow my chain of thought!'

'Yes, ma'am!' the Duke said meekly.

Lady Eleanor looked suspiciously at him but his expression remained quite bland.

'Well, naturally enough, Clarissa Verey suggested that both Jane and the friend she has brought with her from the country should make their curtsies to me! Clarissa had already ordered tea, and mentioned in passing that Jane had a sweet tooth so, coupled with Philip's comments, I made the obvious connection that the girl ate too many cakes!'

'Naturally enough!'

'Then the door opened, and a divine child tiptoed in and curtsied to me! She was tiny, all pink and white, with golden curls! A veritable angel!'

'The friend from the country?'

'Of course,' Lady Eleanor said, discontentedly. 'Miss Sophia Marchment! It's a tragedy!'

'That the friend is so pretty and Miss Verey not?'

'No!' Lady Eleanor glared. 'Really, Alex, how you do leap to conclusions! No, the tragedy is that Philip has made even more of a fool of himself than we had imagined. For then, Miss Verey herself came in. Oh, dear!'

'Pray compose yourself, ma'am,' the Duke said, lips twitching. 'I am desperate to hear the end of the tale!'

'Why, but she is quite beautiful! Quite distractingly lovely!' Lady Eleanor said crossly, reaching for a handkerchief and blowing her nose hard. 'And the sweetest of girls! How could Philip do such a thing? How *could* he?'

The Duke was accustomed to his aunt's slightly long-winded and sometimes circuitous route when approaching a subject. There was no doubt, however, that he had not been expecting this.

'The girl is beautiful?' he echoed, dumbfounded. 'Are you sure?'

'Of course I am sure! How can you be so nonsensical? She is beautiful and charming and intelligent! They are the perfect foil for each other, the one so fair and the other so dark! They'll break all the hearts in Town!'

There was a silence. Alex got to his feet and strolled over to the window, hands in the pockets of his beautifully cut bottle-green coat. Lady Eleanor viewed his tall figure hopefully. If anyone could think of a way to bring them out of this mess, it had to be Alex. He was as cool-headed and resourceful as Philip was rash and quixotic. In fact, Lady Eleanor regretted that he sometimes seemed too cold, too passionless.

It had not always been thus. She could remember the youthful Alexander, Marquis of Hawarden as he was then, flushed with happiness and good humour on his wedding day some fourteen years before. Before his parents had died so tragically in a carriage accident, before he had had to take on the upbringing of his five siblings and before his beautiful young Duchess had disgraced his name with her open affairs, her gambling and the drinking which had lead to her premature death some six years after their marriage…

'Are you still of a mind for Philip to wed, Alex?' she asked a little hesitantly, as her godson seemed sunk deep in thought.

'I am.' Alex shook himself, turning away from his contemplation of the view of Berkeley Square. 'He has to be made to conform, Aunt Eleanor, and what better way than by a respectable marriage and a brood of infants? And the Verey match is a good one! You may remember that it was my grandfather's dearest wish that there should be an alliance between the Delahayes and the Vereys! I even went to Ambergate myself a few years ago to speak to Verey about it! All was set fair, and now Philip—' He broke off, his lips tightening in exasperation.

'You went to Ambergate?' Lady Eleanor sat forward. 'I had no notion! Did you meet Miss Verey whilst you were there?'

'I did not. I saw her, but I did not speak to her. She was unaware of my visit since her father wished to keep the proposed marriage a secret from her at the time. I believe she was but fifteen and no doubt he did not judge her of an age to be considering her future husband!'

Lady Eleanor raised her brows. In her experience young ladies with far less than fifteen years in their dish were pre-occupied with their marriages.

'What was your opinion of her?'

Alex shrugged as though he did not have an opinion. 'Her looks were pleasant enough, I suppose, although she was a little plump. She seemed a bright, lively girl and hardly the frumpish dullard Philip is suggesting!'

Lady Eleanor frowned. 'How could he have been so mistaken in her? I can scarce believe it! Why, the girl he described and the one that I met cannot be the same person!'

Alex was also frowning now. 'Yes, I confess that that is the part that exercises me the most! I have every respect for your judgement, Aunt—' he flashed her a grin '—and were it a choice between your assessment and Philip's, I should settle for yours any time! But the fact remains that Philip describes Miss Verey in terms of pungent denunciation whilst you have seen her to be a veritable angel! One of you must be mistaken!'

'My dear Alex,' Lady Eleanor said trenchantly, 'the whole Town will shortly see that *my* description is the accurate one! And not only can I vouch for Miss Verey's personal charms, I know she has wit and style to match!'

'Then,' Alex Delahaye said slowly, 'Philip must be lying. I can only assume he made up this outrageous fabrication to strengthen his refusal of the match. Perhaps he thought that I would relent if I believed Miss

Verey to be utterly unpresentable! Evidently he is prepared to go to extreme lengths to avoid the marriage!'

'Foolish,' Lady Eleanor said shortly, 'and dangerous. It only needed for Miss Verey to come to Town
for him to be seen to be a liar and a scoundrel! I am
surprised at Philip! He may be a loose fish but he is
no fool!'

'No,' Alex said, 'he is no fool. Which is why—'
He broke off and Lady Eleanor looked at him curiously.

'What is in your mind, Alexander?'

'I am thinking that there are various strands to be
resolved here,' the Duke said thoughtfully. 'I am still
of a mind to try to save the Verey match if I can.
More importantly, I must speak to Philip about the
sudden transformation in Miss Verey's person and
character. It is that, dear ma'am, which interests me
the most.' His dark gaze, reflective but with a faint
hint of humour, rested on Lady Eleanor's puzzled
face.

'We have assumed that it is Philip who is at fault
here,' he enlarged, 'but no one has yet thought to ask
of Miss Verey's reaction to the proposed match. I
imagine that you had too much delicacy to mention
it to her, Aunt?' Then, as Lady Eleanor nodded in
bewilderment, he continued.

'You say that she has wit and charm. Supposing,
dear Aunt...just supposing...that Miss Verey herself
has objections to Philip's suit, objections that have
been set aside by those making the match. She might
have told her mother that she did not wish to marry,
only to be overruled. Would she perhaps take matters
into her own hands? And take any steps within her
power to make herself displeasing to him?'

Lady Eleanor gasped, recoiling, grasping her parasol as if for comfort. 'Alex! What a suggestion! How could she possibly—?'

'Anyone may play the fool if they choose,' Alex said drily. 'It is more difficult to appear ugly if one is not, but scarcely impossible with a little disguise! And Philip is not very discerning! I wonder...'

'Are you truly suggesting that Miss Verey has tricked Philip?' Lady Eleanor looked as though she would be reaching for the hartshorn next. 'No! Oh, no, I cannot credit it!'

Alex smiled. 'I may, of course, be doing Miss Verey the greatest injustice. But it should be possible to discover the circumstances under which she and Philip met, the witnesses, the words that passed between them. I believe that I could find out quite easily whether or not Philip has been cozened!'

Lady Eleanor was still looking confused and deeply reproachful. 'Alex, you have the cunning of the devil even to think of it!'

'Thank you, Aunt Eleanor!' Once again, Alex grinned at her. 'I confess to a certain curiosity about Miss Jane Verey! It is stimulating to suspect that I may have met an adversary as devious as I!'

'No, it is impossible! Not that sweet girl!'

'Well, we shall see!'

'How do you intend to go about it?' Lady Eleanor asked with misgiving.

'I will make inquiries,' Alex said slowly, 'and I intend to meet Miss Verey. I will judge for myself if she be innocent angel or cunning jade!'

'Oh, Jane, is this not fine?' Sophia sighed in ecstasy. 'Such beautiful shops! Why, not even Bath can rival it! I declare, I could spend an entire day just looking!'

Jane stifled a yawn. She already felt as though she had spent a whole day doing precisely that. This had to be the twentieth shop that they had visited that afternoon.

When the shopping trip had been mooted after breakfast, Jane's brother Simon had looked horrified and had taken refuge at his club. Jane wished that she had a similar choice. It was not that she disliked shopping, precisely—she paused to watch her mother and Sophia agonising between two exquisitely painted fans—it was simply that she grew bored with it so very quickly. The silks and taffetas, slippers and shoes, hats and gloves that so fascinated her friend could not hold her attention for long. Now, if only it had been books... Jane smothered a giggle as she remembered the look of pained disapproval on her mother's face when she had tentatively suggested that they visit James Lackington's 'Temple of the Muses' in Finsbury Square.

'Temple of the Muses!' Lady Verey had repeated. 'Why, it sounds like a house of ill repute rather than a bookseller's! I cannot believe it a suitable place for us to visit unescorted!'

So Jane had been obliged to enlist her brother's help to buy the books she wanted and was denied the pleasure of browsing amongst the galleries of bookshelves and of watching the other bibliophiles thronging Mr Lackington's 'lounging-rooms.'

Lady Verey and Sophia had moved on to consider a very pretty straw hat adorned with blue ribbons. Jane's eye was caught briefly by a silky scarf of emerald green, and she moved over to take a closer look, letting it run through her fingers like water. Beyond the wide bow windows, Charles Street was busy with ladies and gentlemen strolling in the sunshine. Across the road was a spirit booth, with crystal flasks of every shape and form, cunningly lit from behind so that the different coloured spirits sparkled alluringly. Jane smiled. Now there was something worthy of her time; glass and china were fascinating commodities and she hoped to visit Mr Wedgwood's emporium in Great Newport Street, where she had heard that the displays of china were arranged especially to amuse and intrigue the visitor...

There was a gentleman standing across the road just to the left of the spirit booth. His very stillness caught Jane's notice and, once she had looked up, she found that his intent gaze appeared to be directed through the bow windows of the shop and fixed upon her person. It was oddly disconcerting, not least because she was certain that she had seen him before. He was very tall and very dark, and his penetrating gaze locked with her own. Suddenly it was as though they were only a matter of feet apart, with no glass window between them, nor bustling street, nor indeed any barrier of any kind. Jane found herself unable to look away and break the spell.

His gaze pinned her to the spot, so searching and intent that Jane felt the colour coming up into her cheeks.

Then a dray cart came between them, the carter shouting to his horses and blocking the view, and Jane drew a shaky breath and turned away from the window.

'Jane?' Lady Verey had noticed nothing amiss. 'Come here, my love, and tell us which is the finer of these two shawls. Sophia has a fancy for the pink with the lace, but I am not sure—' Her eye fell on the scarf, which Jane was still clutching unknowingly in her left hand.

'Oh, how pretty! You must have it, my love, for it matches your eyes to perfection! What excellent taste you do have, Jane! Now, tell me what you think of this shawl…'

Both the shop assistant and Sophia were looking at her expectantly. Jane obediently looked where her mother pointed but she was scarcely thinking of fripperies and furbelows.

It was him! she thought, still a little breathless inside. I recognised him. I *know* it was him.

Gradually her fluttering pulse stilled and her breathing slowed. No doubt she had imagined it. One dark stranger might look very like another and London was full of people. It seemed foolish to think that she would recognise one man, glimpsed four years before at Ambergate and never seen again. All the same…

She was still puzzling over it as they came out of the shop and on to the sunlit pavement.

'Now then, girls,' Lady Verey said, shepherding them into the street, 'the milliner's is just across from here—'

'Oh, look, ma'am!' Sophia exclaimed, clutching Lady Verey's arm. 'I did not see those gloves! Oh, they would be perfect for tomorrow night! I positively must have them! Jane—' she turned anxiously to her friend '—you do not mind?'

Jane smiled a little. Sophia would be spending all her allowance in one morning at this rate!

'I shall wait for you out here in the sun,' she said. 'It is a pleasant day and there is no need to hurry.'

'Stay in sight of the window, Jane,' Lady Verey instructed, turning to follow Sophia into the shop. 'I wish to keep you in view. And should anyone accost you, I pray you to come straight back into the shop—'

'Yes, mama,' Jane said patiently, gesturing to her mother to follow Sophia. 'I can come to no harm in full view!'

The shop door closed behind Lady Verey and Jane turned to scan the street. Although her acquaintance in London was still small, she recognised the lady and gentleman who were strolling along the opposite side of the road, for they were neighbours of the Vereys in Portman Square and had been most welcoming. And just beyond them... Jane took an involuntary step forward as she saw the dark gentleman again, pausing before a gunsmith's, his back turned to her.

There was a sudden, irate shout and she spun around in alarm. A cart was passing close by and she felt her skirts snag on something, tugging hard and catching her off balance. She slipped on the cobbles, her skirt hopelessly entangled in the cart's left wheel, and felt herself dragged to the ground. It all seemed to happen in the blink of an eye before Jane could scramble back to safety.

'Oh!' It was Jane's dignity that had suffered most, but tears of shock swam in her eyes. Her hands felt bruised from the sudden contact with the ground and she had bumped one knee painfully as she fell. Tumbled in the gutter in a heap of petticoats and rubbish, she struggled to recover herself.

'Allow me to help you, ma'am.' A quiet voice spoke in her ear at the same time as the gentleman slid a supportive hand under her elbow and helped her to her feet. 'Are you injured at all?'

Jane looked up and experienced her second shock. This time there could be no mistake. It was certainly the man that she had seen at Ambergate, though this time more formally dressed in immaculate buckskins, top-boots and a mulberry-coloured jacket. At such close quarters he was disturbingly attractive, a man quite outside Jane's limited experience. He was certainly handsome, with wicked, dark good looks that quite took her breath away, but there was a rather austere expression in those very dark eyes that contradicted the impression of slightly rakish attraction. There was also an aura of strength about him and an impression of power held under tight control that was instantly reassuring.

He was holding her very gently with an arm supporting her about the waist and there was concern in his face and something else…an extraordinary tenderness, surely, that made Jane feel suddenly faint. She swayed a little and his arm tightened.

'You should sit down, I think, to recover from the shock. Where did your companions go?'

'I thank you, sir, I am quite well,' Jane said shakily, catching sight of her mother's face peering in horror through the shop window. The carter chose the same moment to start justifying himself to the gathering crowd. His diatribe on foolish young women who did not look where they were going was silenced by one glance from the gentleman.

Jane realised that she was bruised but not badly injured. She felt foolish and embarrassed. She noticed that one of her hands was resting confidingly against the lapel of the mulberry jacket, whilst the gentle-

man's arm still held her close. It was most comforting, but surely rather improper. Dark eyes smiled
down into her hazel ones. Jane felt her knees tremble
again.

'Thank you for your help, sir,' she said again, trying to extricate herself. 'You have been most kind,
and I am quite well enough to—'

'Jane!' Lady Verey and Sophia came dashing out
of the shop, accompanied by the modiste and half of
the staff, adding to the confusion on the pavement.
The carthorse started to stamp and rear, disturbed by
the noise. Sophia helpfully removed a cabbage leaf
from her friend's skirt.

'Jane!' Lady Verey said again. 'Are you hurt?
Whatever has happened—' She broke off, staring in
sudden confusion at the gentleman. 'Your Grace!'

The gentleman removed his arm from Jane's waist
at last and executed a bow. 'Lady Verey. How do you
do, ma'am.' Jane thought that she could detect the
very slightest hint of rueful amusement in his voice.
'I do not believe that Miss Verey has come to any
lasting harm, but perhaps she should be conveyed
home for a rest. I shall call a hack for you.'

'Yes of course, but—' Lady Verey's gaze was dart-
ing from Jane to her rescuer. 'I had no notion that
you were the gentleman who had come to Jane's rescue. We had no idea that you were even in Town! Is
your brother with you? You must permit us to call
and express our sense of obligation—'

'Of course, ma'am, I should be delighted.' The
gentleman cut her short in the politest, most defer-
ential manner possible. 'I shall not detain you any
longer. Good day...'

He bowed again and the crowd parted to let him

pass as though obeying some unspoken authority. The cart pulled away and a hackney cab took its place. Jane, bewildered and shaken, allowed Sophia to help her solicitously inside.

'Who was that gentleman, ma'am?' she heard Sophia ask Lady Verey as the cab set off in the direction of Portman Square. 'He seemed quite…' Sophia hesitated, but Jane knew just what she meant. The gentleman in question had seemed quite awesome. She felt again the power of his glance, the tender strength with which he had held her. Jane shivered.

'That was the Duke of Delahaye,' Lady Verey was saying composedly, 'the elder brother of Lord Philip. Jane…' she saw her daughter's pale, stricken face '…are you sure that you are quite well? You must go to bed as soon as we reach home or you will not be well enough for Almack's this evening! I am sure that the accident must have overset you!'

'Yes, Mama,' Jane said submissively. 'I confess I feel a little shaken.'

'Well, perhaps we should not go tonight—' Lady Verey broke off, looking torn. 'But on the other hand it could be construed as a snub to the patronesses…oh, dear, how provoking! I do not know what to do!'

'I shall be better directly, Mama!' Jane said, leaning back and closing her eyes. 'I pray you, do not consider cancelling our attendance…'

'I had no notion that the Duke was in Town,' Lady Verey said, smoothing her gloves. 'He is seldom in London, you know, for he much prefers the country!' She frowned. 'How odd! And how curious that he should be passing just when you fell, Jane!'

Jane, remembering the way in which the Duke of

Delahaye had stood watching her from across the road, was tempted to say that he had hardly been passing. She held her peace. The whole episode had been most disconcerting. Why had the Duke been watching her beforehand and what could account for her strange reaction to him? The colour flooded her face as she remembered the sensation of his arm about her. She had met plenty of personable gentlemen in the past week, but never before had she been so aware of a man's touch. She closed her eyes. It was best to forget it, best to forget him. It seemed that, between them, the Delahaye brothers were causing her nothing but trouble.

It was Simon Verey who heard the rumours first. Whilst the ladies were out shopping he had had a meeting with Pettishaw, his man of business, and had then spent a convivial afternoon with Lord Henry Marchnight, one of his oldest friends. They had met by chance at Tattersall's and, as the evening advanced, made their way to Brooks.

'Covered yourself with glory on campaign, I hear,' Henry said with a lazy grin, after they had tried the claret and considered it more than tolerable. 'Whatever will you find to do with yourself here that could compare?'

Simon laughed. 'I intend to enjoy the pleasures of Town for a little, then turn into the complete country squire! Ambergate will be back in good order soon, but I don't want to be an absentee landlord for too long!'

'A country squire needs a wife and brood to look the part!' Henry observed. 'Plenty of pretty girls out this Season!'

Simon grimaced. 'So my mama keeps reminding me! She is forever pushing likely heiresses under my nose! It will be a little while yet before I set up my nursery, though I don't deny I'm looking out for a potential bride!' He shot his friend a look. 'If Mama becomes too pressing I suppose I could always offer my hand and heart to Lady Polly Seagrave—'

Lord Henry's gaze narrowed. 'She wouldn't have you! Lady Polly has just turned down her seventh suitor this Season!'

'And it would be a shame to ruin our good friendship,' Simon murmured, signalling for more wine.

Lord Henry relaxed infinitesimally. 'As you say…'

'Are you settled in Town for the Season or do you travel again?' Simon thought it wise to turn the conversation away from his friend's unrequited passion for Lady Polly. The Earl of Seagrave's daughter had rejected Henry's plea to elope some three seasons before, but Simon knew that, despite Henry's apparent indifference, his friend's feelings were still deeply engaged.

Lord Henry shook his head slightly. 'My plans are uncertain…I must go abroad again shortly and I think that there may be trouble brewing closer to home but…' he shrugged '…I seldom know where I will be sent from week to week!'

Simon let it pass. He knew that Lord Henry worked for the government in various shadowy capacities and equally knew that his friend wished that to remain a well-kept secret. They paused in their conversation as a couple of slightly inebriated young men staggered past on their way to the card tables.

'Are you staying for a hand of whist?' Henry asked.

Simon shook his head. 'Promised to look in at Almack's tonight. M'sister and Miss Marchment are making their debut. Bound to be a crush!' He put his glass down and got to his feet. 'Damned slow, squiring one's own sister about Town!'

'You're too kind-hearted,' Henry mocked. 'Can Miss Marchment be the reason for this generosity?'

Simon stared. 'Sophia? Hardly!' He realised that he sounded less than gallant and flushed at the sardonic light in Lord Henry's eyes. 'Miss Marchment is a charming girl, but I know her like my own sister and besides…I prefer women a bit more—'

'Voluptuous?'

'Intelligent!' Simon finished, on a note of rebuke. 'Unfashionable it may be—boring it ain't!'

'Miss Verey is highly intelligent,' Lord Henry murmured.

'Jane?' Simon paused. 'Well, I suppose that she reads a lot—'

'Not just intelligent—clever. Clever enough to evade marrying Philip Delahaye, by my reckoning, and making him look churlish into the bargain!'

Simon sat down again. 'You've lost me, Harry. What are you trying to tell me?'

'You were still away when Delahaye went to Ambergate to pay court to your sister, weren't you?'

'Came back a few weeks later,' Simon confirmed. 'Mama said Philip Delahaye had cried off. Jane didn't seem to mind and I was always a bit uncomfortable about the match, to tell the truth. I knew it was mooted—knew m'father had been keen and that the Duke was pushing for it to go ahead.' He shifted in his chair. 'Thought that was the end of the matter.'

Lord Henry shook his head slowly. 'Better that you

hear it from me, Simon, than through rumour and falsehood. There are a hundred-and-one stories circulating about Philip Delahaye's visit to Ambergate because he arrived and left again so swiftly. Everyone knows that he intended to make Jane an offer and the speculation is all about what made him change his mind. The worst matter is that Philip himself appears to have encouraged the rumours by saying that he cried off because—'

'Verey!' Lord Henry had broken off as someone stumbled against Simon's chair and hailed him at a volume more suited to a hundred yards than the three feet actually involved.

'Cheriton,' Simon said, with a cold inclination of the head for the painted dandy before him, 'how do you do?'

'Well, old fellow, very well! I'm for Almack's—I hear that your lovely sister is to be there! I can barely wait to make her acquaintance!' Lord Cheriton gave a crack of laughter. 'You will have heard what a fool Philip Delahaye has made of himself by disparaging Miss Verey! The *on dit* is that Delahaye was so foxed when he arrived at Ambergate that he mistook some pox-faced serving wench for your sister! We had a fine laugh at his description of her! Pudding-faced, freakish, barely literate—' Cheriton's shoulders shook. 'He said that he would rather starve than tie himself to her in marriage! Then Freddie Ponsonby met Miss Verey in Charles Street and said that she was divinely beautiful with a wit to match, don't you know! Philip could not believe it and swears he'll be at Almack's to see for himself! We gave him a roasting he'll never forget and all he could think of was that he must have confused her with some serving doxy! He was paying his addresses to a damned serving maid!' Cheriton sauntered away, still chuckling.

The detail might have been confused but the gist of Cheriton's words was all too clear. Simon was half out of his chair and Henry Marchnight laid a restraining hand on his arm. As was often the way, a hush had fallen over the room as everyone else, sensitive to the slightest scandal, strained to hear what was going on.

'Simon, think a little!'

Simon sank back into his chair, his face flushed with sudden fury. 'I suppose that this was what you were about to tell me, Harry? That Philip Delahaye has been bandying my sister's name about Town—'

'Well, not precisely…' Lord Henry bit his lip. Cheriton's tactless interruption had made it well-nigh impossible for him to explain to Simon that he suspected Jane of tricking Philip Delahaye. Henry had known Jane since childhood and had the greatest respect for her quick mind. As soon as he had heard Philip's lurid description of his encounter with Miss Verey, Henry had immediately remembered the ugly stepmother of the pantomime held at Ambergate so long ago. After serious consideration, he had thought it only fair to warn Simon. His friend needed to know of Philip's inexcusable slander, but also to be alerted to the fact that Jane might have deceived him. Matters seemed somewhat delicate. It only needed for Jane and Philip Delahaye to meet for the most almighty row to develop.

As Henry hesitated over his potential disclosure, another voice broke the silence.

'May I have a moment of your time, gentlemen…?'

Neither Simon nor Lord Henry had noticed the arrival of the newcomer, yet when they looked up they both wondered how they could have missed the atmosphere of tension in the room. The slightly malicious eavesdropping of a few minutes before had given way to something approaching incredulity. Astonishment was mingled with awe. Then Simon caught the whisper:

'It is the Duke of Delahaye—Alexander Delahaye...'

A faint smile touched Alex's mouth as he took the third chair at the table. 'I must apologise for interrupting your conversation, gentlemen, but my business is pressing.'

'Simon, this is Alex Delahaye,' Henry murmured, covertly assessing the interest they were arousing from their peers and smiling wryly. Any minute now, Cheriton would be offering to serve the wine in his attempts to overhear. 'Alex, Simon Verey. Forgive my informality but I guessed that you would wish to cut straight to your business!'

The two men shook hands. 'You were correct, Harry,' Alex said drily. ' A pleasure to meet you, Lord Verey. I have heard a great deal about your exploits on campaign. Just now, however, there are matters closer to home that demand our attention! Have you, perhaps, heard the rumours?'

'Heard about them just this instant,' Simon confirmed grimly. 'A small misunderstanding over your brother's courtship of m'sister!'

'You are all generosity to describe it thus,' Alex said ruefully. 'I am most concerned to avoid any further cause for general speculation. The rumours are highly coloured and as inaccurate as these things usually are! My major preoccupation, however, is that

Philip is to be at Almack's tonight, where, I understand, he will undoubtedly meet Miss Verey again. I do not wish it to be turned into a public spectacle!' He cast a quick look round the crowded room and drew his chair in closer. 'Every ear in the place is strained to overhear us, I see!'

'They're taking bets,' Henry said cheerfully. 'Evens on a public row in Almack's, two to one that Miss Verey will cut Lord Philip dead and twenty to one that Philip's description was accurate after all— saving your presence, Simon!'

Both Simon and Alex Delahaye winced.

'How did this happen in the first place?' Simon demanded. 'Pudding-faced, freakish, illiterate... Those were Cheriton's words and, devil take it, there's no smoke without fire! Your brother must have been damned disparaging, Delahaye!'

Alex gave him an enigmatic glance. 'I confess that that is one aspect of the case that does interest me. Without a doubt, Philip has been more outspoken in his opinions than he should have been, although I am persuaded that the *ton* has far exaggerated his comments and turned the whole thing into a bear garden. But having met your sister, Lord Verey, I can see that the description could not be less appropriate!'

Simon grinned, not noticing that he had been deflected from his original question. 'Well, for all that I'm her brother, I can see that Jane's grown into a devilish attractive girl! The only effect of this is to make your brother look foolish, Delahaye!'

'Absolutely,' Alex Delahaye murmured. He drained his glass. 'I hope that Philip will accept that he has only himself to blame. But in case he does not, I believe we should have a plan.'

Henry raised a brow. 'You mean to stage a diversion, distract attention?'

'Precisely. If we three go to Almack's, make an entrance, draw attention to ourselves and spike Philip's guns, I think that we may successfully defuse the situation. What do you say? It is almost eleven and they will be closing the doors on us if we are not careful!'

There was general acquiescence to the plan.

'I did not think to see you turning your attention to domestic disputes, Alex!' Lord Henry said pensively, as they got up to leave. Alex flashed him a smile of genuine amusement.

'More difficult than diplomacy between nations, Harry, I assure you!'

'I had no notion that the two of you were in the same line of business,' Simon observed quietly to Henry as Alex paused for a word with an old friend on his way to the door.

'Oh, Alex is way above my humble station,' Henry said cheerfully, eyes twinkling, 'but keep it to yourself, old fellow! He wouldn't thank me for giving the game away!'

'He is somewhat forceful,' Simon said, with a grin. 'I imagine it would be uncomfortable to be in opposition to him!'

Lord Henry held his tongue. He could have said that Miss Jane Verey was the only person he knew who had successfully opposed the Duke of Delahaye's plans. Despite Alex's self-proclaimed desire to prevent further gossip, Henry reckoned that he had a secondary motive. He was almost certain that Alex intended to get to the bottom the mystery of Jane's apparent change of appearance and personality. Stifling a grin, he found himself possessed of a sudden, surprising enthusiasm to visit Almack's again. He had a healthy regard for Jane Verey's wit and charm, but if they were placing bets on who would prevail in this struggle, his money would have to be on Alex Delahaye every time.

Chapter Three

Jane was dreading her come out at Almack's. Her encounter with the Duke of Delahaye had made her realise that she had been naïve in the extreme to imagine that she could avoid Lord Philip. In such a small circle of society, where one brother went the other must inevitably follow. She had already heard that, although Lord Philip was generally held to be a rake and a gambler, all but the highest sticklers opened their doors to him. Perhaps he might even be at Almack's that very evening.

Jane could imagine all too well what might happen when they finally met. She knew that it would be dreadful. They might come upon each other in a crowded ballroom and Lord Philip would declare before hundreds of onlookers that she was an impostor and not the real Jane Verey at all. Or perhaps he would denounce her for playing a trick on him and the *ton* hostesses would turn their backs on her. He might demand an explanation that would be almost impossible to give and Lady Verey and Simon would be both horrified and disappointed in her when they knew the truth. She would be packed off back to Ambergate in disgrace and would have ruined matters for Sophia as well as herself.

Then there was the Duke of Delahaye himself, a man who had come to Ambergate to look her over as though she had been a prize horse. Whilst Jane was supposed to be resting that afternoon, she spent the whole time thinking about him. There was no doubt that the Duke was the man she had seen four years previously at Ambergate. The memory of that night was etched on her mind forever; the candlelight, the handsome stranger, the mysterious way in which he had appeared and then vanished. It had all seemed so romantic, and yet it was proved to be nothing but a sham. He had come to do business with her father, come and gone again in secret, and his sole intention had been that she should marry his brother. Everything that had followed was his fault. Jane felt this very strongly. The unwelcome proposal, the necessity of deceit, the problems that now arose…the blame for all of this could be laid directly at Alex Delahaye's door. Arrogant, overbearing man! Jane sat up, all prospect of rest vanishing. She could feel her anger swelling again, and with it a curious feeling of desolation that she should have come to know Alex Delahaye through this particular set of circumstances.

She started to prepare for the ball as slowly as possible, in the hope that something untoward would happen to prevent their departure. Perhaps the carriage would have a wheel loose, or the horses would have colic, or Lady Verey would decree that Jane was too ill to go, although this was unlikely in view of the fact that she had told her mother that she was very well…

Jane frowned a little as she allowed the maid to

help her into an exquisite white dress embroidered with tiny violet flowers. For some reason she had started to think of the Duke of Delahaye again, remembering how powerfully attractive she had found him. Honesty prompted her to admit that this was the other reason that she dreaded her come out. The thought of meeting Alex again was a disturbing one, filling her with a mixture of anticipation tinged with fear that was entirely uncomfortable. She could not account for the effect the Duke had had on her other than to hope rather half-heartedly that it had in fact been the shock of the accident that had made her pulse race in his presence.

'Oh, if only we had not come to Town!' Jane lamented, as she watched the maid finish dressing Sophia's hair. 'I feel quite *sick* with nerves!'

Sophia checked her reflection for one last time and thanked the maid prettily. She patted Jane's hand, giving her an anxious look.

'Oh, Jane, but it is all so thrilling! You must try to enjoy yourself! Why, I declare I do not know whether to faint with nerves or burst with excitement!'

Even Sophia's high spirits seemed a little dampened, however, as they crossed the famous threshold. Jane, for her part, was almost silent, a state of affairs so unusual that even Lady Verey noticed and fretted.

'Come along, girls! Try to look animated! No, not like that, you merely look half-witted! Oh, dear...'

The rooms were decidedly shabby but the company clearly had a good opinion of itself. Young ladies stood about in small groups, their eyes bright and malicious as they surveyed new arrivals. Their mamas looked harder and more acquisitive still and the young men appraised the girls boldly but without warmth. Snatches of conversation ebbed and swirled around them.

'Thirty-two if she's a day...'

'Only two thousand a year, my dears, and who is to make a respectable match on that?'

'They say her grandfather was a coal merchant...'

'Positively paints her face, but should try to make a better attempt at it. One can see where the face ends and the neck begins, for they are two different colours!'

The spiteful words cut like shards of glass.

'Oh, dear,' Sophia said under her breath, and Jane knew from her tone that her friend suddenly felt as small and uncertain as she, 'I am not sure that I shall like this place after all!'

They were greeted fulsomely by Lady Jersey, who swam towards them in a diaphanous robe of eau-de-nil, brown eyes alight with excitement and intrigue. The sophistication of her dress made Jane feel like a frump in her debutante white and the warmth of her greeting seemed suspicious in itself.

'My dears!' Lady Jersey took Jane's hand in one of hers and Sophia's in the other. 'I am so very glad that you have decided to come! What courage in the face of such unkind gossip! I do so admire you! And how charming you look, Miss Verey! All the gentlemen will soon see that Lord Philip was fair and far out in his remarks! Still, he is such a slow-top that I dare swear 'tis true he mistook the serving maid for a lady!'

She wafted away, leaving Jane, Sophia and Lady Verey to look at each other in consternation.

'Whatever can she mean?' Lady Verey fretted,

fidgeting with the beaded fringe on her shawl. 'Oh, I do wish that Simon were here! He promised! Everyone is looking at us and this is so awkward!'

Jane knew that her mother was feeling countrified and dowdy amongst the exotic throng and it was true that everybody did appear to be paying them a great deal of attention. It was early, so the rooms were not yet crowded, and they could see few of their acquaintance amongst the assembled guests. It was many years since Lady Verey had been to Town and she had no fashionable relatives to sponsor them. Jane began to perceive that it might be awkward to be an object of curiosity and yet to see no friendly face ready to help them. Then Lady Verey sighed with relief.

'Oh, thank goodness! It is Lady Eleanor Fane!'

The redoubtable Lady Eleanor came up and kissed Lady Verey, bestowing a look of approval on Jane and Sophia. 'Charming,' she observed. 'Quite charming and a credit to you, Clarissa!'

'Eleanor, the most extraordinary thing!' Lady Verey began. 'Lady Jersey made some strange remark about Lord Philip Delahaye and some rumours about Jane! And everyone is staring! Do you know—?'

Jane saw a look akin to annoyance cross Lady Eleanor's face. 'That woman!' she said crossly. 'There has been a little talk about Lord Philip's hasty departure from Ambergate, Clarissa, that is all!' She smiled approvingly at Jane and Sophia. 'The best way to refute the gossip is simply by being here and looking so delightful. I know I can rely on you girls! Now, look—' she took Lady Verey's arm in a firm grip '—my cousins the Applefords are approaching. Do smile, Clarissa! You would not wish to put off the girls' partners with that mournful face!'

Mrs Appleford, her daughter Paulette and son Roger arrived at that moment. Roger soon asked Jane to dance and from that moment both girls seemed to be besieged by a flood of eager admirers. Lady Verey's strained social smile soon relaxed into one of genuine enjoyment as Lady Eleanor introduced her to what seemed like half the *ton*, all of whom seemed flatteringly eager to make her acquaintance.

Jane, dancing with young Lord Blakeney, had almost forgotten her apprehension about the evening when fate finally caught up with her. A group of four young men had come into the ballroom; even from her place amongst the dancers, Jane could see everyone craning to watch. A few glances were cast in her direction and with a sinking heart she realised that one of the men was Lord Philip Delahaye. She saw one of the others lean close to Lord Philip and he turned towards her, scanning the ballroom.

Jane tried to make herself as inconspicuous as possible, shrinking amongst the other dancers. Unfortunately the set was coming to an end and she was obliged to accept Lord Blakeney's escort back to her mother and Lady Eleanor. She watched Lord Philip draw closer, he and his cronies strolling with lazy disdain across the floor towards them. Her breath caught in her throat. What on earth was she going to say?

'Lady Verey.' Lord Philip's bow was much more punctilious than on the occasion of their previous meeting. 'Aunt Eleanor.'

Lady Eleanor frowned slightly. Lord Philip was no favourite of hers. 'How do you do, Philip? It is a surprise to see you here! I thought that you had little time for Almack's!'

Lord Philip looked vaguely discomfited. A hint of colour came into his face. Jane suddenly thought how young he looked, for all his dandified appearance. He could only be a couple of years older than she was. His fair hair flopped across his brow with carefully arranged disorder and his shirt points inhibited him from turning his head too much. He looked a little like a schoolboy trying to appear grown-up. Jane stifled a smile.

'Came to pay my respects to Miss Verey again,' he muttered, his colour rising higher. He turned to Jane. 'How do you do, ma'am? I hope that you will spare a dance for me later.'

Jane dropped a slight curtsy, avoiding his gaze. 'How do you do, sir,' she responded colourlessly. 'I should be delighted.'

There was an awkward silence. Lord Philip's friends began to fidget behind him. They had expected far greater sport than this. Murmuring their excuses, they drifted away, leaving Lord Philip marooned and looking very uncomfortable.

'Very pretty, Philip,' Lady Eleanor approved with deliberate tactlessness. 'Everyone will see now that those silly rumours are nothing more than empty gossip! Now, may I make you known to Miss Sophia Marchment, a friend of Miss Verey's from Wiltshire? Miss Marchment—Lord Philip Delahaye.'

Lord Philip turned to look at Sophia properly for the first time. Jane, watching with sudden sharpened interest, saw the first moment that he truly saw Sophia and the arrested expression that came into his eyes.

Sophia, for her part, blushed adorably and curtsied most gracefully.

'How do you do, sir? I am most happy to meet you!'

Lord Philip was still holding Sophia's hand as though he had forgotten that it rested in his. His blue gaze was fixed on her face with a half-dazed, half-wondering look.

Well! Jane thought, both amused and a little concerned. Perhaps there was some virtue in Lord Philip after all, if he were able to recognise Sophia's innate beauty and goodness at a single glance.

'Good God!' Lady Eleanor said suddenly and it was a measure of her shock that she used the phrase at all. 'It is your brother, Philip! Alex is here! I am sure...I have no recollection of him *ever* attending Almack's!'

The habitual sullen expression replaced the wondering look on Philip's face. 'Keeping an eye on me, no doubt, ma'am!' he said, with a tight smile. 'Miss Marchment—' he turned back to Sophia urgently '—will you grant me this next dance?'

'Of course, sir.' Sophia looked shy and confused. 'I should be honoured—'

Lord Philip had already drawn her away on to the floor before she could finish her sentence. Lady Verey, Lady Eleanor and Jane looked at each other with varying shades of surprise.

'Well!' Lady Eleanor said explosively, but Jane was no longer listening. All her attention was riveted on the tall figure of Alexander Delahaye as he came towards them across the ballroom. In full evening dress he looked magnificent, the black and white stark but elegant. As dark as Lord Philip was fair, his silky black hair gleamed in the light with the dark resonance of ebony. Jane dimly registered that her brother Simon and Lord Henry Marchnight flanked the Duke on either side and that their arrival was creating the biggest stir of the evening, bigger by far than that caused by Lord Philip and his friends.

'Alex!' Lady Eleanor had regained her *sangfroid* by the time they arrived. 'Must you create such a commotion wherever you go?' She turned to smile at Simon and Lord Henry. 'Gentlemen...allow me to congratulate you on turning an evening at Almack's into an event! If you are the cavalry you are sadly late, but fortunately there is no need of rescue! Philip has been before you and has done the pretty!'

The Duke raised his black brows. 'I saw that Ponsonby, Malters and Cheriton were expecting a show!' he said drily. 'I trust there were no problems, ma'am?'

Lady Eleanor smiled at him, in perfect understanding. 'Now, Alex, not even Philip would show such bad *ton* as to make a scene at Almack's!'

'I wish someone would tell me what all this is about!' Lady Verey said plaintively. 'I have heard nothing but veiled hints and mysterious remarks all evening!'

Simon cleared his throat. 'I'll go and find a drink, then, if the crisis is over! Harry? Alex? Can I fetch anything for you?'

Alex! Jane thought. It had not taken the Duke long to achieve a friendly footing with Simon! That did not augur well for her plans at all. She was aware that Henry Marchnight was looking at her thoughtfully and suddenly she felt rather hollow. Harry knew her well enough to guess at what she had done to get rid of Lord Philip at Ambergate. Would he give her away? Worse, Alex Delahaye was clearly no fool and he was watching her with a mixture of amusement and speculative consideration that was far more disturbing than Henry's friendly scrutiny. Suddenly Jane felt as though all her difficulties had caught up with her with a vengeance.

'Miss Verey.' Alex drew her to one side, speaking softly. 'I hope that you are recovered from your accident earlier. It seems that you came to no lasting harm, for you are in excellent looks this evening!'

Jane caught sight of Lady Eleanor looking absolutely stunned, her eyebrows almost disappearing into her hairline. Evidently the Duke of Delahaye paid a compliment as rarely as he attended Almack's, but Jane did not flatter herself that he meant it. She had a deep conviction that he was making the opening moves in a game he was intent on playing with her.

'Yes, I thank you, your grace. I am much better and I must thank you for your help.' Jane was glad that she still sounded so composed when her heart was racing.

The Duke shrugged negligently. 'I am glad that I was able to be of service, Miss Verey. Now, I see Lady Sefton approaching. May I ask her to grant you permission to waltz with me?'

Even Lady Eleanor, for all her town bronze, gasped at that one. Jane met the Duke's dark gaze and saw the laughter lurking there. So she had been correct in thinking that he was making a game of her! The temptation to respond was very strong, to show him that she was no milk-and-water miss. However, that was too dangerous. She would not play.

'I thank you, your Grace, but I do not waltz,' she said steadily.

She had the satisfaction of seeing the lazy amusement fade from his eyes, to be replaced by shrewd calculation. Lady Verey, unaware of the by-play, stepped in hastily to smooth over any awkwardness.

'Oh, Jane, you need have no concern as to that! It is perfectly proper for you to waltz if one of the patronesses of Almack's gives her permission—'

'Thank you, Mama.'

Jane, exasperated by her mother's well-meaning intervention, looked up to see the Duke's eyes still on her and, worse, that he had read her thoughts. The amusement was back. She knew that she had been checkmated.

'Lady Sefton,' Alex said clearly, turning to the approaching patroness, 'will you present me to Miss Jane Verey as a suitable partner for the waltz?'

Lady Sefton's good-natured agreement and Jane's acquiescence followed. It had to—she knew that he would brook no refusal. Meanwhile, across the ballroom another intriguing tableau was developing as Lady Jersey, not to be outdone, could be seen giving an eager Lord Philip her permission to waltz with Sophia.

Lady Verey, suddenly becoming aware that she had been neglecting Sophia in her concern for Jane, gave a little gasp. 'Oh, Eleanor, he has asked her for a second dance and immediately after the first! I am sure that Sophia knows how to go on, but I feel she should have a little more care! Besides...' her gaze swung back to Jane '...Lord Philip should surely be dancing with Jane!'

Jane dropped a neat curtsy. 'Oh no, Mama!' she

said sweetly. 'If I am favoured with the Duke's attention I can have no complaint!'

'Then come along, Miss Verey,' Alex said gently, in a tone that suggested he would have liked to call her a minx, 'for the music is starting!'

Jane took his hand, with a feeling that she was about to step right out of her depth. The gossip was deafening. Part of her was aware of the hum of discussion all around, but most of her senses were concentrating on the experience of being in Alex Delahaye's arms.

The sensation of closeness was intimate but in no way unpleasant, more intense than it had been that afternoon. One of Jane's hands rested lightly on his broad shoulder whilst the other was clasped in his. The touch of his fingers threatened to disturb her, for she found that she was very aware of him, and she tried to shut her mind to it. It would never do to make a fool of herself at Almack's!

Jane tried to concentrate on the steps of the waltz. She was a good dancer and it was easy to waltz with Alex because he, too, was so good at it. Besides, it gave her the excuse to stay silent and avoid looking up at him, which she was sure would unsettle her completely. Instead, she looked around at their fellow dancers, noticing that Sophia was whirling around and chattering nineteen to the dozen to Lord Philip. He was smiling and looked boyish and happy. It was an extraordinary transformation.

'It is not really so bad, is it?' the Duke said ironically, after they had circled the room twice in silence. 'I realise that, given a choice, you would not have danced with me, Miss Verey, despite your pretty little remark just now! You have a neat way of administering a set-down! It was a salutary experience for me!'

Jane raised her eyebrows, biting back a smile. The twinkle in his eyes was infectious. 'You surprise me, your grace! I would imagine your self-esteem to be much more resilient than that!'

Alex Delahaye smiled, looking suddenly as boyish as his younger brother. 'But appearances can be so deceptive, Miss Verey! Do you not find that?'

Jane was suddenly on her guard. There was no reason to read anything into his words and yet she was wary. He was too perceptive and she could not afford to trust him.

'I must allow that to be true sometimes, I suppose,' she said carefully. 'This is not a society where one sees much below the surface.'

She saw his smile broaden with real amusement. 'Indeed, Miss Verey! Yet sometimes it is the surface itself that is misleading! Take my brother's visit to Ambergate, for example!'

Jane felt herself jump in his arms and was sure that he had felt it too. She cast one swift glance up into his face and saw that the smile held a hint of challenge now.

'I have no notion as to your meaning, your Grace,' she said, with more composure than she was feeling, 'but I cannot regret the outcome of Lord Philip's visit. I am persuaded that he and I should not have suited at all!'

'Or was it that you took steps to ensure that you should not suit?' the Duke asked, his lazy gaze still watchful. 'As I say, I have the oddest suspicion, Miss Verey, that you have made a fool of my brother!'

'Oh, no, your Grace!' Jane avoided his gaze, her

eyes fixed on the swirling dancers. 'Whatever your brother has achieved has been on his own account!'

The Duke's arm tightened momentarily around her waist. He gave her a look of brilliant amusement. '*Touché*, Miss Verey! You are quite right that Philip's indiscreet descriptions of his visit have been most ill bred. But perhaps he was provoked? Perhaps you gave him a very different impression of Miss Jane Verey from the one that is on show tonight?'

Jane hesitated. She had no way of knowing how much he knew and what was mere guesswork. How she wished that she had never started this! In deception one could give oneself away so easily…

Whilst she hesitated, the Duke said blandly, 'Philip has already described your meeting, of course. Perhaps you would care to give me your version of events?'

Jane made up her mind. 'I think not, sir. That would be…embarrassing and unnecessary. You have seen that all has been forgiven and forgotten tonight!'

The Duke nodded. 'Of course,' he murmured, 'it may be better to let sleeping dogs lie. But indulge my curiosity, Miss Verey! How did you disguise yourself? You must be an accomplished amateur actress…'

The colour flooded Jane's cheeks as her guilty conscience, fully awake now, gave her a prod. He might as well have called her an accomplished liar!

'Please, your Grace, may we not change the subject?'

'I can see that it might not reflect well on you!' the Duke agreed. 'The disguise, the deceit…'

'Sir—'

'No, no,' the Duke murmured, 'say no more, Miss Verey! I would not wish to cause you mortification!'

Jane's eyes flashed with annoyance. 'But surely it was your intention to do precisely that, sir! And you have succeeded!'

'No, indeed!' Alex's expression of virtuous indignation was as good as anything Jane could have achieved. 'Surely you mistake, Miss Verey! It is never the lady who is at fault in these situations!'

Jane forced out a smile from between gritted teeth. Somehow—she was not at all sure how—Alex had managed to pin the blame on her neatly whilst turning the whole situation around to make it appear as though he was sympathising with her!

'I do believe that you are spoilt, your Grace,' she said unwisely. 'Surely the real cause of your ire is that you are so accustomed to people falling in with your plans that you cannot bear to be gainsaid!'

She saw Alex's eyes narrow in incredulous amusement, then he laughed. 'What an acute young lady you are, Miss Verey, and one who dares much! You have my measure—I have a great aversion to being thwarted! And unfortunately your astuteness only serves to convince me that you are exactly the right bride for my brother!' This time there was steel beneath the silky drawl. 'I intend the marriage to go ahead despite your best efforts to prevent it!'

Jane almost stumbled over the steps of the waltz. She had never contemplated that the Duke would still be of the same mind and insist that the match be made despite all that had happened. Surely she had made it clear by both her words and her actions that she would not marry Lord Philip? Yet it seemed that Alexander Delahaye had either not heard her or had disregarded her words. His final, patronising comments had suggested that he viewed her as no more than a precocious child who might be humoured a little but whose final obedience was taken for granted.

'I am sorry to hear you say that, your Grace,' Jane said slowly. 'I was in earnest when I said that Lord Philip and I should not suit and my mind is unlikely to change.'

'But you see,' the Duke continued softly, 'Philip needs a clever wife and you have proved yourself to be eminently suitable, Miss Verey! Where a man lacks certain…qualities himself, it is most beneficial if his life partner can supply what is missing! A perfect combination!'

Once again, Jane caught sight of Sophia and Philip, fair heads bent close, laughing at something Philip had just said. She felt a pang.

'Would it not be more beneficial for Lord Philip to choose his own bride, sir?' she said, a little desperately. 'He might feel a greater commitment to the match under those circumstances!'

'Happily, his wishes need not concern us,' the Duke said a little grimly. 'You are my choice, Miss Verey, and Philip knows it well! The financial rewards of such a marriage are his prime consideration!'

Jane could feel her temper slipping at his arrogance. 'But they need not be mine, I thank you, sir!'

The Duke laughed a little harshly. 'No, but there are other levers… I have immense social power, Miss Verey. A word here, a hint there… A reputation is so fragile. Think of the distress to your mother if doors were to be closed to you. I am persuaded that you would not want that. And Miss Marchment…she would be tainted by association, of course.'

Jane looked at him for a long time in silence. She could hear the music sweeping on in the background but it was as though she and Alex Delahaye were quite alone. His face was expressionless.

'I do believe that you are threatening me, sir,' she said slowly. 'Despite our differences I had considered you a man of integrity, but perhaps I mistake you. And I should warn you that I am not easily susceptible to coercion!'

'No, that was clumsy of me,' Alex agreed affably. 'I would not stoop so low, Miss Verey, and I beg your pardon. But perhaps you are more amenable to persuasion from your own family? Investment in Ambergate would be a great help to your brother. Were we to be related, I could assist him…'

Jane glared at him. 'I saw the ease with which you had gained his confidence! Simon does not deserve false friendship!'

The Duke's arm tightened about her waist. Jane felt quite breathless, as though the music was whirling faster and faster.

'Oh, my friendship would be offered in earnest,' he said pleasantly. 'I have the greatest respect for your brother and would never offer him Spanish coin! I only wished to point out to you that there are different ways to influence a situation! I must warn you to beware of crossing swords with me, Miss Verey. You cannot possibly win…'

Jane was rather afraid that he was correct. The combined wishes of the Duke and Lady Verey would be difficult to oppose, particularly if he enlisted the support of Lady Eleanor Fane and Simon as well.

Together they could chip away at her resistance, ignoring her wishes in their desire to achieve a mutually beneficial alliance. Jane caught sight of Lady Jersey's fascinated face as she watched them from the edge of the dance floor. She manufactured a dazzling smile. 'I shall bear your warning in mind, sir!'

'I am still curious, Miss Verey,' Alex said slowly. 'You seem most adamant in your refusal to wed. Can it be that your affections are already engaged?'

'No, sir,' Jane said steadily. 'They are not.'

'Then perhaps you are of a romantical disposition? A pity—I should have thought you much more practical than that! I did not expect sentiment from you!'

'I do not consider it sentimental to expect to make a match where mutual respect, if not love, is present,' Jane said hotly. She seemed to have stumbled from one conflict directly into another! Would this wretched dance never end? She could hardly walk off the floor in the middle of a waltz. 'Perhaps it is your Grace whose ideas of marriage are prejudiced! Your own experience, perhaps, has led you to reject romantic love out of hand!'

She knew that she had overstepped the mark even before the flash in those dark eyes suggested that she had hit a raw nerve. Madeline Delahaye and her notorious infidelities were common knowledge amongst the *ton*, but Jane knew it had been ill bred in the extreme to speak of it to the Duke. She closed her eyes briefly and awaited the set-down she knew that she deserved. It was one thing to engage in a spirited defence of her own ideals and behaviour, but quite another to touch on his personal tragedy.

'Perhaps you are right, Miss Verey,' the Duke of Delahaye said bitterly. His mouth was set in a tight, angry line, but Jane could read unhappiness in his face and felt a sudden uprush of misery. It had never occurred to her that he might have loved his wife so much that she still had the power to hurt him eight years after her death. And then that she had so carelessly raked up matters best left undisturbed…

'I am sorry—' She began, only to be harshly overruled in tones that held more passion than anything that had gone before.

'Do not be, Miss Verey! Do not seek to pity me! I do not require that from you!'

Jane felt close to tears. It was bad enough to be thought deceitful without Alex Delahaye believing that she had deliberately sought to hurt him. She would have tried to apologise once more, but there was something in his harsh, set expression that forbade it.

The music finished and Jane dropped a very deep curtsy. She found that she was shaking from their encounter, an explosive mix of anger and misery flooding through her. Part of her was burning with fury at Alex's high-handed behaviour and part was ashamed of what she had said to him. Yet her overriding feeling was shock at the sheer physical impact he had made on her. It was very distressing. Worse was the fact that she could not retire, could not escape the prying eyes and intrusive questions of her companions. Her dance card was full and she had to smile through the rest of the evening. She even had to smile when Lord Philip sulkily and belatedly presented himself for a country dance. By the end of the evening, Jane was wishing the entire Delahaye family to perdition along with the rest of polite society.

*   *   *

Alexander Delahaye, strolling back to Haye House
in the early hours beneath an absurdly romantic full
moon, found himself beset by various unfamiliar
emotions. He had declined an invitation to return to
Brooks with Simon and Henry, but had agreed to
meet them there the following evening. Just now he
was aware only of a need for solitude.

Miss Jane Verey… She had practically ignored him
after their passage of arms during the waltz and he
could not blame her for it. He was deeply ashamed
of his behaviour towards her and considered it unforgivable. One did not go to Almack's in the expectation of threats and bullying. Miss Verey was young
and inexperienced and, whatever she had done, she
did not deserve to be treated so harshly.

The trouble was that she had read him all too well.
It was true that he had been angry because she had
overset his plans. Alex's calculations had not allowed
for Jane's feelings at all, but now that he had met her
he could ignore her no longer. Ignore her! He gave a
mirthless laugh. There was no possibility of that!

Alex squared his shoulders. He was unaccustomed
to being made to feel guilty. Miss Verey had done
that and had made him question his own judgement
into the bargain! Well, Philip had to marry; he was
still resolved on that. The Verey match had been his
grandfather's dearest wish and who better to manage
Philip than a girl who had already shown her quick
wit and devious ways? Besides, he was persuaded that
Miss Jane Verey would soon relent. A spell in Town
would make her realise that Philip was quite a good
catch. All young ladies were anxious to marry well,
after all, and why should Miss Verey be different? A

show of reluctance was probably required for form's sake, but would be followed by meek acquiescence.

The matter was settled. Alex let out a long breath. He would continue to promote the betrothal, although perhaps in a more subtle way. Miss Verey would soon conform and then all this fuss could be forgotten. Alex frowned. The decision should have cleared his mind, but for some reason he still felt vaguely dissatisfied. This had to be Jane Verey's fault in some vague way that he could not specify. What a stubborn and opinionated chit! Who would have thought that the henwitted Clarissa Verey would have bred so unconventional a daughter?

He had reached the portico of Haye House and as he was about to start up the steps an extraordinary thing happened. He suddenly remembered with perfect clarity the softness of Jane Verey's body within his embrace, the translucent radiance of her skin and the dazzling challenge in those wide green eyes. His imagination, normally firmly subject to his reason, presented him with the further image of Jane held naked in his arms, her lips parted beneath his own. It was so vivid and shocking an impression that he stopped dead. The immediate ache in his body told him that the idea held instant appeal.

'Damn it all to hell,' Alex said forcibly, and raised his hand to knock with far more violence than was necessary.

'Oh, Jane!' Sophia curled up on the end of Jane's bed, leaning her chin on one hand. 'Was that not the most exciting evening you have spent in an age? And is not Lord Philip the most—' She broke off, blushing a little. 'I know that he left Ambergate with indecent

haste,' she said in a rush, 'and he has admitted to me
that his behaviour was not that of a gentleman,
but...oh, surely he cannot be all bad! He seemed to
me to be charming and lively and...oh, everything a
high-spirited young man should be!'

Jane put down her hairbrush with a smile, looking
at her friend in the mirror. 'I saw that you were enjoying his conversation,' she teased. 'I think that you
had a better evening than I!'

Sophia's eyes sparkled in the candlelight. 'Yes, for
you were obliged to be kind to that awesome Duke!
Oh, but Lord Philip and I had a hundred-and-one
things to talk about! It seemed as though we had
known each other forever!' A slight frown entered her
eyes. 'Dearest Jane, you do not mind, do you?'

Jane shook her head. 'No,' she said with perfect
truth, 'I do not mind for myself. But...' she hesitated
'...did Lord Philip tell you that his brother has plans
for his future—very definite plans?'

'Yes—' Sophia hugged her knees '—but I am persuaded that I need have no concern over the Duke's
plans to marry Lord Philip off! You see...' she looked
suddenly shy '...Lord Philip can marry no one but
me! Oh, Jane, he is the man I dreamed about all those
years ago on St Agnes Eve! As soon as I saw him I
recognised him at once!'

Chapter Four

Jane stared at her friend in stupefaction. 'Oh, no! Surely that was just a childish game!'

As soon as she had spoken she saw Sophia's face fall.

'But, Jane, I thought that you did not mind! You just said—'

'I know!' Jane put out a hasty hand to touch Sophia's. 'I do not mind for myself, dearest Sophia, for you know that Lord Philip and I would not suit! But the legend of the Eve of St Agnes is just that—a legend! It cannot be true!'

Sophia was looking distinctly obstinate. 'All I know is that I dreamed of Lord Philip that night and now I have met him! It seems quite simple to me!'

Jane knew that there was no arguing with her. Sophia was a sweet girl but she could be frighteningly stubborn at times. Besides, who was to say that it was not true? Sophia had dreamed of a handsome young man and now she thought that she had met him. She had certainly tumbled into love. What was more surprising was that Lord Philip appeared equally smitten. Jane, remembering the bad-tempered young man who had visited Ambergate, suddenly wondered whether it had been frustration and anger that had made Philip behave as he had. Certainly Alexander Delahaye was imperious enough to try the patience of a saint, as Jane herself had discovered, and if he had pushed Philip beyond endurance…

She moved over to give Sophia an impulsive hug. 'Oh, Sophy, I'm sorry! I did not mean to appear disbelieving! I am very happy for you!'

Sophia hugged her back, her spirits restored at once. 'Jane, it is so exciting! I am just sorry that you did not dream of your future husband that night! That would have been marvellous!'

Jane tried not to smile. 'Well, to tell the truth I did dream of a man that night, but—'

Sophia clutched her. 'Jane! Why did you not tell me? Who was he?'

Jane dropped her gaze. 'It was nothing, Sophy! I woke in the night and saw a man in the corridor and then I dreamed about him, but it turned out that he was just one of my parents' guests…'

Sophia's brow was furrowed. She focused on the one point of importance. 'Yes, but, Jane, who was he?'

'It was the Duke of Delahaye,' Jane said reluctantly.

Sophia squeaked and clapped her hand to her mouth. Above it, her eyes were huge and round. 'Jane! The Duke! But—'

'I told you that the legend could not be true!' Jane said urgently. 'Besides, I was awake when I saw him, and although I dreamed of him later I am sure that it does not count.'

Sophia was not so sure. She shook her head stubbornly. 'But you went to bed without supper? You did not look behind you?'

'No,' Jane admitted, wishing she had never mentioned it. 'It's true that I did those things, but—'

'Then it must be true!' Sophia's blue eyes widened even further. 'Oh, Jane, the Duke of Delahaye! Only think!'

Jane was thinking. With a shiver that was half-fear, half-pleasure, she remembered the curious attraction that Alex Delahaye held for her. Would it be so terrible to be married to him? Then she remembered that he wanted her to marry his brother and that he was still in love with his dead wife. How many reasons did she need to prove that it was all foolish superstition? She slid into her bed.

'It has to be nonsense, Sophy,' she said firmly. 'If Alexander Delahaye proves to be my future husband you may have that pair of silk gloves of mine that you so admire—yes, and the straw bonnet with the matching ribbons! That is how certain I am that it will never come true!'

It seemed that Sophia was as anxious to see Lord Philip again as Jane was to avoid him. Jane heard her friend humming at the breakfast table and noticed a distinctly dreamy look on Sophia's face as she picked at her buttered eggs. When the visitors started to arrive, Sophia's blue gaze was riveted on the door in much the same way as a dog watches for its master, her face falling as each new arrival proved not to be the man she wanted to see. A whole procession of sharp-eyed mamas and their hopeful daughters were filling up the pink drawing-room and still Lord Philip did not come.

The hum of conversation and clash of teacups grew ever louder. Several ladies noted Lord Philip's absence and teased Jane about it, their false smiles not quite reaching their eyes. A number of the daughters were casting a thoughtful eye over Simon, who had the look of a man wishing he could remember a pressing engagement elsewhere. More than one debutante was sighing soulfully over Alex Delahaye and his sad romantic history.

The door opened and Lord Philip came in. The assembled ladies cooed a little with pleasure. Jane moved unobtrusively across to a group of debutantes and inserted herself in the middle, making sure that there was nowhere for Lord Philip to sit. She saw Lady Verey glance over in her direction with a meaningful look, then turned her shoulder and pretended to be engrossed in the conversation. When she looked up again, Jane saw that Lord Philip had taken the seat by Sophia, who was pink with suppressed joy.

Lady Verey was not so pleased. When the drawing-room had emptied of their guests, she took her daughter firmly to task.

'Jane Verey, I do declare you can be the most provoking girl!' she chided. 'Lord Philip came here especially to see you! If you think to provoke his interest by appearing unconcerned, you are only being foolish! A gentleman needs some encouragement—a smile here, a soft word there. Try to be more pleasing!'

Jane bit back the retort that Lord Philip was receiving as much encouragement as he needed from a different source. Sophia had turned quite pale at Lady Verey's attack and was now trying to pretend that she could not hear. With a murmured word of excuse, she slipped out of the room. Lady Verey barely seemed to notice.

'Surely, Mama,' Jane said mildly, 'you can see that Lord Philip has no wish for my company—no more than I have for his! We are not suited.'

Lady Verey looked affronted. 'Not suited! What nonsense is this? It is my dearest wish that Lord Philip should renew his attentions! Now, he will be at Lady Winterstoke's dinner tomorrow and I expect to see an improvement in your manner towards him, Jane! Pray show him some partiality!'

'Excuse me, my lady.' Golding, the butler, had soft-footed into the room. 'There is a posy here for Miss Jane.' He snapped his fingers and the footman hurried forward, carrying a small but exquisite bouquet of tight pink roses.

Lady Verey's irritated face broke into a smile. 'From Lord Philip, no doubt! I expect he was too shy to present it himself, the foolish boy!'

Jane took the posy, wondering at her mother's championing of a man who had been so offensive to her only a month before. No doubt Lady Verey had conveniently ascribed Lord Philip's behaviour to a temporary aberration or boyish high spirits. She had to agree, however, that the flowers were beautiful, each tiny bud a deep pink colour and on the point of unfurling. She extracted the card and handed the flowers back to the footman to put in water. Much as she would like to send them back, it seemed a churlish gesture and Lady Verey would never permit it. She could not resist a certain curiosity to see the message. What could Lord Philip say to her that would not appear either rude or insincere?

The bold black writing had come from another pen,

however. It was not an apology, only a name: Alexander Delahaye.

Jane caught her breath and pressed the card to her chest in case her mother was about to snatch it from her. Lady Verey was still twittering on about Lord Philip and his thoughtful choice of flowers and Jane did not contradict her. She excused herself as quickly as possible and flew up the stairs to her bedroom. The posy was already on a side table by the window, its pink buds just tinged with gold. Jane hesitated. She could have torn the card into pieces and thrown it away, but instead she placed it carefully in a drawer, on a bed of silk ribbons.

The sensation at Lady Winterstoke's dinner was caused not by the presence of Lord Philip Delahaye but by that of his elder brother. For years the hostesses of the *ton* had tried to entice the Duke of Delahaye from his self-imposed seclusion, offering him the most tempting food and the best company. For years he had rejected all invitations. Yet that evening he arrived with Lord Philip in a convincing show of brotherly unity and caused Lady Winterstoke positively to crow with triumph.

Jane's heart had sunk when she saw them come in. It seemed that the Duke and his brother must be forever dogging her steps and spoiling things for her. After all, it was Alexander Delahaye's avowed intent to wear down her resistance until she capitulated and agreed to the marriage. She had spent much time thinking of the bouquet he had sent her and had come to the practical conclusion that it was an attempt to soften her feelings towards the match. Well—her pretty face set into lines of obstinate disapproval—it would not work! No matter how romantic it had seemed at first, in truth it was just another means by which Alex Delahaye hoped to manipulate her!

Accordingly, she was looking very severe when Lady Winterstoke brought the Duke and Lord Philip over to them as the guests assembled before dinner.

'I was about to inquire how you were enjoying yourself, Miss Verey,' Alex said lazily, once greetings had been exchanged, 'but you look so forbidding that I hardly dare! Can it be that Town does not agree with you?'

Jane checked to see whether her mother was listening. Fortunately Lady Verey was intent on engaging Lord Philip in innocuous conversation and deflecting his attention from Sophia. She gave the Duke a dazzling smile. 'Well, your Grace, it is not all bad, I suppose! The theatres and concerts are great fun but the company is sadly lacking—it seems to be the same people saying the same things to each other at the same events!'

Alex smiled. 'That's frank, Miss Verey! You are not afraid to blight your social position by appearing an eccentric? Young ladies are meant to be bowled over by the sophisticated charms of the Town, you know!'

'It seems to me that a lot of nonsense is talked about Society!' Jane said judiciously. 'If people enjoy the company and the entertainments then so be it, but if they prefer other pursuits then they should be allowed their choice!'

'How singular,' Alex said thoughtfully, 'and how true! You are quite fearless, are you not, Miss Verey? I know of no other lady who would express such a view even if they believed it!'

'Yet you yourself do not succumb to the charms of Society a great deal, if the stories are true,' Jane pointed out, feeling at the same time that her tongue was probably running away with her again. 'I had heard that the Duke of Delahaye chooses to immure himself in his northern stronghold with only his books for company!'

'And his faithful dogs,' Alex added. 'Do not forget the dogs, Miss Verey! What else do they say of me?'

'Oh, many things,' Jane said, plying her fan, 'but none of them appropriate for a young lady to repeat in company!'

They laughed together, stopped together and stood looking at each other in a silence that seemed curiously loaded. Only a foot away, Sophia was chattering to Philip and Lady Verey was gossiping with one of her acquaintances. Jane made an effort to break the silence.

'I must thank you for the flowers, sir. They were very beautiful.'

'They reminded me of you,' Alex said abruptly. 'Excuse me, Miss Verey.'

Jane was left feeling breathless and disconcerted. She had imagined him a man accustomed to paying light compliments, but his unexpected words and hasty departure had none of the polish that might have been expected. Frowning a little, she watched him cross the room, spare a word for a distinguished gentleman in uniform, then be artfully ambushed by a dashing blonde in a clinging scarlet silk dress. Jane felt a vague depression settle on her.

Excusing herself to her mother, Jane slipped away to the ladies' withdrawing room so that she should not be obliged to make stilted conversation with Lord

Philip. Whilst tweaking her curls back into place, she reflected that the Duke was likely to be one step ahead of her in arranging for his brother to escort her in to dinner. The seating would no doubt be in order of precedence but, at a word from Alex Delahaye, Lady Winterstoke would gladly rearrange her table plan. Peeking down the corridor to confirm that she was not being watched, Jane decided to detour via the dining-room and examine the place cards.

Her suspicions had been justified. Lord Philip's place was set beside hers and he was a long way away from Sophia for good measure. Jane made a little adjustment and was on her way back to the drawing-room when, in the doorway, she collided abruptly with a broad chest.

'Oh!'

'We meet again, Miss Verey,' the Duke of Delahaye said, in the deceptively soft tones that Jane had already come to distrust. 'Have you lost something?'

'No!' Jane knew that a guilty blush was staining her cheeks. 'That is—I lost my way!'

'I see. I had thought that your penchant for food had led you to try to steal a march on the rest of us!'

Jane looked surprised. 'Who told you that I enjoyed my food, sir?'

'Why, I believe that it was my aunt, Lady Eleanor. She commented that you had a sweet tooth.' Alex offered her his arm and they strolled back across the hall towards the drawing-room. 'No doubt it was ungallant in me to mention it, but I have to confess that you look very good on it, Miss Verey! Not all young ladies are fortunate enough to be able to eat as they choose and not look the worse for it!'

Jane, relieved that he had not discovered her activ-

ities in the dining-room and guilty at spinning another
tale, started to colour once again. Alex was watching
her with undisguised interest.

'I am not sure whether it is guilt or pleasure that
makes you look so, Miss Verey! If only it were my
poor compliments that put you to the blush!'

Jane found herself unable to resist responding in
kind. 'I am sure that most young ladies would be
overcome to be the object of your gallantry, your
Grace!' she said sweetly.

'But not you, Miss Verey? No doubt that is your
implication!'

'Alas, I have always been told that I am not like
all the rest!' Jane said innocently. 'You said so yourself!' She dropped him a neat curtsy and went to join
her mother, managing not to look back at him over
her shoulder.

Alex watched her go. 'No, indeed,' he said softly,
under his breath. 'You are not like anyone else, Miss
Verey! I would venture to say that you are completely
original!'

The butler arrived to announce that dinner was
served. Jane was delighted to see Alex move away to
attend to his duties as escort to a Dowager Countess
in regal purple. She confidently expected that that
would leave the field clear for her to exchange partners. Next, Lady Verey was claimed by an elderly
baronet, who seemed flatteringly pleased at his good
luck. That got rid of the final obstacle to Jane's plan.
All it required now was for Lord Philip to be recalled
to his duty as her escort. Unfortunately he seemed
disinclined to leave Sophia's side. Jane wondered
whether he meant to cut her anyway, and thought this
would be rather funny after all the trouble she had

gone to. But no, Sophia was gently encouraging her
beau to relinquish her and escort her friend. As Lord
Philip approached, Jane stepped forward to intercept
him.

'I am so very sorry, my lord, but I fear that there
has been a mistake,' she said, with a winning smile.
'I happened to see the table plan and I fear that Lady
Winterstoke has made an error, for she has placed
Miss Marchment by your side rather than myself.'
She saw Lord Philip cast an incredulous glance in
Sophia's direction and added, 'I am sure that we
would not wish to embarrass our hostess, so the best
thing would surely be for us to exchange escorts. I
hope that Lord Blakeney could be prevailed upon to
accompany me, if you would be so good as to offer
Miss Marchment your arm.'

'Miss Marchment! Yes, of course!' Lord Philip had
regained Sophia's side in less time than it had taken
Jane to suggest it. She saw him speak earnestly in
Sophia's ear, saw her friend look dubiously towards
her and gave them a little smile and a nod of encouragement.

'I am so sorry, Lord Blakeney,' Jane said, turning
to the young peer, 'you will have to make do with
me rather than Miss Marchment! All in a good cause!'

It had indeed been Lady Winterstoke's intention
that Lord Philip should escort Miss Verey in to dinner
and she was mortified by the social disaster that had
so nearly occurred.

When she saw Philip tenderly seating Sophia beside him, saw Jane with Blakeney and realised that
the place cards were all in the wrong order, she could
only bless the strange fate that had led the girls to
accept the wrong escorts. No doubt the maids had

jumbled the cards, which was irritating for she had given them the strictest instructions! Such social ineptitude would have been death to her reputation as a fashionable hostess!

Heaving a sigh of relief, Lady Winterstoke applied herself to the watercress soup. She cast a look at the Duke of Delahaye, bearing in mind that it had been his express wish that Lord Philip escort Miss Verey. She saw that Alex was also watching Jane Verey and there was a look of mingled exasperation and amusement on his face.

Jane was also aware of Alex's scrutiny. She knew that he had guessed that she had engineered the change of placements and had also exchanged escorts with Sophia. Thinking back, he would remember meeting her in the dining-room and immediately realise that she had told him yet another falsehood. The thought made her feel more miserable than she would have expected. She set her jaw firmly. She had warned him that she would do everything in her power to avoid Lord Philip. If the Duke thought badly of her, it would only reinforce his existing opinion that she was a liar and cheat.

After dinner there was impromptu dancing in the salon, which the older guests watched indulgently whilst the younger took part. Jane, whirling around the floor in Lord Blakeney's arms, decided that she had enjoyed the evening very much. A moment later she caught sight of the Duke of Delahaye talking to the elegant blonde woman again, and changed her mind. The evening had been a sad bore after all.

'Lady Francine Dennery,' Blakeney said, in answer to Jane's unspoken question. 'She's the widow of the

Eleventh Earl of Dennery and the scourge of the Twelfth Earl! He don't approve of his wicked stepmother! Not sure where she came from, but we can all guess where she's going! She aims to crown her career with ducal strawberry leaves!'

It seemed that Lady Dennery had her quarry well within her sights. Her blonde head was bent close to Alex Delahaye's dark one and there was a provocative little smile on her red lips. As Jane watched, Lady Dennery brushed her fingers swiftly across the Duke's hand, an intimate little gesture full of meaning. Jane hastily looked the other way.

The last dance of the evening was a quadrille and Jane had promised it to Henry Marchnight. She was not a little taken aback to find the Duke of Delahaye approaching her instead.

'Marchnight has asked me to present you his apologies and myself as a poor substitute,' Alex said, smiling at Lady Verey in a manner that Jane was annoyed to see made her poor mother melt completely. 'His sister has torn a flounce and twisted her ankle, and demands to be taken home at once! I promised him that I would try to make amends!'

'I am sure that Jane is greatly flattered, your Grace,' Lady Verey said, when Jane had singularly failed to provide any response of her own. 'Come, Jane,' she added sharply, 'thank the Duke for his condescension!'

Jane thought that she saw Alex wince. 'I assure you that the privilege is all mine, ma'am,' he murmured, 'but if Miss Verey does not care for my company…'

Jane met his eyes. She had been expecting to see mockery there and was taken aback that he was not even smiling. For some reason she felt a need to hurry in and reassure him. It seemed ridiculous—he was a Duke and had all the assurance that his fifteen years' seniority could give him. Surely he did not need a green girl to convince him that she appreciated his company! And yet...

'Thank you, sir,' she murmured. 'I should be very glad to dance with you.'

Alex took her hand and looked so genuinely pleased that Jane felt her heart leap. She almost drew back, appalled to find her pulse racing at his touch. It was shocking to feel so vulnerable to him, both mentally and physically, and she had no notion how to deal with her feelings. She only knew that she was becoming involved in something too complex to handle.

'The evening has been quite a triumph for you, has it not, Miss Verey?' Alex said quietly, so that only she could hear. 'I did appreciate your manoeuvre at dinner—a masterful piece of strategy! I find that I have to admire you for that!'

The figure of the dance separated them at that moment.

'Thank you, your Grace,' Jane said when they came back together again.

Alex gave her a broad smile that Jane found deeply disturbing. 'No pointless denials, Miss Verey? I admire that too!' The smile faded and his gaze became as brilliant as a sword thrust. 'You are ahead on points, I cannot deny it, but the game is not yet over! We shall see who triumphs in the end!'

Jane's heart skipped a beat but she gave him a look of limpid innocence. 'No doubt we shall be seeing a great deal of you then, sir.'

'I expect so.'

'Do you attend Lady Aston's masquerade on Thursday? I believe that your brother is invited!'

'A masquerade!' Alex looked quizzical. 'Such potential for dissembling, Miss Verey!'

The dance ended. Jane dropped a little curtsy. 'Indeed, sir! We are all looking forward to it! I have a pink domino that I am told is all the crack!'

Alex took her hand and kissed it, his eyes laughing at her. 'Giving secrets to the enemy, Miss Verey?'

'Perhaps so, perhaps not!' Jane withdrew her hand before he could feel it tremble and realise his effect on her. That was one secret she did not intend to give away. She was not at all sure why she had mentioned the masquerade, for it would have suited her plans better for Alex not to be present. Yet the urge to see him again had been a powerful one, a dangerous one. She did not like to examine the reasons for it too closely. As he escorted her back to Lady Verey's side, Jane saw Lady Dennery catch his eye with a significant little glance. At once, Jane felt young and naïve to have succumbed to the charm of a man who evidently preferred more sophisticated company. No doubt he would deliver her to her mother, then forget all about her. It was foolish to expect anything else and she had only herself to blame for being such a starry-eyed innocent.

Simon was alone in the Breakfast Parlour when Jane came down the following day. He was dressed for riding and was flicking through the *Morning Post*, but cast the paper aside with a smile when his sister slid into the seat opposite.

'Good morning, sis! How are you?'

He poured her some chocolate whilst Jane helped herself to a large portion of kidney and bacon.

'I am very well, I thank you.' Jane fixed him with a businesslike eye. 'Simon, I need to ask you something. How is it that you and the Duke of Delahaye are become such firm friends so quickly? It is particularly unfortunate, because I need your support against him in this ridiculous plan to marry me off to Lord Philip!'

A slight frown marred Simon's brow. He was accustomed to his sister's painful directness, although several years away from her company had lulled him into a false sense of security. He looked at her critically as she despatched her breakfast with an efficiency that argued a hearty appetite, if a certain lack of delicacy. He was forced to admit that Jane had grown into a strikingly attractive girl, with her jet black hair and the flyaway black brows that seemed only to emphasise the bright intelligence in those green eyes. Jane was no country mouse, nor could he imagine her playing the part just to find a husband in the marriage mart of *ton* Society. As for the suggestion that she make a marriage of convenience to Lord Philip, well, it seemed absurd. Except that he knew that his mother's heart was set on it and Alex Delahaye seemed insistent… He sighed unhappily.

The impatient drumming of Jane's slender fingers on the tablecloth reminded him that she was still awaiting his reply.

'Alex and I are not particular friends—' Simon prevaricated.

'Alex!' his sister interrupted, investing the word with scorn. 'You seem to be on first-name terms, at the very least!'

Simon sighed again. The martial light in Jane's eyes suggested that this was going to be difficult. 'Alex Delahaye is a friend of Harry Marchnight's,' he said carefully. 'He asked Harry to introduce us because he was concerned to avoid any… difficulties…that might have arisen as a result of Lord Philip's behaviour towards you. The trip to Ambergate and the rumours…' He could feel himself floundering.

'Difficulties?' Jane was momentarily distracted. 'Simon, what exactly did Lord Philip say about me?'

Simon shifted uncomfortably and avoided his sister's eye. He had no intention of stirring up the malicious gossip again. 'Why, nothing much to the purpose! It's better to forget it all now that everything is smoothed over! But Alex was anxious to avoid misunderstandings, or the possibility of me calling Philip out—as though I would waste my time on such a silly young cub!'

'I see.' Jane stirred her chocolate slowly. 'Then as you think him of so little account, you will understand my rejection of his suit! I may count on your support!'

Simon began to perceive that he had made a tactical mistake. Jane's mind was evidently more alert than his at ten in the morning. He smiled reluctantly.

'The trouble is…' He hesitated. He knew she was about to make mincemeat of him. 'The difficulty lies in a business transaction that is to be completed this very morning…' He watched Jane put her cup down and fix him with an unnervingly wide green stare. 'Knowing of my financial constraints at Ambergate, Alex has arranged to advance me a considerable sum on generous terms—'

'You sound like Pettishaw,' Jane said, with deceptive calm. 'Are you trying to tell me that you have sold me into marriage with Lord Philip in return for a loan to help you renovate Ambergate? I know the house is in sad need of repair, but surely your sister's happiness is too high a price to pay?'

'Dash it, Jane, you're running on like a novel from the circulating library!' Simon spluttered, his conscience pricking him. 'I mean no such thing! Of course you don't have to marry the man if you do not wish, but...' he risked a look at her face '...if you could just be nice to him for a few weeks it would help me immensely! Truth is, I'd never get the chance of such good terms from anywhere else and as Alex has seen fit to offer his help—'

'Yes, I wonder why that should be?' Jane marvelled in an innocent tone. Alex Delahaye's words to her at Almack's rang in her ears. *It would help your brother if there were investment in Ambergate... There is always a way...* 'Take care when you sign the agreement, Simon, or you may find your inheritance disappearing into the vast Delahaye estates!'

Simon looked affronted. 'What the devil has Alex done to deserve such opprobrium? You make him sound like a dashed moneylender! From all I hear he's as straight a man to do business with as one could wish!'

Jane shrugged, feeling a little ashamed of herself. She could hardly tell Simon of Alex's threats at Almack's and, as the Duke had seen fit to apologise, it seemed ungracious of her to continue to suspect him. And yet it made her uncomfortable. To think that he had an interest in Ambergate and a growing friendship with Simon brought him a little too close for comfort. It was almost enough to put her off her toast. She eyed the dish of butter with disfavour. This really was not to be borne! Alex Delahaye had achieved what no other man had ever done, and put her off her food!

After Simon had gone out, secretly relieved that his sister had not made more of a scene, Jane poured herself another cup of chocolate and sat back to consider matters. She had believed the Duke entirely when he said that the game had only just begun. It would never do to underestimate him and, rather disconcertingly, she thought that he already had her measure. The patronising attitude he had assumed at Almack's had been replaced by something far more dangerous—the watchful respect a man might show a real adversary. The barriers seemed formidable. Ranged against her to a greater or lesser degree were her own family, who would be happy to see the match made with Lord Philip, as well as the Duke and Lady Eleanor. Worse, she would have to guard against her own wayward heart, which, despite her opposition to him, was inclined to consider Alexander Delahaye with far more warmth than was at all prudent for her peace of mind.

Chapter Five

'Oh Jane, is this not splendid?' Sophia said. Her eyes behind the mask were as bright as stars as she watched the dazzling company mingling in Lady Aston's ballroom. She smoothed her rose pink domino with excited fingers. 'I cannot wait for the Duke and Lord Philip to arrive! I have a wager with Lord Philip that he will never find me in this crush!'

Jane looked at her friend's radiant face and reflected that it would take Lord Philip all of two minutes to identify Sophia, for all that she was masked. There seemed to be some irresistible attraction that drew them directly to each other's side at every opportunity.

Their party was somewhat diminished that evening, for Lady Verey had suddenly succumbed to a sick headache, making it impossible for her to accompany them. Jane and Sophia had been consigned to the somewhat erratic care of her cousin, Mrs Brantledge. Mrs Brantledge had a daughter of her own to launch into society, a young lady who might unkindly have been considered to be firmly on the shelf at twenty-three. Fortunately a suitor had recently swum into

view and both Miss Brantledge and her mother were
hellbent on encouraging him. Simon Verey had been
prevailed upon to accompany his sister, but had made
a purposeful beeline for the cardroom and showed
every sign of staying there all evening. This left Jane
and Sophia very much to their own devices, which
suited Jane admirably, since she was free to pursue
her strategy without interference.

Sophia clutched Jane's arm. 'Jane! He is here! Lord
Philip is here!'

Jane was amazed that Sophia could distinguish
Lord Philip in the crowd about the door and yet her
friend seemed quite certain. In a few moments, Sophia was proved correct as Lord Philip, dashing in a
black domino, was beside them.

'Miss Verey?' he said cautiously, addressing himself to the pink domino. 'Will you do me the honour
of dancing with me?'

'Happily, sir,' Sophia replied softly.

Lord Philip stiffened. His gaze went from the pink
domino to Jane, in sapphire blue, who smiled en-
couragingly but did not speak. Lord Philip turned
back to Sophia and his tone changed completely, softened. 'It is a great pleasure to see you again, ma'am.
I trust that you are well? It has been too long since
we last met!'

'I am very well, I thank you.' Sophia sounded as
breathless and happy as he. 'But for shame, sir! It is
all of a day since we were last together!'

'Does your brother accompany you tonight, sir?'
Jane could not help asking. She convinced herself that
she needed to know for strategic reasons, but felt her
heart sink with disappointment as Lord Philip shook
his head.

'I fear that Alex has cried off! Some party of Lady Dennery's contriving, I believe. He tells me that a trip to the opera is far more suitable for someone of his years.' Lord Philip spread his arms out. 'He gave me his domino and told me to dance with the beautiful lady in the pink domino and I intend to take his advice!' He turned to Sophia and offered his arm, and they moved away towards the dancing.

Jane sighed. The sharp pang of disappointment that had assailed her when she heard of the Duke's absence was something that she did not care to think about. She felt oddly flat, as though all the excitement had already gone out of her evening. She frowned at her own perversity. What could be better? Lady Verey and the Duke were absent, Simon preoccupied and no one there to notice that she and Sophia had exchanged dominos!

On her left, Mrs Brantledge was chatting to another chaperon, deeply engrossed.

'Such a suitable connection for my dear Evelyn! Mr Coomberson's father made a vast fortune but he is a man of both leisure and good education, with a fine estate in Hertfordshire! I am persuaded that they will make a match of it!' And she fell to discussing Evelyn's prospects further.

It seemed to Jane that she was the only one without a beau, a situation that would not have distressed her unduly were it not for the irritating preoccupation she appeared to have with the Duke of Delahaye. It was inexplicable that her thoughts should centre on him, for she had met several young men of good family and unblemished reputation at her come out, and many more men of a shadier sort, yet none of them had interested her in the least. Whereas Alex Delahaye, far beyond her reach and completely uninterested, was constantly in her mind.

Still, there was always the food as consolation and she was already hungry… Excusing herself to Mrs Brantledge, Jane slipped out of the ballroom. A huge buffet supper was laid out on a long table in the next room, with small chairs dotted about so that the guests could gather in informal groups whilst they ate. The table was piled high with the most wonderful food and the smell was very appetising. Jane's mouth watered.

The room was completely empty. Jane tiptoed forward and reached tentatively for a slice of cold chicken pie. It was absolutely delicious, light and creamy with a flaky pastry crust. She licked her fingers, looking dubiously at the gap left on the plate where the slice should have been. Someone would be sure to notice the space.

'All alone, my lady?'

Jane jumped violently. She had not heard anyone approach, despite keeping a wary eye out for attentive servants. Yet the gentleman in the dark green domino was standing almost directly behind her.

The dark gaze behind the mask moved from Jane's guilty, flushed face to the pie dish. 'You could rearrange the remaining slices,' he suggested with a hint of a smile. 'I am sure that no one would notice. But only if you also removed this—' And he stretched out a hand and touched Jane's cheek. A crumb of pastry floated down to the floor.

He had not been wearing gloves and his touch seemed to burn Jane's skin. For a moment her startled gaze locked with his, then she took a hasty step back. She knew at once who he was, despite the disguise

of the domino and mask. She had known as soon as
he had touched her.

A footman and maid came in, bringing huge silver
dishes of fruit, and the silence between them was broken.

'Perhaps I should escort you back to the ballroom,'
the gentleman said gently, and there was a note in his
voice that Jane did not understand. He offered her his
arm and she took it without a word. She felt as though
her whole body was tingling, alive to his touch. The
recognition between them was not a matter of names
or even faces, but something far deeper.

'You must tell me how I may address you,' the
Duke said lazily, steering her purposefully along the
colonnade that skirted the ballroom, and away from
Mrs Brantledge's curious gaze. 'It is important to settle such matters early on at a masquerade, for you
could equally be a Duchess or a milkmaid in disguise!'

Jane smiled a little, remembering the curious pleasure she had felt when he had called her 'my lady'.
It seemed that they were to pretend to anonymity,
which was, after all, the purpose of a masked ball.
She had no objection, but she was certain that he had
recognised her all the same. And she was wary. Why
had he pretended to be engaged elsewhere and then
attended the masquerade? What was his intention in
seeking her out? And had he remembered that she
should have been wearing a rose pink domino?

'Oh, I am nothing so exciting as either of those,'
she said, with a smile, playing for time. 'I am only a
young lady who has but recently come to Town!'

'Then it seems I must be formal, madam, if that is
all the help you will give me.' Alex's gaze was warm

with appreciation as it dwelt on her face. 'A young lady I could have guessed—a beautiful young lady, perhaps... Does your mama know how dangerous it is to allow you to wander unattended at a masquerade ball? There are plenty of gentlemen less scrupulous than I who would be eager to take advantage!'

Jane could see that this might well be true. Before they had arrived that night she had wondered at the appeal of a masked ball. Now she was experiencing it for herself. Freed by the disguise of a mask and domino, one might pretend to be whomever one pleased and flirt as one chose. It was strangely seductive, even to so level-headed a girl as Jane.

'I prefer to keep my name a secret, sir,' she said, 'just as you do yours, so you must call me what you will!'

'Ah...' she could see that he was smiling now '...but then I might offend you by having to call you sweetheart! Such endearments suit you well!'

'I thank you, sir, that is quite enough!' Jane realised that a strategic retreat was necessary already—he moved far too quickly. 'I said that I was a young *lady*—' she stressed the word '—and you must believe it, sir! No doubt my chaperon will be so good as to reinforce the point when you return me to her!'

The gentleman inclined his head. 'Your point is well made and well taken, ma'am! And that being the case, may I not keep you from her side a little longer? It is seldom one has the chance to match wits with a diamond of the first water!'

'A diamond, sir?'

'The sharpness, ma'am, as well as the beauty—do not tell me that you do not understand me. Diamonds cut diamonds, they say.'

Jane caught her breath. She could not deny that this was an intriguing skirmish, but it was hardly wise. She remembered her mama's strictures that ladies should never appear to be too clever, 'For you have a distressingly *mathematical* turn of mind, dear Jane, and I do beg you to dissemble it as much as possible. The gentlemen will not understand, nor wish to humour you…'

Yet the Duke of Delahaye had always expressed himself delighted to have the chance to pit his wit against hers, just as he was doing now.

'Have we met before, sir?' she asked innocently, testing how far he might take the pretence.

'No, indeed,' the Duke said smoothly, 'for I should not have forgotten!'

'How odd! I could have sworn… Then it is strange—'

'To feel such recognition, ma'am? I am flattered that you should think so!'

'I was about to say that it is strange that you should seem to presume on a longer acquaintance, sir!' Jane finished sweetly, and heard him laugh.

'Do you know, ma'am, I have the oddest feeling that the more time I spend in your company, the more I shall have to accustom myself to such set-downs!'

'Then pray do not put yourself through the experience, sir,' Jane concluded gently. 'My chaperon is just a few steps away and may take me off your hands!'

There was a silence. The pillars cast long shadows and Jane suddenly experienced the illusion that they were quite alone, rather than within feet of a ballroom full of four hundred people.

'Your suggestion holds little appeal, I fear, ma'am,' Alex said silkily. 'I would far rather dance with you!'

Jane opened her eyes wide. 'A most autocratic invitation, my lord!'

'You attribute a rank to me, ma'am?'

'A high one to suit your manner, sir!'

He laughed. 'Come and dance with me, if you please!'

The music was just striking up.

'A waltz!' Jane hung back.

'I collect that you must have danced at Almack's?' Jane realised that he was teasing her. Who would know that better than he?

'As you know, sir! But—' Jane was suddenly wary. It was too late. He had swept her on to the floor with an expertise that was very familiar.

There was also a difference between verbal fencing and this altogether more disturbing intimacy, Jane thought breathlessly. Clasped so close to the Duke, the dancers around them dipping and swirling, she felt frighteningly powerless. The awareness that was flooding her body was familiar and exciting, threatening to sweep her beyond common sense. The atmosphere of the masquerade, daring and raffish, could only encourage such abandonment.

'The supper dance is next,' Alex remarked, reclaiming Jane's attention from her wayward thoughts as the last strains of the waltz died away. 'You will not be wanting to miss that.'

'No, indeed.' Jane blushed at the memory of being caught with her mouth full of chicken pie. 'I am promised for that dance, sir. I must beg you to return me to my chaperon.'

'A pity. Remember to hurry into the supper room

at the end of the dance and you may be able to take another piece of pie before anyone notices,' her escort said smoothly. 'Otherwise there will be endless speculation on who the mystery eater could be—one of the servants may even be dismissed as a result!'

'You are unchivalrous to remind me, sir,' Jane murmured. She could see her partner for the supper dance approaching Mrs Brantledge. 'What could be more humiliating than being found stealing the food?'

'But it shows an interesting trait of character, perhaps…'

'That I like food?'

'That you will take risks to achieve what you want, ma'am.'

Their eyes met again, a quizzical expression in his. Jane wrenched her gaze away. What was this peculiar affinity that threatened her, this attraction that was like nothing she had ever experienced before? She had told herself that it was only common sense to try to keep out of his way, but the shaming truth was that she had no wish to do so. She was not at all certain of his next move. It was like an engrossing game of chess, but with an added edge of sensual awareness between the two of them. Jane frowned. His Grace of Delahaye might well be accustomed to playing such sophisticated games, but she was not at all sure that she would be able to carry it off!

'Lord Harvey is waiting for me, sir,' she said, a little at random. 'Please excuse me.'

He bowed. 'Certainly, ma'am. I shall see you later, perhaps.'

Jane, trembling inside, hoped that that was unlikely. Now that good sense had reasserted itself, she intended to do everything in her power to avoid him.

From the dance floor she watched the green domino skirt the edge of the room and take up a position by the door of the supper room, resting his broad shoulders against the wall as he watched her with undisguised interest. Jane shivered a little. She was becoming too entangled in this! Her feelings were hopelessly engaged and it seemed that Alex did not intend to allow her to withdraw.

Lord Harvey's bland presence was soothing. He made few conversational demands upon her and Jane began to relax as the country dance progressed, although Alex's continued scrutiny was unsettling. It was only as they progressed through the set that Jane realised that Philip and Sophia were also dancing, Sophia resplendent in the pink domino that should have been Jane's own. Jane risked another glance across at Alex and saw with a sinking heart that his gaze was also following Philip and Sophia. She knew that he would not be slow to put two and two together.

Jane realised that Simon had abandoned the card tables and was also dancing, his partner being a slender girl with very fair hair. Jane did not recognise her and wondered who she could be. There was a look on her brother's face that arrested her attention, for all that he had the protection of the mask. Jane sighed silently. So Simon was also succumbing to Cupid's arrow! It seemed that she was surrounded by romance and her own foolhardy heart had to choose an entirely inappropriate subject for its affections!

For once Jane did not enjoy supper, not because she was worrying about the piece of pie but because she was like a cat on hot bricks trying to locate the Duke of Delahaye. It seemed, however, that the green domino had vanished and, once fortified by food, Jane felt a little better. Her dance card was full and the rest of the evening fled, until Sophia touched her arm late on in the evening.

'Jane! It is only ten minutes to the unmasking! Are we to exchange dominoes?'

They slipped away to Lord Aston's study. There, the pink and the blue dominoes were hastily exchanged and Sophia hurried back to the ballroom to be blamelessly at Mrs Brantledge's side at the unmasking. Jane tarried a moment, so that they should not be seen returning together. She smiled a little, thinking of the neatness of her plan and how well it had worked in the end. Lady Verey knew that her daughter's domino had been pink and Sophia's blue. Now there would be plenty of people to report to her that Lord Philip had spent all evening dancing attendance on the pink domino... Her smile faded as she thought of the Duke of Delahaye. He too had known that her domino was supposed to be pink. That meant that either he had not recognised her earlier, and would flirt with any pretty girl he met, or that he was just playing along with her to see where the deception was leading, or that she had been mistaken and the green domino had not been the Duke at all... Jane gave up. It was a tangled web and she was becoming hopelessly confused.

She checked the clock and decided to give Sophia another minute before she followed her back to the ballroom. Lord Aston had a carved marble chess set on a round table before the window. Jane moved the Queen idly.

'All alone at the unmasking, Cinderella?'

She had not heard anyone come in. Whirling

around, her heart pounding, Jane caught her breath on a gasp.

'Oh, sir, you startled me! I was about to go back to the ballroom…'

The green domino's gaze fell on the chessmen.

'It is a fine set. Do you play?'

'Yes,' Jane said, 'my father taught me.' She put the Queen back in her appointed place.

'A game of cunning and strategy.'

'If played well…' Jane saw the glimmer in his eyes and smiled back in spite of herself. 'I make no claims to be a good player…'

'I am sure you are not doing yourself justice, ma'am! What other games do you play?'

'I do not gamble, sir, if that is what you mean…' Jane's breath caught a little. She knew exactly what he meant. Any moment now he would identify himself and upbraid her for her latest trick. He *must* know now that she had exchanged dominoes with Sophia and that it was Sophia, not she, who had spent the evening with Lord Philip.

'Excuse me, sir.' She was glad that her voice did not betray her. 'I think I should rejoin my party. They will be missing me…'

The long-case clock in the corner chimed the hour, making her jump.

'It is time for the unmasking,' the green domino said, his eyes intent on her face. 'Am I to be denied knowledge of the identity of so fascinating a companion? I assure you, it is the only reason I have lingered so long at the ball…'

He put out a hand to pull back the hood of Jane's domino, reaching for the ties to her mask.

She could feel his fingers amongst her tumbled

black curls and her whole body started to tremble.
The mask came away and Jane felt as though she
were naked. There was no chance of escape now. To
play the innocent could be her only defence.

'You have the advantage of me, sir...' Her voice
was husky. His hand brushed her cheek for a moment,
sending more quivers of sensation along her nerve-
endings. He pulled his own mask away with a quick,
impatient gesture.

'Not so, Miss Verey. You have known my identity
all evening, have you not?'

Jane cleared her throat. 'All evening, sir?'

Alex's dark eyes pinned her to the spot. 'Come
now, Miss Verey, where is your much-vaunted honesty? Are you denying that you spent some time in
my company earlier?'

Jane's wide green eyes met his virtuously. 'How
could I know, sir? All the guests have been masked...'

She could see from his expression that he did not
believe her and he looked to be torn between laughter
and exasperation. He took a step forward and Jane's
heart leaped into her throat. Her instinctive movement
away caused the pale candlelight to shimmer for a
moment on the rose pink domino; the shadows shifted
and then Alex stood back suddenly, his voice changing abruptly.

'A pink domino, Miss Verey?'

'As you see, sir.'

'No doubt Miss Marchment is in blue?'

'Indeed she is.'

'But you were wearing the blue domino earlier this
evening?'

'You might well have believed that, your Grace.'

Alex looked as though he was uncertain whether

to shake her or kiss her. For a moment Jane was held captive by the expression in his eyes, then he said,

'Oh, Miss Verey, I believe that it is not safe to let you from my sight!'

He sketched a slight bow and watched her positively run from the room. The oak door latched with a firm click behind her.

Alexander Delahaye slumped into an armchair, running a hand through his rumpled black hair. It was only with the greatest effort of will that he had made himself let Jane Verey go. His instinct, more powerful than anything he had felt in a very long time, had prompted him to crush her to him and kiss her until she could no longer stand.

As soon as he had met her in the supper room he had recognised her, blue domino or not. He remembered her references to wearing a pink domino and suspected that she had tricked him again. When he saw Philip paying court to the lady in pink, he had been certain.

Nevertheless, some impulse had led him to flirt with her, a whim that he barely understood but was forced to admit he had found deeply enjoyable. Jane's quick wit and willingness to cross swords with him were most stimulating. She was an intriguing conundrum, at once so daring and yet so innocent, risking a little then drawing back! Alex sighed. These were not the feelings he should be having for his brother's future bride! He stretched out his long legs and looked covetously at the decanter of brandy standing on Lord Aston's bureau. Suddenly he needed a drink.

Simon Verey was having a bad evening. He had lost the angelic beauty who had granted him one dance earlier in the evening and now his sister had disappeared as well. Belatedly remembering that he had promised his mother that he would look after Jane and Sophia, he started to search the ballroom for them.

A blue domino was visible in one of the alcoves, talking to a gentleman in black who looked completely besotted. Simon frowned. Had Jane been wearing pink or blue? Was that Sophia? Her face was turned away from him but the fair hair curling from beneath the hood certainly suggested that it could not be Jane.

Scowling, Simon ventured into the empty supper room and out into the conservatory. There were plenty of people strolling there, but none of them were Jane. Finally Simon stepped out into the garden, where the cool night air was refreshing after the humid atmosphere in the house. Giggles and rustling from behind the bushes suggested that the most amorous of the party-goers had decided to further their acquaintance in the relative privacy of the darkness. Simon did not for one moment believe that his sister would be amongst them, but he was almost ready to strangle her anyway. He retraced his steps to the terrace.

'I beg you, sir, to let me go! Your suggestions disgust me!'

Simon swung round abruptly. He knew that it was not Jane, but he recognised the voice. The shifting shadows of the terrace moved a little to show the slender shape of a girl struggling violently in the grip of a burly individual almost twice her size. There was a ripping sound and an exclamation from the man, who appeared to be bending her back against the parapet until it seemed she must break in half. Simon hurried forward and took him by the collar.

'You heard the lady, sirrah! Be off with you!'

The man was very drunk. He let go of the girl abruptly and swung his fist at Simon, making contact instead with the stone coping. With a howl of mingled rage and pain, he stormed off into the night. There was a silence. The girl smoothed down her torn domino, which was showing a dress of silvery gauze beneath.

'You're very kind, sir.' Her voice shook a little with agitation and Simon put out an instinctive hand.

'You must let me take you back to your chaperon,' he said gruffly. 'However appealing a breath of fresh air may be, it is not safe to be alone out here.'

He thought he saw her smile a little in the darkness. 'Oh, I have no chaperon to take care of me,' she said, with bitter amusement, 'but I thank you for your concern, sir.'

Simon stared at her through the darkness. Her words suggested that she was married or worse—better?—that she was a Cyprian who had attended the masquerade in the hope of attracting a rich protector. It was scarcely unknown, but Simon's whole being rejected the idea. She neither spoke nor acted like a courtesan and she had had every opportunity to try to engage his interest earlier, yet she had made no push to do so. Nor, indeed, had she encouraged the drunken overtures of Lord Hewetson, whom he had just seen off…

'Who are you?' Simon asked abruptly. 'You must be here as part of a party, you must have some protection! Let me escort you back inside—'

'I thank you, but no.' The girl's voice was low but firm. There was some kind of accent that gave it an added charm, elusive but very sweet. 'You misunderstand me, sir. I am quite alone, but I have no need of your escort. Please excuse me...' And she walked away, her footsteps fading away across the stone terrace.

Simon followed more slowly, determined to keep her within view and puzzling over what she had said. He had completely forgotten his intention of finding Jane and Sophia and escorting them home.

The girl could be seen hurrying along the edge of the ballroom towards the main door, her torn domino flapping behind her. She kept the hood up, held closely about her face, but her long silver-gilt hair streamed behind her. For the first time Simon reflected that she might have told him the literal truth when she had said that she was attending the ball alone. If so, she *had* to be a barque of frailty, for no respectable girl would ever attend a ball like this unescorted. And yet—

A scream pierced the air. Startled, Simon saw that the girl had checked in the doorway, restrained by the clutching hands of the Duchess of Merrion. The girl was pulling in one direction and the Duchess in the other, and they were making a comic spectacle of themselves. The Duchess was still screaming.

'My dress! She's wearing my dress!'

Everybody was staring. The Duchess had a very loud and penetrating voice. Simon tried to push his way through the gathering crowd.

'Dear ma'am, there must be some mistake—' he heard the girl say as she tried to prise herself free. Her hood had fallen back and strands of the silver fair hair tumbled over her shoulders. Her face was thin with high cheekbones, like a drawing from a fairy story. She still had her mask on and behind it her eyes shone with a blue fire. Simon stared, completely bewitched.

The old Duchess clung tighter. 'Mistake! I promised a fortune to Celestine for that dress! The only one, she said! It was to be delivered tomorrow! Where did you get it from? Who are you?'

With a gasp the girl wrenched herself free and ran into the hall. Her jade green domino slid from her shoulders and crumpled on the floor.

'Stop her, she's stealing my dress!' The Duchess shrieked, completely over-excited. For a moment no one moved, then a babble of conversation broke out, but no one made any move after the girl.

'Kitchen maid tricked up in her mistress' dress...' someone said.

'Dashed pretty girl...'

'Any old riff-raff at these events...'

People began to move away. Simon bent to pick up the discarded jade green domino. A faint sweet scent still clung to its folds, immediately evocative of its wearer. Simon was astonished to feel desire stirring in him. He knew that he had to find her. Whoever she was, he had to see her again.

Chapter Six

The trouble with the Season, Jane thought, as she prepared for yet another evening's entertainment, was that it gave one so little time to think and plan. She could well believe Miss Brantledge's smug assertion that she had attended fifty balls, twenty-six dinners and fourteen picnics the previous year. Miss Brantledge would be sure to have counted every one. And since the object of the entire exercise appeared to be to wear oneself to a thread as well as find a husband, Jane could see that it worked very well. However, the social demands gave her no chance to develop her scheme for avoiding the marriage with Lord Philip. Jane snapped her fan together sharply in frustration, causing one of the struts to splinter. That evening they were to be the guests of the Duke of Delahaye for a concert at Vauxhall Gardens. Jane's natural pleasure in visiting so exciting a place was tempered by the thought of close chaperonage and the embarrassment of being in Alex's company for the first time since the masquerade.

The memory of that evening a week ago was still disturbing to Jane. She had promised herself that she would think of it no more, but she could not help herself. There had been a moment, there in the darkened study, when Jane had been sure Alex was about to kiss her. The look in his eyes, compounded of exasperation and tenderness, had held her rooted to the spot. And she had wanted him to kiss her, had quite ached to be in his arms, with a desperation that puzzled and worried her. Surely it was not at all refined to be subject to such strong feelings? The mutual respect and comfort she had hoped to find one day in marriage were pale and cold in comparison.

Yet evidently Alex had not felt the same. He had had plenty of opportunities to seek her out in the past week—even if it was only to ring a peal over her for her conduct—and he had not chosen to do so. Clearly she had read far more into his behaviour than he had ever intended; the flirtation that she had found so exciting had no doubt seemed tame to him, a diversion quickly forgotten. It was shaming now to remember how his touch had stirred her senses and how much pleasure she had taken in his company.

Besides, Alex was now too occupied with the odious Lady Dennery to have a moment's thought for Jane. The whole of society was talking about them; they had been seen driving in the Park and Alex squired her to any number of events. Sighing, Jane tried to fix the splintered struts of her fan together again, then cast it away in exasperation. No doubt Lady Dennery would be there that evening and the prospect did not entice.

In one respect only were matters shaping quite well. Lord Philip and Sophia were clearly smitten with each other and therefore quite willing to give Jane as much tacit support as she needed. It only re-

quired for her to suggest that she and Sophia
exchange partners for a dance, or escorts for a walk,
and the substitution was accomplished. However, this
could not be achieved as often as Jane would wish
under Lady Verey's beady gaze. She was obliged to
endure several tedious dances with Lord Philip during
which he spoke in monosyllables, if at all. Jane decided that she would soon need to seek his more ac-
tive participation in her plans.

They approached Vauxhall by river that evening
and the gardens looked remarkably pretty in the fading dusk, with their lantern-lit walks and arbours. Jane
thought that it looked very romantic and her sense of
humour was tickled at the thought of their ill-assorted
party. Lord Philip and Sophia were surely the only
true romantics in the group and even if Lord Philip's
intentions were of the purest, he could not declare
them openly. Lady Dennery was hunting Alexander
Delahaye with a single-minded concentration that had
very little to do with romance, as far as Jane could
see. Simon seemed forlorn and quiet, and she herself
felt quite out of step with the brightly coloured illusion all around.

The concert and the supper were both excellent,
despite Lady Dennery's somewhat sharp asides.

'What charming children!' she had said to Lady
Verey when first introduced, for all the world, Jane
thought, as though she and Sophia were still in lead-
ing-reins! Lady Dennery then took it upon herself to
intersperse intimate little remarks to Alex with obser-
vations on the conduct of young ladies, until Jane was
heartily sick of her.

'Why, Miss Verey, you have a most robust appetite!' she said archly, picking at her dessert and smil-

ing at Alex. 'You will find that the gentlemen prefer young ladies who show less partiality for their food! No doubt Lord Philip will bear me out!'

Philip, who had been gazing soulfully at Sophia and had not heard the comment, grunted non-committally. Jane's cheeks flamed. Lady Dennery's laugh tinkled out as her sharp gaze appraised Jane's neat figure. 'Lud, Miss Verey, I think you should restrain yourself now! Over-indulgence at the table is often a sign of a sadly unsteady character! There is no knowing where such a lack of discipline will lead you later!'

Lady Verey and Lady Eleanor exchanged a horrified look at such vulgarity. Fortunately Jane and Sophia were both looking quite blank, for neither of them had taken her ladyship's coarse allusion. Simon, catching his mother's eye, got up and suggested a short stroll in the interval before the concert resumed. He offered his arm to Sophia and in short order Jane and Lord Philip had joined them. The others declined the exercise, making Jane almost burst as she tried to repress a remark on the benefits of activity for a healthy figure.

They admired the little pools and grottoes and sauntered amidst the crowds. All of them studiously avoided speaking of Lady Dennery and more particularly of the possibility that she might become the next Duchess of Delahaye.

Sophia and Philip paused to admire a group of marble statuary whilst Simon and Jane walked on ahead.

'Are you enjoying all this or do you miss Ambergate, Janey?' Simon asked suddenly, gesturing at the crowded gardens.

Jane smiled. 'A little of both, I suppose! I am enjoying the Season, but I shall not be sorry when it ends.' A shadow fell across her face as she realised that the matter of the marriage to Lord Philip would have to be resolved once and for all by then. In an effort to be cheerful she turned a smile on her brother.

'What about you, Simon? I suppose you'll be going home in a couple of months?'

'I'll spend some time at Ambergate,' Simon agreed, 'but Alex has invited me to Yorkshire for the shooting in August.'

'Has he!' Jane realised that she was out-of-proportion cross. The Duke of Delahaye seemed to interfere in everything! 'After you have helped him marry me off to his brother, I suppose!'

Simon flashed her an ironic glance. 'We shall have to be quick about it then, or else Philip will have eloped with Sophia!'

Jane sighed, sliding her hand through his arm. 'So you have noticed it! Yes, their affection is becoming a little too apparent! And whilst it would solve one problem, I suppose—'

'It would only cause another,' Simon finished grimly. 'Alex would be furious and matters would be off to a very bad start!'

'Yes…' Jane looked round to see if Sophia and Philip were within earshot. To her surprise they were nowhere to be seen. The empty walks stretched away on either side of the gravel path, dark with their high hedges.

'Oh! It is too bad! They should have more sense than to slip away together at a place like this! Sophia should be more careful of her reputation and if Lord Philip does not have honourable intentions—' Jane broke off, afflicted by a powerful guilt. She was all too aware that she had encouraged the couple to spend time together.

Simon was frowning as he scanned the crowds.

'They cannot have gone far. We may see them if we walk towards the pavilion—'. He broke off suddenly, staring over the heads of the crowd. 'Well, I'll be…'

Jane saw that her brother was watching a slender blonde girl who was walking swiftly away from them. At her side, a portly man in a striped red and white waistcoat appeared to be talking to her urgently, almost running to keep up with her. Jane saw her shake her head once, decisively, then the man tried to catch her arm. The couple turned down one of the dark walks, and at the same time, Simon dropped Jane's arm and darted off after them without another word. Jane stared in stupefaction.

To have gone from being in a party of four to being alone seemed strange and vexatious, but Jane was a sensible girl and realised that she could find her way back to the rotunda with little trouble. There were plenty of people about and she felt quite safe. Far more provoking was Simon's erratic behaviour. Evidently he had recognised either the girl or her companion, but as to why he had rushed off without a word… Jane started to walk slowly back towards the rotunda. As she passed the pool with the statuary, she thought she saw Philip and Sophia just disappearing around the corner of one of the walks to the right of her. At the same time, Jane glimpsed the tall but unmistakable figure of the Duke of Delahaye coming towards her. She was not sure if he had seen her, but did not want to wait and find out. The first difficult explanation—why she was alone—was linked too closely to the second—where Sophia and Philip were. And if his Grace of Delahaye should come across Lord Philip with Sophia down one of the dark walks... Without further ado, Jane whisked around the hedge and hurried after the disappearing couple.

Although the crowds were thick only a few yards away, here between the high hedges it was dark and silent. Jane came to a crossroads, where a marble nymph reclined in a mossy bower. Looking around, she felt as though she had entered a maze. Any moment she would lose her sense of direction and become completely lost. She was about to abandon Sophia to her fate, turn around and retrace her steps, when she heard a faint noise.

Jane realised that the walk was not as deserted as she had at first thought. The portly gentleman she had seen earlier crossed her view briefly as he turned down a parallel path. The girl was no longer with him and he was skulking in the shadow of the hedge. For some reason Jane shrank back, praying that the gossamer white of her dress would not betray her. There was something so furtive in the man's behaviour that it made her deeply uneasy.

Then she froze. There was a summerhouse ahead of her at a point where five of the walks converged, and she had just noticed Alex's tall figure stride into the centre in order to scan the crowds thronging along the main walks. And she could also see the portly gentleman, stalking as quietly as a cat, up the shadowy edge of the nearby path. The moonlight glinted on the white stripes of his waistcoat and on the silver blade in his hand. It seemed ludicrous, yet there was a stealth about the man that was infinitely frightening, and each step took him closer to Alex's unsuspecting back.

Jane did not wait another moment. She flew down the walk, making as much noise as possible, raced up the steps and tumbled into Alex's arms. To her left she heard the rustle of leaves and saw the shadows move as the man slipped away as silently as he had come.

'Your Grace!'

'Miss Verey? I have been looking for you!' There was a lazy amusement in Alex's voice. 'Whatever can you have—?' His tone sharpened as he felt her knees give way and she sagged against him. He took her by the upper arms and shook her slightly.

'What has happened? Has somebody hurt you? Answer me!'

'No! Oh, you must come away...' Jane could hear her voice breaking shamefully. Now that the immediate danger was over she found that she was able to neither stand nor speak properly. Alex's face was very close to hers, his eyes blazing. If he had not held her, she knew she would have fallen.

'Jane? You must tell me what is wrong!'

Jane took a deep breath. 'You must come away from this place, your Grace! There is a man with a knife—'

Alex took a swift look around. 'A pickpocket—'

'No!' Jane said, beating her hands against his chest in her agitation. 'A murderer! He has a knife!'

'Very well. We will go at once.' Alex captured both her hands in his own, infinitely reassuring, grip. His voice was very calm. He saw that she was shaking and wrapped his cloak close about her, at the same time urging her forward and down the summerhouse steps towards the crowded paths.

'Can you manage to walk back to the others, Miss Verey? It is but a step and you are quite safe.'

With Alex's arm around her and one of her hands still resting in his, Jane managed to walk shakily back towards the main path. Once they had rejoined the press of people wandering back towards the rotunda, Alex let her go and offered her his arm in a more circumspect manner. Jane let out a huge shaky breath.

'Oh, thank goodness! What a horrid thing to happen!' She glanced up at Alex's face and saw that he was frowning. He drew her into one of the lit alcoves and helped her to a seat.

Seeing her look of surprise, he said quickly, 'We shall go back to the others directly. But first, Miss Verey, can you tell me what happened?'

He was so matter of fact that Jane was determined not to be missish. 'I saw the man earlier when I was walking with Simon,' she said, as calmly as possible. 'He was a fat man in a bulging waistcoat, not some ragged pickpocket. Then, just before I saw you in the summerhouse, I heard a noise and saw him creeping down the walk towards you. He had a knife in his hand! I saw it!'

Alex remained silent. His dark brows were drawn and he looked to be thinking of something far beyond the brightly lit pleasure gardens. Whatever his thoughts were, Jane could tell that they were not pleasant. She shivered.

'An opportunist thief,' Alex said easily, after a moment. 'It was foolish of me to step aside from the crowds, for Vauxhall is well known for its petty thieves and criminals. I am sorry that you should have had such a shocking experience, Miss Verey, but I beg you to forget it. The man missed his chance and will be long gone by now.'

Jane did not reply. Something in her wanted to protest that the man had been no simple thief, but what proof did she have? It was the most obvious explanation. After all, who would intentionally seek Alex out with murder in mind? The idea seemed ridiculous.

'I think,' Alex added, very deliberately, 'that we should not worry the others with this story, Miss Verey. The ladies, in particular, would be most distressed. Which reminds me to ask…' the frown deepened on his brow '…whatever were you doing alone in the dark walks?'

Jane hesitated. This was tricky, since she had no wish to cause trouble for the others. 'I became separated from the others by accident,' she said evasively, 'and was looking for them again when I saw you— and the thief.'

'I see,' Alex said drily. 'How very vague, Miss Verey! You *were* alone, I suppose?'

'What do you mean—?' Jane broke off and blushed. 'Your Grace!'

'Well?'

'Would it have been preferable for me to have been accompanied or alone in such a situation?' Jane asked spiritedly.

Alex raised an eyebrow. He got up and helped Jane to her feet. 'Ah, now I know that you are feeling more yourself, Miss Verey! And there you have me, for I am not at all sure!'

They walked back to the rotunda slowly. The music had already started again. Sophia and Philip were sitting several feet apart, looking on her part demure and on his suspiciously cheerful. Simon caught Jane's eye. His own expression was sheepish. Jane raised a cautionary finger to her lips and he kept obediently silent. She did not wish him to say anything that might contradict the sparse tale that she had already told Alex.

It was only as she was turning back to the orchestra that Jane realised that Alex had also seen her clandestine gesture and was watching her with a look that was both interested and deeply speculative.

Lady Eleanor Fane called at Haye House the following morning at a time that most members of the *ton* would have considered quite uncivilised. As she let the knocker fall she had a moment of doubt, for she had just remembered how much attention Alex had been lavishing on Lady Dennery the previous night. If she had managed to fix Alex's interest he would scarcely be receiving guests that morning... Lady Eleanor set her lips firmly as the door started to open. Too late!

Tredpole's impassive face gave nothing away.

'I will inquire if his Grace is at home,' the butler murmured, his stately progress across the hall suggesting that though the answer to his question might be in doubt, he would be equal to any eventuality. Left alone to wait in the drawing-room, Lady Eleanor peered critically into the mirror and fidgeted with her silver-topped stick.

Fortunately the Duke was receiving and did not keep her waiting long.

'His Grace begs you to join him in the library, my lady,' Tredpole murmured, preceding Lady Eleanor across the hall.

'Humph!' Lady Eleanor replied, secretly relieved not to have found her godson *in flagrante*.

Alex was sitting at his desk, slowly sipping a cup of coffee, the pungent fumes of which Lady Eleanor could smell across the room. She sniffed appreciatively.

'Tredpole, another cup, if you please!' Alex said with a grin, coming forward to kiss his aunt. 'What can bring you here so early, Aunt Eleanor? You might have found me otherwise occupied!'

Lady Eleanor fixed him with a repressive gaze. 'Perhaps that accounts for your deplorably high spirits, Alexander!' she said tartly. 'I shall not inquire!' Then, as her nephew's grin broadened, she added, 'It is another lady I have come to speak about—Miss Verey! I have been thinking that Philip's suit progresses very ill. According to Maria Winchester, Philip was spotted in the dark walks with Miss Marchment last night! I begged Maria to keep quiet for the sake of our friendship, but if Philip is pursuing other game… Meanwhile, the *on dit* is that Blakeney is hoping to fix his interest with Miss Verey, engagement or no! He has certainly been very attentive of late!'

Alex's smile faded. 'Blakeney? Are you sure, Aunt Eleanor?'

'What does it matter if it is Blakeney or some other gentleman?' Lady Eleanor demanded discontentedly. 'First the business at Lady Winterstoke's dinner and now this! Why, it seems to me that the little minx is running rings around you!'

Alex sat down on the corner of his desk, one leg swinging. 'Do you think so, Aunt Eleanor? It is early days yet, you know!'

Lady Eleanor took a reviving draught of the strong coffee. 'Decisive action is what is called for here, Alex, not shilly-shallying! Why, anyone would think that you enjoyed crossing swords with the chit!' She drained her cup, thereby missing her godson's fleetingly rueful expression. 'Whilst you are playing games, Philip is engaging the affections of another lady entirely! I should have thought that *that* would exercise your mind considerably!'

Alex did not seem either surprised or disturbed by this statement. 'I collect that by that you mean Miss Marchment? Philip has fallen in and out of love more times than I care to count, Aunt! You know that! It means nothing—he will marry where the money dictates!'

'Miss Marchment is no lightskirt to help Philip while away the time until he weds!' Lady Eleanor snapped. 'The girl has fallen head over ears in love with him and this time…this time, Alex, I do believe that Philip may feel the same!'

Alex was examining a paperweight, turning it over in his hands so that the light struck sparks off the deep blue interior. His head was bent and Lady Eleanor could not see his expression.

'I am certain that you must be mistaken,' he said levelly. 'Philip has never shown any sign of attaching himself to a respectable female!'

'Never before!' Lady Eleanor tapped her stick on the floor in her agitation. 'If you do not act quickly, Alex, the Verey match will be lost forever and then how will you square your promise to your grandfather with events?'

Alex looked up, the expression in his dark eyes quite unreadable. 'No doubt I should think of something…' he murmured. 'But I suspect that you had more in mind than to come here to berate me for my lack of action, did you not, ma'am? Unless I miss my guess, you have a plan!'

Lady Eleanor smiled reluctantly, soothed by both her nephew's teasing and the excellent coffee.

'Well, well…I thought to lend a helping hand! I had the idea of inviting the Vereys to Malladon!'

Alex put the paperweight down gently. 'You intend for me to open up Malladon for a house party? Now? In the middle of the Season?'

'Precisely!' Lady Eleanor leaned forward. 'It would not be a party Alex, only a few guests, and not for long! And I would act as hostess for you!'

'Good of you, ma'am!' her nephew murmured with irony.

Lady Eleanor was not to be deterred. 'I know it is the middle of the Season, but I thought that a few days in the country would be the very thing! The trouble with the Season is that too many people are milling around! It is easier to concentrate attention in a smaller group!'

'One of Miss Verey's tactics has been to employ others as a distraction,' Alex observed thoughtfully. 'It is true that she would find it less easy to be so evasive in so small a group. You realise, however, that Miss Marchment will have to be invited too? Courtesy demands that she should be included.'

'I suppose we cannot leave the wretched girl behind,' Lady Eleanor concurred, 'and really it is too bad of me to describe her thus, for she is the sweetest child, only a threat to your plans!'

'Plans can always be changed, ma'am,' Alex observed, but before his aunt could ask for further clarification, he continued. 'I am gratified to see, however, that you have come round to my way of thinking! Originally you were berating me for believing Miss Verey to be anything other than a witty and charming girl!'

Lady Eleanor smoothed her skirts. 'Well, I confess that at first I had difficulty in imagining Jane Verey as the artful schemer you described, Alex! But now I have seen the evidence with my own eyes! Oh, she is both witty and charming, I do not dispute that, but therein lies the problem! Girls these day,' Lady Eleanor said severely, 'can be too clever for their own good! A little feminine modesty would be more becoming!'

'Come now, Aunt Eleanor…' Alex straightened up and strolled over to the mantelpiece '…you are too harsh! Miss Verey is not precisely immodest! And she may be wilful but she is still beautiful and engaging—' He broke off as he saw the arrested expression on Lady Eleanor's face and finished a little hastily, 'The perfect wife for Philip, in fact!'

'For Philip! Of course!' Lady Eleanor's lips twitched a little as a certain truth made its presence felt. 'I am persuaded that Miss Verey will settle quickly enough once the match is made. I am anxious only to avoid a monstrous scandal if Philip takes it into his head to elope with Miss Marchment! That could not be borne, for although the girl is from an entirely respectable family, they have no estate or connections or fortune, and it could not be deemed suitable! So Philip—and Miss Verey—must be brought to the point as soon as may be!'

'Indeed!' Alex turned away. 'I believe that you are correct in thinking that the more intimate atmosphere of the house party might promote our cause. Besides, if the signs are not auspicious, we can always contrive to compromise Miss Verey sufficiently for a betrothal to follow!'

Lady Eleanor looked appalled. 'Alex! You would not! Your deceit—'

'Is matched only by that of Miss Verey, I assure you! If she can outwit me then I shall concede defeat gracefully. If not—well, we shall see who is the winner!'

Lady Eleanor said no more, but as she took her leave she found herself scanning once more her nephew's impervious features and wondering whether she had imagined the moment earlier when Alex had betrayed his own interest in Jane Verey. The way his voice had softened as he spoke of Jane's beauty and charm, and the indulgent note she had detected... Lady Eleanor suddenly remembered Alex's sharpened interest when she had mentioned Lord Blakeney paying court to Jane. She smiled a little as she stepped out in the direction of her home in Lower Brook Street. Perhaps she had dreamed it, but she did not think so. And if Alex was already aware of his own feelings, just what did he have in mind for Jane Verey? Certainly not marriage to his brother! The more she thought about it, the more equivocal some of Alex's remarks seemed, to the point where Lady Eleanor suddenly wondered just which of the Delahaye brothers Miss Jane Verey would be compromised into marrying.

Unaware of the unexpected invitation that was about to come their way, Jane, Sophia and Lady Verey spent the morning in Bond Street attending to some essential shopping. Most improbably, Simon had expressed a wish to accompany them. He had murmured some excuse about needing a new hat and Jane, unusually distracted by the purchase of a white evening gown with an overdress of pale gold, did not at first notice the piercing looks he was giving to all the staff in the modiste's shop. It was only when her brother had peered behind a curtain and startled a shop assistant who was preparing to model a dress for them that Jane had dragged him to one side.

'Simon! What on earth are you doing?' she whispered fiercely. 'You will have us all expelled from the shop if you keep spying on models in their undergarments!'

Her brother gave her a harassed look. 'This is Celestine's, isn't it, Jane?'

'Yes of course! That is Celestine herself over there glaring at you! But what is that to the purpose?'

Simon glanced at his mother and Sophia, who were chattering over a dress of pale green. 'Come outside for a moment and I will tell you.'

The whole story of Simon's encounter at the masquerade came tumbling out, including how he had danced with a girl then lost her for a while, only to find her again out on the terrace in need of his help.

'She was the most beautiful girl I had ever seen, Jane,' he said unselfconsciously. 'At first I thought she was a Cyprian come to the masquerade to—' Simon broke off, grinning at his sister's rapt expression. 'Anyway, she ain't. I could tell. So then I thought she might be a maid, tricked out in her mistress' dress for the ball, but...' he wrinkled up his nose '...she was no servant. I could tell that too.'

Jane stepped to one side to allow a couple to squeeze past them on the pavement.

'Yet she would not give you her name?'

'No, only that she had come alone to the ball. She ran away from me,' Simon finished. 'After I'd saved her from Hewetson she simply walked off. Her domino was torn in the struggle and the old Duchess of Merrion spotted her, and thought she recognised the dress underneath. It was extraordinary, Jane! The Duchess was ranting and raving, swearing that the girl had stolen the dress because Celestine had promised her that there had been only one, then the girl just turned on her heel and left, and everyone was speculating about her identity... Can't think how you missed it!' He frowned. 'Where were you, anyway?'

Jane, realising that she had been closeted in the study with the Duke of Delahaye whilst this drama had been unfolding, chose to ignore this question. It would involve too many difficult explanations and also involve an examination of her own feelings. She shrugged, trying to look vague.

'Goodness knows... But what size was she, Simon?'

Simon looked confused. 'Size? Who? The Duchess of Merrion?'

'No, of course not! Your wits have gone a-begging along with your heart!' Jane said severely. 'I refer to your young lady! If she was small and slender then a dress made for the Duchess might well have fitted her. The Duchess of Merrion is a short woman, after all! But if she was taller then it is unlikely that it was the same dress, in which case the Duchess might well have made a mistake!'

Simon looked totally baffled. 'Don't know what the

deuce you're talking about, Jane! All I know is that I must find her again! Last night—'

'Yes!' Jane said wrathfully, remembering that she had not yet had the chance to take him to task for deserting her at Vauxhall. 'What did you mean by leaving me all alone like that? Why, anything might have happened!'

Simon looked self-conscious. 'Yes, I do apologise, Janey! I thought I saw her again, you see, so I had no thought but to rush after her! Anyway, it was no good, for she had disappeared. But you must see that I have to find her!'

'Why?' Jane asked bluntly. 'Have you truly thought about this, Simon? You say she was no servant, but how do you know? She might be a governess or a confectioner's assistant or—'

Simon blushed bright red. 'Never put you down as a snob, Jane!'

'Oh, don't be so foolish! That was not what I meant!' Jane frowned at him. 'Think about this, Simon—what would such a girl believe, if a peer of the realm came to find her and tell her that he wished to pursue an acquaintance with her?'

'Why, that—' Simon stopped dead.

'Exactly,' his sister said drily.

'Then I should persuade her of my good intentions—'

'Intentions? Then you wish to marry her?'

Simon thrust a hand through his fair hair. 'Devil take it, Jane, I don't know! All I know is that I need to find her! I—' He broke off, realising that he was about to say that he loved her. It seemed so extraordinary. He had seen the girl twice, for such a brief time. He did not even know her name, and yet...

'I suppose you think me run quite mad,' he finished glumly.

Jane looked a little rueful. Privately she thought that her own feelings for Alex made her ill-equipped to judge anyone else. 'Not really, Simon. I can only respect your feelings. So I shall go and ask Celestine if she can help us. Wait here for me!'

Presently Jane, Sophia and Lady Verey all came out of the modiste's talking nineteen to the dozen. As they strolled slowly up the pavement in the sunshine, Jane caught her brother's eye and fell back a little. She took his arm as Lady Verey and Sophia walked on ahead.

'Well?' Simon could scarcely contain himself.

'I spoke to Celestine,' Jane said softly. 'There is a girl—her name is Thérèse.' She felt his arm jerk under her hand, as though she had shocked him. 'Try to look as though we are talking of something inconsequential,' she added humorously, 'unless you wish to acquaint Mama of your plans at this early stage! I hope we are speaking of the same person,' she added. 'Slender and very fair?'

Simon nodded speechlessly.

'Celestine says that she did piece work for her. Bits and pieces of sewing,' Jane added, seeing that her brother was looking puzzled. 'It is cheaper for the modiste to employ people only when she needs them. She says that Thérèse was a very good seamstress but that she had to dismiss her because of a complaint from the Duchess of Merrion. Apparently Thérèse borrowed the Duchess's gown for a masquerade and the Duchess threatened to take all her custom elsewhere…'

They walked on a little in silence.

'Thérèse…' Simon said slowly, '…is she French?'

'Yes, an *émigrée*, Celestine said. She knows little more about her,' Jane warned. 'She said that Thérèse kept very much to herself and told no one of her circumstances.'

'But did she have an address for her? Surely she must…'

Jane gave him an old-fashioned look. 'You think that she would be anxious to part with such information? She was already deeply suspicious of me and your peering into cupboards and around doors hardly helped! For all that I told her that Thérèse had been recommended to me and I wished her to do some work for me, I believe she thought me a procuress!'

'Jane!'

Jane delved into her reticule. 'This is the address she gave me. Do not be surprised if she has already sent to warn her—'

Simon grabbed the paper and held it triumphantly high. 'Thank you, Jane!' He kissed her cheek and dashed off down the street.

Lady Verey and Sophia turned to look at Jane in astonishment.

'Simon has forgotten the hat he wanted,' Jane said foolishly, grasping at the first excuse that came into her head. 'He has the details written on the piece of paper. He will join us later for luncheon.' And he may bring you your new daughter-in-law, she added silently, looking at her mother's unsuspecting face and wondering a little apprehensively what on earth would happen if he did.

Chapter Seven

In the event, Simon did not reappear for the whole day. Jane was left torn by speculation and worry. She would have warned her brother to be prepared for disappointment, but she knew that he would not have heeded her words. Simon had been alight with excitement and anticipation, and nothing she could say would have touched him. Of more serious concern to Jane was Simon's assertion that he had seen Thérèse at Vauxhall the previous night. If she had been the girl with Alex's assailant, Simon could be getting himself into more trouble than he bargained for. Jane's mind fretted away at the problem and she was so quiet that Lady Verey asked if she was feeling unwell.

In the afternoon Jane accompanied her mother on a series of visits to friends and on their return prepared for the musical soirée they were all promised for in the evening. As her maid helped her into the new white and gold dress, Jane caught herself wondering whether Alex would be at the soirée. What did it matter if he was—no doubt Lady Dennery would be hanging on his arm! Whilst Cassie brushed her hair the regulation hundred strokes, Jane viewed her despondent face in the mirror. Every so often she would forget that the Duke of Delahaye intended her to be his brother's wife, and when she remembered, the depression of spirits was greater than she had ever experienced before.

Simon was waiting with Lady Verey and Sophia when Jane joined them in the hall. He looked flushed and not particularly happy. Jane's heart sank further. That must mean that his trip had not met with success and worse, he appeared to have been drowning his sorrows as a result. The smell of alcohol hung about him and Lady Verey pointedly opened the carriage window and gave her a son a look of deep disapproval.

As they all entered Mrs Wingate's drawing-room, Jane caught her brother's arm. He almost over-balanced.

'Simon! What happened to you this afternoon?' Jane demanded. 'Are you foxed?'

'Devil a bit,' her brother muttered. He slipped into the seat next to hers. 'One or two li'l drinks at White's…met Harry Marchnight—'

Jane's lips tightened. 'I would have hoped Harry would keep you out of trouble!' she whispered crossly, trying to hold a clandestine conversation and make it look as though she was not doing so. 'What happened? Did you not find Thérèse?'

'I went to the address,' Simon muttered. 'It was dreadful, Jane—such a poor and dirty street, and—' He broke off. 'This is hardly the time… At any rate, she was not there. An old crone opened the door and denied that she knew anyone called Thérèse, but I did not believe her.' He drove his hands into his pockets and scowled. 'I know she lives there!'

'How do you know?' Jane asked, wondering whether her brother was just blindly refusing to admit defeat.

'Because as I was about to go, someone from within called out in French and the crone shut the door in my face,' Simon said with dogged logic. 'So you see it must be an *émigré* household.' He stumbled a little over the word *émigré*. 'I will go back—again and again if I must, until she agrees to see me! It's just so damned—dashed—frustrating, Jane!'

'Which was where the drink came in, I suppose! Do try to sober up!' Jane said, still cross, waving away a servant who was trying to press some wine on them. 'Really, Simon! I thought that you had more self-control! Reeking of drink is hardly the way to a young lady's heart!'

Simon looked crushed. 'I know! I just felt so miserable…'

Jane glanced round, but no one appeared to be attending to them. The musicians were tuning up in a corner and the Duke of Delahaye was just ushering the striking Lady Dennery into a seat in the front row of the audience. Jane thought sourly that her ladyship was set upon making a show. Her blonde hair was dressed high with diamonds and her plunging blue gown left little to the imagination. She was trailed by a crowd of admirers and gossiping cronies, all intent on drawing as much attention to themselves as possible. Jane shrank in her seat and reflected bitterly that she need hardly have wasted her time thinking about Alex. He evidently had more on his mind than an ingenuous schoolroom miss!

Mrs Wingate came forward to announce the start of the recital and the chatterers were obliged to hush. The music was very good and once or twice the pathos of the arias brought a lump to Jane's throat and made the tears tickle behind her eyes. In contrast, Simon disgraced himself by falling asleep and had to be nudged by Jane when he snored in the quiet parts.

'The Duke and Lady Dennery look very intimate, do they not,' Sophia murmured in Jane's ear as the interval was announced and the gossip and chit chat broke out again. 'But, oh, Jane, did you ever see anything like that dress! I am sure she has damped it, and for a small musical soirée!'

'Very bad *ton*!' Lady Verey said, overhearing. 'I am glad Lady Eleanor is not here tonight! I cannot believe that she would wish for such a connection for the Delahayes!'

Lord Philip was also missing that evening and Sophia was noticeably less cheerful as a result. Jane, with her downcast friend on one side and her morose brother on the other, began to feel trapped under her own small rain cloud. Worse, Lady Dennery was directly in view and, having despatched the Duke to fetch her some syllabub from the refreshment room, was engrossed in flirtation with another gentleman.

Jane got up, excused herself to the others, and made a beeline for the food. The thought that it was her only solace restored her spirits a little. It was better than resorting to drink, as Simon had done!

'Good evening, Miss Verey. Are you enjoying the music?'

Jane had been hesitating between the ice cream and the fruit pudding when the Duke of Delahaye paused by her side. His query seemed no more than mere politeness—indeed, she could see his gaze straying over her head to where Lady Dennery sparkled as brightly as her diamonds. Jane castigated herself for spending even a moment thinking about him when it was clear that the Duke had barely given her one moment's attention.

'Good evening, your Grace,' she said coldly. 'The music is very pretty, is it not? Or perhaps you have not noticed?'

Alex's gaze came back from Lady Dennery and focussed on Jane's face with sudden intentness. He gave her a glimmer of a smile that set her heartbeat awry despite her intention to resist his charm.

'Oh, I have noticed several things, Miss Verey! More, perhaps, than you might think! I have observed that your brother is not himself tonight, that Miss Marchment appears to have lost some of her sparkle and that you are cross about something—would you care to enlighten me?'

'No, thank you!' Jane said smartly, secretly taken aback at his perspicacity. She allowed her own gaze to drift back to Lady Dennery, who was laughing as she allowed one of her admirers to feed her with grapes. 'Would that we were as perceptive of our own circumstances as you are of other people's, your Grace!'

'Ah, true!' Alex smiled whimsically, not one whit put out. 'It is always so difficult to see the beam in one's own eye, is it not, Miss Verey! Now, lest I forget, I believe that Lady Eleanor will be calling on you tomorrow to deliver an invitation to my home at Malladon. We had a sudden urge to escape the pleasures of Town and seek some country quiet!'

Jane eyed him suspiciously. This sudden invitation

seemed most questionable. She had a horrid misgiving that the net was closing in around her; that Alex had tired of her resistance to the match with Philip and was now planning to put an end to her games. He had allowed her some latitude, had even played along to a certain extent, but now he had lost patience. She looked at him through her lashes. He was smiling blandly, but there was a hint of challenge in his gaze that only confirmed her doubts. Clearly there was some plan that hinged on Malladon.

'I am not certain that Mama would wish to leave Town whilst the Season is in progress,' she said cautiously, testing the water. Despite her words, she knew that it was very unlikely that Lady Verey would refuse. She would be too flattered, too grateful for such a sign of Lady Eleanor's regard.

Alex's smile grew. 'Oh, I am persuaded that she will accept the invitation!' he said easily. 'And it will only be for a short while! The benefits outweigh the drawbacks, you know, for I am sure your mama's main purpose in bringing you to Town is to see you suitably settled by the end of the Season! In that she and I are as one!'

Jane's feeling of entrapment pressed closer about her. He had summed up Lady Verey's reactions so accurately! Jane knew that her mama had never made any secret that she wished to revive the Delahaye match and such a sign of encouragement and approval from the Duke and Lady Eleanor could not be rejected. The three of them were united in the attempt to wear down Jane and Lord Philip until they capitulated.

'I am sorry that you are not more enthusiastic, Miss Verey,' the Duke said mockingly. His gaze had not left her face once and now Jane felt so frustrated she was sure that it must show. Vexed, she bit her lip.

'Checkmate, Miss Verey?' Alex added softly. 'You know that you must concede soon! We are all ranged against you!'

Jane's stormy hazel eyes locked with his.

'Check, perhaps, but not checkmate, sir! Beware that your complacency does not catch you out!'

Alex laughed. 'How stimulating it is to cross swords with you, Miss Verey! I never knew an opponent who could look defeat in the face and yet persist in opposing me!'

He bowed and sauntered back to Lady Dennery, insinuating himself at her side and displacing several of his rivals with what seemed the greatest of ease. It made Jane feel even more annoyed. He obviously did not care that he had to share Lady Dennery's affections with so many others! It was all a little too sophisticated for Jane to either understand or appreciate.

The music was starting again. She slipped back into her seat beside Sophia and observed the droop of her friend's mouth as she contemplated the rest of the evening without Lord Philip. With a further spasm of despair Jane realised that the success of the Duke's plan would mean the death of all Sophia's hopes. She set her chin. She needed some allies now and she was already starting to plan her next strategy.

Jane had intended to plan her next move once she was in bed that night, but in the event she fell asleep almost as soon as her head touched the pillow. She awoke again, suddenly, and for no apparent reason, and lay in the dark, wondering what it was that had disturbed her.

Then there was the sound of gravel spattering against the window and a whisper, 'Jane? Jane, are you there?'

Jane slipped from the bed and leaned out, the curtains billowing behind her.

'Who's there? Harry? What on earth—'

Lord Henry Marchnight was in the street below, supporting another figure whom Jane recognised with deep foreboding as Simon.

'Harry? Is Simon hurt?'

'Of course not,' Henry said tersely. 'Come down and open the door, there's a good girl! I don't want to wake the whole house!'

Obscurely reassured, Jane dragged on a robe and sped downstairs. A single light burned in the hall, and from behind the door leading down to the servants' hall she could hear the low murmur of voices. She slid the bolts back softly.

'Thank God!'

Henry was already outside the door and strode in to deposit his burden in the hall with scant concern for Simon's welfare. Jane recoiled from the smell of drink as her brother lurched towards the stairs, missing the handrail and slumping on to the bottom step. She had thought that Simon had recovered his sobriety during the soirée that evening, but evidently he had made up for it immediately afterwards with a trip to his club.

'Good heavens! He's three parts disguised!'

'Just be grateful you didn't have to bring him all the way home as we did,' Henry said bitterly.

The door closed and Jane spun around with a gasp. She had thought Henry was alone, but the tall figure emerging from the shadows was as familiar as it was unexpected.

'Can you get him upstairs on your own?' the Duke of Delahaye was asking Henry. He cast Jane one single dark glance. 'I need to have a word with Miss Verey.'

'I can call Simon's valet to help—' Jane said. She had already stretched out a hand towards the servants' door when Alex's fingers closed around her wrist.

'No,' he said, and there was such a note of authority in his voice that Jane fell silent. For the first time, her gaze moved from Henry to Alex, noting their extraordinary appearance. Gone were the gentlemen of *ton* Society, and in their place were two rather disreputable characters in shabby black and white. Henry, with his tumbled fair hair and billowing white shirt, looked rather like a poet fallen on hard times, whilst Alex's sinister black cloak made him look like the archetypal highwayman. Jane had to press a hand to her mouth to stop herself laughing. Above it her eyes were bright.

'Oh, dear! You look—'

'Thank you,' Alex said drily. 'Your face says it all, Miss Verey! Henry, please—before we wake the whole house—'

But it was already too late. The door from below stairs opened and Cassie stepped into the hall, holding her candle high. She gave a muted squeak.

'Lord save us! Miss Jane! And the young master! Foxed again! George,' she shouted back down the stairs, 'come and help the young master to bed! He's as tight as an owl!'

Jane realised that Alex was still holding her wrist. In the ensuing confusion he pulled her round to face him. Suddenly she saw that for all their comical appearance their business was deadly serious. Alex was looking both grim and determined.

'Miss Verey—may we speak in private?'

Jane's eyes widened. 'Now? We cannot!'

A hint of a smile lightened the grimness of Alex's expression. 'I fear we must! I assure you, you are quite safe with me! I simply need to ask you a few questions!'

Jane's startled gaze searched his face. 'Surely it can wait until the morning—'

'I am afraid not,' Alex said, very definitely.

'Best do as he asks, Janey,' Harry Marchnight said soberly. He was helping the servants to manoeuvre Simon up the staircase and suddenly Jane and Alex were alone in the shadowed hall. Alex dropped her wrist and stood back to allow her to precede him into the drawing room, picking up the candelabra as he followed her in. The door shut with an unnerving click.

'Your Grace, this is very improper...' Jane said faintly, curling up in an armchair and drawing her robe more closely about her.

'I know.' Alex smiled with sudden and devastating charm. 'Needs must, Miss Verey! I shall not keep you long and this is very important.' He took the chair opposite and sat forward, fixing her with a stern look that almost made her shiver. 'Is Simon in some kind of trouble?'

Jane met his eyes very directly. 'I am not aware of it, your Grace. What kind of trouble?'

Alex shifted a little. 'We found Simon far from his usual haunts, in circumstances that suggested foul play. He was slumped in the gutter, in severe danger

of having his pockets picked—or worse! He is not in
the habit of getting blind drunk and hanging around
street corners in Spitalfields, so—' He broke off, his
eyes narrowing on Jane's face. 'Do you know anything about this, Miss Verey?'

Jane knew that her expression had given her away.
She had assumed that Simon had over-indulged at his
club, but as soon as Alex mentioned Spitalfields, she
realised that Simon must have returned to look for
Thérèse, just as he had sworn he would. As she hesitated, Alex said drily:

'I see that you do know, Miss Verey! You have
the most expressive face! So what is this all about?'

Jane resented his high-handed tone. 'What business
is it of yours, your Grace? Forgive me, but you and
Harry Marchnight are the ones who have been creeping around London like Mohawks!'

Alex gave her a reluctant smile. '*Touché*, Miss
Verey! I can see that our behaviour must look suspicious! However, have you considered that your own
actions are also most questionable?'

'Mine!' Jane looked incredulous. 'I have no notion
what you mean—'

'No?' Alex was not smiling any longer. His face
looked as cold and carved as stone. 'Consider the circumstances. I find you skulking in the dark walks
alone last night at Vauxhall. You tell me a very thin
tale to explain the situation. When you are reunited
with your brother, you give him a sign to say nothing.
I had already seen him in very dubious company last
night and tonight he is found dead drunk in a low
neighbourhood. And I believe that you know what is
going on.' He brought his clenched fist down with

heavy emphasis. 'This seems most suspicious to me, Miss Verey!'

Jane's head was spinning. 'I assure you, there was nothing remotely suspect about my behaviour last night! I only gestured to Simon to keep quiet because—' She broke off, suddenly aware that any explanation would incriminate Sophia and Philip in some way. Alex was waiting patiently, his dark gaze riveted on her face.

'You appear to be in some difficulty, Miss Verey,' he said after a moment. 'The natural consequences of chicanery, I fear! And can you be surprised at my distrust? You have, after all, proved yourself adept at deception!'

Jane gasped. 'How dare you, sir! I have done no such thing!'

'No?' Alex said again. 'What about the exchange of partners at Lady Winterstoke's dinner, the change of dominoes at the masquerade... I do not believe that you are to be trusted, Miss Verey!'

Jane found that she was on her feet with no real idea of how she got there. She reached for the door handle, but Alex was before her, resting one hand against the panels and blocking her path.

'Oh, no, you don't,' he said pleasantly. 'Not until you have told me what I need to know!'

'This is outrageous!' Jane realised that her voice was shaking. 'You cannot behave in this high-handed manner, sir! How dare you accuse me of deception when all I have done is oppose your plan to marry me off to your brother!'

'Perhaps we may discuss that on another occasion, Miss Verey,' Alex said smoothly. 'Just now it is very

important that I know what it going on. The company
your brother is keeping is dangerous—'

'I know that!' Jane glared at him. 'I told you that
that man was trying to kill you!' She stopped suddenly, seeing the flash in his eyes and realising that
she had been provoked into saying rather more than
she had intended. She bit her lip.

'And just how much do you know about that, Miss
Verey?' Alex said, very softly.

Suddenly Jane was frightened. There had always
been something exciting about crossing swords with
Alexander Delahaye, but now she realised that she
was completely out of her depth. This was real, and
dangerous and threatening. She thought of the way in
which he had casually referred to her deceit, the fact
that he did not trust her, and the tears stung her eyes.

Alex stood back with an ironic bow, gesturing to
her to sit down again. Jane sat without a word, curling
up as tight as she could for both warmth and comfort.

'Shall we start again, Miss Verey?' Alex said.

There was a little silence. The candle flame flick-
ered. Jane capitulated.

'Very well! There is no mystery! It is misfortunes
in love rather than anything else that trouble Simon.'

'Indeed. What matter of the heart could take him
to Spitalfields?'

Jane's eyes flashed at his disbelieving tone. 'Something far less dubious than your own activities, I am
sure, your Grace! Simon is looking for a young lady
by the name of Thérèse, who apparently lives there.
He wishes to marry her.'

There was a sharp silence. 'Does he, by God!' For
the first time, Alex seemed startled. 'Mademoiselle
Thérèse de Beaurain?'

'Mademoiselle—' Jane broke off. 'Is that her other name? You know her?'

'I know of her,' Alex admitted. 'She is the daughter of the late Vicomte de Beaurain, who lost his head in the Revolution. Her mother fled to England with her daughter when the child was very young. I imagine that she must be about twenty years of age now. Her mother is an invalid and Mademoiselle de Beaurain supports both of them on a pittance from sewing. How did Simon meet her?'

'She was at the masquerade ball,' Jane said, in a small voice. Suddenly Simon's Thérèse had become a real person and had taken on her own character. Jane looked at Alex, troubled.

'Simon saw her again at Vauxhall last night, and rushed off to try to speak to her. She was with the man in the striped waistcoat, the one who—' She broke off. 'Oh, I do hope that Simon knows what he is doing... I would not like to think that Miss de Beaurain is involved in something criminal...'

'Do not worry,' Alex spoke quietly. 'As far as I know, Mademoiselle de Beaurain is quite innocent. She has nothing to reproach herself for except a stubborn pride which I understand has led to a rupture with the English branch of the family!'

'Oh, how unfortunate!' Jane's sympathies were already thoroughly engaged with the young *émigrée* girl who had to struggle so hard to care for herself and her parent. 'You mean that she has relatives who might help them?'

'Yes, indeed, very respectable ones! Her mother is a distant cousin of General Sir John Huntington, who heard of their plight several years ago and summoned Thérèse de Beaurain to offer them a home.' Alex smiled. 'I only know of this because I heard him telling all and sundry of his kind condescension in offering a home to destitute relatives! Truth to tell, he was so patronising that I can only imagine he offended the girl mortally. Anyway, the whole *ton* was later regaled with the story of how he had had his generosity spurned and that the family could rot in hell for all he cared! Not a pretty tale!'

Jane shivered. 'So they have been left to make shift as best they can? How cruel!'

'It seems very harsh, certainly. But if Simon can rescue her from all that—' Alex shrugged. 'But we are becoming distracted from the main point. I am relieved to know that there is so innocuous an explanation for tonight's escapade, although I suppose finding Simon drunk outside his beloved's house is a sign that his suit is not prospering!'

'No,' Jane said cautiously, 'I believe that it is not!' She took her courage in both hands. 'But Simon's misfortunes are not the main concern, are they, your Grace? It was only coincidence that brought him into contact with the man in the striped waistcoat—oh, I wish I knew his name, for to refer to him as such sounds so foolish! But he is clearly the one who is dangerous!'

'His name is Samways,' Alex said, stirring the fire to a fresh blaze, 'and he is, as you have surmised, Miss Verey, a dangerous man. I do not know what led you to disbelieve my excuse that he was merely a common pickpocket. I thought I was a better liar than that!'

Jane smiled faintly. 'I am not really sure why I did not believe you, but—it was his demeanour, I suppose, and the fact that he did not look as though he intended to rob, but to kill.' She shivered convulsively, despite the warmth of the fire. Looking up, she found that Alex was watching her with a thoughtful regard.

'I suppose that you cannot tell me what this is all about,' she finished, a little forlornly.

'You suppose correctly, Miss Verey.' Alex gave her a slight smile. 'It really is safer that you do not know! Take comfort from the fact that Simon's Thérèse is innocent and that her association with Samways is not a close one!' He sighed. 'It seems unfortunate that Simon should choose this of all times to visit Spitalfields! It is not a healthy place to be!'

Jane had other fears. 'Upon my word,' she burst out, 'you do not seem very concerned that someone wishes to murder you! One might almost believe that you encounter such situations every day!'

Alex grinned. He got to his feet and stretched. Jane hastily averted her gaze.

'You would be surprised, Miss Verey!' he said easily. 'Thank you for your help tonight. I regret that I cannot enlighten you on the reason for my interest and once again I must beg you to keep quiet about this. One day, perhaps, I will tell you why…'

His gaze travelled over her, lingering on the soft hair tumbling about her shoulders and the slender curves of her body beneath the thin robe. Jane, who had been about to uncurl from the chair and stand up, kept very still. Suddenly there was an expression on Alex's face that she did not understand, but it turned her throat dry and started her heart racing.

'I must also thank you for your concern,' Alex said slowly. His voice had dropped several tones. 'I do believe that you are genuinely upset at the thought of someone sticking a knife in me!'

'Of course it concerns me!' Jane's voice had risen, anxiety overriding her natural reticence. 'A strange creature I should be if I took pleasure in thinking you stabbed to death by some dangerous criminal!'

Alex put out a hand and pulled her to her feet. His touch lit something inside of Jane, something that made her tremble. They were standing very close and she could not tear her gaze away from his.

'Even though we are in opposition?' Alex queried softly. 'You would still wish me no harm?'

Jane cleared her throat. For some reason she was finding it very difficult to breathe. 'I have never had any wish to be in opposition to you, your Grace.'

Alex's voice was caressing. 'I do believe that we could be in the most perfect accord, Miss Verey.'

His mouth was only inches away from her own and he was still holding her lightly, but with a touch that burned her blood with sensuous awareness. Yet only ten minutes before he had spoken of her in terms of the deepest scorn, called her deceitful and untrustworthy, and Jane was not about to forget that.

She stepped back.

'I collect that you mean we are both accomplished in dissimulation,' she said coolly, covering the turbulence of her emotions with a strategic withdrawal. 'I think that you should leave now, sir.'

Jane opened the door and pointedly stood holding it for Alex to leave. He did not move. She felt his gaze, as powerful as a physical touch, searching her face.

'Well,' he said ruefully after a moment, 'I suppose

that I deserved that! I can only apologise for my remarks. I said it mainly to provoke you—'

'Oh! That makes it much more acceptable then, sir!'

Alex laughed, conceding the point. 'We'll talk about this again! Good night, Miss Verey.'

The clock struck two. Jane took the candelabra in one hand almost as though it was a shield. By its flickering light she could see that Henry Marchnight was loitering in the hall, but otherwise the house was dark and silent. Conscious of Henry's thoughtful look resting on her still-pink face, Jane avoided his eyes and made a business of shepherding them towards the door. The night was fine and the moon hung low in the sky. Jane shivered a little.

'Go back inside,' Alex said, abruptly. 'Harry and I will make all secure.'

Henry bent forward and kissed her cheek and after a moment Alex followed suit, taking her hand and drawing her to him as his lips brushed her skin in the lightest of caresses. Jane, scurrying back to the sanctuary of her room with one hand unconsciously pressed to her cheek, reflected wryly that she would be the most envied girl in London if anyone found out. To have been kissed by both Harry Marchnight and the Duke of Delahaye! It was enough to make one swoon, and all in one evening, too! As she slipped between the chilled sheets, Jane paused long enough before sleep to wonder why one salutation had left her totally unmoved whilst the other felt as though it had been branded on her skin with fire.

Chapter Eight

It was Henry Marchnight, not Alex Delahaye, who called first in Portman Square on the following morning. Simon had not yet risen from his bed but the ladies were assembled in the parlour, Sophia and Lady Verey sewing placidly and Jane watching the clock and wondering at what hour any visitors would call. She jumped when the bell rang and her disappointment on seeing Henry rather than Alex was acute. Henry, a twinkle in his eye, came across to sit by her.

'Your servant, Miss Verey. I hope that you are recovered from last night!'

'Oh. Lord Henry, I daresay that I should not mention it, but I must thank you for your help in bringing Simon home,' Lady Verey said eagerly. 'A most unfortunate occurrence, but gentlemen must be allowed, I suppose…'

Henry stretched out his long legs and gave her the smile that always worked on Dowagers. 'A small transgression and very rarely committed, Lady Verey…'

Lady Verey fluttered. 'Of course! And he would come to no harm at his club—'

'At his club!' Henry's gaze touched Jane's innocent face briefly. 'Of course!'

'So good of you and Alexander Delahaye,' Lady Verey burbled. 'Such good friends!'

'Yes, ma'am, but I beg you not to mention it to Delahaye—he is rather a reticent fellow!'

Henry smiled at Jane again. 'I see you have been singing our praises, Miss Verey!'

Jane cast her eyes down modestly. 'There was some speculation about last night's activities, sir... I simply did my best to quash it. How fortunate that I heard the hack draw up and came down to see what was happening!'

'Fortunate, indeed!' Henry murmured. Under the cover of the refreshments being served he added, 'I see you have no need of me to concoct a story, Miss Verey!'

The door opened again and Alex Delahaye came in. Jane saw the infinitesimal nod that Henry gave him before Alex came across with easy grace to bow over Lady Verey's hand and inquire of her health.

'I am here to bring your formal invitation to Malladon,' he said, with a smile. 'Lady Eleanor had hoped to call herself, but she is slightly incommoded with a cold in the head. Oh, not enough to spoil your visit,' he added, seeing Lady Verey's look of concern. 'I am sure she will be better directly! But as we were planning to travel on the morrow I did not wish to delay any longer. You will, I hope, be able to accept?'

Jane saw that Lady Verey was fluttering and recognised it for a bad sign. Her mother was flustered, which meant that she was inordinately flattered by the invitation and would not dream of refusing.

'Oh, your Grace…such condescension, we should be delighted…tomorrow, you say? Well, I dare say it can be arranged…'

Alex's eyes met Jane's and she saw the wicked twinkle in them that said that her plans had been foiled. 'I am so glad,' he murmured.

Jane had, in fact, almost forgotten the invitation to Malladon in the mystery that had happened the previous night. She had been too tired to consider it when she had got back to bed, but that morning she had lain awake for quite some time puzzling over the nature of the business that could have taken Henry and Alex to Spitalfields. Clearly they had been involved in something that they preferred to keep secret, but the thought that they might be entangled in criminal activities seemed ludicrous. It was far more likely, Jane thought as she sipped her tea, that they were working to foil some illegal enterprise. She had known for years in a vague sort of way that Henry Marchnight worked for the government, which led logically to the idea that Alex might too…

'Will it still be convenient for your Grace to spare the time to host us at Malladon?' she asked limpidly, her eyes innocent.

'Oh, certainly, Miss Verey,' Alex responded, the laughter lines deepening about his eyes. 'I should not miss it for the world! Do not forget that Philip will also be there to squire you about!'

This was another unwelcome reminder for Jane and she saw that Sophia, who had been very quiet that morning, looked flushed and unhappy. All in all, it was not going to be a comfortable trip.

* * *

Malladon was only half a day's drive from London, set in the lush Hertfordshire countryside. It was the least favoured of the Duke of Delahaye's estates, for he considered it too close to the capital and the countryside too bland for his tastes.

'Philip tells me that his brother prefers Hayenham to all his other establishments,' Sophia had reported shyly to Jane as they packed their bags for the unexpected trip to the country. 'It is a medieval castle on a wild northern cliff, Philip says, and the Duke locks himself up in there for months at a time! Only fancy!' Sophia shivered with enjoyable fear. 'It sounds quite Gothic! What a very odd man he is!'

Jane, looking out of the carriage window as the verdant scenery sped past, reflected that it seemed very much in keeping with Alexander Delahaye's character that he should prefer the untamed reaches of the North to more gentle climes. There was something about him that suggested, for all his eminent title and position, that he scorned the conventions of polite society. The elements of danger and restlessness were well hidden behind the veneer of authority and sophistication, but they were there nevertheless. Like Sophia, Jane shivered a little. She knew that she had pitted her wits against an opponent worthy of the name and that this unexpected invitation, seized on with such excitement by Lady Verey, had been the Duke's way of raising the stakes in their game.

Lady Verey had fallen asleep, lulled by the movement of the coach. Ahead of them, Lord Philip was driving Lady Eleanor with exemplary skill and care, whilst the Duke's own phaeton headed the expedition, the fair Lady Dennery at his side. No one had had the indelicacy to refer to Lady Dennery's presence in the party, but it had been an unwelcome one for all that. Lady Eleanor had set her lips tight in clear disapproval when the Duke had bowled up with his companion, and Lady Verey had worn the anxious look of a chaperon who knows that her innocent chicks are in danger. Jane's own predominant feeling was one of jealousy, which she both despised and despaired of. It seemed that Alexander Delahaye was bringing out the worst in her in more ways than one.

It was an oddly assorted party, Jane reflected. Simon had declined to join them, preferring to stay in Town and, she suspected, pursue his quest for Thérèse. Lady Eleanor had bemoaned the lack of a young man for Sophia, making Jane horribly aware that the intention was to throw herself and Philip together as much as possible. She had noticed that both Lady Eleanor and Lady Verey had started to bracket their names together as though it were the most natural thing imaginable. Sophia had also noticed and was looking ever more strained and upset, although she had not reproached her friend for the circumstance. Oh, dear, Jane thought, as they rumbled through a picturesque village and turned into a long driveway, this is not going to be at all pleasant!

The others had just arrived as their carriage drew up on the gravel sweep, and Lady Dennery was intent on giving instruction to the harassed servants over the care of her luggage.

'You, there! Take this portmanteau! No, not like that, like this, you dolt!'

Lord Philip was standing watching with a look akin to horror on his face and Jane, who still remembered his own churlish behaviour at Ambergate, was sur-

prised to feel a certain sympathy. Unquestionably
Lord Philip did not welcome this potential sister-in-
law!

Matters did not improve at dinner. There were only
seven of them around the imposing polished table and
Jane had been firmly placed next to Lord Philip whilst
Sophia was acres away, next to the Duke. So cowed
was she by his magnificent presence that she barely
said two words and Jane noticed how Lady Dennery,
on the Duke's other side, took no more notice of Sophia than to bend a patronising smile on her every so
often. Lady Dennery was saving all her attention for
Alex, touching his sleeve with intimate little gestures,
smiling into his eyes and hanging on his every word.
It made Jane feel so sick that she was barely able to
do justice to the excellent dinner. At her side, Lord
Philip chewed moodily, spoke little and gazed fixedly
at Sophia.

Jane was up betimes the following morning. She
had excused herself to bed immediately after dinner
in order to avoid Lord Philip's unwilling company
and by the morning she was feeling very restless. It
was a beautiful day. Throwing back the shutters, Jane
could see the green parkland shimmering in the early
sun and the glitter of a lake in the distance. She resolved on an early morning stroll.

The house seemed silent as she slipped outside. It
was a very pretty building, small but elegant, red-
brick and foursquare. Jane stood on the drive to admire it, before taking a well-mown grassy track that
cut across the park towards the lake.

It seemed that she was not the only one up and
about early that morning. As she emerged from the

shadow of the trees on to the gravel path that circled the water, Jane saw a figure standing in the shade of the summer pavilion. Another moment helped her to identify it as Lord Philip Delahaye. This was surprising. It was very early and Lord Philip was renowned as a late riser, never up before midday. As Jane hesitated, he turned his head and saw her. For a second she saw the expression of unhappiness on his face, clear in the bright sunlight, before he schooled his features to indifference.

'Good morning, Miss Verey.'

It seemed he was about to pass her without another word, but Jane put out a hand.

'A moment, if you please, sir!'

Lord Philip paused. 'Madam?'

'I need to speak to you, sir,' Jane said clearly, determined not to lose her nerve. 'It is a matter of extreme importance!' She saw that he was about to refuse and added, 'Please!'

Lord Philip gestured to her to fall into step with him on the gravel path, but his expression was not encouraging, nor were his words. 'Well, Miss Verey?'

'It concerns our projected marriage, my lord,' Jane said, fixing her gaze firmly on the plane trees in the far distance. 'I do not wish to marry you and I have observed that you do not wish to marry me, so I propose that we join forces to avert a horrid fate!'

There was a startled silence.

'Are you always so outspoken, Miss Verey?' Lord Philip said, tight-lipped. He cast her a quick sideways glance, which she met with a blithe smile.

'Always! I find it is much better to be honest, or one might find oneself married to the wrong person! I have been quick to notice that you have a certain admiration for Miss Marchment, a regard which might lead you to wish *me* in Hades!'

Lord Philip swallowed convulsively. They had reached the summerhouse and he paused, turning to look at Jane properly for the first time.

'Has Miss Marchment...? That is...did she say that she—' He broke off, looking suddenly boyish and eager. 'She is the most delightful creature, Miss Verey! A veritable angel! When she smiled on me that night at Almack's I believe I counted myself the most fortunate man in the room!' A shadow fell across his face as he realised the absurdity of addressing such sentiments to his intended bride. 'I beg your pardon,' he muttered. 'You are most fortunate in your friends, Miss Verey!'

'Pray do not apologise!' Jane said sweetly. 'I am very fond of Sophia! She is the dearest girl imaginable and I wish to see her happy. Which is why I wanted to talk to you, sir! Let us sit down together and put all to rights!'

They sat on the seat in the shade of the summerhouse veranda. 'Let us be straight with one another, sir,' Jane said practically. 'Neither of us wish to be joined in matrimony with the other, but we need not repine. If we work together we may be able to thwart your brother's plans for us!'

Lord Philip's face had brightened, only to fall again. 'I appreciate your plain-speaking, Miss Verey, but if I may be equally blunt, it is a matter of money! Alex will only pay my debts if I marry you!'

He drove his hands into his jacket pockets. 'It is not that I am extravagant, precisely, although I do find that Alex keeps me on a ridiculously tight allowance, but...' he frowned a little '...the matter cannot be avoided. For whatever reason, he favours this match and no other. I fear we are doomed!'

It was at that exact moment that Jane looked up to see the Duke of Delahaye, magnificent on a raking chestnut hunter, approaching them down the ride. He sat the horse with negligent skill. He had not seen them yet, but Jane knew that it was only a matter of time.

'If we can persuade your brother that all looks set fair for a match between us, we have the advantage,' Jane pressed. 'Trust me, sir, I will think of a scheme to avoid the marriage *and* to pay your debts! Then you may marry Miss Marchment and we shall all be happy!'

Lord Philip was looking slightly stunned at this *force majeure*. 'Can you contrive such a plan?' he asked weakly.

'Indeed! Look how easily I hoodwinked you!'

Lord Philip tried to look disapproving, but could not prevent a smile. Jane realised that she was warming to him.

'Yes,' he said reluctantly, 'you took me in magnificently, Miss Verey, and by rights I should be out of charity with you for such a shabby trick!' He cleared his throat. 'I have a bad conscience about that night, however. I know I behaved churlishly, but I was so angry with Alex for forcing me into the situation! I did not mean to denigrate your home and hospitality, or—'

He broke off and flushed bright red.

'I heard the maid come up to your room,' Jane said helpfully. 'Let us not speak of it, nor of the unfortunate rumours about me which circulated about Town after your visit...'

Lord Philip looked mortified. 'Miss Verey...' He was positively stammering, 'I did not mean... how did you...?'

'Forgive me, I know I should not have mentioned it.' Jane was trying not to laugh. She was starting to feel a real affection for Lord Philip, who reminded her of nothing so much as an overgrown schoolboy. 'Let us start afresh,' she added, in kindly fashion. 'I can understand that your brother must be a sore trial to you!'

'Oh, Alex is a good enough fellow,' Philip said grudgingly. 'It's just that he can be rather forceful at times! Perhaps you have observed it, Miss Verey!'

Jane could see the Duke approaching now. She smiled blindingly. 'Perhaps his Grace is not accustomed to polite society,' she agreed sweetly. 'His address certainly lacks polish!'

Philip gave a crack of laughter. 'Well, that's the first time I've heard Alex criticised for his skills in the petticoat line, Miss Verey!'

They were still laughing together when the Duke reined in beside them.

Philip turned to his brother with a grin. 'Morning, Alex! Lady Dennery not riding with you?'

'Her ladyship does not care to ride,' Alex said, unsmiling. 'Good morning, Miss Verey. Are you walking unaccompanied?'

'Obviously not, Alex! Miss Verey is walking with me!' Philip said with a grin, throwing himself into the part of Jane's beau with convincing alacrity. 'We are becoming better acquainted! Don't spoil sport, I beg you! Miss Verey and I wish to converse alone!' He saw his brother's lips tighten angrily and added, 'It is all perfectly respectable!'

Jane was aware that Alex Delahaye's penetrating gaze had hardly wavered from her even when he was speaking to his brother. There was something disturbing about such single-minded attention, nor could she understand why he was bestowing it on her. Did he suspect of them of play-acting? She had to admit that it was a rather sudden turnabout, but since this was precisely the outcome the Duke wished for, she could not understand why he was looking so furious!

'Forgive me,' he said through his teeth. 'I had no intention of interrupting a romance! I will see you at breakfast if you can tear yourselves away from the beauties of nature! Good day!'

'Well, we brushed through that rather well,' Lord Philip said, seemingly unaware of his brother's anger as the Duke galloped away. He stood up and held out a hand to help Jane rise, giving her a look of genuine admiration. 'What a capital girl you are, Miss Verey! I had no idea!'

Alex Delahaye was able to work off much of his bad temper on a gallop across the parkland, but as he trotted into the stableyard in more decorous fashion he was aware that a niggling irritation still troubled him. He slid from the horse, patted its heaving flank with appreciation and handed it over to the groom with a word of thanks, before turning towards the house. Lady Eleanor was waiting for him at the top of the wide terrace steps and her eyes were alight with satisfaction and a certain complacent self-congratulation.

'I told you so!' she said in greeting. 'I knew that a week in the country would do the trick! Miss Verey and Philip are out walking together and looking absolutely *épris*! I told you!'

'You did indeed!' Alex said wryly, feeling all his bad temper return with a rush. He could see his brother and Jane Verey wandering slowly up the path from the lake and appearing to be engrossed in each other's company. Jane's hand was tucked through Philip's arm in a way that seemed positively confiding and their laughter was for themselves alone. Alex felt a pang of something that was uncommonly like jealousy...or possibly pain.

He had felt nothing akin to it since the terrible time, years before, when his wife had told him that his unsophisticated ways bored her and she had taken a lover to provide some entertainment. He could still remember the look in her eyes: the hard cruelty, daring him to reproach her, goading him to lose his temper. It had seemed inconceivable to him that matters between them had altered so desperately. They had been entwined in love when they had married, Madeline eighteen, he twenty, but the pursuits and entertainments of Town had undermined that love. Madeline was weak and easily led; soon she became a spendthrift, complaining when Alex had tried to reason with her and finally scorning him publicly as an old-fashioned and tedious husband, old before his time. He might have come to accept that they shared no interests, but her taunts had hurt and the blow of her infidelity had destroyed Alex's still-cherished belief that all might be saved. If only they had never gone up to London, if only he had taken her back to Hayenham before it was too late, if he had been stronger...

Alex followed Lady Eleanor back into the salon,

allowing the door to slam behind him with unwonted ferocity. At least Francine Dennery would not rise for another couple of hours—that was one irritation that he was spared! Lady Dennery's increasingly unsubtle hints about their relationship had aroused nothing but indifference in him and he was already regretting the impulse that had led him to invite her to Malladon. Lady Eleanor had implied that it was tantamount to a declaration and Alex was annoyed to think that she might almost be correct. It was a complication he would rather do without. For a moment his imagination compared the slender but devastatingly desirable curves of Jane Verey with the overblown charms that Lady Dennery was trying to place at his disposal. Jane would be so soft and sweet, innocent but waiting to be awakened. He felt himself suffused with so potent an desire that he had to turn away.

The door opened again to admit Jane and Lord Philip. With curiously sharpened observation, Alex noted the pink colour in Jane's cheeks, whipped up by the breeze, the way that one windswept black curl rested in the hollow of her throat, the brightness of laughter in her eyes. His fists clenched as some nameless emotion clutched him by the throat. It was just that she had disappointed him, he told himself. She was like all the other debutantes after all, a little wilful, perhaps, but ready to see the benefits of a good match in the end. Lady Eleanor had been right when she had predicted that Jane Verey would settle down and accept the betrothal. Alex had just not believed that it would be so easy.

He told himself that his disappointment stemmed from the fact that the game was over before it had really started. He had expected that Jane Verey would been made of sterner stuff and he felt obscurely discontented to have been proved wrong. He knew that he was lying to himself. The problem was that he had already started to consider an alternative plan for Miss Jane Verey, and now apparently it would not be needed. He would have to treat her as a sister-in-law after all. Ironic, when he had promoted the Verey match so actively, but that had been before he had realised that he wanted something else—

Lady Dennery's fluting voice suddenly impinged on his notice.

'God damn it!' Alex said violently under his breath and, before any of his startled relatives could utter a word, he had turned on his heel and walked straight out of the door again. They did not see him again until dinner.

'You are perfectly sure that you are happy about this, Sophia?' Jane asked, as they reined in their horses at the top of the hill and looked down on the roof of Malladon nestling in the valley below. 'You do not feel uncomfortable with Lord Philip apparently paying open court to me? For if you do, you have only to say the word and we will stop at once!'

Sophia threw back her head and laughed. Her face was flushed and her blue eyes sparkling. She was in excellent looks and Jane was surprised that no one else had spotted the improvement in her friend's spirits, but then she could only be grateful that it was so. To rouse the suspicions of Lady Eleanor—or worse, the Duke—would defeat her plan utterly.

They had been three days in Hertfordshire and matters were progressing precisely as Jane had intended. Lord Philip was playing her devoted suitor to the top

of his bent in company and, whilst ostensibly monop-
olising his attention, Jane had in fact been engineering
opportunities for him to court Sophia. Lady Verey
and Lady Eleanor were lulled and off their guard, and
with Jane drawing all the attention, Sophia's actions
went almost unnoticed. Lady Dennery had also
proved a staunch if unknowing ally, for she had kept
the Duke occupied throughout.

Jane smiled contentedly. She could see Lord Philip
galloping towards them up the hill, having set off for
a ride before them with the intention of meeting up
once out of sight of the house. Lady Verey had felt
reasonably at ease in allowing the girls to go riding
together within the estate, for both Jane and Sophia
were country-bred and unlikely to come to harm so
near to home.

Lord Philip drew up beside them and raised his
whip in salutation. He smiled at Jane before turning
to Sophia and engaging her in conversation. The
horses walked on slowly, with Philip and Sophia a
little ahead and Jane careful to stay out of earshot.
She was well pleased with her strategy, for it had the
additional benefit of keeping Lord Philip in a very
good mood indeed and with both him and Sophia as
allies, Jane felt immeasurably stronger. The only
problem was not getting caught out…

'I saw Alex driving Lady Dennery over to Moreton
Hall,' Philip said over his shoulder, with a grin for
Jane. 'He looked in a very black mood, but he only
has himself to blame for foisting that creature's company on to us! A more ill-bred, rapacious woman
would be difficult to find!'

Sophia hushed him reprovingly. 'Philip! At the
very least we may be grateful to her for keeping your

brother occupied!' She shivered. 'It frightens me to think that he might find us out!'

'I'll protect you, my love,' Philip said cheerfully, and Jane saw Sophia blush becomingly at the endearment. Once again she felt a moment's concern as she watched them ride on ahead together down the track between the beech trees. It would be a dreadful thing to be conspiring in the romance if Lord Philip was not in earnest! But surely she could not have mistaken his sincerity? Jane frowned. She was certain that it was only the need for secrecy that held Lord Philip silent and that as soon as he could he would make Sophia a declaration...

The Duke had returned in time to witness the three of them riding into the yard together at the end of their expedition, with Lord Philip very firmly at Jane's side by this time. Alex had been leaning over the stable door and chatting to the head groom, and he straightened up as they clattered past, a frown descending on his brow. Jane noticed it and reflected that he seemed to have frowned far more since she had reached an understanding with his brother. He had been noticeably better tempered when they were at odds!

Dinner that evening was a far from comfortable meal. Lady Dennery had evidently indulged in some disagreement with the Duke and vented her spleen through sharp comments on how slow the country was and how poor the company. Alex barely bothered to respond to her barbs and, with such a lack of amity between them, the others fell quiet and ate in almost total silence. When the ladies withdrew, Jane thankfully took the opportunity to slip away to the library for a little peace. She selected a tattered copy of *Tom*

Jones and Maria Elizabeth Jackson's *Botanical Dialogues* from the shelves and curled up on a window seat.

It was a good hour and a half before the sound of footsteps recalled her from the pages and then a dry voice said,

'Escaping into literature, Miss Verey? No doubt you find it more congenial than the atmosphere in the drawing-room!'

Alex Delahaye was standing before her, a quizzical lift to his black brows as he assessed her choice of reading matter.

'Are you a student of botany, Miss Verey? There have been some interesting studies in recent years.'

Jane nodded. 'I have read a few of the books and done a little studying at Ambergate,' she admitted.

'It is certainly an interesting contrast to *Tom Jones*,' Alex observed. 'I scarcely think that your mama would approve, Miss Verey!'

Jane put her book to one side with reluctance. 'No, indeed she would not! She particularly told me that I should not read it before I married! But—' She broke off, on the edge of giving herself away by saying that she believed she would never marry. That would never do, given her supposed affection for Lord Philip! She had a sudden conviction that Alex could accurately follow her every thought process and see right through the deception. A guilty blush stole into her cheeks and she stood up hastily.

'Excuse me, your Grace. I should rejoin the ladies.'

She was about to slip past him, when he put hand on her arm. 'A moment, Miss Verey. I will escort you back, but there is something I would like you to see first.'

He drew her across the room, to where a huge oil painting hung in a recessed alcove. Jane had noticed it when she had first entered the room but it had been wreathed in shadows and she had not paused to study it. Now, as Alex moved a lamp so that more light fell on the picture, she stood still and considered it.

The subject was a lady, fair and delicate, dressed in the high fashion of a decade before. She looked very young. She was reclining with languid grace on a chaise-longue, one white hand resting on the collar of a small dog that was gazing up at her with undisguised adoration in its eyes. Jane considered it a poor painting, studied and artificial, and yet there was something compelling about the beauty of the sitter and the sweetness of her expression. So this was Madeline Delahaye! No wonder the Duke was still so attached to the memory of so gentle and gracious a lady. Looking at the vacant, painted face, Jane wondered what had happened to change so unspoilt a girl into the selfish pleasure-seeker who had apparently betrayed her husband with such blatant disregard for his feelings and public opinion. Remembering Alex's bitterness when they spoke at Almack's, Jane thought she understood. Evidently he had chosen to ignore his wife's infidelity and concentrate on the happier times they had experienced when first married. The fact that he had kept this early portrait in so prominent a position seemed to underline his attachment to her and his determination to keep her memory alive.

A sort of anger took possession of Jane that Madeline Delahaye could have taken Alex's love and treated it with such contempt. If she had had the love of such a man... The painting shimmered in a sudden wash of tears. All Jane's feelings locked in a tight pain in her throat. It was so unfair that Alex should still have such strong feelings for his dead wife, for how could anyone else ever compare? With a smothered sob she pulled her arm from his grasp and ran from the library.

She heard Alex say, 'Jane, wait!' but her pride would not permit him to see her tears.

Later, as she sat dry-eyed in her room and acknowledged to herself for the first time that she loved him, she thought bitterly that pride was indeed all that she had now.

Chapter Nine

'Is this not fun!' Lady Eleanor Fane said, a twinkle of repressed mirth in her eyes as she surveyed her ill-assorted guests as they sat on picnic rugs and under parasols.

There was Lady Dennery, a little worn and over-dressed in the unkind light of day, picking petulantly at her food. Beside her sat Alex Delahaye looking, Lady Eleanor thought, decidedly bored and moody. Oddly, it was as though he had reversed roles with his brother, for Lord Philip seemed happy and at ease as he laughed and talked with Jane Verey. A little distance from them sat Sophia, being charming to Lord Blakeney and apparently enjoying herself immensely. Lady Verey, a contented smile on her face, dozed in the sun.

Well! Lady Eleanor thought now, with secret amusement, if Miss Verey does not like Philip she is making a very good pretence at it! All seems set fair! And the Marchment girl, whom Philip seemed so taken with before, does not appear concerned! I wonder… Her gaze slid to Alex, who was leaning forward to attend to something Francine Dennery was saying.

If Alex allows himself to be caught by her, then more fool him, Lady Eleanor thought astringently. Yet there was very little of the lover in Alex's demeanour and every so often his gaze would rest on Jane Verey in a completely unfathomable regard.

The arrival of Lord Blakeney had been most opportune. He had called at Malladon on the fourth day of their stay, after visiting a rich old uncle in the neighbourhood and hearing that the Duke was in residence nearby. Philip, conscious of a certain constraint in the party, had pressed him to join them and Blakeney had taken little persuading.

'Whole countryside's buzzing with the news,' he had confided to Jane, on the first evening. 'Delahaye never comes to Malladon; now he's not only here but he's brought a party as well!'

Jane considered that it had been a decidedly odd week. On the surface, all had been delightful. There had been riding in the countryside and walks in the park and visits to friends and neighbours. There had even been an informal dinner and dancing in the evening, but now Alex Delahaye had signalled his intention to return to Town and the picnic was the last event before they all drove back the following day.

Beneath the surface matters had not been quite so straightforward. Jane, made hopelessly self-conscious by her behaviour in the library and the discovery of her feelings for Alex, had gone out of her way to avoid him. He had seemed preoccupied by estate matters and plagued by Lady Dennery's increasingly broad hints about the future, and scarcely seemed to notice her anyway. Lady Verey had been dropping broad hints of her own, and Jane had suddenly awoken to the fact that her mother was expecting to

announce the betrothal to Lord Philip as soon as they
returned to Town. Meanwhile, Sophia and Lord Philip
were moving inexorably towards their own conclusion, which Jane devoutly hoped entailed an engagement of their own. Suddenly it all seemed intolerably
complicated and bereft of hope and enjoyment.

Jane swotted an eager wasp that was attacking her
lemonade and tilted the broad brim of her hat forward
a little to shade her face. She had also become aware
of the unsettling nature of Alex's gaze as it drifted
over her. Certainly he could object to nothing in her
manner, for she was behaving towards Philip with the
greatest cordiality and he was responding effortlessly.
Yet she sensed that there was something angering
Alex, something she could not comprehend. It was
very puzzling and she had been aware of it for almost
the whole week.

She looked up and caught Philip's eye. They had
already agreed that Jane should manufacture a reason
for a stroll and that Sophia and Blakeney should help
distract attention. Sighing inwardly, Jane got to her
feet and dusted the crumbs off her skirt.

'Gracious, I feel quite in need of some exercise to
walk off the effects of all that delicious food! Would
anyone care to join me for a turn about the park?'

Lord Philip, taking his cue, scrambled up with alacrity. 'I should be glad to, Miss Verey! Miss Marchment, Blakeney, do you care to come?'

'Oh, yes, that would be delightful!' Sophia agreed
eagerly. She allowed Lord Blakeney to help her up
and adjusted the ribbons on her bonnet. Jane took her
shawl from Lord Philip with a pretty word of thanks.
Lady Verey smiled indulgently to see such harmony.

'You may discount me, my love,' she said sleepily.

'I am happy dozing here in the sun and I do not doubt that Lady Eleanor will keep me company. But perhaps the others…'

Jane saw that the Duke was frowning quite darkly. Some imp of perversity prompted her to extend the invitation as her mother had suggested.

'Would you like to join us, your Grace? Lady Dennery?'

She saw Philip looking quite appalled and tried not to laugh. It seemed a safe gamble, for Lady Dennery was looking quite horrified. 'Oh, no, I do not care to walk at all!' she said as though Jane had suggested some activity in bad taste. 'I am persuaded that Alex will stay here with me, for we may have a delightful coze together!'

Jane smiled brilliantly. 'Just as you wish, my lady!' She did not dare to look at the Duke for his reaction.

'You run along, my dears,' Lady Eleanor said comfortably. 'We older folk will do very well here in the peace and quiet!'

Lady Dennery was now looking quite affronted to be classified with the ancients and the Duke's frown had not lifted. He looked almost murderous. Jane dropped a mischievous curtsy.

'Thank you, ma'am!'

The four of them wandered off, chatting happily amongst themselves.

'Oh, I shall not be sad to return to Town,' Sophia sighed. 'The country is all very well, but it has not the same excitement! I believe Lady Jersey is hosting a ball next week that promises to be the highlight of the Season!'

'Heard about that myself,' Blakeney confirmed. 'Word is that the theme will be classical myths and legends! The talk in the clubs was that Francine Dennery intends to appear in little more than a sheet!'

'Won't be the first time!' Lord Philip guffawed, then caught Sophia's look of innocent bewilderment and cleared his throat loudly.

Jane stopped abruptly, turning to Lord Blakeney urgently.

'Oh, no! I have left my parasol behind and Mama will be furious with me if I catch the sun! She considers freckles most unladylike! Lord Blakeney, would you be so good as to run back and fetch it? I should be so grateful...'

Lord Blakeney was as amiable as he was undiscerning. Expressing himself honoured to be of service, he trotted obediently back in the direction from which they had come. Jane watched him go, then turned to her companions with a smile.

'Pray walk on ahead! There is no sense in all of us waiting here! Lord Blakeney will only be a moment and we will follow you when he returns!'

Sophia and Philip needed no second bidding. Jane, moving into the shadow of a group of trees, saw them stroll away slowly, deep in conversation. She smiled in spite of herself. She would do a great deal to secure Sophia's happiness and it was a joy to see her strategies working so effectively. Splitting up the group meant that Sophia and Lord Philip were, to all intents and purposes, alone, yet within view and perfectly respectable. Lord Blakeney would be back shortly, but Jane would ensure that she did not walk quickly enough for them to catch the others up. Really, she felt that she had the tactics to match any of the King's generals!

Jane frowned a little as she contemplated the next

stage of the plan. Matters were likely to become decidedly tricky from now on. For a start, she knew that
Lady Verey intended the announcement of her betrothal to Lord Philip to be sent to the *Morning Post*
as soon as they returned to Town. That had to be
avoided at all costs. Then a way had to be found to
solve Lord Philip's financial difficulties and promote
the match with Sophia. Jane was forced to admit that
she did not have any ideas at present...

At that point her musings were interrupted by a
completely unforeseen hitch.

A figure was striding towards her across the grass
brandishing her parasol in his hand like an avenging
angel. It was not the slightly corpulent Lord Blakeney, but the altogether more impressive figure of the
Duke of Delahaye. In a sudden panic, Jane turned
round and plunged deeper into the trees, heedless of
the sudden slope and the muddy ground beneath her
feet. She was not sure whether she was intending to
run away or to hide; she only knew that she was about
to be caught out and that she did not appear to be
able to think quickly enough to explain herself.

In the event she was able to neither run nor hide,
for Alex caught up with her with unnerving speed.

'Miss Verey! What is this nonsense about a lost
parasol? And where are my brother and Miss Marchment?'

Jane was at something of a disadvantage. The hem
of her skirt was an inch deep in mud and her bonnet
had slipped to one side, making her look like a dowager who had taken rather too much port. She was
out of breath and flushed, and Alex's proximity and
the altogether furious look on his face increased the
fluttering nervousness inside her.

'There is no nonsense, your Grace,' she said with more composure than she was feeling. 'Why, you have the parasol there in your hand! Be careful that you do not attack that branch!'

She watched the grim expression on Alex's face ease slightly as he lowered his arm and handed the offending parasol to her.

'And my brother and Miss Marchment?' he asked, with a dangerous calm.

Jane gave him a winning smile. 'I suggested that they strolled on ahead. There was no point in all of us waiting! Indeed, I was expecting to catch them up when Lord Blakeney returned!' Her tone managed to convey reproach that it was he, and not Lord Blakeney, who had appeared. 'I expect they are back with the others by now!'

'I am surprised that Philip could bear to be from your side,' Alex said drily. 'He has stuck like a burr all week!'

'Yes, is it not delightful?' Jane said blithely. 'You must be so pleased that your brother and I have reached an understanding!'

'It is the nature of the understanding that concerns me,' Alex said affably. 'You had me fooled for quite a little while this time, Miss Verey, but not any more!'

'I have no notion what you mean, sir!' Jane said, managing to preserve her air of injured innocence.

Alex caught her arm and swung her round to face him. 'Oh, come now, Miss Verey! I used to admire your honesty! The truth is that you have managed to enlist the support of my disgraceful brother—and Miss Marchment, no doubt—in your scheme to thwart the marriage plans! It was so obvious,' Alex mused, a smile starting to curl the corners of his mouth, 'I cannot think why I did not see it before! To think that I believed that you had meekly accepted the plans made for you! My wits must have gone a-begging!'

There was a long silence. Jane's intellect, which had served her so well up to that point, suddenly seemed to have deserted her, banished by the insistent pressure of Alex's touch. Worse, although her mind was frighteningly blank, her senses seemed unusually sharp. She was conscious of the plaintive sweetness of the birdsong, the rustle of the leaves and the cool caress of the breeze on her hot cheeks. Her gaze was held by his and no power on earth could have broken the contact.

Jane saw the amusement fade from Alex's eyes, to be replaced by an expression that made her shiver.

'Am I to test my theory and the strength of your feeling for my brother?' he asked softly. 'It is irresistible, I fear...'

Jane had plenty of time to move away from him and she knew that he would not have tried to stop her had she done so. She could not have said what it was that held her captive, unless it was that fatal curiosity of hers; it had prompted her to wonder secretly what it would be like to be kissed by Alex, and now she wanted to know the answer. Whatever the reason, she stayed quite still, and Alex leant forward and kissed her.

The touch of his lips on hers was deceptively light, almost casual, were it not for an undercurrent of sensuality that sprang shockingly to life as soon as they touched, elemental as sheet lightning. Jane felt a surge of sensation wash over her, leaving her weak with a most delicious pleasure. She knew a moment when she was sure that Alex was about to sweep her into his arms, then, to her great disappointment, he released her and stepped back.

'My apologies, Miss Verey,' Alex said expressionlessly. 'I fear I succumbed to an impulse that has been troubling me for some time.'

Jane took a deep breath. She was dizzy with the memory of taste and touch of him, torn by disappointment that he had let her go.

'Well!' she said, with incurable honesty. 'I do not see that it is at all the thing to kiss your brother's intended bride, your Grace!'

'No...' Alex slanted a glance down at her '...I agree that it would not be at all appropriate—were you to be that bride, Miss Verey! Now, permit me to escort you back to the others before anything else befalls you!'

After a moment's hesitation, Jane took his proffered arm and they walked slowly through the dappled shade towards the edge of the copse. Her shaken nerves were beginning to settle again, but she was still acutely aware of Alex's physical presence. She reflected a little ruefully that Alex himself seemed quite unmoved, almost as though he had forgotten what had passed only a moment before. In fact he suddenly seemed a great deal more cheerful than he had for the entire week.

'So,' he said conversationally, 'will you concede the truth? It is all a scheme, is it not?'

Not even Jane found herself brass-faced enough to tell a direct lie. 'It was all working so well!' she said a little plaintively. 'You said yourself that you had been taken in!'

'Yes, I must have been very slow,' Alex agreed

pleasantly. 'In truth, I thought I knew you far too well to be deceived again!'

Jane cleared her throat. For some reason his words and tone had disturbed something in her. They created a feeling of intimacy that stirred emotions already aroused by their encounter. For some reason he did not sound accusatory—there was too much warmth in his voice.

'You have said before that you knew I was untrustworthy,' she began, a little bitterly, but Alex stopped and turned to face her properly.

'I did say that, and I am sorry for it. I said it only to provoke you at the time and the fact that it worked does not make it any more admirable! The truth is, Miss Verey—' his tone dropped '—I have long admired your strategies and your determination not to give in!'

There was a silence broken only by the chatter of the birds and the running of the brook. Jane felt the colour sting her cheeks and dropped her gaze, and Alex, sensing her discomfort, started to walk again.

'Tell me, what did you plan to do next?' he asked. 'Your plan was a good one in the short term, but dangerous as well! You must realise that your mother in particular is planning an announcement as soon as we reach Town!'

'Yes...' Jane was glad to be distracted from her own complicated feelings '...I own that was a problem! I had not quite fathomed how to avoid the formal engagement!'

'No doubt you would have thought of something,' Alex said, so consolingly that Jane looked up sharply to see if he was teasing her. He was smiling at her, but without mockery.

'I expect so,' Jane said dolefully, 'but now that you know the truth—'

'Yes, we shall have to think of something else!'

'I only wanted Sophia to be happy,' Jane said, still following her own train of thought. 'That is,' she added scrupulously, 'I did not wish to marry Lord Philip, but when it became apparent that Sophia *did*, I hoped for a happy outcome! Do you think—' she glanced at Alex hopefully '—that you might permit...?'

Alex was looking preoccupied. 'I shall have to think about it, Miss Verey,' he said.

Jane left it at that. She wanted to make a push for Sophia's future, but knew full well that Alex was hardly a man who could be pestered into agreement. Besides, she wanted to escape the leafy shade, for being alone with him was making her nervous. The strength of his arm beneath her fingers, the brush of his body against hers...she was very aware of him and had no wish to betray her feelings.

They stepped out into the bright sunshine and Jane nearly gasped with relief.

'I see Miss Marchment and my brother ahead,' Alex said, matter of factly. 'As you predicted, Miss Verey, they are almost back with the others!'

'Oh, by all means let us hurry to catch them up!' Jane said thankfully. She had no wish to prolong this unsettling encounter. Alex, however, appeared to have other ideas.

'Oh, let us not rush back,' he said lazily, with an amused look down at her. 'It would not do for you to go hurrying about in the full sun!'

'I have my parasol now,' Jane said pertly, unfurling the lacy white material, 'and I am no fragile flower!'

'No, indeed, a most resilient root, Miss Verey, although that is scarcely a flattering description of you! I would never underestimate your resourcefulness!'

Jane tilted her head to look at him. 'You are speaking in riddles, your Grace!' she said bluntly. 'It is most disconcerting!'

Alex gave her a smile that was even more disturbing. 'Forgive me! I thought, perhaps, that you would understand me, being so accomplished in strategy! I simply meant that though I have seen through your current plan, I would not put it past you to devise another! I must beg you not to do so. You see, I already have one of my own in the devising, and though it will take a little time to sort out, I have high hopes that it will come to fruition!'

'I hope that it is not along the lines of your other tactics, sir,' Jane said tightly and not entirely truthfully. 'I consider them indefensible!'

'If you mean the kiss, it was not an intentional part of my plan,' Alex admitted, still smiling, 'but now that I have found it so effective and enjoyable I may have to employ it again! Now, Miss Verey, tell me if you would protest! *That* is an interesting test of your honesty!'

Jane's stormy gaze locked with his but she was not able to respond because of the proximity of the others. She did not like to imagine what they might have read into her expression. The picnic had been neatly packed away and Lord Philip was assisting Lady Verey and Lady Eleanor up into the gig that was to convey them back to the house. Lady Dennery, her face as thunderous as it had been earlier, was standing a little apart from the others and tapping her parasol angrily on the grass.

Lord Philip hailed his brother with a deeply suspicious innocence. 'Alex! We had all but given up hope of you and imagined that you had spirited Miss Verey away!'

'Tempting,' Alex said under his breath, with a limpid look for Jane. He raised his voice. 'Is everybody ready to go back?'

'I have been ready this past hour!' Lady Dennery snapped. 'Have you no thought for others, Alexander?' Her contemptuous gaze raked Jane. 'Or perhaps you were lost in your pastoral idyll with that little—?'

'Have a care, Francine!' The Duke's tone was soft but with an undertone that made Jane jump. For a moment she saw a flash of some vivid emotion in his eyes, before he turned to her with scrupulous courtesy.

'Miss Verey, do you care to walk back or would you prefer to drive?'

Before Jane could reply, Lady Dennery made a rude and derisive noise and stormed off in the direction of the house.

'Shocking *ton*!' Lady Eleanor was trying not to smile at Lady Dennery's downfall. 'I fear it is about to rain, Alex—perhaps you should go to her aid?'

The Duke raised one eyebrow. 'I am persuaded that Lady Dennery will find her own way home,' he said easily. 'No doubt she prefers to be alone!' He turned back to Jane and his smile was dazzling in its warmth. 'Miss Verey?'

'I will drive, I thank you, sir,' Jane said hastily, although she would indeed have enjoyed the walk through the parkland. She allowed him to help her up into the second gig and squeezed in next to Sophia.

'Oh, Jane,' her friend whispered, 'did you see the look that the Duke gave you? I do believe…and Lady Dennery clearly thinks you a rival! Oh Jane, I do believe that the Duke of Delahaye is developing a *tendre* for you!'

'Poor Lady Dennery,' Sophia said the following morning, as the summer dust settled on the drive behind her ladyship's coach, 'she had such high hopes and finds them all dashed! It must be very hard for her—'

'To be a rich widow?' Jane asked, a little waspishly. 'She may not have managed to attach the Duke, but there will be plenty of other suitors!'

She came away from the bedroom window and moved rather restlessly across to the portmanteaux that her maid had already packed. They were all returning to Town that morning, but Lady Dennery would not be accompanying them, for she had been invited to stay with friends in Buckinghamshire and had high hopes of a certain elderly Marquis who would be of the company. Jane felt that the journey back would be rather more comfortable without her ladyship, but it was only a small relief amongst the other matters that preoccupied her.

Sophia was looking at her friend with concern. 'Are you quite well, Jane? You seem sadly out of sorts today!'

Jane sighed, unpacking half of the clothes that Cassie had already put away as she rummaged for a favourite pair of gloves. 'I'm sorry, Sophy! You are right in thinking me like a bear with a sore head! It is just all so difficult…'

She sat down and Sophia came to sit beside her on the bed.

'Tell me what is troubling you,' she urged. 'Is it that Lady Verey plans the betrothal announcement for as soon as we return to Town? I'll allow that it is a little difficult…'

Jane made a sound that was halfway between a sob and a laugh. 'Oh, Sophy, you have such a talent for understatement! The truth is that my mother wishes to promote my engagement to a man who should by rights be marrying you! I have come up with no plan to solve Lord Philip's financial difficulties and can see no solution to the whole problem other than that you elope with him!'

Sophia had paled a little. 'Oh, Jane, I do not think that a very comfortable solution! Why, the Duke would cut Philip off altogether and then everyone would be unhappy!'

Jane got to her feet and moved restlessly across the window. 'The Duke knows that my apparent affection for Lord Philip is all assumed!' she said over her shoulder. 'That is the worst part of the situation! He challenged me about it only yesterday and warned me to make no more plans! There is nothing to be gained by further deception!'

'He is a most perceptive man,' Sophia said with a shiver. 'All the time that I was smiling on Blakeney, I was convinced that he knew the truth!'

'A guilty conscience!' Jane said bluntly. 'The Duke had no notion until he took Blakeney's place and brought me the parasol yesterday. Then, when he saw that you and Lord Philip had walked on together— *then* he knew the truth! I tried to persuade him to look upon the two of you with kindness, but—' She

broke off, not wishing to raise Sophia's hopes unnecessarily. After all, Alex had told her that he had a
plan, but it might not be one that would make everyone happy.

'But perhaps—' Sophia avoided Jane's eye '—the
whole matter may be solved if the Duke has feelings
for you, Jane—' She broke off and looked hopeful,
bursting out, 'Oh, if he were to love you then he
would no longer wish you to marry Philip and his
heart might be softened towards us—'

But Jane was shaking her head. 'No, Sophy, I fear
you have it all wrong! I know that you thought yesterday that the Duke had developed something of a
tendre for me, but I am certain that you are mistaken!'

Sophia looked stubborn. Jane realised that this was
because she so desperately wanted it to be true. It
would solve the whole problem of the projected marriage to Lord Philip and they might all live happily
ever after… Jane made a wry grimace.

'I am sorry, Sophy, but it really isn't true.'

'But I saw the way that he was looking at you,
Jane! And when Lady Dennery made her ill-bred remarks he gave her the set-down she deserved for
slighting you! Surely—'

Jane took a deep breath. There was only one way
to convince Sophia.

'I know it cannot be true for the Duke kissed me
yesterday and thought so little of it that he had forgotten it the next second!'

Sophia gave a little squeak. 'I beg your pardon,
Jane?'

'He kissed me,' Jane repeated, with a hint of irritation.

'Oh, Jane!' Sophia's eyes were huge. 'Was it truly dreadful?'

'No,' Jane said slowly, 'it was not. I am obliged to admit that it was rather nice!' She smiled suddenly, against her will. 'Which is very confusing, but progresses our situation not at all!'

'Oh, Jane!' Sophia said again, breathlessly. 'But if he kissed you—'

'It was only part of the game!' Jane said, the light dying out of her face. 'I told you—he was completely unmoved by it! It is all a game to him!'

Sophia was looking at her with blank incomprehension. 'A game?'

Jane decided that she could not begin to explain the complicated steps in the encounter between herself and Alexander Delahaye. Pitting her wits against his had been amusing at first, a challenge that had had an underlying current of excitement. She had never dreamed that it would ever have the power to hurt her. Yet now…

She decided to opt for the easier explanation.

'I believe that the Duke of Delahaye is still in love with his wife,' she said, 'and that is why no other lady would have the chance of engaging his affections. He showed me a picture of her, Sophia—she was very beautiful and the picture is displayed so prominently that I think it must be a sign of the regard he still has for her.' She turned away, closing the portmanteau lid and struggling with the straps in order to hide her confusion. Her feelings were currently too raw to allow her to confide.

'Oh, Jane,' Sophia said, and there was pity in her

voice, as though she has guessed Jane's state, 'what are you going to do?'

'Avoid him, I should think,' Jane said bleakly. 'I will not marry Lord Philip, but nor shall I have any further dealings with his brother!'

Chapter Ten

Alex's opposition to this plan became apparent almost immediately. Whilst Jane was intending to avoid him, he seemed to seek her out deliberately. When they met in the entrance hall for the journey home that afternoon, he expressed the aim of taking Jane up in his phaeton whilst Philip drove Sophia and the ladies of more mature years travelled in the carriage. This was sufficiently improper for Lady Eleanor to raise an eyebrow, but no one contradicted him. Lady Verey was too much in awe of him, whilst Jane saw no point in arguing only to be overruled. Sophia and Philip both looked a little stunned by this public sign of approval and as Sophia went out onto the carriage sweep she gave Jane a look of mingled doubt and pleasure. Interpreting this correctly, Jane thought that Sophia was now convinced of Alex's partiality and would quiz her mercilessly about it later.

They bowled down the drive and out on to the road in the wake of the carriage. It was very pleasant to be driven so expertly. The phaeton was very well sprung, the view enjoyable and day fair. Jane was relieved to discover that they could chat inconsequen-

tially on various topics as wide-ranging as her childhood at Ambergate, her interest in botany and many
other subjects of mutual interest.

'I hope that you have enjoyed your stay, Miss
Verey,' Alex said a little formally, after an hour or
so and for some reason it felt as though they had
moved from impartial to more personal subjects.

'Yes, thank you,' Jane said cautiously. 'It has been
pleasant to be in the country again and Malladon is a
fine house.'

Alex laughed softly. He cast her a sideways glance.
'No mention of the entertainments or the company,
Miss Verey?'

Jane shifted a little uncomfortably. 'I find it difficult to spend any length of time in the same company,' she admitted. 'Everyone seems to live in each
other's pocket! I believe that there must be some fault
in me that makes me intolerant of the society of others!'

'Why do you suppose I spend so much time at
Hayenham?' Alex said, with a crooked smile. 'I am
the least sociable of creatures, Miss Verey, and find
the demands of the Season or the houseparty a severe
trial! Perhaps we are kindred spirits, you and I!'

Jane did not trust herself to answer directly. 'I certainly find the country preferable to London. I fear I
must be a sad trial to my mother, for all that she tried
to turn me into a perfect young lady!'

'Well, don't change!' Alex said abruptly. 'Indepen-
dence of mind is a quality seldom found in a young
lady, let alone valued as it ought to be! I lose count
of the number of vapid, feather-brained girls one
meets every Season and it appals me that they are
encouraged to act so!'

'You are very ungallant!' Jane said severely. 'What do you suppose is their opinion of you, your Grace?'

Alex looked startled. 'A good question! Apart from as a rich Duke in need of a wife?'

'Upon my word! But then, I suppose there are some young women who will tolerate any number of faults for a title and a fortune!'

Alex smiled as the point went home, but he did not rise to her comment. 'You would not count yourself amongst them, Miss Verey?'

'No, indeed! You have not answered my question,' Jane pointed out. 'Perhaps you are so quelling that all the young ladies you meet are over-awed by you!'

'Then it is fortunate that I do not ask them to bear with me,' Alex said laconically. 'Though you, Miss Verey—' He broke off with an exclamation.

Following his gaze, Jane saw that the wheel of the carriage in front was wobbling wildly and even as Alex shouted a warning to the coachman, there was the sound of rending wood and the vehicle lurched violently to one side. The wheel rolled off into the ditch and the carriage sat marooned like a fat dowager in the middle of the road.

Philip, whose phaeton was at the front of the procession, reined in and turned back hastily. By the time that Alex and Jane had drawn level, Lady Eleanor had already been helped down and Sophia was comforting her by the roadside whilst Philip and the groom tried to aid Lady Verey.

It quickly became apparent that Lady Verey had fallen awkwardly when the coach had tipped up and seemed to have sprained her wrist. She had fainted from pain and shock, and as she was no lightweight the two men were having some difficulty in extracting her from the carriage. Eventually they managed to pull her out, by which time Alex had sent his own groom to fetch a physician and had driven to the nearest inn to alert them to the accident. They laid the invalid on the travelling rugs at the side of the road and stood around a little helplessly as they waited for her to return to consciousness.

'Hartshorn!' Lady Eleanor said triumphantly, after rummaging in her reticule. 'My poor Clarissa! She looks as white as a sheet!'

Jane suspected that Lady Verey was better off unconscious, at least until the doctor arrived to have a look at the injured arm. Fortunately Alex returned at that moment, bringing a makeshift stretcher made out of a tavern bench. They wrapped Lady Verey up and carried her to the inn.

It seemed to Jane, watching with anxiety tinged with amusement, that Alex's presence seemed to smooth all possible obstacles. In the space of a few minutes, Lady Verey was carried to a bedchamber, a parlour and refreshments were bespoken for the other guests and the physician arrived to set the broken limb. The damaged carriage was brought in and a wheelwright set to work whilst the ostlers attended the horses. It was all achieved with maximum speed and minimum fuss. Jane sat with her mother whilst the doctor was busy and presently went down to the parlour where the others were waiting, standing around a little awkwardly as they awaited some news.

'My mother is much better now that her arm is bandaged,' she confirmed in response to Lady Eleanor's anxious enquiry. 'She is sleeping now, for she is quite worn out, but declares that she will be quite well enough to return home tomorrow. Perhaps—' she turned instinctively to Alex '—you would be so good as to give my brother a message when you return to Town, sir? If he could come to fetch us tomorrow we shall do very well, and need not delay your departure any further.'

Her words were met with a storm of protest. 'We cannot leave you here alone, child!' Lady Eleanor said astringently. 'No, indeed, we must all stay!'

Sophia added her own concerns. 'Oh, Jane, it is impossible that you should stay here! Why, everyone knows that inns are most dangerous places! You would be ravished in your bed!'

'It is natural that Miss Verey would wish to remain to look after her mother,' Alex said smoothly, stifling a smile. 'I have already spoken to the landlord and they have only three rooms altogether, so it is clearly impossible for all of us to stay. It would be better for you to return to London, Aunt Eleanor, for I am assured that the carriage wheel has been mended already. Philip can escort you and Miss Marchment. She will need to stay with you tonight, for she cannot return to Portman Square and be alone with Lord Verey! I shall stay here with Miss Verey and her mother.'

Jane opened her mouth to object at the arrogant way in which Alex had taken charge. She closed it again as he shot her a quelling look. Lady Eleanor looked affronted. 'Well, upon my word, I see that you have it all worked out, Alex!'

'Yes, Aunt Eleanor,' Alex agreed, shepherding her towards the door, 'but it really is all for the best! There is little we can do for Lady Verey until tomorrow and there is Miss Marchment to consider as well. Philip—' his brother came forward with alacrity

'—please take Lady Eleanor and Miss Marchment out to the carriage. And let Simon Verey know what's happened, there's a good chap...'

Jane escaped upstairs. Alex's high-handedness had evidently won the day and for the moment she did not wish to confront him. She was certain that he had manoeuvred matters so that they would be alone together and she was tempted to spend the rest of the day in Lady Verey's chamber in order to avoid him.

Lady Verey was asleep, showing none of the signs of incipient fever that the doctor had warned against. Jane sat with her for a few hours until night fell outside and Jane's stomach began to rumble and remind her that she had not eaten for a number of hours. Whilst she was hesitating over whether or not to venture down to bespeak supper, there was a knock at the door. The landlord's daughter poked her head in.

'His Grace's compliments, miss, and will you join him for dinner in the parlour? I am happy to sit with your mother whilst you are away.'

Jane was tempted to refuse but it seemed that Alex had already removed the most obvious excuse by engaging the girl to sit with Lady Verey. She washed her face and hands slowly, and made her way downstairs.

The parlour was cheerful with a small fire burning in the grate and an enticing smell of food. Jane's spirits began to revive a little. Alex was standing before the fire and came forward at once to hold a chair for her and to ask after Lady Verey. Jane realised that she felt nervous; the strangeness, intimacy even, of their situation, suddenly struck her. He passed her a glass of madeira and, after a moment's hesitation, Jane took a sip.

'You are very quiet, Miss Verey,' Alex observed, after she had made no effort to speak during the entire first course. 'I hope that the distress over your mother's accident has not overset you?'

'Oh, no!' Jane tried to pull herself together. 'That is…I am very sorry for Mama, for it was a dreadfully unlucky thing to happen, but I believe that she will recover well. I must thank you for your help, sir. You have eased our difficulties considerably.'

'Even if the price is having to accept my company?' Alex said, with an unrepentant smile. 'I saw that you disapproved of my high-handedness, Miss Verey!'

Jane bit back an answering smile. 'You are very frank, sir.'

'I deal straight, as you do, Miss Verey. Perhaps you would have preferred to stay here alone, facing whatever dangers Miss Marchment feels lurk in such places?'

'I do not believe that I would have been in any great peril,' Jane said judiciously. 'However, your Grace evidently felt it necessary to provide protection, for which, no doubt, I should also thank you!'

'It was nothing. I have my own reasons.'

'I do not doubt it,' Jane said, a little crossly. 'Does everyone always fall in with your plans, sir?'

'Almost always!' Alex said cheerfully. 'Except for you, Miss Verey! You are the one notable exception and it has been a salutary experience for me!'

Jane met his eyes squarely. 'I collect that you refer to my refusal of your brother's suit? If you thought to spend your time this evening persuading me, I should warn you now that it would be a waste of time! I am still of the same mind!'

Alex considered the deep ruby red of his wine. 'Oddly enough, Miss Verey, that was not my intention.' He looked up suddenly and Jane's heart did a little flip as their eyes met. 'Though I should be gratified to know why you are so adamantly against the match.'

Jane looked away. 'It is simply that marriage is a very serious business, your Grace. I esteem your brother—we are fast friends—but we have little in common on which to base a life together.' She blushed. 'Must we speak of this? I have no wish to prolong the subject!'

Alex inclined his head. 'Then we will not do so. It would be ungallant of me to persist with a topic you find distressing.' He paused. 'However, your reluctance did lead me to wonder whether your feelings were already engaged. I asked you before, of course, but now that we know each other better you might be willing to confide...'

Jane stared at him, her pie congealing on the plate in front of her. Of course! Why had she not thought of that for herself? It would have been the obvious delaying tactic! She could not believe that it had not occurred to her to invent a secret fiancé, or indeed to plead guilty to an affection that was not returned! There was only one problem—the identity of her secret love...

'Harry Marchnight, for instance,' Alex was saying, carefully expressionless. 'I have observed that you are very fond of him, but perhaps your feelings are of a deeper nature than mere affection...'

Dark eyes and hazel met and held. Jane trembled on the edge of committing herself. Henry was a perfect candidate for her unrequited love, handsome, dashing… Yet there was something in Alex's gaze that compelled her honesty.

'Oh, I have known Harry for an age,' she said, as carelessly as she was able, 'and I love him like a brother! I wish I could claim that you are right, sir, but it is not true and I shall not pretend otherwise.'

She thought she saw Alex relax infinitesimally, but could not imagine why. The silence between them suddenly seemed oddly significant.

'Let us speak of other matters,' she said impulsively. 'Tell me about Hayenham, sir. I have heard that you spend most of your time there.'

Alex's description of his Yorkshire home took most of the rest of the meal and by the end Jane could almost taste the sea spray and feel the wind in the heather.

'I can tell that you love it very much,' she said, a little wistfully. 'It sounds so very beautiful! Yet I would have thought that a man like you would still need other employment…some sort of gainful activity—' She broke off and flushed at the look he gave her. 'I beg your pardon, sir. I was thinking aloud.'

Alex was smiling. 'So you do not think that my estates provide sufficient interest or occupation, Miss Verey?'

Jane blushed all the more. 'I did not intend… I suppose that I see you as needing more of a challenge…forgive me,' she finished hastily. 'I am tired, I think, and should retire.'

Alex put out a hand to detain her. 'A moment. This is interesting—an interesting insight. What would you see me doing, Miss Verey?'

Jane made a vague gesture. 'Well, take Harry Marchnight as an example—'

'Must we? I am fast becoming tired of his name!'

'Nonsense! Harry is the perfect example! He gives the impression of being a rake and a gamester and yet he is nothing of the sort!'

Alex's gaze was suddenly very intent. 'What do you mean, Miss Verey?'

'Why, that Harry is forever disappearing on mysterious errands and pretending that he is nothing but a pleasure-seeker, but anyone who knows him must realise he is no dilettante! It is obvious that he must be engaged upon secret government business. Just as you—'

Jane broke off and blushed scarlet. 'Excuse me, sir. I have said too much. My imagination runs away with me.'

Alex leant forward. 'What does your imagination see for me, Miss Verey? A self-proclaimed recluse using his somewhat eccentric reputation to cover— what?'

Jane shrugged. 'I know not, sir. I promised that I would keep quiet about that night at Vauxhall—and about your activities in Spitalfields—and I have kept my word! But I do not have to be a bluestocking to calculate that there is some strange business afoot! Only…' she frowned, aware that her glass was empty and her mind slightly fuzzy from drink and tiredness '…I do believe that you should be careful, sir. It cannot be right that someone is stalking you armed with a knife!'

'I will take your advice, Miss Verey,' Alex said gravely. 'I do take it. And once again I am touched at your concern for me. What does that betoken, I wonder?'

Jane suddenly realised how very tired she did feel.

The food, the warmth of the fire and most of all the wine, had filled her with a sudden lassitude. She stood up. It seemed very late. The shadowed room was far too intimate for comfort and Alex was coming far too close to the truth. It was best to retire before she gave away all her secrets.

'I hope that my mother may stand as chaperon even though she is asleep in bed,' Jane said doubtfully. 'I do not think that this is at all respectable, your Grace!'

Alex smiled. 'Perhaps you are right! Certainly I could argue that you are hopelessly compromised!'

Jane blinked at him a little owlishly. 'Surely it is your brother who has the rake's reputation!'

Alex's gaze was bright with mockery. 'Perhaps,' he said again, 'but you have had the proof that I am not safe, have you not, Miss Verey?'

The room suddenly seemed far too small. Jane edged towards the door. Alex stood up and stretched with a lazy grace. 'Allow me to escort you to your room…'

Jane started to protest, but to her horror she found that she was so tired she could not be bothered to form the words. She grasped the back of a chair to steady herself.

'Oh, dear…'

'It is just a reaction to all the events of the day,' Alex said practically, and before Jane could object, he had swept her up into his arms. 'I will take you upstairs.'

'Oh, no!' Jane's eyes opened wide, sobriety suddenly restored. 'You cannot do that!'

He was laughing openly at her, the mocking tone still very much in evidence. 'You are quite safe, Miss

Verey! I have never had to stoop to seducing young ladies in alehouses…'

'No, but…' The effort of argument was almost too much for Jane, whose eyes seemed to be closing of their own volition. 'If somebody saw us—'

'Then you would have to marry me. It is a perfectly simple solution.'

Suddenly it all seemed perfectly simple to Jane also. Various pieces seemed to slot together in her mind. 'Yes,' she said sleepily, 'because that is the real reason that I cannot marry your brother, sir…'

She opened her eyes. Alex's face was very close above her own, his eyes so dark she imagined that she might drown in them. The firelight cast its shadow along the hard line of his jaw, his mouth…

'Why is that, Miss Verey?'

'Because it is you that I…'

Jane's eyes closed. Her head rested against his shoulder. She thought she heard him say, 'You stopped at the most interesting moment, Miss Verey!' Then he was holding her even closer and she felt his mouth brush her hair with the lightest of touches. She could not protest, could not even open her eyes. She felt warm and safe and by the time he had carried her up to her room, Jane was fast asleep.

It was very late when Jane awoke the following day. The sounds of the voices upraised in the kitchen floated up to her room mingled with the rumble of wheels on the cobbles of the yard. Jane stretched. She felt warm and content—until she remembered the events of the previous evening. She had been very sleepy…what had she said? She must have fallen asleep in the parlour and Alex… She was in her shift!

With growing horror, Jane saw that her clothes were neatly folded over the back of a wooden chair by the window. She closed her eyes in dread. Certainly she could not ask…

'Miss Verey!' The landlord's daughter had knocked briskly at the door and stuck her head inside. 'Your mother is asking for you and your brother is already arrived! Do you care for some breakfast, madam?'

When Jane reached her mother's chamber it was to find Lady Verey was up and dressed, partaking of breakfast and in a surprisingly buoyant mood.

'I am very well, my love,' she said in answer to Jane's inquiry, 'though the arm pains me a little. Of all the foolish accidents! Your brother is come to take me back to Town and the Duke has graciously agreed to drive you—'

Jane flushed bright red. 'Oh, no, Mama! I am persuaded that it would be better for me to accompany you and Simon to tend to your comfort—'

'Your mother will be more comfortable with the additional space in the carriage,' a smooth voice said from the doorway behind her. 'Lady Verey, your servant, ma'am! I can scarce believe I find you looking so well!'

Lady Verey fluttered becomingly. 'Oh, your Grace! So unfortunate an accident, but I thank you for all your help…'

'It was nothing,' Alex said easily, smiling at her. His gaze travelled to Jane and lingered. 'Good morning, Miss Verey. I believe you were just evincing a desire to be rid of my company?'

Jane dropped a slight curtsy. She did not choose to

be diplomatic that morning. It was so very frustrating to find that he was ahead of her at every turn!

'Just so, your Grace. Excuse me, I must go and greet my brother.' Before Lady Verey could reprove her she had slipped from the room.

When the time came to leave, it seemed that her feelings were not to be taken into account. Lady Verey and Simon took the carriage whilst Alex handed Jane up into his phaeton as though she had never expressed any disinclination for his company. Jane found herself so annoyed by this that she was uncharacteristically cross and silent. Her feelings were already rubbed raw by a self-consciousness in Alex's presence and her mind was worrying over the events of the previous night. Had he…? No, surely it was impossible… The memory of the pile of neatly folded clothes came back to haunt her. No one would know, least of all herself…

'I do believe that you are quite out of charity with me this morning, Miss Verey!' Alex said cheerfully, observing her stony face. 'You must allow that it is better for Lady Verey to have plenty of space. She needs a cushion for her arm, you see—'

'I am perfectly aware that my mother requires not to be squashed!' Jane snapped. 'It is simply—'

'That you did not wish to travel with me. I am aware. What can I have done to have given you so strong a dislike for me?'

Jane turned her face away and gazed unseeingly at the passing countryside. Her tormentor was not silenced.

'Perhaps you are regretting the things you said last night,' he said softly. 'Such an avowal of affection…'

Jane turned to him, her hazel eyes huge and stricken. Oh, why could she not remember? 'I made no such avowal!' she said hotly. 'How dare you, sir!'

'Oh, but indeed you did!' Alex took his eyes off the road to consider her flushed and furious face. 'You said that you could not marry my brother because—'

'I beg you,' Jane said hastily, in a fierce tone that belied her words, 'not to put me to the blush, your Grace! I swear you are no gentleman!'

He shot her a smile. 'Gentleman enough to leave you to the tender mercies of the landlord's daughter rather than acting as lady's maid myself! Though the temptation—'

Relief and anger washed through Jane in equal measure. Why did he have to be so provoking? And how could this laughing man be the same austere Duke of Delahaye whom everyone described as cold and remote?

'Your Grace!' she began stormily. 'Pray show a little decorum!'

'Very well.' Alex lowered his voice. 'We shall talk about it another time.'

'I have no ambition for it,' Jane said, turning her shoulder. Her hands were shaking and she pressed them together to still them. It was with the most profound relief that she realised they were already driving through the outskirts of London and she did not speak again until they were in Portman Square.

'I wondered if I might call on you tomorrow,' Alex was saying, effortlessly casual, as he helped her down from the phaeton. 'Would ten o'clock be convenient? It is early, I know, but then my business is urgent.'

'I…yes, of course.' Jane tried to think of an excuse

and totally failed to do so. More than half of her wanted to see him, but the timid part of her was still urging her to withdraw before it was too late. 'That would be quite convenient.'

'Good.' Alex smiled at her and the glimmer of humour in his dark eyes set her pulse awry. He kissed her hand. 'Until tomorrow, then, Miss Verey.'

It was good to be home again. Whilst the servants fussed over Lady Verey and led her away to rest, Jane cornered Simon over a cup of chocolate in the drawing-room. She had thought that her brother looked strained and tired in the brief time she had seen him before their departure from the inn. Now she was shocked as the harsh morning light showed just how hollow-eyed he had become.

'How did you fare whilst we were away, Simon?' she asked lightly, only the expression in her eyes betraying her concern.

'Very ill, Janey.' Simon's smile and his use of the childhood diminutive confirmed her worst fears.

'Have you seen her?'

Simon turned away, making a pretence of scanning the *Morning Post.* 'I collect that you mean Thérèse? No, I have not seen her. She would not see me!' He turned back sharply and his face was full of so much misery that Jane could feel his unhappiness. 'For the first three days they continued to deny that she lived there, then they said that she would not see me and finally she told me to take my foolish flowers and leave her alone!'

'You sent her flowers?'

'By the barrowful,' Simon confirmed grimly, casting the paper aside. 'She didn't want them, nor the food I sent, nor any of the things I could offer…' His mouth tightened. 'So in the end I thought, what's the point? She don't want me but there must be hundreds who would! So I thought to throw myself into the party spirit—'

'Oh, Simon!'

'—and I've been entertaining myself ever since! Plenty of pretty girls out this season, and ladies of another sort for other sport—' He caught himself up. 'Sorry, Janey, feeling a bit rough…'

'Go and sleep it off,' his sister advised unsympathetically. 'And you need a shave!'

'No time!' Simon said, with an attempt at a jaunty grin. 'I'm engaged to take the divine Miss Shearsby driving!'

Jane sighed. She was hardly fooled by Simon's assumed insouciance and knew it hid a deeper pain. It seemed that Thérèse de Beaurain simply did not wish to know and, Jane thought, there was no possible way to make her care for Simon if she did not.

'What about you?' her brother asked, pausing in the doorway. 'Am I addressing the future Lady Jane Delahaye?'

Jane looked affronted. 'No, Simon! I have *told* you that I will not marry Lord Philip! I have told everyone and no one is listening!'

'Thought that was the point of your trip to the country,' Simon said, tactlessly but with truth. 'Mama seemed to think that it would bring matters to a head! She and Lady Eleanor were banking on it!'

'Well, they will have to accept it! Philip is to marry Sophia—I have it all planned!'

Simon raised an eyebrow. 'Then you may solve the problem by marrying Alex,' he said easily. He eyed his sister's sudden blush with frank interest. 'Oh, dear, it seems I have struck a nerve there, Janey! Well, you have my blessing! I should like above all things to have Alex as a brother-in-law!'

'Oh, go away!' Jane hustled her brother out of the room, suddenly anxious to see the back of him. Simon knew her well enough to suspect the truth and she did not want him to realise just how much his suggestion had appealed to her. 'Go and devastate poor, unsuspecting Miss Shearsby! Though why she would wish to be seen with so disreputable a character defeats me!'

Alex Delahaye was not at Lady Sefton's ball that night. Sophia Marchment and Philip Delahaye danced with each other three times, to the delight of the gossips. Simon Verey behaved quite scandalously, flirting with any lady who glanced in his direction, and Jane Verey sat quietly in a corner, wondering what on earth the Duke was going to say to her the following morning.

Chapter Eleven

The following day was bright but cooler than previously and Jane was glad of the warmth of her red riding habit when she and the Duke of Delahaye rode out. She had been awake for hours, but in the event, Alex was early and he brought with him a horse from the livery stables.

'We can take the phaeton if you prefer, Miss Verey, but I wondered if you would like to ride,' he said. 'You seemed to enjoy your country rides so much at Malladon that I took the liberty of bringing what I hope is a suitable mount for you!'

He had chosen a horse that was sufficiently spirited to keep Jane occupied through the busy streets and they did not speak much until they reached the quieter environs of the Park. It was still very early and there were few people about. Jane noticed that Alex had instructed the groom to ride a long way back, where there was no danger of them being overheard.

The cool, green expanse was very welcoming and Jane had to curb a sudden urge to gallop away.

'Thank you for thinking of this, sir!' she said spontaneously. 'It was a delightful idea!'

Alex smiled. 'I thought that you might enjoy it, Miss Verey. It is not quite the same as being in the country, but nevertheless…'

'Nevertheless, it brings a sense of freedom that one seldom finds in Town,' Jane allowed, her eyes sparkling. 'It is very pleasant to escape sometimes!'

'The country has, perhaps, fewer diversions?'

'Just different ones, I think,' Jane said, smiling a little.

'Some might argue that Town is more exciting.'

'That,' Jane said serenely, 'depends on one's interests. If excitement is derived from creeping through the streets cloaked in black and carrying a pistol—'

Alex burst out laughing. 'You will not let me forget that, will you, Miss Verey?'

Jane looked at him. Today he was in black again, but with a very different appearance from the disreputable and sinister figure of that strange night. His jacket was cut by a master and fitted without a wrinkle. His linen was a pristine white and his boots had a high polish.

Jane privately thought that he looked devastatingly handsome.

'How is Simon?' Alex was asking. 'Did his suit prosper whilst we were away?'

Jane shook her head. 'No, indeed, it goes very ill for him. Mademoiselle de Beaurain has told him to take his attentions elsewhere!'

'I am sorry to hear that. I imagine it must have made him very unhappy.'

Jane looked resigned. 'Oh, he pretends that he does not care and, indeed, to see him at Lady Sefton's ball last night one would have believed it! However I think that he feels it very keenly... It is too bad! Everyone is in love with the wrong person!'

Alex cast her a sideways glance. 'Everyone, Miss Verey?'

'Oh, Simon with Thérèse and Philip with Sophia!' Jane said, greatly daring. 'Matters so seldom progress in the way one would wish!'

'Very true. And what of yourself, Miss Verey?'

Jane, who had steeled herself to answer this question suddenly found it more difficult than she had imagined.

'I?'

'Who are you in love with?'

Jane blushed and hated herself for it. 'I am in love with no one, sir. I told you when we—I told you that night at the inn...'

'Of course,' Alex said smoothly. 'I remember! This touches on the matter I wished to discuss with you, Miss Verey. Would you care to dismount? I will ask Dick to walk the horses.'

Jane looked dubious. 'I am not at all sure that we should. We have been away some time. Mama will be worrying—'

'I will square matters with her later. I must crave your indulgence, Miss Verey. This is important.' There was an imperative note in Alex's voice. He had already dismounted, summoning the laggardly groom with a wave of the hand. As the man took the horse's bridle, Alex helped Jane down.

'Walk the horses for a while, would you, Dick? Thank you...'

He offered Jane his arm and they walked slowly along one of the winding paths. There was no sound but for the clop of the horses' hooves, growing more distant as the groom led them away.

'I no longer wish to promote the match between Philip and yourself, Miss Verey,' Alex said abruptly. 'You mentioned Philip's affection for Miss Marchment and indeed, I have seen you promoting that romance most zealously! So...' He shrugged. 'I am not entirely heartless! I realise that you and my scapegrace brother are very amicable, but scarcely romantically inclined! Whereas Philip behaves as though Miss Marchment is the very pattern of perfection! So I will give the match my blessing!'

Jane felt as though her breath had been taken away. To have connived and schemed for just such an outcome and then to have it put so suddenly into her hands... It was scarcely to be believed.

'Sophia is indeed the sweetest girl,' Jane said warmly, 'and if you are to allow them to wed then I must give you credit for greater sensibility than I had previously thought, your Grace! I am quite overwhelmed!'

'Thank you,' Alex said gravely. He was smiling a little. 'You have not, however, heard the second part of my proposal.'

'There is more?'

'Indeed. In permitting Philip to wed Miss Marchment I am no longer able to honour the commitment I made to my grandfather. Would you permit me to explain a little of the background, explain why I wished for the match at all?'

'Of course,' Jane said, feeling a little at sea. If Alex was no longer interested in the Verey-Delahaye alliance, why should he need to explain? She was suddenly uncertain where this was leading.

Alex squared his shoulders. 'I believe that it was our paternal grandfathers who formed the idea that an union between the two families would be beneficial. They were both in the diplomatic service and met in Vienna. Did you know that they had formed a friendship?'

Jane shook her head. 'My father's father died when I was but young, sir. I had no idea he planned a grand family alliance!'

'Unfortunately there was no one appropriate in our parents' generation,' Alex said drily. 'My own mother and father were already married and I believe the other children were either promised or unsuitable in some way! Nevertheless, the grandfathers were not deterred!'

'They planned to skip a generation?'

Alex smiled. 'Precisely, Miss Verey! My grandfather summoned me before he died and acquainted me with his plan. I was already married but Philip was still a bachelor and already giving cause for concern with his wild antics. My grandfather knew that your parents had married late and that you were still in the schoolroom. Nevertheless, he suggested that it might be a good match. So I went to Ambergate to find out whether your father liked the idea.'

'I know.' Jane said. 'I saw you.'

Alex looked startled. 'You *saw* me? At Ambergate?'

'Four years ago,' Jane said. 'I saw you one night going along the corridor past my room.'

For a moment the memory of the night came back to her: the dancing candle flame, the dark stranger, the legend... Jane felt suddenly resentful, all her bitterness over the arrangement with her father flooding back, reminding her that Alex had sought to use her as a pawn to further his own ends.

'I suppose you had come to look me over and negotiate with my father as though I were some commodity!' she said sharply.

Alex winced. He drove his hands into his jacket pockets. 'I concede that the plan was ill conceived. I was trying to honour my grandfather's wishes and find a solution to Philip's wildness. I did not think—' He broke off, to resume:

'I must be honest and admit that I thought nothing of your hopes and wishes! Oh, it was old-fashioned of me to wish to arrange a match, but I had the best of intentions. I really thought that it would be the making of Philip!'

'And so it will be,' Jane said stoutly, 'immeasurably more so now that he has been allowed to choose his own bride!'

'Yes.' Alex slanted a look down at her. 'I suppose my reasoning was at fault in thinking that marriage was the means to compel Philip to settle down. He would no more accept a forced match than he would reform of his own accord! Yet now that he has attached himself sincerely to a young lady, he is a changed character!' Alex shook his head ruefully. 'I admit that I have made some bad mistakes in this business.'

Jane was prey to mixed feelings. It seemed from Alex's words that matters were now settled. Philip and Sophia would be permitted to marry and Jane would no longer be obliged to scheme and plan to avoid her fate. She could return to Ambergate, perhaps, and then she would never need to see the Duke of Delahaye again…

'Of course,' Alex was continuing, 'that leaves me with the difficulty of resolving my pledge to my grandfather. Then I thought that if one plan could not suffice, another might.'

Jane realised that they had stopped walking. They were in the shadow of a huge clump of cedars and the figure of the groom seemed suddenly far away. There was no one else in sight. Her throat had gone dry. She could read his intentions in his face…

'Oh, no…'

Alex gave her a whimsical smile. 'Is it so horrifying a prospect, Miss Verey? You must be quite honest, as I know you can be! You do not wish to marry me? It is such a neat solution!'

The breeze caressed Jane's hot cheeks. Her mind was racing.

'Oh, I could not! I am…you are so—' She stopped before she could say anything she regretted. She was not entirely sure what she had meant to say. For all her feelings and half-formed wishes, the whole idea was so shocking, so sudden, that she could not comprehend it. Yet Alex was looking quite composed, almost lazily amused, as though her confusion pleased him.

'Oh!' Jane burst out. 'This is so like you! To replace one outrageous suggestion with one even more monstrous! After all the trouble I went to—'

'To thwart me?' Alex was laughing openly now and it only added to Jane's distraction. 'But surely you did not wish to marry Philip?'

'No, but—' Jane almost stamped her foot with frustration. 'Nor did I plan to have to reject you, your Grace!'

'Then do not…' Alex had taken her gloved hand

in his and his touch was almost too much for Jane to bear. She realised that something strange was happening to her. The combined shock and the heady influence of Alex's presence threatened to sweep away her good sense. It would be thrilling to give in to her instincts and accept him. For a moment she revelled in the idea, before sanity intervened.

There were so many reasons to refuse him. He had admitted that he had proposed in order to fulfil the pledge to his grandfather. Then there had been his bitterness when he had spoken of his dead wife. Alex must have loved her very much, and who could compete with a ghost? Surely not a naïve girl of nineteen! And then there was Francine Dennery…

'What of Lady Dennery?' she said, suddenly forlorn, remembering the Beauty's flagrant charms.

Alex raised his black brows. 'You need not concern yourself over her,' he said cryptically. 'Lady Dennery will not be surprised at our betrothal.'

He was moving much too fast for Jane. Betrothal… She frowned a little at his presumption.

'I do not find that particularly reassuring, sir,' she said candidly. 'Do you imply that Lady Dennery would accept the situation and carry on as before, or that your association with her would be at an end?'

Alex gave her a wicked grin. 'Straight to the point, Miss Verey! Do *you* imply that Lady Dennery is my mistress?'

'I have no wish to discuss your precise relationship!' Jane snapped, fast losing her temper. 'My point was that I would not marry a man who would be unfaithful to me!'

Alex inclined his head. 'I respect your views and

you need have no concern on that score. I do not intend to be unfaithful to my wife!'

His wife... Jane realised that her question had given the false impression that she would accept. Drawing away a little, she turned to look at him. She had to put a stop to this now, before she became further entangled. Alex had viewed the marriage as a neat solution, and on that basis she had to decline. The balance would be too unequal otherwise—she loved him, but he saw her as a way out of a problem...

'I am sorry,' she said formally. 'I cannot accept you, your Grace.'

Alex's face was very still. Jane found herself studying him closely, committing to memory the strong lines of his face, the dark eyes that could lighten so easily to unexpected laughter... Her throat ached with tears as an intense love swept over her. Oh, if only he had said that he loved her!

'May I ask why you have refused?' he said at length, very quietly.

'Because...' Jane cleared her throat '...I understand that it would only be a match of convenience—'

'A match of convenience! What extraordinary ideas you do have, Miss Verey!' Alex stepped closer. 'Surely you must realise that I find you prodigiously attractive?'

Jane gave a despairing squeak. That was not what she had meant at all and now matters were taking a decidedly difficult turn. 'Oh, no, your Grace, that cannot be so! You are funning me! Please do not say any more!'

'Pray do not distress yourself, Miss Verey,' Alex murmured. 'Let me convince you of my good faith!'

Jane was aware that the situation was slipping from her grasp. She had witnessed Alex's potent charm on many an occasion but never imagined that there would be a serious need to defend herself against it. She put out her left hand to ward him off—he appeared to already have possession of her right—but he simply captured it in his and pulled her closer.

She knew that he would release her at once if she appeared truly distressed and yet she discovered that she had not real inclination to pull away from him.

He freed her hands only to draw her more closely into his arms and Jane found that, instead of pushing him away, she was leaning confidingly against his chest. His cheek grazed hers, rough against the softness of her skin and Jane gave a pleasurable shiver, breathing the delicious male scent. She had a sudden urge to turn her face against his neck and inhale deeply until she was intoxicated with the essence of him, but Alex was kissing her already and this time it was very different from at Malladon. Gone was the gentleness, to be replaced with a real urgency that was both exciting and a little bit frightening at the same time.

The stretch of parkland, the tall trees and the cool breeze all receded from Jane's consciousness. She was aware of nothing beyond the powerful circle of Alex's arms and the melting warmth that was invading her body.

Her lips parted instinctively beneath the skilful pressure of his own and Jane felt herself tremble in response. Nor did Alex seem unaffected by the embrace as she had thought him at Malladon, for she could feel the racing of his heart where her hand still rested against his chest. She slid her arms up around his neck and felt him draw her all the closer until she was resting against the whole length of his hard, muscular body. The kiss deepened into a dizzying spiral of desire, easing after an immeasurable time only as Alex let her go a little to catch his breath.

Jane swayed a little within his arms, aware that she would have fallen without his support. She was still trembling and her blood was alight with a strange mixture of heat and ice-cold excitement.

Jane struggled to free herself, suddenly overcome with emotions she could not understand.

'Oh, please—'

Alex let her go at once. He was pale and breathing hard, and for a moment Jane saw the reflection of an emotion in his eyes that she found deeply disturbing.

'I am sorry,' he said expressionlessly. 'I forgot that—' He broke off. 'I did not intend to frighten you, Jane.'

'I was not frightened precisely,' Jane said, incurably truthful, 'only a little shocked to know how it felt. I am told that young ladies should not be subject to violent emotions...' She looked away, too shy to admit that she had found the encounter as enjoyable as it was disturbing.

Alex tucked her hand through his arm and steered them back towards the path. 'I have heard that said too, and thought it so much nonsense!' he said cheerfully. 'I should feel flattered and more encouraged were you to admit to taking pleasure in the experience!'

'Oh!' Jane cast a dubious look at him. 'More encouraged?'

There was a wicked glint in Alex's eyes. 'My dear Jane, I wish to repeat my actions on plenty of future occasions, but will not do so if you hold them in strong dislike! However, I cherish a hope that my advances were not entirely unwelcome, and as your fiancé—'

Jane felt her spirits sink a little. The delicious pleasure of Alex's embrace had helped her to forget temporarily that he had other motives for the marriage, motives that had little to do with love. She frowned a little. For a moment she hesitated on the edge of confiding her concerns in him, then there was a spattering of gravel and she realised that the groom had returned with the horses. A carriage crossed her line of vision, then two ladies on horseback. The Park was beginning to wake up.

'Have you changed your mind?' Alex asked quietly, as they turned the horses towards the gate. 'Will you marry me?'

Jane's troubled green gaze searched his face. 'I do not know...I am not sure...there are reasons...'

She saw the shadow that touched his eyes, before he said with constraint, 'Is that a definite refusal, Miss Verey?'

'No, I—' Jane knew instinctively that she had hurt him, although Alex's dark face was carefully expressionless.

'I am sorry,' she said wretchedly. 'I need to think. If you could allow me a little time...'

'Of course,' Alex said with a scrupulous courtesy that was somehow chilling.

They rode back to Portman Square in silence.

'I have business to attend to,' Alex said, still with the same cool civility, after he had helped Jane down and the groom had set off back to the stables, 'but I shall hope to see you tomorrow night, Miss Verey.

Perhaps you will be able to give me an indication of how long you need to consider my offer.'

Jane's face crumpled as she tried to hold back the tears that threatened to ambush her. Somehow this had all gone wrong and she felt dreadful, as though she had casually inflicted some great hurt on Alex and had damaged for ever the relationship between them. She could not understand how it had happened.

She put an instinctive hand on his sleeve. 'Wait!'

'Yes, Miss Verey?' Alex said, with the same distant politeness.

'I...that is...please be careful,' Jane said, her words coming out in a rush. 'If your business is part of what has gone before, you could be in danger and—' She knew she was making a wretched mess of this and felt even more desolate.

Surprisingly, Alex's grim expression had lightened considerably. One gloved hand covered Jane's briefly as it rested on his sleeve.

'Thank you for giving me hope, Miss Verey,' he said very softly. Before Jane could even guess his intention, his arms had gone around her and he had kissed her hard on the mouth.

She was released, breathless and ruffled. 'Oh! For shame! In the street!'

Jane had seen the stealthy movement behind at least half a dozen curtains, including the ones of Lady Verey's drawing-room.

'Yes,' Alex said, his good humour apparently restored, 'you will have to marry me now, Miss Verey! Think about it! I will see you tomorrow!'

And with a deplorably cheerful wave of the hand he turned and strolled away.

* * *

Simon Verey, crossing London Bridge, saw a slender, fair girl hurrying along in front of him, a covered marketing basket over her arm. He started forward. It had happened so many times in the last two weeks—he would see a fair girl and hurry to accost her, only to find that he was confronting a total stranger. But this time…

'Thérèse!'

She turned and he was looking into the cornflower blue eyes that he remembered. His heart started to race.

'Thérèse,' he said again. He put out a hand but she flinched back. Her eyes were bright and angry.

'Leave me alone! Why must you be forever pestering me? Coming to the house…upsetting *Maman*…fine gentlemen asking for her daughter.' Her tone was scornful. 'What do you think I am, *monsieur*? Because I am penniless and you are a rich lord—'

Simon was stung by the injustice of this. 'That's not fair! I only wanted to see you, to talk to you.'

She shrugged carelessly. 'We have nothing to say to each other, *monsieur*! If you are in earnest, the best thing you can do for me is leave me alone!'

She turned to go, but Simon caught her arm, beyond caution. 'It cannot be true that you do not care! I cannot be alone in feeling thus!'

For a frozen minute they stared into each other's eyes and he saw the doubt and the hesitation and, behind it all, a flash of emotion so vivid that he almost pulled her into his arms there and then. He knew that he had not misread her. Thérèse did care, but—

'It is immaterial how I feel,' Thérèse said, so

fiercely that Simon almost stepped back, yet so softly he could barely hear. 'There are reasons why I cannot have anything to do with you, my lord—'

'Is the gennelman bothering you, miss?' asked a burly carter, and Simon dropped Thérèse's arm, suddenly conscious of the attention their raised voices had attracted.

'No, I thank you.' Her composure was flawless. The moment of intimacy, when he had seen into her soul, might never have been. Simon felt triumph and despair in equal measure. 'The gentleman is about to go. Good day, sir,' and she walked away across the bridge, without a backward glance.

Henry Marchnight called late at Haye House that night and was met by Tredpole the butler, wearing his most lugubrious expression.

'I regret that his Grace is unwell, my lord,' Tredpole said, his face completely blank. 'He is not receiving visitors.'

Since Alex had never had a day's illness in all the time Henry had known him, he treated this with polite incredulity.

'Come now, Tredpole, you can tell me the truth. Where is he?'

'His Grace is in the study, my lord, but—' Tredpole shook his head '—I would counsel against disturbing him!'

Light dawned. 'You mean that he is foxed, Tredpole?' Henry hesitated, suddenly aware that he might never have seen Alex ill, but he certainly had never seen him drunk.

The butler cleared his throat delicately. 'A little

cast away, my lord, and I have seldom seen him in a blacker temper—'

The door of the study crashed open making the hall chandelier vibrate. Alex, his hair ruffled, his clothes dishevelled, was leaning against the door jamb.

'Tredpole? Where the devil are you, man? I'll have died of thirst before I get that second bottle! Who the hell are you chattering to?'

Henry thought that he saw the butler wince. It was impossible to imagine the stately Tredpole chattering to anyone.

'Lord Henry Marchnight is here, your Grace,' the butler said austerely. 'I was informing him that your Grace was not receiving.'

'And I was telling him not to be such a damned fool!' Henry said cheerfully. 'How are you, Alex? Think I'll share that second bottle with you!'

Tredpole moved noiselessly away to fetch a second glass. Alex stood aside with exaggerated courtesy to allow Henry to precede him into the room and gestured him to a chair.

'Well, Henry?'

Henry raised his eyebrows. 'My apologies for interrupting you! Seems you wish to go to the devil on your own!'

That won him a brief smile. Alex pushed the brandy bottle towards his friend.

'I hear you were riding in the Park with Miss Verey this morning,' Henry continued.

The smile vanished. Alex frowned. 'You take a keen interest in Miss Verey's concerns, Harry!'

Henry, his unspoken question resolved, relaxed and sat back in his chair. 'Don't be an arrant fool, Alex!

I love Jane like a sister, but that's all!' He paused, then added, 'Unlike you!'

Alex did not deny it. 'How the hell did this happen?' he said morosely.

Henry poured himself a generous measure. 'No one is immune, Alex,' he said. 'Your mistake was probably to think that you were.'

Alex ran a hand through his hair, still frowning darkly. 'I told her that I had decided it was a mistake to force Philip to marry her. Do you think Philip genuinely cares for Miss Marchment, Harry?'

'Yes, I am sure that he does. Everyone has observed it. What did Jane say to that?'

'She was very happy. Not so happy when I put forward my alternative, which was that she should marry me.' Alex drank deeply. 'What should I do, Harry?'

'Don't ask me, old fellow. You know I'm the last person to ask for advice!' Despite the joking tone there was a deeper bitterness in Henry's voice.

'I collect you refer to Lady Polly Seagrave? You could put that to rights if you chose!'

Henry shrugged. 'Maybe so, but we are talking of your romantic difficulties, not mine! I do not immediately perceive the problem, however. You proposed to Miss Verey and—what happened? Did she refuse you?'

'Not outright,' Alex acknowledged, 'but who wants an unwilling bride? Not I! I am to wait until tomorrow to know my fate!'

'Jane is scarcely indifferent to you,' Henry said with a grin, savouring his brandy. 'And she is very young. Give her time!'

'I have—until tomorrow. This is damnably hard on my pride!'

Henry laughed. 'Come on, Alex, your pride can take it! I see that you intend to spend the entire time three sheets to the wind!'

Alex grinned reluctantly. 'It seems a sound enough plan, Harry! But perhaps a game of faro would be an alternative.'

Henry inclined his head. 'Why not? I may stand a chance of winning for once!'

And they settled down to make a night of it.

Chapter Twelve

The following day saw huge excitement in Portman Square. Lord Philip had arrived at an improbably early hour and had asked, with barely restrained impatience, to speak with Sophia alone. He had followed this with a brief meeting with Lady Verey, after which both she and Sophia erupted into the drawing-room, where Jane had been pretending to read.

'Oh, Jane!' Sophia burst out. 'It is so wonderful! The Duke has given Philip permission to pay his addresses to me and he has come at once to ask me to marry him! He is posting to Wiltshire in a couple of days to see my parents! Oh, Jane!'

'Jane, my dearest, dearest child!' Lady Verey cried simultaneously. 'I am so very happy for you! A Duke! Who would have thought it!'

Jane, who was hugging Sophia, eyed her mother with misgiving. 'Whatever can you mean, Mama?'

'Why, Lord Philip tells me that his brother wishes to marry you, you little goose! Surely that was the purpose of his meeting with you yesterday? Why did you say nothing to me? I knew he was developing a *tendre* for you! You are the most fortunate girl in all of London!'

Jane winced.

'Philip says that we are to be married in four weeks and that he cannot believe his good fortune!' Sophia burbled, her blue eyes huge. 'I have written at once to my mama, begging her to return to Town with him and help me to choose my bride clothes! You will help me too, won't you, Jane? Oh, Jane, we shall be sisters! I am so happy!'

'I told the Duke that I would not marry him,' Jane said.

There was a silence. Sophia's smile faded and she stepped back, staring at her friend in disbelief. Lady Verey turned pale. A pained spasm crossed her face.

'Jane? What are you saying?'

'I told the Duke that I would not marry him,' Jane repeated, wishing that the ground would open up and swallow her whole. It was not precisely true, but she did not want her mother becoming carried away and announcing the two engagements at the same time. Besides, her heart was sore that Alex had apparently disregarded their conversation and decided that the marriage would go ahead. Why had he told her that he would wait for her decision when he evidently intended to ride roughshod over her feelings?

Lady Verey eased her way backwards into the elegant Louis Quinze *fauteuil* and sat down rather hurriedly. Sophia went swiftly to the sideboard to fetch her a drink.

'Time...' Lady Verey said faintly. 'You need time... overpowered by excitement...accustomed to the idea... Thank you, child,' she added, as Sophia pressed the glass into her hand.

'I am sorry, Mama,' Jane said, taken aback that her mother had not pressed for the marriage more stridently. She seemed more saddened than angry. And Sophia—

'Oh, Sophy, I am so sorry!' Jane was overcome by remorse. 'I am so selfish! This is your special day and I would not spoil it for all the world!'

'Never mind that,' Miss Marchment said severely, showing her practical streak. 'I am so very happy that nothing could spoil my mood! But I wish to know what it is with you, Jane—we were all so very sure that you are in love with the Duke, you see!'

'All?' Jane repeated faintly, sitting down rather suddenly in much the same way as her mother had.

'Yes indeed, dear child!' Lady Verey sat forward, fixing her daughter with her wide myopic eyes. 'We have all observed it! Sophia and I were quite certain and even Lady Eleanor was coming round to the same view! And Sophia will tell you that Lord Philip is quite convinced that the Duke is smitten by you! Tell her, Sophia!'

'It's true, Jane!' Sophia said eagerly, coming to kneel by her friend's chair. 'Lord Philip said that Henry Marchnight, who as you know is well acquainted with the Duke, said that—'

'Wait, wait!' Jane besought. 'Has everyone been discussing this?'

'Well, yes, my love!' Lady Verey frowned a little. 'It was quite clear to me at Malladon that Lord Philip and Sophia were set fair to make a match of it and when I mentioned it to Eleanor Fane she told me that I was not to regard it, for she was sure that Alex Delahaye intended you for himself! They say that he has never attached himself to any woman since the death of his first wife,' Lady Verey said triumphantly, inadvertently making the situation worse. 'She was a great beauty, of course, but we all know that her behaviour scarcely graced the Delahaye name!'

'I believe, however, that the Duke was most sincerely fond of her,' Jane said dolefully.

Lady Verey stared. 'But since she is dead, my love, you have no need to think of her at all!'

There was a rustle and Sophia took Jane's hand in hers.

'Dear Jane,' she said gently, 'tell me what is the matter!'

'He does not love me, Sophy!' Jane let out a desolate sigh. 'He is still in love with his dead wife! Oh, I seem to amuse him and he indulges me, but I know he is only wishing to marry me to honour the pledge to his grandfather!' She turned to look at her mother. 'So I will *not* marry him, Mama, for all that I love him so much!'

Sophia's eyes were huge. 'So you do love the Duke! Jane, are you sure? He is so…frightening!'

'Oh, he is not so bad when one gets to know him a little! Yes, of course I love him!' Jane said crossly. 'I love him but he does not love me and I will *not* marry a man who does not love me!'

'Heigh ho!' Lady Verey said philosophically, getting to her feet. 'Fine sentiments, my girl, but you have forgotten a couple of things!'

Both girls looked up at her inquiringly. 'One!' Lady Verey enumerated. 'If Lord Philip has told us you are betrothed to Alex Delahaye he will have told everyone and it will be all over Town! Two! If Alex Delahaye wishes to marry you, I defy even you to withstand him!' And so saying, she swept grandly from the room.

Word of Sophia's engagement spread like wildfire that day, mainly because Lord Philip was proclaiming it from the rooftops. It was something of a sensation. The little country miss, with no money and nothing to recommend her but her pretty face, had caught the younger brother of a Duke who was a hardened rake to boot. Not everyone was kind. Jane knew that Sophia missed none of the nuances, though she smiled bravely throughout until her face ached. Nor was Jane able to do much to help, for many of the malicious remarks made reference to her own short and ill-fated courtship by Lord Philip, so that Jane ended up being the butt of the spite as well.

'Oh, it is not to be borne,' Sophia stormed, her good nature quite banished by a particularly sharp remark from Miss Brantledge. 'I declare I will make Philip live in the country all year round if people cannot curb their tongues! To suggest that I stole Philip from under your nose is the outside of enough!'

Both girls were feeling on edge by the time they reached Lady Marfleet's ball that evening. Jane was very grateful that Lord Philip had decided to postpone his departure to Wiltshire and was there to give her friend some much-needed support. Smoothing down her lilac and silver dress, she wondered whether Alex would also be there. It seemed like days rather than hours since she had parted from him and she knew that he would be awaiting her answer. Her nerves tightened at the thought.

'Miss Marchment!' Lady Jersey, malice incarnate, billowed up to them as soon as they entered the ballroom. 'I must congratulate you, you sly little puss! And Miss Verey! I hear your own triumph is to be announced soon! Such a relief for your dear mama that you will not be eclipsed by your friend!' And with a sharp little smile she glided away to spread the gossip.

It was, in fact, at least three-quarters of the way through the evening when the Duke of Delahaye finally deigned to make an appearance. Jane had not been short of partners and Lord Blakeney was particularly attentive. Nevertheless, she found that she had missed Alex's company more than she had imagined. It did not make her feel any happier, especially when her first view of him was with Lady Dennery hanging on his arm and whispering in his ear. Jane turned a particularly brilliant smile on Lord Blakeney, who blinked with surprise.

'Is this not most enjoyable, my lord?' she gushed, making sure that her smile was even broader as they whirled past the Duke and his fair companion. 'I declare I could dance all night!'

''Pon my word, Miss Verey, I could partner you the whole time too!' Blakeney said, quite carried away by her enthusiasm. 'Splendid idea! Are you free for the next?'

The next dance was a progressive country dance which Jane had intended to keep free for a well-earned rest. Now, seeing Lady Dennery persuading Alex on to the floor, she scorned the idea. So this was what he meant when he said that she should not concern herself with Lady Dennery! He intended to carry on as he had before and she was supposed to close her eyes to it! The hurt and anger rose inside her.

It was some time before the movement of the dance

brought her together with Alex and by then Jane had had plenty of time to think about how she would deal with him. Accordingly, she gave him the very slightest of acknowledgements when he greeted her and she smiled ravishingly at Lord Blakeney further down the set.

'How do you do, your Grace? I was—' Again she broke off as Blakeney passed in front of her and she paused to exchange a few words.

Alex was speaking. Jane turned a vague, questioning face to him. 'I beg your pardon, your Grace, I was not attending…'

'No.' Alex sounded quite expressionless. 'I was only observing that Blakeney is a universal favourite! Only last week it was Miss Dalton who was waxing poetic about him!'

'Oh, he is most charming!' Jane agreed airily. 'Lord Henshaw has also been most attentive this evening—'

'Spare me a recital of your admirers, Miss Verey,' Alex said, with the first hint of irritation he had shown. 'I had thought to claim the right to banish such suitors!'

Jane raised her brows. 'Had you, your Grace?'

It was the perfect moment for Blakeney to claim her again, as the figure brought him back to her side and obliged Alex to move on. For the rest of the dance she was aware of his inscrutable dark gaze resting on her from time to time and there was something calculating in it that made her very nervous.

The dance ended and Jane very prettily accepted Lord Blakeney's escort back to her mother's side. They did not get far.

'Sorry to cut you out, old fellow,' the Duke of Delahaye drawled, blocking their way, 'but Miss Verey is promised to me for the next. Miss Verey...' There was a very definite challenge in his eyes.

Jane picked up the gauntlet, taking his arm a little gingerly and allowing him to steer her to an alcove at the side of the dance floor.

'Now, Miss Verey,' Alex said pleasantly, 'you will explain to me why you are playing Blakeney on your line just to thwart me.'

Jane's lips closed tightly. 'I have no notion what you mean, your Grace. I am sure that it would be ungracious in me to deny Lord Blakeney my company when he seeks me out!'

'Indeed! It would do no harm for you to be a little more moderate in your undertakings! Blakeney, Henshaw, Farraday...you will soon have a name as a flirt!'

Jane's eyes narrowed. She had thrown Blakeney and Henshaw in his face and could therefore not complain if he reproached her for it, but poor Mr Farraday, who would not say boo to a goose...

'If we are speaking of flirtations, your Grace, you would do well to look to yourself!'

Alex caught her wrist in a tight grip. They had both forgotten the crowded ballroom and the press of people so close at hand.

'I collect that you mean to censure me for my relationship with Lady Dennery,' he said levelly. 'I should have realised that it was jealousy that prompted your remarks—'

Jane's eyes flashed. This was particularly provoking as it was true.

'I do not care if Lady Dennery wishes to rehearse

her *amours* before the whole Town! I only condemn your hypocrisy in ringing a peal over me!'

'And I do not care to see the likes of Blakeney hanging on your coat-tails! I shall take steps to prevent it in future!'

Their eyes met and held, locked in furious confrontation. Then Alex shook his head slightly.

'I cannot believe... Jane, you try my patience sorely, but I suppose my own behaviour is scarcely exemplary! To tell the truth, I met Lady Dennery in the ante-room, that is all. What I said this morning is true—you need have no concern for her! Now, admit you would not care what company I kept if you did not like me a little!'

The logic of this was hard to refute. His fingers had relaxed their grip and had slid down to take her hand in his. His touch was warm and seductive, reminding Jane of their encounter in the Park. She could feel a smile start to curve her lips.

'Your Grace—'

'Please call me Alex, now that we are betrothed.'

'Yes!' Jane said, suddenly remembering that she had an issue to raise with him. 'I understand that you have already told your brother that we are to wed! That was not well done, sir! I asked for a little time!'

'I know it.' The pressure of Alex's fingers had increased infinitesimally, sending quivers of sensation along Jane's nerves. 'You are mistaken, Jane. I said nothing to Philip, although he may have drawn his own conclusions when I gave my blessing on his match with Miss Marchment! I would not do that when I had given you my word that I would wait for your decision.' He stepped closer. 'Will you give me your answer now, Jane? I do most ardently hope that you will accept me…'

Jane felt as though she was trapped in the tantalising web of her feelings. Alex was smiling with a warmth that did strange things to her equilibrium; she could read in his eyes that he wanted to kiss her and she felt a little dizzy.

'Perhaps I will… But this is Sophia's night, not mine, your Grace. I would not wish to steal her thunder—'

His expression told her that he knew she had capitulated. She saw the blaze of triumph in his eyes, shadowed by a less definable emotion. Jane was swept by excitement followed by near-terror. Alex turned her hand over and kissed the palm, then a dry voice from beside them broke the spell.

'Alex, I am persuaded that you would not wish to draw any further attention to Miss Verey, at least not yet!' Lady Eleanor Fane said.

Alex tore his gaze away from Jane. 'As usual, you are quite correct, Aunt Eleanor,' he said abruptly. 'I will bid you goodnight, Miss Verey.'

'I assume that you have just agreed to make Alex the happiest of men,' Lady Eleanor said comfortably, tucking Jane's arm through hers and steering her towards Lady Verey. 'It is an open secret, particularly the way that the two of you looked this evening! When you were quarrelling I scarce knew whether it would end in tears or kisses! As good as a play, and good to see Alex on his high ropes when usually he is the most moderate of men!'

Jane smiled, accepted the approval and the good-tempered teasing, but a small, cold corner of her heart reminded her that one thing was missing. It seemed that, despite his pleasure at the engagement, the Duke of Delahaye was still not able to tell her that he loved her.

The following day was bright and summery enough to banish even the most melancholy of reflections. They were engaged for a trip to Richmond to watch a balloon launch and Lord Philip and the Duke had offered their escort, before Philip took himself off to Ambergate next morning.

They arrived in the country to discover a crowd already gathered, strolling in the sun and watching the stripy silk balloon rippling gently in the breeze. Four burly men were anchoring it to the ground with thick ropes. Jane jumped down from the phaeton, her troubles forgotten.

'Oh, how wonderful. I would so love to fly!'

'Why don't you stand in the basket and see what its like under the canopy, miss?' one of the aviators suggested. 'Here, let me give you a hand up the steps.'

A few of the crowd clapped as Jane stepped over the side and down into the well of the basket. After a moment, Alex followed her, jumping down inside. It was surprisingly roomy under the huge silk canopy, with strong leather straps that Jane imagined the aviators must hold on to during the flight. There was room for at least three people in the basket and the edge was so high that Jane could barely see over the top. She looked up into the balloon's canopy and wondered what it would be like to feel the ground drop away and watch the countryside receding below you.

A sudden gust of wind caught the canopy and

whipped under the basket. There was a shout and then the crowd was scattering, drawing back. For a moment Jane wondered what was happening and then she felt the edge of the basket tip up, throwing her to the floor. The basket started to drag across the field, lifting from the ground one moment, bumping over the tussocks the next as the wind filled the canopy.

'Oh!' Jane tried to scramble to her feet, but their progress was too rough to allow her to regain her balance. She felt as helpless as a rag doll, tumbled in a heap of petticoats on the floor, tossed from side to side.

'Hold on!' Alex had managed to grasp one of the leather straps in one hand and bent down to pull Jane closer. The basket lifted from the ground and with a whimper Jane clutched at his jacket, turning her face into his chest. Gone were her ambitions of being a fearless aviator. Suddenly solid ground seemed much more appealing.

The basket hit the ground for a final time, shaking Alex's grip from the strap so that he fell with Jane in a heap on the floor. There was silence. Silence and stillness. Jane opened her eyes. Above her the huge canopy was snagged on the branches of a tall oak and as she watched, it gradually crumpled down on top of them, blotting out the blue of the sky.

She felt as though she was covered in bruises, every bone in her body shaken from its socket. Her hat had come off and she had evidently sat on it at some point for it was completely flattened. Her hair was tumbled about her face and she suddenly became aware that her skirts were up about her knees, revealing far too much of her legs to Alex's appreciative gaze. She tried to sit up, only to find that the angle of the basket prevented it.

Jane pushed the hair out of her eyes and tried to straighten her clothing. Her dress had slipped from one shoulder, showing the upper curve of her breasts, and she was sure that she looked like the veriest Cyprian with her hair about her shoulders, her skirts riding up and her dress descending to meet it.

She turned her head to see Alex watching her with a lazy grin that made her heart skip a beat.

He was looking no less dishevelled than she, his black hair hopelessly tousled, his jacket creased and his neckcloth awry.

'You look very nice,' Alex said slowly.

The silk canopy descended with a sudden whoosh, throwing them into a twilight world. In the distance Jane could hear shouts and voices calling, but she paid no attention.

Alex put out one hand and tumbled her back into his arms. Before she could say a word his mouth came down on hers.

It was suddenly like another world, a fantasy world. The shock, the fear and the sudden relief combined in a heady brew. Instead of pushing him away, Jane found herself pulling Alex closer so that their tangled limbs were inextricably entwined. Her lips parted in invitation and she felt the same dizzy, melting sensation invade her limbs as though her whole body was just waiting for his touch.

The kiss deepened with a searing intensity but Jane was no longer afraid. She shivered as the dress slipped further from her shoulders and Alex's fingers skimmed her bare skin. Desire coursed through her. His mouth left hers to trace the line of her neck and the curve of her breast with agonising, irresistible slowness, pausing only as it reached the place where the last wisps of material still covered her. The excitement lit her blood with wildfire. Alex's mouth was rough and urgent as it returned to hers and Jane revelled in its sensuous demand. She had lost all concept of time or reality, only knowing the greatest relief and joy at being safe and in the arms of the man she loved.

Neither of them heard the voices or footsteps approaching and only came to their senses as the silk curtain lifted to reveal the anxious faces of the balloonists and half the crowd. Alex had sufficient time and presence of mind to straighten Jane's dress, but they were still in each other's arms when it seemed that they were surrounded by people exclaiming and crying and reaching in to the basket to help them out.

Alex picked Jane up and handed her out of the basket to the first of the waiting men. Her legs crumpled as she was put gently on the ground and when Alex jumped down and scooped her into his arms again, she made no demur. The fresh breeze cooled her hot cheeks and the bright light made her blink. Suddenly she could feel every ache and bruise, and she did not want to face the barrage of questions and the curious eyes of the crowd. She felt the tears come into her eyes and turned her face against Alex's shoulder. She was not sure whether it was reaction to the accident or the sudden realisation of what she had done that made her want to cry.

Alex strode across the field, making short shrift of the questions of the crowd. It was only when they reached Lady Verey and the others, almost prostrate with anxiety, that Alex allowed his pace to slow.

'Miss Verey is bruised and shocked but otherwise unhurt,' he said, giving a tearful Lady Verey his most reassuring smile. 'We must return home at once, for she needs to rest.'

'What a terrible thing to happen!' Lady Eleanor, normally so resilient, had aged visibly. 'When we saw that the men had had the ropes snatched from their hands, we thought you would take off straight into the sky!'

'Not without the burners going, ma'am,' Lord Philip said practically, 'but it must have been very unpleasant nevertheless. Alex, put her down here.' He gestured towards the seat of his carriage. 'Can you drive, or would you prefer someone to take your phaeton back for you? I notice your shoulder is giving you a little trouble.'

Alex hesitated. 'Thank you, Philip. I must confess that it pains me a little. If you could take my team, perhaps Blakeney would drive your curricle back?'

'I'm flattered you trust me with your cattle,' Philip said a little drily. 'I've been waiting for a chance to try my hand with them, although not, perhaps, under these circumstances! Lady Eleanor, perhaps you and Sophia could travel with me? Lady Verey, I am persuaded that you would wish to remain with your daughter? As would Alex, I make no doubt…'

Lady Verey was already in the carriage, chafing Jane's cold hands and peering into her daughter's face.

'No harm done,' Philip said bracingly, proving himself a staunch support in times of need. 'We'll have you all back in Portman Square in no time!'

Sophia bent to kiss her friend, her blue gaze troubled.

'Oh Jane,' she whispered, 'everyone is talking! They all saw the two of you in the balloon basket and…' she blushed '…they say that he was making love to you! Oh, Jane, you'll have to marry him now!'

Chapter Thirteen

'You'll have to marry him now.'

Jane slept deeply that night; when she awoke, Sophia's words were still ringing in her head. She slipped from her bed and moved across to the window, leaning on the sill. It was still early. The street was deserted and beyond the rooftops the sky was a pale, misty blue and very beautiful.

Jane sighed. She knew that what Sophia had said was true. To be found kissing and hugging in the basket of a hot-air balloon was an extraordinary circumstance that the *ton* would savour to the full. Alex had already made his declaration and now, for the sake of her reputation, the announcement would need to be made as soon as possible...

She opened the window and took a deep breath of the cool air. She ached a little from the balloon accident, but not as much as she had expected. Evidently she had been very lucky.

The house was silent. Jane could imagine what would happen once Lady Verey was awake. Her mother would erupt into her bedroom, insisting on a public announcement of the engagement forthwith, planning the wedding, talking and talking about bride clothes…

Jane dressed quickly and quietly. She had a few difficulties with the buttons of her dress but managed by twisting around as far as she could. It was hopeless to try to arrange her hair on her own, so she tied it back with a ribbon and bundled it under a chip bonnet. Folding her cloak over her arm, she went softly from the room and down the wide stairs.

A housemaid was scrubbing the doorstep and looked up, startled and taken aback, to see the young mistress out and about so early.

'Oh, miss—' she began, but Jane put a finger to her lips.

'Hush, Hetty! I shall not be gone long! Pray do not tell Mama…'

'But, Miss Jane—' the maid protested, only to find she was speaking to thin air. Jane's hurrying figure could just be seen, disappearing down the street and turning the corner. The maid watched dubiously, then, with a sigh, she returned to her scrubbing.

For several days, Jane had had in her mind a half-formed plan to go to Spitalfields and find Thérèse de Beaurain. Simon had maintained that he would not force his attentions on Thérèse since she quite evidently did not welcome them, but Jane loved her brother a great deal, knew that he was unhappy and was determined to try to help him. If Thérèse truly did not care, then Jane was prepared to accept that, but she could see that it would be easy for the French girl to misunderstand Simon's intentions. Jane was sure that she could make Thérèse realise that Simon was entirely honourable, and perhaps persuade her to agree to a meeting.

There was only one fly in the ointment and it was a formidable one. Jane knew that Alex would never agree to her visiting Spitalfields and, now that they were to be officially betrothed, she was sure she would never be able to slip away on her own. This was her only chance.

Jane had thought that it would be only a step to Spitalfields, but that was because she did not really know where it was. She turned down Oxford Street and, by the time she reached St Giles Circus, she felt as though she had been walking for hours. She was obliged to pause for a rest, for her feet had started to ache and, as the morning awoke and the pavements filled, she was starting to attract some curious glances. A young man driving a cart called across to her, but Jane raised her chin and turned haughtily away. She was now far from Portman Square and for the first time, the imprudence of her plan struck her.

'Cab, lady?'

A hansom had drawn up beside Jane. The driver, a fatherly-looking figure, was eyeing her with concern.

'Can I take you home, miss? You should not be wandering about on your own...'

Jane smiled. 'Thank you, sir. You can take me to Spitalfields, if you please.'

The driver looked dubious. 'It's no place for a young lady alone. Be sensible, ma'am, and go home. Where's it to be? Grosvenor Square? Queen's Square?'

For a moment Jane reflected crossly on her lack of foresight in forgetting to borrow some of Cassie's old clothes. It seemed that a young lady was as instantly recognisable on the streets of London as a Cyprian might be. She had not laid her plans particularly well this time, and felt keenly that Alex was to blame for this. She had become so preoccupied by him that it had left little room for other schemes.

'I have business with another lady in Spitalfields,' she repeated. 'Be so good as to take me there, sir.'

The driver scratched his head doubtfully. Then, clearly thinking that Jane was safer with his escort than without, he reluctantly agreed and they set off along High Holborn.

Jane watched in fascination as the streets passed by. Narrow cobbled alleys gave glimpses of cramped squares and tumbling buildings leaning towards each other. Shop signs swung in the breeze and sprawling taverns already seemed packed with humanity. Crowds jostled the coach, good-humoured in the sunshine, peering curiously into the interior. Jane could not have created more of a stir had she been preceded by a butler announcing her progress.

'This is Crispin Street, Miss,' the driver said, in tones of deepest disapproval. 'Whereabouts do you wish to me to set you down?'

Jane's throat was suddenly dry. 'I am not precisely sure—' she began, then broke off as she saw a fair girl emerging from a house a little way down the street.

'Oh, there she is! I am sure of it! I pray you…' she fumbled in her reticule for a coin '…wait for me here! I shall not be long!' She thrust the money into his hand and turned back to the street.

'Thérèse! Wait!'

The fair girl had been about to pass them by with no more than an inquiring look, but at Jane's words she hesitated a moment and her intensely blue eyes rested in puzzlement on Jane's face.

'*Mam'zelle?* I beg your pardon—do I know you?'

'No…yes!' Jane found that she seemed out of breath, her thoughts tumbling. It had all happened too quickly. How was she to find the words to explain? The cab driver was listening with unconcealed interest and a couple of passers-by had stopped to watch. Across the street, a portly man, bulging out of an embroidered waistcoat, lounged in a doorway and watched them out of the corner of his eye.

A frown wrinkled the girl's forehead as she considered Jane's simple white dress and elegant bonnet. 'I think you are a long way from home, *mam'zelle*… Perhaps you would be better to return.'

Jane thought that she was probably right. She suddenly felt very odd, cast adrift in an entirely unfamiliar world. Yet the stubbornness that had brought her this far would not allow her to give up now.

'I am Jane Verey,' she said clearly. 'I believe that you are acquainted with my brother Simon, Miss de Beaurain. I must speak with you.'

The girl's blue eyes had narrowed. 'You are his sister? Can he have sent you here? But no, it is impossible!'

She had started to turn away, but Jane caught her arm in desperation. 'Please! I beg you to listen to me!'

A murmur ran through the growing crowd. Thérèse eyed them with exasperation, her expression becoming even more irritated as it returned to Jane's flushed but determined face. 'Very well, Miss Verey! You had better come with me before they tear the clothes from your back! This way…'

She ushered Jane through a narrow doorway and

up a steep stair. The air was musty and dim out of the sunshine, and Jane blinked as her eyes accustomed themselves to the comparative darkness.

There was one room only at the top of the stairs, a long room resembling an attic, with bare boards and high windows. To the side of the stairs was a table with materials scattered across it—rich silks and taffetas in red and gold, a contrast to the bare austerity of the room with its single chair and wooden bed pushed up against the wall. The bed was occupied, but Jane did not like to stare with ill-bred curiosity at the recumbent figure.

'My mother is too ill to be disturbed,' Thérèse said abruptly. 'I beg you to speak softly, Miss Verey, and do not wake her! Now, how may I help you?'

Her tone was not encouraging. Jane looked about her helplessly. She wondered suddenly whether she was making a dreadful mistake, then she remembered Alex's words. The proud daughter of the Vicomte de Beaurain had already rejected one offer of help. She would need every ounce of persuasion she possessed to make Thérèse de Beaurain even listen to her.

Jane sat down on the workbench beside the dress that was clearly Thérèse's latest commission. The room was spotlessly clean and tidy, the floor swept and the bedclothes neatly folded around the invalid on the bed. Jane dragged her gaze away and found Thérèse watching her with a mixture of pity and exasperation.

'I do not know what can bring you here, *mam'zelle*,' the French girl said impatiently. 'I have already told your brother, the good Lord Verey, that I do not wish to encourage his interest. He has been here—sitting in the street, begging entry to the house!

I cannot believe that he has sent you to plead his case!
I repeat, I have no wish be his lordship's mistress!'

The colour flamed in Jane's face. Thérèse's tone
had been heavily ironic, but there was anger in her
eyes—anger and a kind of hopelessness that Jane did
not understand. For two pins she would have rushed
from the house, but the memory of Simon's strained
and despairing face was before her eyes. She spoke
firmly.

'Mademoiselle de Beaurain, I beg you to hear me
out. Firstly, my brother has no notion that I have
sought you out today. I am here because I care about
his happiness and I thought—erroneously, perhaps—
that you might do so too. Secondly, I do not believe
that Simon ever suggested that you should become
his mistress! He is far too honourable a man to do
such a thing!' The sincerity in her voice rang out. 'I
thought that if I could see you...explain to you that
he was desperately unhappy...you might relent and
at least grant him an interview... He loves you!' she
finished desperately.

There was silence. Thérèse had sat, head bent,
whilst Jane spoke, but now she looked up with a flash
of her blue eyes. 'Do you know who I am, Miss
Verey?'

'Yes! You are the daughter of the Vicomte de
Beaurain, who fled France at the Revolution! You
used to do sewing for Celestine and you were at the
masquerade ball at Lady Aston's, which was where
my brother fell in love with you! You are related to
General Sir John Huntington, who offended you by
trying to offer you charity! I assure you that I am
offering no such thing!'

This time there was reluctant humour in Thérèse's

voice. 'I believe you, Miss Verey! You are remarkably well informed! And is your brother similarly aware of my history?'

'No!' Jane spoke more hotly than she had intended. 'Simon knows nothing and cares even less! He is not concerned over your ancestry or current occupation! He would not care if you were a Duchess or a chambermaid! But I cannot convince you of that.'

A bout of coughing from the bed interrupted them and Thérèse jumped up, hurrying across to hold a beaker of water to her mother's lips. They spoke briefly in French, too softly for Jane to hear, then the Vicomtesse turned on her side, smothering another paroxysm of coughs in her pillow. Thérèse straightened the covers about her mother's form, then came back to Jane, a deep frown on her brow.

'Forgive me, Miss Verey, but I must ask you to leave now. My mother has need of more medicines and I was on my way to fetch them when you arrived.' Her gaze rested on the luxurious silk dress. 'I have my work to do, as you see. You have done your best for your brother, but—'

'Will you not see him at the very least?'

Thérèse was shaking her head. There was a mixture of frustration and anger visible on her face. 'Miss Verey, you do not understand—'

There was a peremptory knocking, then the door burst open to admit a florid man whose yellowing smile Jane immediately distrusted. He was well dressed in a rather gaudy manner, with lace at the throat and wrists, and although he affected the manner and pose of a gentleman, there was something vaguely threatening in his appearance. Jane immediately sensed something defensive in Thérèse's demeanour as the girl stood up, shielding her from his view.

The man executed a bow. 'How d'ye do, my lady? I am come as promised to collect my debt!'

'I told you that the money would not be available before Tuesday,' Thérèse said calmly, but Jane thought she detected a hint of nervousness in her voice. She gestured towards the table. 'I have the work to finish before I am paid and only then can I pay you!'

The gentleman did not seem convinced. He paced the boards, walking over to peer with ill-concealed curiosity at the figure on the bed.

'I see your mother is not in plump currant,' he observed unctuously. 'How would it be if I sent out for the medicine for her—at a price?'

Thérèse cast Jane a swift look. She spoke stiffly. 'I have told you before, sir, that the price is too high for me!'

The gentleman stepped neatly around Thérèse and stopped before Jane. His gooseberry-green eyes, bloodshot and slightly protuberant, appraised her with sharpened interest. With a sudden jump of the heart Jane recognised him. This, she was sure, was the man she had seen at Vauxhall advancing towards Alex with a knife in his hand. He had been with Thérèse when she and Simon had seen them in the gardens, but later he had been alone, creeping down the dark alleys with murder in his mind... She shrank back.

'Barely saw you there, my dear!' the man was saying cheerfully. 'Thérèse, introduce me to you friend!'

'My friend was just leaving, sir,' Thérèse said, and this time there was no mistaking the sharp anxiety in her tone.

'Not so swift, my sweet!' There was an edge to the unctuous voice now. 'So charming a companion! Pray make me known to her!'

Thérèse paused. 'You must excuse us, Mr Samways. Your money will be ready on Tuesday as agreed. Now, by your leave—'

The gentleman stepped forward and grasped Jane's sleeve. She came to her feet with a gasp of shock. There was no mistaking the cupidity and excitement on his face.

'I do believe that you have the real thing here, Thérèse, my dear! Who is she—some society lady come to consult about a new dress? But no...' he peered closely into Jane's face and she could smell his stale breath '...she is too young! A golden child! A pretty pigeon for the plucking!'

'You mistake, Mr Samways,' Thérèse spoke hurriedly. 'My friend is nothing and no one! She cannot interest you—'

'On the contrary!' The gentleman's eyes were avid on Jane's face. 'She interests me extremely! There must be an anxious family somewhere and I am determined to take care of her for them!'

'You will not hurt her!'

There was taut anxiety in Thérèse's voice. Jane, only part-understanding, grabbed her cloak and tried to step past the gentleman. He was too quick for her, grasping her arm.

'A moment, my dear! You are too hasty!' He bent his face close to hers. 'Who are you, eh?'

'I am no one, sir, as Miss de Beaurain has said,' Jane said hurriedly, a catch in her voice. 'I beg you to let me go now! I will be missed!'

'Why, that's just what I'm saying!' Jane could not

mistake the menace underlying his voice now. 'There'll be those who'll pay handsomely to get you back, my dear! Now, be a good girl and tell me who they are! The sooner you do, the sooner you'll be going home!'

Jane's eyes met Thérèse's in a look of horror. It seemed impossible that her errand had brought her into such sudden and unexpected peril. Despite what Alex had said to her about Spitalfields, it had never occurred to her that she might be in any physical danger. It was daylight and there were plenty of people about, and although she had felt uncomfortable in this unfamiliar environment, she had not for a moment thought that there might be those who saw her as a prize, a means of gaining some money... All her thoughts had been concentrated on the interview with Thérèse and the necessity of convincing her to meet Simon again, rather than the hazards that might lie along the way. Now, she realised that she had been naïve and foolish in the extreme.

'I suppose you have brought your jackals with you!' Thérèse was saying furiously. 'How dare you use me to further your dirty little plans! I have told you I shall have no part in your filthy games!'

The gentleman gave her a look of admiration. 'Spoken like a true noblewoman, my dear, a true aristocrat! I ain't offended! Truth to tell, you had your chance to share in my good fortune! I've accepted that you ain't interested, but you'll pay your dues like the rest and keep your mouth shut!'

Thérèse said a rude and idiomatic phrase, the meaning of which Jane could only guess at. Samways was still holding her arm, and now he dragged her over to the wooden chair, thrusting her down on to it.

'I've plenty of time, my dear, but have you? Wouldn't you rather be restored to the bosom of your family?'

Tears stung Jane's eyes. She had only herself to blame for getting into such a ridiculous and dangerous situation.

'I do not understand you, sir!' she said, scrubbing angrily at her eyes. 'This is tantamount to kidnap!'

'No, no, my dear!' Samways swung a chair round and straddled it, resting his arms along the back. 'I have no intention of kidnap or abduction! This is a business transaction—I will keep you here safe until your family can reclaim you!'

'At a price!' Jane said furiously.

Samways shrugged expansively. 'It costs to keep a young lady safe in these parts! You ask the high-and-mighty French missie there!' He nodded at Thérèse, who was standing irresolute, biting her lip. 'She pays me to keep her from the brothels and the whore-houses, which—' He thrust his face close to Jane's '...is where you'll be if your loved ones don't come through with the cash!'

For a moment Jane stared at him, her eyes bright with fury. She was enraged to find herself in such a position of weakness, but there was a strong practical streak in her as well. Common sense suggested that it was in Samways's interests to keep her unhurt whilst he extracted a ransom. She knew her family would pay. Therefore it was sensible to make the process as painless as possible—and face the consequences once she was free. For a moment Alex's face swam before her eyes. She could picture his anger, the black brows drawn with fury, the blistering words that would be heaped on her head.

'I am Miss Jane Verey of Portman Square,' she said haughtily. 'If you approach my brother, Lord Verey, he will see to it that you are...rewarded...for restoring me to him unharmed.'

Samways was out of his chair even before she had finished speaking, rubbing his hands together in anticipation of rich pickings. The sister of a lord! Even better than he had imagined!

'Don't go getting any ideas, now,' he warned, pausing at the door. 'Dolbottle and Henty are watching the house and will persuade you against leaving. If your brother is fond of you, Miss Verey, I reckon you should be home by nightfall!'

'If we are not to go out, you had best fetch the medicine for Madame de Beaurain,' Jane said crossly. 'I do not see why she should suffer unnecessarily!'

Fortunately, Samways seemed much amused by this. 'Medicine for the Frenchies! Yes, milady!'

There was a silence after he had gone out. Madame de Beaurain was asleep and snoring softly. Thérèse moved across to the window and looked out into the street.

'He spoke the truth. His men are everywhere.' Her blue gaze lingered thoughtfully on Jane. 'That was very wise, Miss Verey. You have more sense than most of your contemporaries, who would be having the vapours by now!'

'Thank you,' Jane said coolly. 'Please call me Jane.'

There was a hint of amusement in Thérèse's gaze. 'And you must call me Thérèse. I am sorry that a compassionate errand has put you in such an awkward position, Jane.'

Jane's hazel eyes were bright as they rested on Thérèse's face. 'What did that unpleasant man mean when he said that you paid him to keep you out of the brothels?'

A hint of colour stole into Thérèse's cheeks. 'Just that,' she said shortly. 'Mr Samways is a business man, a man of many and varied interests! One of them is the ownership of a number of whorehouses. I did not care to be amongst his women, Jane, though he offered me the privilege of being his own mistress! So instead I pay him so that I need *not* be a whore! A neat reversal, *n'est ce pas*?'

Jane was momentarily silenced. 'But what…could he..?'

'Oh, yes,' Thérèse said drily, 'he could! He runs this neighbourhood, Jane, and everyone must contribute in some way!'

She sat down and stoically started to stitch the hem of the taffeta dress. Jane stared at her. After a moment Thérèse looked up and gave her a faint smile.

'Does my sang-froid offend you, dear Jane? But you see, it is the way of the world! It is simply that you are usually protected from its harsh realities! Have no fear, Samways will quickly find your family, they will pay handsomely for you and you will be on your way home! A storm in a tea cup!'

'I am not offended,' Jane said, not entirely truthfully. 'If you will pass me the underskirt, Thérèse, I shall occupy myself in helping you. I am not so neat a seamstress as you, but if you give me the bits that do not show…'

There was reluctant admiration in Thérèse's eyes as she pushed the skirt across to Jane.

For a while they sewed in silence, but after a little, Jane said, 'Perhaps you could tell me a little of yourself, Thérèse, to pass the time. I could chatter but I would prefer to hear about you, if you do not mind…'

Thérèse laughed. 'Very well, Jane. Would you like the tale of my life? It starts in gilded luxury in Blois, where I was the pampered only child of the Vicomte and Vicomtesse de Beaurain. I had wardrobes of pretty clothes and servants at my beck and call. I remember nothing of those days for when I was still a baby my father was guillotined and we were forced to flee abroad. We went by night, running away, hiding like thieves… We came to England, where my mother worked for years as a teacher of French and later took in sewing when her health began to fail.' She cast a swift, affectionate look across at the humped figure in the bed. 'I did not go to school— my mother taught me until I was old enough to work, telling me all the time that I should try to better my position and remember whose daughter I was. What I remember is nothing of richness and luxury and everything of poverty and struggle.' Despite the words her face was serene, untroubled.

'Then I became French governess to a family in Kent…' Thérèse shrugged a little. 'It is the old story. I was young and the master of the house was old and importunate and the mistress unable to believe that he was resistible… I was turned off without a reference and for my next governess role I was obliged to take a job further down the social scale with a Cit who wished his daughters to become little ladies…' Another shrug. 'I have no time for rank and fortune—

how could I, given my own circumstances? What value has rank been to me, the penniless daughter of a French nobleman? But these people were not even pleasant—petty, small-minded… In the end they dismissed me because they said they found my manner too high and mighty, but really they were uncomfortable to have a servant higher born than they. So I came back to London and took to sewing, like my mother.' She bit her thread with sudden violence. 'My mother's health was deteriorating. It was that that prompted me to contact the Huntingtons and ask for help. Nothing else would have induced me to beg, for I am too proud.' She met Jane's eyes and smiled a little. 'I know it is my besetting sin! Anyway, we received a grudging invitation to visit. Have you met the family, Jane? They are as proud as we, stiff and unbending, and they were not warm to their French cousins. Well, it would never have worked… I cannot be a poor relation—I would rather earn an honest wage. And so there was talk of ingratitude and pride, and we came back and took a room here. My mother became too ill to work and her medicine costs much, but we manage.'

'And then, a few weeks ago, you went to Lady Aston's masquerade,' Jane said softly. Thérèse put down her sewing slowly. There was suddenly a distant look in her eyes. 'Yes. Oh, Jane, it was a beautiful dress, that one. I have worked for years with silks and velvets, and never felt tempted, but that dress… The old Duchess—' she gave a naughty smile '—I fear she could not do it justice. As soon as I saw it coming together under my hands I had to have it! I tried it on…and then I thought, why not? No one would know…so I ran up a domino as well and went to the masquerade. I had heard the Duchess mention it. And—' she shrugged '—the rest you know.'

'You danced with Simon,' Jane said thoughtfully. 'I saw the two of you. You looked very happy.'

Thérèse evaded her eyes. 'I was enjoying myself. It was like a fairytale and the deception added spice to it all! Just for once…' She shook her head. 'Oh, I cannot say that I was mingling with my equals, in a place I was meant to be, for fate has decreed otherwise! But it was lovely. Then that toad of a man tried to importune me and your brother came to my aid…' Her voice trailed away.

'You like Simon, don't you?' Jane said perceptively. 'Regardless of what you have said, I do believe…'

Thérèse looked away. She was silent for a moment. 'Perhaps if things had been different… Yes—' suddenly she pushed the dress away from her and stood up '—when I met him I thought—there is a man…' there was a smile in her eyes '…and truly, I was tempted for the first time ever, but…'

'But Simon does not want you to be his mistress!' Jane objected. 'He would never insult you so! He wants to marry you!'

'Even worse!' Thérèse said briskly. 'Can you imagine people asking your mother about her daughter-in-law and she being obliged to say that it is the girl who made her dresses?'

'Our family does not care about such things!' Jane said staunchly.

Thérèse suddenly looked very tired. 'Everybody cares about such things, Jane! But there is worse! You have seen Samways—can you imagine him coming to Portman Square and blackmailing me with threats to tell the *ton* how I paid him to stay out of his whore-houses... What a delicious scandal that would be! Now, would you like to share my luncheon? It is only bread and cheese, but the cheese is French!'

Chapter Fourteen

The afternoon dragged by. Shortly after lunch, a man brought some medicines for the Vicomtesse de Beaurain, and she roused herself sufficiently to take a spoonful at Thérèse's coaxing.

'What is the matter with her?' Jane whispered softly, as Thérèse returned to the sewing-table. She did not wish to pry, but there was something unbearably touching about the patient devotion with which the daughter nursed her sick mother.

'She has a weak chest and is forever suffering inflammation of the lungs,' Thérèse said. 'She needs to go to a hot climate, or to a spa, perhaps, to cure her.' For a moment the tears shone in her eyes, then she blinked them back. 'Now come! I need to finish this dress so that I may pay Samways!'

They talked some more. Thérèse spoke about her experiences as a governess and Jane told Thérèse about her childhood at Ambergate, managing to talk quite a lot about Simon in the process.

'It sounds a delightful place to live,' Thérèse said dreamily, when Jane had finished describing the rolling Wiltshire hills and lush fields. 'But I suppose that all young ladies must come to London to make a suitable match. Are you betrothed yet, Jane? It would seem very likely!'

Jane blushed. She had managed to avoid speaking of Alex and even succeeded in not thinking about him for at least five minutes at a time.

'No! Yes, that is, I suppose I am, in a manner of speaking…'

'*Tiens!*' Thérèse said, amused. 'Are you or are you not, Jane? You do not seem certain!'

'Well…' suddenly Jane felt like confiding. 'There is a gentleman who made an arrangement with my father that I should become betrothed to his brother.'

Thérèse nodded. 'That I can understand. That also is the way of the world! And then?'

'I did not wish to marry the brother,' Jane said, 'and then he fell in love with my dearest friend.'

'And what happened about the arranged match?'

Jane blushed again. 'Well, the gentleman—he is a Duke—wishes me to marry him now instead of his brother, in order to preserve the family alliance. It was not a good enough reason to persuade me. Unfortunately yesterday we became…in short, I appear to be compromised and will have to agree.'

It sounded quite extraordinary when described in those bald terms and indeed Thérèse was staring at her in the greatest astonishment.

'*Mon Dieu*, Jane, do not tell me half the story! Who is this Duke, and what is he like, and how on earth did so innocent a girl as you become compromised?'

Jane could feel herself blushing all the more. 'The gentleman is the Duke of Delahaye. He is—oh, how can I describe him? He is accustomed to people falling in with his plans and was not at all pleased when

I opposed them! He is handsome but seems a little grave until one gets to know him, and he has a reputation as a recluse, which some consider to be most odd! But I think—'

Jane broke off, aware that she was smiling and that she had given herself away entirely.

'So you are in love with him,' Thérèse said shrewdly, 'in which case why did you refuse his proposal?'

Jane hesitated. 'Why do you refuse to see Simon?' she countered. 'The reasons are not always simple, are they, Thérèse?'

Their eyes held for a moment, then the older girl smiled and shrugged a little. 'I like you, Jane Verey! I should not, but I do! *Mon Dieu*, why must the Vereys make things so much more difficult for me?'

Jane was glad to turn the subject away from herself. She knew that she had given herself away too easily. It did not matter that Thérèse suspected that she was in love with Alex, but at all costs she had to guard against him finding out the truth. It would be too demeaning, when his affections still lay with his dead wife. With a little pang of apprehension, Jane realised that she would have to face Alex at some point and explain why she had disregarded his warnings to avoid Spitalfields. It was a nerve-racking thought.

'We saw you with Samways at Vauxhall Gardens,' Jane said suddenly, her thoughts of Alex bringing her back to the man who had threatened him there. 'Surely you did not go there with him, Thérèse?'

Thérèse laughed. 'No Jane, you may acquit me of complaisance in Samways's dirty schemes! I had gone to Vauxhall on my own—I was playing truant again, I confess! Samways caught up with me there and tried to persuade me to join him in a spot of enterprise. He was engaged in lifting plump purses from unsuspecting victims and wished to pass them on to me for safe-keeping! I gave him the rightabout and saw no more of him!'

Jane hesitated on the edge of telling Thérèse about Samways's attack on Alex, but held her peace. For all the older girl's worldliness and air of cynicism, Jane suspected that she would be shocked. It was not comforting, however, to think that she was in the power of a man who was so ruthless. Jane hoped profoundly that Simon would pay what was demanded and that she would be home within a few hours.

They chatted a little more, then Thérèse made some broth for their supper and managed to persuade her mother to take a little. A soft conversation in French followed, then Thérèse called Jane over.

'Miss Verey, may I make you known to my mother, the Vicomtesse de Beaurain? Mama, this is Miss Jane Verey.'

The Vicomtesse had the waxy pallor of the very ill. Her slight body made barely a dent under the thin covers. Her eyes, a faded blue that had no doubt once been as vivid as Thérèse's own, were sunk deep and shadowed with pain. Nevertheless, they rested on Jane with interest and warmth. She took Jane's hand in her own.

'*Enchantée, mam'zelle…*'

'I am sorry that you are so unwell, ma'am,' Jane said sincerely. 'It must be horrid for you. If I can do anything to help—'

The Vicomtesse opened her blue eyes very wide. 'You can help, Miss Verey. You can persuade my foolish daughter to give your brother a hearing. She is pining for him, yet absurd notions of rank and pride keep her silent—'

'*Maman!*' Jane was amused to see that Thérèse had blushed bright red. 'You should not give me away!'

'Pshaw!' The Vicomtesse made a vague gesture, lying back and closing her eyes. 'I want what is best for my daughter, Miss Verey, and I recognise love when I see it. Seven times your brother has come here to speak to Thérèse and each time she has sent him away. Yet afterwards, she cries…'

'*Maman,*' Thérèse said again, beseechingly, 'it is not so simple—'

'Nonsense! It is as simple or as complicated as you wish to make it! That's French practicality!' The Vicomtesse smiled faintly. 'Now let me rest, child, and think on what I have said!'

The candle had burned down. Thérèse started to tidy the room and folded up the sewing with neat, practical movements. 'It is very late,' she said. 'Perhaps Samways will not be back tonight. You should try and rest…'

She dragged out a pallet from under the Viscomtesse's bed and gestured towards it, but Jane was shaking her head.

'I should not sleep,' she said with truth. 'I will doze in the chair—'

The door opened and Jane's heart leaped in her throat. Samways came in, grinning at Thérèse as she looked down her nose at him.

'Good evening, Princess! Well, now, it seems I have a tastier bait than I had thought at first!' He swung round on Jane, who instinctively drew back. 'It seems,' Samways said gloatingly, 'that this little lady is the betrothed of the Duke of Delahaye!'

Jane caught her breath as he came towards her and raised one calloused hand to run it down her cheek. She flinched away. 'I have a grudge against that man,' Samways continued. 'At first I wondered whether it would suffice to send you back to him after an instructive night in one of my clubs... It's a sweet notion!' His shoulders shook at Jane's look of disgusted horror. 'But then I thought not—I'm not a vindictive man—I'll just use you to bait the trap! He will come to save you, will he not?'

'Let us hope he thinks it worth it!' Jane said, with more cold composure than she was feeling. 'I was telling Mademoiselle de Beaurain earlier that it is an arranged match. I pray that his Grace will put himself to the trouble!'

For a moment Samways hesitated, then showed his teeth in a yellow grin. 'You had better pray so, miss! Now, you will stay here whilst I send to his Grace of Delahaye, telling him to meet me here to negotiate the terms of your freedom...'

With a sick flash of memory, Jane saw again that night at Vauxhall, the moonlight glinting on the knife blade. She knew what would await Alex when he came to keep the meeting. Thérèse stepped closer, as though she were afraid that Jane would faint, and put a comforting hand on her shoulder.

'It will be all right, *chérie*...'

Jane swallowed hard. 'What is your quarrel with Alex Delahaye, sir? If you intend to use me in your revenge I believe I have a right to know!'

For a moment she thought that Samways would refuse, but then he smiled again. 'The man robbed me of fortune, that it what I hold against him!'

'Robbed you?' Jane sounded as amazed as she felt. She had not expected this.

'Aye.' Samways passed his handkerchief across his florid face. 'There was a time when I was a gentleman, set fair to marry one of his Grace's relatives! Rich she was—a rich widow ripe for the picking, and sweet enough on me to make the business easy! That was before the Duke saw fit to put an end to it and lose me a fortune into the bargain!'

'A rich widow—' Jane was almost whispering.

'Aye, Lady Eleanor Fane!' The hatred in his voice was almost tangible now. 'That oh-so-respectable society lady was willing to throw her bonnet over the windmill for me—until Delahaye turned me off! All that fortune that would have been mine—none of this scraping and scratching a living...'

Jane sat down rather quickly, her thoughts whirling. It was an extraordinary story. The thought of the severe Lady Eleanor being thwarted from making a runaway match with an unsuitable man at least ten years her junior made the imagination boggle. Yet Samways had said that he had been a gentleman once and his hatred of Alex was all too real...

Dimly she registered that Samways was leaving and instructing one of his men to stay with the girls. Thérèse was objecting at this invasion of her home but was being overruled. The door slammed behind and the man settled himself in the armchair, fingering his knife and grinning wolfishly at Jane. Thérèse, who appeared to have accepted the situation with sudden and suspicious equanimity, was offering him a drink of wine. Jane watched as she moved across to pour it and, behind the man's back, added some of her mother's medicine. Jane stared, then, obedient to a fierce glare from Thérèse, looked away.

They settled down, Jane taking the pallet that Thérèse had indicated and Thérèse herself lighting another candle and sitting at the workbench as though prepared to sit out the night. The presence of Samway's henchman prevented any kind of discussion. On the bed, the Vicomtesse sighed a little in her sleep.

For what seemed like hours, Jane lay rigid on the hard pallet, her thoughts going round and around in her head. It was bad enough to have put herself in a position where Simon could be asked for money for her safe return, but to have brought Alex into danger was an entirely different matter. She wondered whether Samways had contacted him yet, what he would do, whether he could escape the threat and if so, what would happen to her... She knew her thoughts were quite profitless but she could not escape them. A couple of tears squeezed from beneath her eyelids.

'Jane!' Thérèse was shaking her by the shoulder and Jane opened her eyes, dazzled for a moment by the candle flame. 'Come quickly! He is asleep!'

'What—?'

'The poppy juice!' Thérèse said impatiently. 'I thought it would never work!' She stood aside so that Jane could see the slumped figure of the guard, sound asleep and snoring loudly. 'Now, listen. You must get out of that window and climb along the ledge to the end of the building. There is a staircase there that leads down to the street. Samways's men will be about, but in the dark you may be able to slip past. If not, there is a family in the end tenement who will hide you! I would come too, only I cannot leave *Maman* here! I pray you will not be too late!'

'But when he comes back…' Jane was struggling with the stiff catch on the window. 'What will you say, Thérèse?'

'Oh, that I fell asleep and when I awoke you were gone! If it comes to it, Jane, I will do everything I can to help your Duke of Delahaye, but I hope—I imagine—that he is a man who can look after himself! Now, good luck and godspeed!' She gave Jane a brief, hard hug.

Just climbing out of the window was frightful enough for Jane. She had never been afraid of heights, but in the dark she felt frighteningly exposed and alone. The ledge was wide enough to edge along very carefully but when her dress caught on a nail and pulled her back she almost lost her balance, and had to bite her lip hard to prevent herself from crying out. She found that she no longer cared if all of Samways's men were thronging the street below as long as she could get back on to solid ground.

She reached the end of the building at last and stepped carefully down into the dark stairwell, pausing for her frightened breathing to still. There was no sound or movement close by and she began to hope that she had been undetected. The stairs were unlit and she started to creep down, feeling her way down one wall, each step a venture into the unknown.

When she got to the bottom she paused again, before peering gingerly around the corner and out into the street. It appeared to be deserted, which was odd since Samways's men had been swarming everywhere earlier. Jane started to slip along the edge of the building, keeping in the shadows, intent only on reaching the main street and trying to find someone who could help her. She tried to blot out of her mind the dangers of wandering around London at night, the perils that might befall her, the fact that Alex might even now be walking into a trap...

She reached the end of the buildings and there was a pool of darkness before her, blacker than the surrounding night. Jane darted across, almost tripping over a kerb stone and putting out a hand blindly to break her fall. And then she was caught and held in a merciless grip, strong arms sweeping her up and away from the darkness, but she did not cry out or struggle, for as soon as he had touched her she had recognised who he was.

There was light and warmth, and someone was forcing strong spirit down her throat.

'What the hell do we do now, Alex?' Jane heard a voice say.

Jane coughed and opened her eyes. She was still in Alex's arms, sitting on his knee and held close, which struck her as somewhat improper given that the other occupants of the room were Harry Marchnight and her own brother. She struggled to be free, but Alex held her tightly.

'Jane? Has he hurt you? Are you all right?'

'No, I am not hurt,' Jane said crossly, 'but for you squeezing me half to death!'

She saw Simon's tense face ease into a smile as he exchanged a rueful look with Alex. 'She's quite herself,' he observed.

Alex stood up, placing her gently in the chair opposite his.

'We haven't much time,' he said. 'You really are unhurt, Jane? Tell me the truth!'

'Yes, truly!' Jane was shaken and a little awed by what she saw in Alex's face. 'And Thérèse is quite safe, though we must not be gone long! She drugged the man who was sent to guard us, but how long he will remain unconscious is another matter—'

'That was when you escaped?' Henry questioned swiftly. 'And there was only one man left in the room with you?'

Jane nodded. 'Thérèse would not come with me because she would not leave her mother, but she should not be left to face Samways alone! He said his men were everywhere, but—'

'We've taken out all of those who were guarding the street,' Alex said. 'We were intending to ambush the ones in the house with you, though of course we had no way of knowing how many there were. But you say there is only one, and he has been dealt with by Mademoiselle de Beaurain.' He flashed Simon a grin. 'The next time we consider mounting a rescue we will remember that the two of you are well able to take care of yourselves! What did you have in mind for Samways? Hitting him over the head with a saucepan, perhaps?'

'Perhaps…' Jane shivered. 'We must go back for Thérèse. Whatever she says, she cannot stay there now!'

'No.' Alex consulted his watch '—and we have little time. I am to meet Samways here within the hour—which I shall do, but with the odds weighted more in my favour than he imagines! Simon, will you escort Jane, Thérèse and her mother back to Portman Square? Harry and I will deal with Samways!'

It was Thérèse who opened the door to Jane's knock. The candlelight was behind her, turning her silver hair to a halo, and her face was in shadow.

'Jane? What has happened? *Tiens*—' she suddenly saw Alex and Henry Marchnight '—*messieurs...*'

Alex tucked the pistol into his belt. 'Your servant, Mam'zelle de Beaurain. I am Alexander Delahaye, Miss Verey's fiancé.'

'Jane is most fortunate,' Thérèse said, with an expressive lift of her brows. 'And this gentleman...?'

Henry Marchnight, languidly elegant as ever, came forward to bow over Thérèse's hand. 'Henry Marchnight, entirely at your service, *mademoiselle*. And here is one who most particularly wishes to see you...' He stepped to one side and Simon came out of the shadows, closing the door softly behind him before turning to Thérèse.

It was an extraordinary moment. Jane, standing within the circle of Alex's arm, saw the arrested expression on Thérèse's face and the still watchfulness of Simon's. She had not had the chance to tell Simon anything of the outcome of her conversations with Thérèse, and now she saw that there had been no need anyway. They had eyes only for each other, utterly absorbed in the reaction of one to the other. Jane, Alex, Henry, the sleeping occupants of the room...all might have been invisible.

'Good evening, milord,' Thérèse said, a little tremulously. Her eyes were suddenly full of tears. Jane realised, with a rush of compassion, that she was very nervous.

'Thérèse.' Simon said.

Very slowly they came together. Simon's arms went around her gently, then he was holding her exultantly to him and there was no need for any further words.

'Time for all that later,' Alex said, with a grin. His arm tightened about Jane for a brief instant, then he became businesslike.

'Mademoiselle de Beaurain, you and your mother must leave here at once. Please could you gather your belongings as swiftly as possible. Simon will escort you back to Portman Square with Jane whilst Henry and I stay to keep our appointment with Samways. Please!' Alex added imperatively, as Thérèse had not moved. 'There is not a moment to lose!'

'You will come with us, won't you, Thérèse?' Jane said, moving forward. Thérèse had not let go of Simon's hand and Jane half-expected him to add his pleas to hers, but he remained silent, his eyes never leaving her face.

There was a moment of stillness, then a voice spoke from the bed.

'My child,' the Vicomtesse said, 'if you refuse now I swear I shall disinherit you!'

She struggled to sit up, coughing a little. 'Pass me my wrap, I pray you, *monsieur*,' she instructed Alex. 'I shall then feel respectable enough to undertake the journey!'

Thérèse nodded, a little smile on her lips. 'There is nothing here that I wish to bring,' she said, and Jane thought that she was speaking of more than just her belongings. 'I have a small bag—so...' she pulled it out from under the bed '...and that is all.' She turned to Simon. 'I fear I come to you in nothing but the clothes I stand up in, my lord!'

Simon's smile was full of tenderness. 'That is enough for me, my love! Now, will you go first and

I shall carry your mother down. The carriage is be-hind Crispin Buildings. Harry, if you could help us before you come back to stay with Alex...?'

'What will you do with him?' Thérèse asked, eye-ing the slumped figure of Samways's henchman. It looked to Jane as though he had not moved since she had gone.

Alex laughed. 'We will leave him there! Samways will return to find an empty room, an unconscious guard—and Harry and myself waiting for him!'

At the last moment, before she started down the dark stair for the last time, Jane turned to look back at Alex. She wanted to run to him and tell him to be careful, that she loved him, that if he was killed she could never feel happy again. But there was some-thing stern in his expression, as though he was already thinking of the encounter to come, that made her bite the words back and she could only hope that she had the chance to tell him when next she saw him.

Their arrival in Portman Square was as dramatic as anyone might have wished. The whole house was in uproar, with all lights blazing and all the servants still awake and milling around whilst they waited for news. Jane, whose preoccupation with Alex's safety had almost led her to forget that she had been held to ransom, hung back, suddenly embarrassed.

Simon helped the Vicomtesse from the carriage and sent a startled footman running to waken the doctor. Thérèse followed him into the hall, while Jane brought up the rear.

Lady Verey and Sophia had been in the drawing-room, but both came hurrying as Simon strode into the hall, their strained faces breaking into smiles.

'Jane!' Sophia hugged her friend with heartfelt relief. 'Oh, Jane, we were so worried! How could you do such a thing?'

'Thank God you are safe, Jane! And—' Lady Verey broke off as she caught sight of Thérèse and her mother. 'Who—?' she began, only to have the question comprehensively answered as Simon, oblivious to all around him, swept Thérèse into a ruthless embrace.

'My apologies, madam, for this unexpected intrusion into your home,' Vicomtesse de Beaurain said calmly. 'It must seem most singular and indeed it is, but—' A spasm of coughing shook her and Jane and Lady Verey both stepped forward to help her.

'Do not try to talk any more, ma'am,' Jane said soothingly. 'Mama, Sophia, this is the Vicomtesse de Beaurain and that—' she nodded towards the slender figure of Thérèse, still locked in Simon's arms '—that is her daughter, whom Simon intends to marry!'

'A fortunate thing too, after such a display!' Lady Verey said, trying not to smile. The two mothers exchanged looks of qualified approval. 'Well, well, no doubt we shall hear all about it in the morning! Please come this way, ma'am, and I will show you to your bedchamber. Is that Dr Tovey arriving? Excellent!' And with the air of one who can take any number of surprises in her stride, Lady Verey led her unexpected guests away.

'Oh, Jane! It is so romantic!' Sophia curled up at the end of her friend's bed, her face lit with happiness. 'Why, it is plain to see that they love each other to distraction! And Simon has only met her three times! Barely spoken to her! And yet he knew at once that she was meant for him…' Sophia gave a pleasurable little shiver.

Jane felt tired and wan that afternoon. She had hardly slept for fear that Alex's plans had gone awry and even now he and Harry Marchnight were lying dead in a pool of blood somewhere. She knew that sooner or later she would have to face the repercussions of her actions in going to Spitalfields and bringing all this trouble on them. And the final straw was the air of extravagant romance that seemed to be invading the house, with both Sophia and Simon floating happily on their respective clouds of rapture. Examining her feelings, Jane felt left out and a little envious.

'I came to tell you that your mama utterly forbids you to get out of bed until Dr Tovey has confirmed that you are quite well,' Sophia continued blithely, unaware of her friend's ill humour, 'and that the Duke of Delahaye has sent a message that both he and Lord Henry are quite safe, the man is taken and he will call to see you this evening! I will leave you to rest now!'

Jane lay back against her pillows with a heavy sigh. She had no need of a doctor to tell her that she was tired but otherwise unharmed. It was her heart that was sore. Sophia and Philip had triumphed over adversity to become betrothed and now Simon had found his Thérèse. In comparison her own engagement, based on Alex's desire to make the alliance his grandfather wanted, was distinctly unromantic.

Jane got up and dressed slowly, choosing a dress of pale mauve then discarding it because it made her look sallow. After she had tried a second one of jonquil muslin and a third of pink, she resigned herself to the fact that she was too pale for anything to look flattering and settled for her oldest dress. Cassie arranged her hair in a simple knot and then she was as ready as she would ever be to face the world.

The rest of the family were taking supper when Jane went downstairs, but she did not feel like eating and slipped out into the courtyard garden. It was cool and the sky was just starting to turn the pale blue of evening. She sat by the fountain and listened to the water splashing into the pool below. She could hear Sophia and Thérèse laughing together in the dining-room. They were already fast friends and with the common ground of weddings and trousseaux, they had plenty to talk about. Jane smiled. Sophia had no malice in her and had already accepted Thérèse without reservation. I am lucky in my friends, Jane thought, and for some reason the thought made her sad and a tear trickled from the corner of her eye and ran down her cheek.

'Jane?'

She had neither sensed nor heard Alex's approach and now she jumped, rubbing her cheeks dry with a hasty hand. In the gathering dusk he looked tall and a little unapproachable and as always, Jane's heart gave a little skip upon seeing him. He looked tired, she thought, which was no great surprise. He took a seat beside her on the stone bench, half-turned towards her with his arm along the back of the seat. For some reason his presence suddenly made feel Jane shy.

'I am glad that you are well,' she said softly. 'I have been worrying...'

'Have you, Jane?' Alex gave her a searching look from those very dark eyes. 'I confess I am a little fatigued, but nothing that will not mend. And Samways is taken. You need have no more concern over him.'

'I was more concerned over the danger to yourself than any threat to me,' Jane said, honesty overcoming her reticence. 'You are the one he sought to kill, after all! I confess it reassures me to think him locked away and unable to do you any more harm!'

'You should not seek to minimise the danger to yourself,' Alex said heavily. 'Did he speak to you of his clubs, Jane? Did he tell you about the brothels he owns and the girls he ruins for his own profit? Did he say that if Simon had refused his ransom you would find yourself at the bottom of the Thames? And did you think of any of those things when you went rushing off to Spitalfields on your mission to unite Thérèse with Simon?' There was a note of warm anger in his voice now. 'I can scarce believe, after all I told you of the dangers of that particular neighbourhood, that you chose to go there alone!'

No one had yet reproached Jane on her conduct, for they had all been too relieved that she was safe to blame her for her foolishness. Alex, however, did not seem inclined to let the matter go easily and Jane felt the tears prickling her eyes again.

'I was only thinking of how I might help Simon—' she began defensively, only to be interrupted.

'I can well believe that you thought of nothing else! Nothing of the danger and the difficulties you caused everyone else and the fear of your mother—'

'Oh, do not!' Jane's composure was fading fast. 'I know I have been foolish! Pray do not remind me! And I am sorry for all the trouble I have caused, but I do believe that Samways would have found another way to reach you if it had not been through me! He had his own quarrel with you and I was only the means he tried to use to gain revenge!'

There was a little silence. The water splashed softly. 'Did he tell you the nature of his grudge against me?' Alex asked, at length.

'A little.' Jane looked away, to where a thin sickle moon was rising above the rooftops. 'That is, he told me some tale of Lady Eleanor Fane, which I took to be all a hum! It did not seem in character at all for Lady Eleanor to be taken in by such a man!'

Alex shifted on the seat. 'Part of what he told you is true enough,' he said soberly. 'I would like to tell you the tale if I may, Jane. Peter Samways was the son of a clergyman who held a living from my father. My father even paid for his education on the understanding that Samways would also go into holy orders. When he declared himself temperamentally unsuited to the priesthood my father found him a position in the household of a friend and later, when Lady Eleanor was widowed, he became her secretary. I do believe that there developed between them an affection that flourished despite the disparities of age and position.'

Alex sighed, trailing his fingers in the shallow pool. 'Who can say what might have happened? Certainly Samways believed that the match was his for the making! And Lady Eleanor's wealth with it! I had no doubts that he was a fortune-hunter,' Alex said ruefully, 'but I would never have intervened had I thought she was happy. You must believe that, Jane!'

'I do believe it!' Jane was taken aback by his vehemence. 'Besides, it would have been no wonder had you objected to so unequal a match—'

Alex made a slight gesture. 'Oh, there are many who would not have thought twice about putting an end to his pretensions! And I confess I was uneasy. Yet I would not have interfered. But then Lady Eleanor came to me in some distress, reporting that some small items had gone missing from her household—small sums of money, items of jewellery, including a locket with a picture of her late husband. We suspected one of the servants and we set a trap.' He sighed. 'Samways was caught red-handed. I had to turn him off.'

'He bears a heavy grudge against you for it,' Jane said thoughtfully. 'What happened to him after he left Lady Eleanor's service?'

'I believe that he made a bid to fix her interest despite what had happened,' Alex said. 'No doubt he thought to gamble on Lady Eleanor's affection for him. His failure to win her no doubt added to his bitterness. He took a post as clerk in chambers in Holborn and I heard that he had been dismissed for fraud. I imagine his downward spiral continued from then onwards. Samways dropped out of my sight for many years and I thought of him no more. Then one day a little above a year ago, he sought me out to ask a favour. On the strength of the fondness my father had had for him, he asked for my help in finding gainful employment. Against my better judgement I agreed to help—only to find that he had never intended to pursue an honest career. His intention was to defraud his employer in short order and I was left with the embarrassment of explaining away my lack of discretion to those I had counted my friends. It was profoundly difficult.'

A bird sang close at hand, its golden liquid notes

falling on the still air. The lights of the house were growing brighter now. Alex shifted a little, his face in shadow.

'I had thought that I had seen the back of him, but it seemed that was not so. A few months later he contacted me again with an unsavoury proposition. He implied that there had been some improper relationship between himself and Lady Eleanor all those years ago but promised to hold his peace on receipt of ten thousand pounds. I told him to spread his gossip and be damned. I did not believe it could hurt her—she is too respected and it was a long time ago. Anyway, Samways took his dismissal badly. I do believe that he holds me to blame in some manner for all his bad luck and that was when his resentment was fuelled into a rage strong enough to seek my life.'

Jane shivered. 'When I saw him at Vauxhall—'

'Yes, I think that he would have tried to kill me that night had you not intervened. It was a perfect opportunity—he would never have been caught. And I had already had one "accident" whilst out shooting, when a stray bullet had grazed my arm and the man who had fired it was never found. I began to ask some questions about Samways—with my connections it was not difficult—and I found out about the brothels and the blackmail and all the other unpleasant activities that he has dabbled in.'

Jane shivered again. 'And Lady Eleanor? Does she know anything of this?'

'I am glad to say that she does not. Nor does anyone else except Simon and Harry Marchnight. To them and to yourself I have told the whole truth, but everyone else believes that your kidnap was just the work of an opportunistic criminal.'

'Then I will never tell,' Jane said stoutly. 'As you said before, the escapade reflects no credit on me. The least said, the better!'

'You have kept many secrets for me,' Alex said and there was a smile in his voice now. 'I must thank you for that, Jane! You have been the soul of discretion and I am sorry that I was so angry before. It is simply that when I heard that Samways had you in his power I was so very afraid for you.' He took her hand and the warmth sent little shock waves through her. Absorbed in the tale he had to tell, she had almost forgotten the physical impact he had on her.

'I wanted to speak to you of our marriage,' Alex said, a little huskily. 'I had thought that it might be a little difficult with three weddings in the family, but your mama has hit on a scheme! She thinks that a triple wedding at Ambergate in a month or so would be just the thing!'

'A month!' Jane, suddenly confronted by the imminence of the marriage, felt as though her breath had been taken away. She had imagined that first Sophia and Philip would wed, then Simon and Thérèse and finally, perhaps, she might have to start thinking of her own wedding. Something close to panic rose in her. She would have to explain her doubts to Alex, tell him that she did not feel comfortable marrying him when his affections were still engaged elsewhere. No doubt hundreds of other girls would not care a jot and would be carried away with excitement to be in her position, Jane thought miserably. It was only she, loving Alex as she did, who could not accept second best. She remembered that she had told Alex that night at Almack's that she would be happy to marry where there was respect and liking; no blame could attach to him for thinking that he was offering her precisely that and she should therefore be happy.

'Jane?' Alex was watching her face and there was an expression on his own that she did not understand. His voice was very quiet. 'Is something the matter?'

His very gentleness made Jane wish to cry.

'I am just tired,' she said hastily. 'The shock of the last few days…'

'Of course.' For some reason she thought that he sounded as though he did not believe her. 'Jane, if there is anything wrong you must tell me—'

There was a step on the path and then Sophia's voice said gaily, 'I beg your pardon, but Lady Verey fears Jane will take a chill sitting out here in the dusk! She asks that you both come in and join us in the drawing-room.'

'Of course,' Alex said again. He stood back to allow Jane to precede him and she was very conscious of his regard as she stepped past him. She did not know whether to be glad or sorry for Sophia's intervention, but she did know that, sooner or later, she would have to tell Alex the truth.

Chapter Fifteen

Ambergate, drowsing in the June heat in the middle of its water meadows, seemed just as it had always been. After a whirlwind four weeks that had seemed to comprise of nothing but social engagements interspersed with dress fittings, Jane felt like collapsing into its peacefulness and never waking again.

Life had changed so much as a result of her engagement. She was the recipient of more invitations than there were hours in the day, fêted and courted, her company and opinion sought on everything. It would have been enough to turn her head were she not isolated in a growing misery that seemed to blot out all else. It seemed that the more sought after she became, the more she felt distanced from Alex. It had begun with their conversation on the day after her rescue from Samways and each new day seemed to push them a little further apart.

In public, Alex was an attentive suitor, forever seeing to Jane's comfort, introducing her to new people, guiding her through the minefield of social contact that inevitably awaited the lady he had chosen as his wife. In private—but there was no 'in private'.

Now, when their betrothal might have allowed them a little latitude, they never met alone. Alex never took her driving and did not even call in Portman Square to see her. Jane felt as though they were drifting further apart at the very time they should have been seeking to be closer. Alex had become once more the enigmatic stranger of their first acquaintance, and Jane felt that she had barely managed to glimpse beneath the surface before he had withdrawn from her.

She could not understand it. He was so kind to her when they were in company, so concerned that she should not feel overwhelmed or out of her depth. It seemed that he did care for her, or at least cared that she should be happy. Yet there was no sign of any deeper emotion, nor even a sign of any of the passion that had flared between them in the past. Jane contemplated the idea of an empty, indifferent relationship with Alex and found the thought intolerable.

Her feeling of isolation seemed magnified by the cruel contrast provided by Simon and Thérèse, and Sophia and Philip. Both couples were so blissfully happy and in love that Jane could hardly bear to be near them. Philip was a changed man, relaxed and laughing, watching Sophia with adoring eyes. Simon and Thérèse were still in the first flush of love, their affection tinged by a sense of wonderment. The delight experienced by all her friends, plus their conviction that she should be feeling the same as they, left Jane more lonely than ever and very afraid that her marriage to Alex would be a hollow sham.

On the night before they left London for Ambergate, Alex had hosted a dinner for the family at Haye House. Sophia, her face flushed with excitement, had regaled everyone with the tale of the Eve of St Agnes.

'So Jane and I agreed that we would put the legend to the test and I went to bed without any supper and did not look behind me, just as the tale demanded, and I dreamed of such a very handsome man!' She turned glowing eyes on Philip. 'So tall and fair, and so very much like Philip!'

There was general laughter.

'And what did you dream of, Jane?' Alex asked silkily, an intent look in his dark eyes. Jane looked away.

'I did not dream that night, sir.'

The smiles of the others faded as they sensed the constraint between the two of them, but Sophia was still so buoyed up with the astonishing felicity of the story coming true that she had not seemed to notice.

'Oh, Jane! How can you say that? When you dreamed of Alex—' she blushed a little to use the name of her future brother-in-law '—and now you are betrothed to him! You see! It must be true!'

Jane smiled a little at her friend's vehemence. For a moment she forgot the ring of faces around her, Alex looking at her with the same watchful intent as before. 'The truth of it is, Sophy, that it was the real Alexander Delahaye I saw and no dream! He was visiting Ambergate that night. I peeked around my bedroom door and saw a man in the corridor—a man I thought seemed all darkness and shadows, as though he had stepped straight out of the legend...' She paused. 'I was very young and he looked quite stern and frightening, yet curiously compelling to me. Oh, I thought him handsome! And I went back to bed and he stalked my dreams that night...' Her voice trailed away as she suddenly became aware of the silence around her and how far she might have given herself away. Then Lady Eleanor Fane stirred and said approvingly, 'A charming story, child!' And she realised that everyone had taken this as the proof that she was head over ears in love with Alex.

Henry Marchnight clapped him on the back, grinning.

'You're a lucky man, Alex!'

'Why, so I think,' Alex said expressionlessly, his eyes never leaving Jane's face.

The party had broken up early, for they were all to make the journey to Ambergate the following day—all but Alex, who declared that he had business that would keep him in London for a little longer. Jane's spirits had sunk to such a low ebb that she wondered whether the business could involve Lady Dennery. She had no reason to suspect so, but doubt and jealousy gnawed away at her.

Returning to Ambergate had brought with it some kind of solace. Whilst Lady Verey and Lady Eleanor plotted and planned to make it the biggest and most impressive wedding that the county had ever seen, Jane wandered across the fields or sat in the gardens, looking at the mellow old house where she had lived all her life. Even this, Jane knew, would change on her marriage. She would become the mistress of half a dozen fine houses and Simon and Thérèse would take possession of Ambergate. Lady Verey was already cheerfully contemplating a move to Amber House, the Dower house at the end of the drive.

Jane traipsed back to the house just as dusk was falling. It was two days before the wedding and she could hear the voices of Lady Eleanor and Lady

Verey endlessly extolling the virtues of orange blossom and white lace:

'We will ask dear Jane when she returns. Where has the child got to? I declare, she hasn't eaten all day! It isn't natural, this indifference to her own wedding! Why, both Thérèse and Sophia are *aux anges*, but Jane mopes about as though we were planning her funeral!'

Jane paused in the hallway. She felt too miserable to want any supper and the temptation to seek refuge in her room was overwhelming.

The grandfather clock struck ten. Lighting a candle, Jane trod softly up the stair. She reached the corner at the top and turned down the shadowy passageway. She heard a door open below in the hall, but did not look behind, and once in her bedroom she undressed quickly, blew out the candle and jumped into bed.

Sleep eluded her. For a while she tossed and turned, dozing, her mind full of images of Alex. She heard the rest of the house preparing for bed and then silence. Jane's stomach suddenly gave a loud rumble.

With a sigh she slipped out of bed, reached for her wrap and stole downstairs to the larder. There was half a chicken, some fresh bread and a new pat of delicious butter out on the slab and suddenly she felt ravenous. When she had eaten as much as she could, and washed the whole of it down with a beaker of milk, she felt much better. Picking up her candle again, she retraced her steps into the hall and back up the stairs.

The moonlight was very bright. Somewhere deep in the woods, Jane heard an owl call once, then again. The treads of the stair gave softly under her feet. Suddenly, although the night was warm, Jane gave a shiver. There was the creak of a floorboard behind her and she hesitated. She had a strange conviction that there was someone following her, but it seemed nonsense. She had heard no steps and there were always strange noises at Ambergate, which was a very old house indeed.

There was an unexpected breath of wind and the candle flame guttered, then went out. Jane spun around. This time, she was sure that there was someone behind her, but the whole of the stairs were in shadow. With a little muted squeak, Jane shot down the passage and reached the shelter of her bedroom doorway. Her curtains were not quite closed, allowing a pool of silver to dapple the floor. She turned to shut the door against whatever restless spirits seemed to be abroad that night, but as she did so, a figure slid through the doorway and a hand touched her arm, warm and very much alive.

'Jane?'

'Alex!'

Jane was so relieved that her ghost was, in fact, real that she was almost annoyed with him.

'What ever are you doing here?'

'I could not sleep.' Alex leaned against the door jamb, surveying her from head to foot. 'Nor, it seems, could you?'

'I was hungry,' Jane whispered, putting the candle down on the chest and wondering whether he intended to stay there for long. 'Lady Eleanor is only two rooms away. We must take care not wake her up.'

'Then I had better close the door,' Alex agreed, suiting actions to words.

This had not been precisely what Jane intended. She wondered what on earth Lady Eleanor would think if she knew that her godson was in Jane's bedroom, for all that they were supposed to be marrying in a few days' time.

'I did not even know that you had arrived from Town,' Jane said, still whispering. Alex lit the candle and turned to face her. He was still fully clothed, in casual but elegant garb, and his gaze, as it travelled over Jane, only served to emphasise her own state of undress. She jumped quickly into bed, burrowing her cold toes under the covers, watching with deep misgiving as Alex sat down on the side of the bed facing her.

'I arrived whilst you were out this evening,' he said, still looking at her. 'I was hoping to see you, but when we realised that you had come straight up to your room, I thought that I would wait until the morning. But then I could not sleep and decided to take a walk, as it was such a clear night. It was as I was letting myself back in that I heard a noise and realised that I was not the only one abroad.'

He took Jane's cold hands in his.

'Jane, I know that there is something wrong. You must tell me what it is. Your mother was saying only this evening that you are pining for something, and I knew even before we left London that there were difficulties. Is it that you are sad to be leaving Ambergate? It will be a wrench for you, I know, but I am sure that you will always be welcome here. And you will have a new home of your own.'

A huge lump seemed to be blocking Jane's throat.

She thought of the familiar warmth of Ambergate and the imagined cold vastness of the Delahaye estates, and shivered.

'I do not want a dozen houses of my own!' The words burst from her. 'I do not want to be a Duchess and have people bowing and scraping, people I know would not care a rush for me if I were plain Miss Verey! I want none of it!'

Alex had gone very still. His face was in shadow. He still held her hands and his grip had tightened, though Jane made no attempt to pull away. Her eyes, bright with tears, held his defiantly.

'What do you want then, Jane?'

'I want you to love me!' Jane wailed, bursting into tears as she finally admitted to the root cause of her misery. 'I want you to love me as much as I love you! That's all I have ever wanted and without that the rest is not worth a penny!'

Alex let go of her hands abruptly and pulled her into his arms. Jane was too unhappy to resist and for several seconds she just cried against his chest whilst he murmured endearments into her hair. Then, recalling what she had just said, she pulled back and glared at him.

'Oh! You are forever making me say things that would be better unsaid! How dare you?'

Alex did not reply. He turned her face up to his and kissed her. His lips were very gentle, teasing the corners of Jane's mouth with a featherlight touch before raining a path of tiny kisses along the sensitive line of her jaw and the soft skin of her neck. Jane shivered again, but not from cold. It was fortunate that she was already sitting down, she thought hazily, for the burning sweetness that was coursing through her blood made her tremble.

'Alex—'

'Shh! If you make a noise, Lady Eleanor will hear you and doubtless be scandalised!'

'Oh!' In her strangely weakened state, Jane felt herself fall back against her pillows. Alex leant over her.

'And I do love you,' Alex continued, his words muffled against her throat. 'My darling Jane, I love you so much I would have thought it was utterly obvious to everybody!'

'Oh!'

'Is that all you can say?' Alex smiled wickedly down into her dazed eyes. 'I am used to far more accomplished repartee from you, my love!'

His mouth captured hers again and Jane lay back against the yielding pillows with a little sigh. She reached out to him, sliding her hands over the firm muscles of his back beneath his jacket, feeling the heat of his skin through the linen shirt. It was delicious and intoxicating and entirely improper.

Jane was aware that her nightdress, high-necked and virginal as it was, constituted scant barrier against a determined approach, and already Alex's deft fingers were unfastening the laces, brushing the flimsy cotton aside and drifting gently over her exposed skin. As he traced the curve of her breast, Jane arched in pure pleasure, digging her fingers into his back. Improper or not, she certainly did not want him to stop now.

'Jane, we must stop this now if I am not to break all the rules of hospitality and seduce you in your brother's house!' Alex's voice was hoarse, his eyes glittering with a desire that could not be hidden. 'God forgive me, I never intended it so, but I can scarce help myself!'

He removed himself to the end of the bed, very forcibly. 'I need to talk to you, Jane, but this is evidently not the time and the place since talking is not uppermost in my mind! Now, do you still doubt that I love you?'

Jane could feel herself smiling in the darkness. 'No...'

'And I shall not show so much restraint on our wedding night, I promise you!'

Jane drew the covers up to her chin. She felt warm and happy and very much loved. 'I should think not, your Grace!' she said primly.

They met at breakfast, when both behaved as though the previous night's encounter had never occurred. Thérèse noticed that Jane could not meet her fiancé's eyes, but her rosy colour and slight smile suggested that she was in no way displeased to see him. After the meal they escaped from company with indecent haste and strolled towards the walled garden.

'Why did you ever imagine that I did not love you, Jane?' Alex asked. There was a certain expression in his eyes that made Jane feel suddenly breathless and, as she remembered the events of the previous evening, the colour came into her face again. Her doubts seemed so foolish now, in the bright light of day and secure in the knowledge that Alex loved her. Yet at the time they had seemed horribly real...

'Well, first there was your pledge to your grandfather—'

'What of it? I am sure that I am pleased to fulfil his wishes, but I would not let that dictate my marriage!'

'Oh! But that cannot be so! You said that our marriage would be a neat solution!'

Alex looked rueful. 'I did say that, I know! It is partly correct, of course, but it hid the most important truth, which was that I had wanted to marry you myself almost from the first moment. It took me a little while to realise, for I was not accustomed to seeking the company of women—' He broke off. 'Why the reproachful look, Jane?'

'I did not wish to bring Lady Dennery's name into this,' Jane said, mock-sorrowfully, 'but it seems I have no choice! If you did not seek her company, then how would you describe your conduct?'

Alex laughed. 'Very well, I concede I made a bad mistake there! She threw herself at my head and I— well, I was trying to distract myself from the curious hold you appeared to have over me! Needless to say, it did not work! But,' he added hastily, 'she was never my mistress!'

'Hmm!' Jane looked severe. 'I believe she had her eye on your strawberry leaves!'

'They will look nicer on your head, I think!'

Jane tried not to smile. She had not yet finished her inquisition. 'There is a more serious charge against you, however. What of your love for your wife?'

'For whom? I collect you mean for Madeline? Yes, I suppose I should tell you about her.' Alex stopped smiling and Jane felt her heart start to race. Now, she was sure, he would be honest with her and tell her that no matter how much he loved her, he had never ceased to care for his beautiful Duchess. He gestured to her to sit down in the rose arbour.

'It's true that I loved Madeline very much when I first married her,' Alex said. 'She was beautiful and I was young and not very wise. Even when matters started to go awry between us I kept hoping that I might yet make all well, that I might make Madeline love me again. It was a long time before I realised.'

'Realised what?'

Alex shrugged. 'Why, that Madeline was incapable of loving anyone except herself. She had nothing to give; she wanted more and more, until she was insane with greed. Greed for riches and power and love, but without paying any price in return.' He shook his head. 'It was then that my love, which had been twisted out of all recognition, finally died.' He looked up suddenly to meet Jane's sympathetic gaze and took her hands in his. 'I told you once not to pity me, did I not? That was not because I had any feelings left for Madeline, but because I had already started to care for you! It was not pity I wanted from you, Jane, but something far stronger!' His voice dropped. 'And more passionate!'

'I thought—' Jane stopped and started again. 'At Malladon, when you showed me her picture, I thought you were going to tell me that you still loved her. I thought that you kept the portrait in so prominent a place to remind you…'

'I never go to Malladon,' Alex said simply. 'The house was let until a few months ago and it was never a favourite home of mine. I had forgotten that Madeline's picture hung there! That evening, I was going to tell you what had happened between Madeline and myself, and to tell you that I loved you.

Then you ran away and I thought that it was too soon to make my feelings known!'

'If only I had known! My own reluctance sprang only from the belief that you wanted to marry me for all the convenient and none of the romantic reasons!'

Alex's lips twitched. 'We have made a fine mull of things between us, but I hope that in future we shall achieve a better understanding! I certainly intend to devote a great deal of time to doing so!'

They sat for a while in the sunshine. 'I am so glad that everything is all right,' Jane said contentedly. 'I kept looking at Sophia and Thérèse and feeling so envious of their happiness, when all I wanted was mine for the asking!'

The old church at Ambergate was bright with orange blossom and lilies on the day of the wedding. The three radiant brides emerged on to the village green on the arms of their proud husbands and were showered with rose petals and good wishes. As they paused beneath the lych gate, Lady Sophia Delahaye turned a glowing face to her sister-in-law the Duchess and gave her an impulsive hug. Her eyes were as bright as stars.

'Oh, Jane! I can scarce believe it! Is this not fine?'

*   *   *   *   *

The Rebellious Debutante
by
Meg Alexander

After living in southern Spain for many years, **Meg Alexander** now lives in Kent, although, having been born in Lancashire, she feels her roots are in the north of England. Meg's career has encompassed a wide variety of roles, from a professional cook to assistant director of a conference centre. She has always been a voracious reader, and loves to write. Other loves include history, cats, gardening, cooking and travel. She has a son and two grandchildren.

Chapter One

1816

Perdita Wentworth looked about her with a wondering expression. 'This Almack must be the cleverest man in London,' she announced. 'How on earth has he managed to persuade polite society that this is the place to be seen?'

Her mother hushed her at once. 'Do keep your voice down, darling. I know that you didn't want to come here, but at least look as if you are enjoying yourself. When Lady Castlereagh sent us the vouchers she believed that she was doing us a kindness. She had many other requests for them, you know.'

'I could wish that she had handed them out elsewhere.' Perdita was unrepentant. 'Stale sandwiches and weak lemonade? I'm surprised that there hasn't been a riot.'

'Now, love, you know that food is not the attraction here.'

'Well, it can't be the décor.' Perdita laughed. 'I've

seen many a barn with a more inviting interior. The place is downright shabby.'

'You'll forget all that when the music starts, my dear. You know how you love to dance…'

'I do, but not as an exhibit, Mother. Just look at the old biddies seated by the walls. If they haven't priced each item of my clothing I shall be surprised.'

'Oh dear, and I was just about to join them.' Elizabeth Wentworth twinkled at her daughter. 'Sadly, I've forgotten my walking stick and my lorgnette.'

Perdita laid an affectionate hand upon her mother's arm. 'You had best not let Papa know that you fancy yourself an old biddy,' she teased. 'He would take it much amiss. In his eyes you will always be the girl he rescued all those years ago.'

'Your father does not change, thank goodness,' Elizabeth said fondly. 'Now, my dear, I see Emily Cowper by the door. I must go and speak to her. Your card is filled?'

'For every dance, Mama.' With an effort Perdita refrained from commenting upon her prospective partners, most of whom she regarded as barely out of leading strings.

The gentleman standing behind her was not so charitable. 'Dear God!' he said with feeling. 'What are we doing here? Almack's hasn't changed in all the years I've been away. Let us leave and go at once to White's or Watier's.'

'Adam, you can't!' his friend said bluntly. 'If you wish to launch your ward upon the world, you must make yourself agreeable to the lady patronesses.'

'And which of them do you suggest?' The Earl of Rushmore regarded the seated ranks of ladies with a jaundiced eye. 'Damned if they ain't a bunch of harpies, set on matching up these ninnies with a passel of schoolroom misses.'

The Earl had not troubled to lower his voice, and Perdita heard him clearly. It was unfortunate that at that moment her mother had chosen to seat herself with the other ladies. Her anger flared. To hear herself described as a schoolgirl was bad enough, but she would not tolerate the description of her mother as a harpy.

Stepping back, she trod hard upon the speaker's toes, and was gratified to hear a sudden curse. Smiling artlessly, she turned to face him.

'I beg your pardon, sir,' she said politely. 'How clumsy I must seem!'

The Earl of Rushmore caught his breath. This diminutive creature was quite the loveliest woman he had ever seen. Unfashionably dark, perhaps, with raven-black curls framing the perfect oval of her face, and emphasising a creamy complexion against which a pair of fine eyebrows stood out above huge lustrous eyes.

He didn't know what he had expected. Possibly blushes and maidenly confusion? Instead she looked directly at him. He was quick to make his apologies. 'Not in the least, ma'am. The fault was mine alone. My foot was in your way...' He bowed and turned away.

'So it was!' Something in her tone brought him round to face her again. There was no mistaking the light of battle in her eyes. 'Did I hurt you, sir?'

Rushmore was no fool. He understood her perfectly now. The chit had stamped upon his foot deliberately. His lip curled as he bowed again. 'You'll be delighted to hear that I am quite uninjured.'

His sneering tone brought the colour to Perdita's cheeks. She spun round and began to walk away, but was not out of hearing before she heard his comments.

'Who is the beauty?' The question was so casual as to appear almost uninterested.

'That is Perdita Wentworth. She is quite lovely, isn't she? You'll have heard of the family, of course. The Earl of Brandon is one of her connections. Her father is a younger son, and a naval man. This is the girl's first Season.'

'Has she caught herself a husband yet? With that face and those connections it shouldn't have proved too difficult.'

'I don't think so. Nothing has been announced. Why, Adam, are you thinking of trying your luck?'

'Good God, no! The lady is too obvious for me. I think she knows her worth and is aiming to become a countess at the very least. I've seen it all before—dropped handkerchiefs, twisted ankles, fainting fits, anything, in fact, to effect an introduction. I'll give her credit for one thing. She was, at least, original.'

Rigid with fury, Perdita stood riveted to the spot. Then, wheeling round, she turned to confront the speaker.

'Why, you insufferable popinjay!' she cried. 'You must think yourself the catch of the Season!'

The Earl was startled into silence, but he heard a snort of laughter from his companion. He ignored it. Always aware of his surroundings, he noticed at once that the young lady who stood before him, bristling with anger, had become the focus of all eyes.

With a winning smile, he took her hand as the music started, and led her into the dance. A young man barred their way.

'There must be some mistake!' he said stiffly. 'Miss Wentworth is promised to me for the waltz.'

'The lady has changed her mind.' The Earl's reply was uncompromising. 'She will dance with me...'

Disposed to argue, the young man caught the eye of Perdita's companion and changed his mind, retiring in some haste.

'How dare you?' Perdita struggled to release her hand. 'I won't dance with you!'

'You will, you know!' The grip on her hand and about her waist was too firm to allow of escape. 'Miss Wentworth, pray consider your situation. Every eye in the room is upon us at this moment. A public brawl will do nothing for your reputation.'

'Much I care for that!' she hissed.

'Then you are a fool, my dear.' The Earl swung her into the dance with expertise. 'You may dislike convention as much as I do myself, but we live in this world, and we must abide by its rules.'

As he spoke he was seized with a feeling of self-disgust. Even to his own ears he sounded like a prosy old bore. Clearly his partner shared that opinion.

'Don't glare at me!' he said sweetly. 'A smile would not come amiss. You dance very well, by the way.'

'But not with you!' Perdita slipped out of his grasp and turned, intent on leaving him alone on the dance floor.

It took but the barest hint of a hip throw and she stumbled. Then his arms were about her, lifting her off her feet.

'Make way!' he cried in clarion tones. 'The lady has turned her ankle.'

Perdita was unable to contradict him. A large hand

cradled the back of her head, pressing her face into the fine fabric of his coat. Rushmore strode swiftly to an alcove and laid his fair burden upon a sofa. Then, conscious of the interested spectators, he knelt to examine her ankle.

'Don't touch me!' she cried hotly.

'You must try to be brave!' came the tender reply. Then, using his broad shoulders to shield her from the gaping crowd, he bent his face to hers. 'Use your head!' he muttered in a different tone. 'Do you wish to cause a scandal?'

A hand rested lightly upon his shoulder.

'Thank you so much, my lord,' a clear voice said. 'Pray don't feel obliged to trouble yourself further. I have asked that my carriage be brought round to the entrance so that I may take my daughter home without delay.'

The Earl rose to his feet and turned to face the speaker. There could be no doubt that this was Perdita's mother. They might have been sisters, but it was clear that the girl had inherited her beauty from the stunning creature who stood beside him.

The Earl bowed. 'I fear I am a clumsy dancer, ma'am. It appears that the young lady has turned her ankle. It is not broken, but it must be painful. If you will allow me, I will carry her to your coach. My name is Rushmore, by the way.'

'I know who you are, my lord, and I am sensible of your kindness to Perdita.' Elizabeth Wentworth looked about her. The interested crowd of spectators was pressing ever closer. 'If these people will make way for you…?'

'Mother…! There is no need!' Perdita's mouth set in a mutinous line as Rushmore bent towards her, but an icy glance from her mother silenced her. She was forced to submit to being carried from the ballroom by this giant of a man, much though she detested him. Then she noticed that his chest was heaving.

'Put me down!' she hissed. 'I am too heavy for you.'

'Light as a feather, ma'am!' He choked.

Then she realised to her chagrin that he was laughing uncontrollably.

'You find this amusing?' she ground out.

'Vastly amusing, ma'am! Confess it now, you are hoist with your own petard.'

'I don't even know what that means, but I make no doubt that it is an insult…to add to your others.'

'Not so! I was merely pointing out that your scheme to injure me has rebounded against yourself. And when did I insult you, ma'am?'

'First of all you said that I was a schoolroom miss, and then…and then…you said that I was planning to make myself a countess.'

Rushmore looked down at the vivid little face. It was devoid of guile, but there was no mistaking the dagger-look.

'Unforgivable!' he said gravely. 'I see now that you are a lady of mature years…almost an ape-leader, if the truth be known…and with not the slightest prospect of becoming a countess.'

Perdita could have struck him, but she was helpless in his arms. He was grinning down at her with every appearance of enjoyment. She was tempted to put out her tongue at him, but that would have been childlike. Her chin went up and she turned her head away, determined to preserve what shreds of dignity remained to her.

Her temper was not improved when Rushmore laid her in the coach with exaggerated care, solicitous for her comfort with the most tender of enquiries. Then he stood back to allow Elizabeth to take her place in the opposite seat. He bowed and then, expressing the hope that Perdita would be much recovered by the morning, he stood back to let the coach move away.

Elizabeth called him back.

'My lord, allow me to give you our direction. We are staying with the Earl of Brandon. My husband will be anxious to thank you for your kindness to our daughter, if you should care to call upon us.'

'I shall be honoured, ma'am!' Rushmore caught Perdita's eye and surprised a look of horror. He gave her a charming smile, stood back, and watched the carriage until it was out of sight.

'Oh, Mother, why did you ask him to call upon us? He's quite the most hateful man I've ever met.'

'I asked him for the best of reasons, Perdita. Tonight you made an exhibition of yourself. When, and if, the Earl calls, you will apologise to him for your behaviour.'

'Oh, no! I can't! You don't know what he said.'

'I don't care what he said, unless he made some coarse suggestion to you, which I think unlikely.'

'Of course he didn't. We are all beneath his touch, you know. He said that we were schoolgirls—'

'And you felt obliged to confirm that belief this evening?'

'It wasn't just that. He sneered at everything and he said that the older ladies were a bunch of harpies.'

'So that was why you trod upon his foot? Must I remind you that you had been saying much the same yourself not five minutes earlier? You won't deny that your action was deliberate? I saw you do it.'

'I didn't hurt him,' Perdita mourned. 'My slippers were too soft.' She stole a sideways glance at her mother. 'Are you very angry?'

'Need you ask?' Elizabeth replied in an icy tone. 'That action was bad enough, but it might have passed unnoticed as an accident. Why did you go back to challenge him?'

'He was insulting, Mother. He told his friend that I was trying to attract his notice, in the hope of becoming a countess.'

'*You* knew that wasn't true, so why let it upset you?'

'He is detestable!' Perdita cried. 'Puffed up with pride, and convinced that he is the catch of the Season! Insufferable nincompoop!'

'You gave him your opinion, I make no doubt?'

'I did, but, Mother, I didn't mean to make a scene. I didn't want to dance with him, you know.'

'In another second or two that would have become obvious to everyone in the room. You may thank your stars that the Earl had more concern for your reputation than you have yourself. To leave him alone in the middle of the floor must have given rise to speculation, most of it unpleasant. You were already attracting attention before he led you out. No doubt that is why he did so. You have much to thank him for.'

'He's a stupid creature!' Perdita muttered.

'Indeed! Well, it may or may not interest you to know that the Earl was one of Wellington's most capable commanders. He will, no doubt, be glad to accept your opinion of him in preference to that of the Duke.'

Perdita was silenced.

* * *

Her mother did not speak again until they reached their destination. 'Pray do not allow the servants to help you. I know quite well that you have not turned your ankle.'

Once indoors, Elizabeth turned to her daughter. 'You had best go to your room,' she said. 'I shall speak to your father when he returns, but I can tell you now that he will not be best pleased to hear of this latest piece of folly. We shall see you in the morning.'

It was an utterance which promised little sleep for Perdita that night. Her fiery temper had got the better of her again, and she confessed as much to her sister.

'You are home early,' Amy said brightly. 'What was it like at Almack's? I want to hear all about it. I can't wait to make my own come-out...'

'It was the same as usual,' Perdita said heavily. 'Deadly dull, I must confess, unless one believes all the nonsense spoken by these hopeful younger sons.'

'*I* should not object to being told that my eyes were like stars,' Amy informed her wistfully.

'It's nonsense!' Perdita informed her. 'Stars are high in the heavens, millions of miles away. Are we supposed to believe such rubbish?'

'Oh, you ain't in the least bit romantical. No wonder all your beaux are afraid of you.'

'They are not *my* beaux,' Perdita said with dignity. 'And if they are afraid, I don't think much of their courage.'

Her sister gave her a quizzical look. 'You are crabby tonight. What has happened to upset you? Have you had more offers?'

Perdita shook her head. 'Nothing like that, but I'm in disgrace again. How was I to know that I should find myself beside the most obnoxious man in the kingdom?'

'Another one? You are mighty particular.'

'This one was different,' Perdita said slowly. 'Insulting, insufferable and far too sure of himself.'

'Well, that's a change!' Amy said brightly. 'You mean he didn't quake in his boots when you spoke to him?'

'Far from it! He…he actually laughed at me. I'll make him pay for that!'

'But who was he? You haven't spoken of him before.'

'He's one of Wellington's men, I believe, and just returned to this country.'

'A hero? Oh, love, how wonderful!'

'You would not think so if you met him. Doubtless he is in his element brandishing a sword, or charging over ramparts, or whatever soldiers do. He doesn't appear to much advantage in polite society.'

'But…neither do you. Mother is forever telling you to keep your opinions to yourself, and not to seem so independent.'

'She doesn't mean it, Amy. Mother was a force to be reckoned with, even as a sixteen-year-old.'

Amy nodded. 'Well, what happened tonight? What did you do that was so dreadful?'

Perdita explained. 'Was I wrong?' she asked at last.

'He sounds vile!' Amy spoke with conviction. 'You should have bitten him!'

'I would have, but he held my face against his coat!' Perdita caught her sister's eye and dissolved into peals of laughter. At last she wiped her eyes. 'Oh dear, it really isn't amusing,' she admitted. 'Mother is very

angry with me. I suppose it isn't the kind of behaviour
that one expects at Almack's.'

At that moment Elizabeth Wentworth was expressing the same sentiments to her husband. Perry had
spent a convivial evening at a naval dinner, but his
contentment vanished at his wife's expression.

'What is it, my darling?' he asked in some alarm.
'Are you not well? Sit down, my love! Let me get
something for you—'

'Don't fuss, Perry! I am perfectly well, but we need
to talk.' Swiftly, she related the events of the evening,
and saw with dismay that her husband was trying to
hide his amusement.

'Now, Perry, I beg that you will not laugh!' she
reproached. 'Our daughter was in danger of losing
what remains of her reputation. You shall not encourage her in her folly.'

'She's just a child,' Perry said cheerfully. 'Will you
tell me that Rushmore is in the fidgets because of all
this nonsense?'

'I'm glad you agree that she is still a child,' Elizabeth said gravely. 'We should not have allowed her to
make her come-out, in spite of all her wheedling.'

'Well, we couldn't send her back to school,' Perry
pointed out. 'Miss Bedlington would not have her.'

'Quite! Have you forgot her words? Let me remind
you of them. ''Perdita is the most disruptive influence
ever to enter my doors.'' Half London is aware of it.'

'Lizzie, let me ask you something! Did you blame
her for what she did? We haven't raised either of our
girls to be silent in the face of injustice.'

'Oh, my dear, I love her just as much as you do!'
Elizabeth stretched out her hand to him. 'Perhaps she

was right to throw a bowl of water over Miss Bedlington, but she's a young woman now, and must learn some self-control.'

'I'm glad she soaked the sour-faced old cat!' Perry was unrepentant. 'There was something sadistic about the way that woman took so much pleasure in humiliating the prettiest of her pupils. Perdita wanted to give her a taste of her own medicine, and I, for one, don't blame her!'

'You are incorrigible!' Elizabeth sighed. 'Miss Bedlington was wrong to force Charlotte Ingham's head beneath a tap just because the girl had curled her hair, but Perdita half-drowned her.'

Perry chuckled. 'Do you know, she reminds me strongly of a girl I used to know…I can't quite recall her name…'

His wife had the grace to blush. 'That was long ago,' she demurred. 'Times were different then. Now that we are at peace there won't be so much latitude allowed. Society will become more circumspect.'

'And you approve?' The question was accompanied by a quizzical look.

'I can't change attitudes,' his wife said softly. 'Oh, my dear, don't you see? If we are not careful, our girl will acquire the reputation of a hoyden. Neither of us has an eye to the main chance as far as marriage for her is concerned. She won't be coerced in any way, but we must think of her happiness. It cannot serve to have the world regard her as a pert and wilful girl. She is deserving of much more than that. She has a heart of gold.'

Perry fell silent for a time. Then he gave his wife a rueful look. 'What are we to do?' he asked. 'Perhaps, in Gibraltar…?'

'I think not!' Elizabeth chose her words with care. 'I know that you promised her the trip, my dear, but it would be folly.'

'I don't care to go back on my word,' Perry said stiffly.

Elizabeth looked at him and sighed. When he set his mouth in that mutinous line he reminded her so forcibly of their elder daughter.

'Nor do I, Perry, but it is time that Perdita was taught a lesson. Aside from anything else, can you see her in Gibraltar, setting that bastion of respectability by the ears?'

'She might liven it up!' Perry twinkled, but he received no answering smile.

'I wish you will be serious, love. I think it best to send her to Aunt Beatrice in Bath for the time being. It will get her out of London, and she and Amy can travel together when Amy goes back to school next week.'

'You can't mean it, Lizzie!' Perry looked his dismay. 'Perdita is like to die of boredom in the place. If you worry about her in Gibraltar, how do you suppose she'll go on in Bath?'

'I've thought about it carefully. Bath is not exactly in the depths of the countryside. It is a fashionable place.'

'It was used to be, my love, but that was in the middle of the last century.'

'Nevertheless, we are not condemning Perdita to a life of solitude. She may walk, and ride, and go to balls and picnics.'

'Behaving always with perfect rectitude?' Perry chuckled.

'I'm hoping that the loss of her trip to Gibraltar may cause her to think more carefully before she acts.'

'Are we not being too hard on her?'

'Oh, Perry, she has got to learn that she isn't a law unto herself. I know you hope, as I do, that she will make a happy marriage, but she frightens all the men away with her readiness to speak out.'

'More fools they!' her husband answered with conviction. 'Perdita need not trouble herself to find a husband yet. I'd rather she never wed at all than threw herself away upon some fool who did not value her. In any case, at seventeen she's much too young to think of marriage.'

His wife hid a smile. 'I was younger when we met,' she reminded him. 'You didn't allow that to stand in your way.'

Perry slipped an arm about her waist and hugged her to him. 'I saved you from a dreadful fate,' he teased.

Elizabeth rested her hands against the fabric of his coat and looked up at him. 'I wonder,' she said solemnly. 'Most certainly I did not bargain to be saddled with a fond papa who will not discipline his daughter. Oh, my darling, let me have my way in this. It will be hard for all of us, but it seems to me to be the only thing to do.'

Perry kissed her then. 'She'll be very disappointed, Lizzie, and so will I. I was looking forward to having both of you aboard my ship for this trip to the Mediterranean.'

'There will be another time,' his wife assured him. 'Won't you make do with me alone?'

'That won't be a hardship, love.' Perry kissed her again. 'You won't change your mind about Perdita?'

'I think not, Perry. Nothing we have said or done to date has changed her behaviour in the least. Trust me, my dear. We *can't* allow her to run wild.'

Perry was silent for a time. He wasn't convinced that Perdita's behaviour needed changing. Her disregard for convention always amused him, but he would not see his wife distressed.

'Very well,' he said at last. 'I'll agree if you think it best.' Then a thought struck him. 'Aunt Trixie may not wish to have her, though. Don't she spend her time drinking that filthy water in the Pump Room, playing cards, and gossiping with her cronies?'

Elizabeth saw the hopeful gleam in his eye. 'Perdita need not take the waters, nor need she play cards or gossip. Aunt Trixie loves our girls, you know. She has been begging for this age to have them stay with her. You must recall how good she was when they were at school, taking them out on holidays? She tells me that they brightened up her life.'

Perry repressed a smile. Miss Beatrice Langrishe clearly had no idea just how much brighter her life could become with a lively seventeen-year-old in her care.

Elizabeth read his mind. 'I think you need not fear that Perdita will upset her. She is too kind for that. Perdita thrives on opposition, but I doubt if she will set her will against that of a gentle, elderly lady who sees the best in everyone.'

'Perdita's arrival will mean extra work for her staff,' Perry insisted.

'No, it won't. I shall send Ellen with her.'

Perry whistled. 'By Gad, you mean it this time, don't you? Perdita won't like that. She'll think you're sending her old nurse to keep an eye on her.'

'She will be right. Perdita may dislike the idea, but I shall explain that she mustn't be a trouble to Aunt Trixie. Officially, Ellen will be there to augment the staff.'

Perry raised a quizzical eyebrow. 'She won't believe you, love. Will you not sleep on this decision?'

'I will, but I shall not change my mind. Now, Perry, you must back me up. I sent Perdita to her room. She is not to leave it until we summon her tomorrow.'

Perry took a turn about the room. Then he gave his wife a guilty look. 'I won't be here,' he told her hastily. 'Tomorrow I must make an early start. I have an appointment with my Lords of the Admiralty.'

'How convenient!' Elizabeth's tone was dry. She was disposed to argue and then thought better of it. Perdita could always twist her father around her little finger. Knowing him, Elizabeth realised that his resolve would melt in the face of his daughter's disappointment. It would be best if she spoke to Perdita alone.

'Very well,' she continued. 'You are leaving it to me, my dear. Now tell me about your naval dinner. Did you see any of your old acquaintance?'

It was a clear invitation to change the subject, and Perry bowed to the inevitable.

Perdita was up betimes next day. In spite of her forebodings, she had enjoyed a good night's sleep, and was ready to defend her actions. Her father would take her side. She felt sure of it. Mother would be more difficult, but if she was suitably contrite, all might still be well.

As for the obnoxious Earl of Rushmore—she thought it unlikely that he would trouble to call.

Doubtless, at that very moment, he was congratulating himself upon his lofty position, and denigrating lesser mortals.

She sipped her morning chocolate and nibbled at a roll. A glance at the clock surprised her. She had slept late, it was almost noon. Reaching out, she rang the bell for Abby, her little maid. Abby would dress her quickly. She must be ready when her mother sent for her.

It was Ellen who entered the room.

Perdita greeted her politely, but an enquiry as to Abby's whereabouts was greeted with a grim smile.

'Your ma asked me to look to you this morning, Miss Perdita. No need to rush. She ain't ready for you yet.' The old woman walked over to the clothes press and lifted out a gown.

'Ellen, I haven't decided what I'll wear today,' Perdita said with some hauteur.

'Then you won't have to trouble your head. You ain't going out, I think. This blue will do well enough.'

Perdita's temper flared. She would not be treated as if she was still in the nursery. 'How do you know what I will do today?' she asked. 'I may decide to ride, or to do some shopping, or visit the beasts in the Tower of London.'

'You won't be doing any of that,' Ellen forecast darkly. 'Though it's a toss-up which has the worst temper—you or them beasts. Been up to your old tricks again, have you?'

'I don't know what you mean,' Perdita said with dignity. She slipped out of bed, cast aside her nightrobe, and walked over to the ewer and basin on her wash-stand.

Ellen watched her with a critical eye. 'You could

do with some flesh on them bones,' she announced. 'Been following that Lord Byron, have you? I hear he lives on vinegar and potatoes.'

'I have not. If you must know, Ellen, I have an excellent appetite.'

Ellen chortled. 'Then it's that nasty temper of yours as keeps you thin. Them hip-bones would cut a man to ribbons, if your tongue hadn't done it first.'

'Don't be vulgar!' Perdita said coldly. She sat down at her dressing-table and picked up her hairbrush.

'I'll do that!' Ellen snatched it from her. 'It comes to somethin' if I don't know how to brush your hair.' She set about her task with enthusiasm

'There's no need to knock my head off!' Perdita's eyes were watering.

'Might do you some good—knocking sense in, as you might say.' She paused as Amy burst into the room. 'Well, miss, where's the fire?' she demanded in caustic tones. 'Don't they teach you anything at that fine school of yours? Wasting their time, they are, in my opinion. No lady rushes about as if the fiends of hell were after her.'

'Sorry, Ellen!' Amy was too full of her news to spare more than a winning smile for her old nurse. 'Perdita, you'll never guess. Mother has a morning caller!'

Perdita smiled at her. 'The Prince Regent, at the very least, to judge by your expression?'

'No, not him!' her sister cried impatiently. 'Can't you guess?'

'The Duke of Wellington, Marshal Blücher, the Tsar of Russia?'

'Of course not, silly! It is your enemy…the Earl of Rushmore!'

Perdita stared in disbelief. 'It can't be! Are you sure?'

'Of course I'm sure,' Amy cried indignantly. 'I heard the commotion at the door and went to see who it was. I heard Knox announce him.'

'Who...who did he ask for?' Perdita said in hollow tones.

'He asked for Father first, but Father is gone out. Then he asked for Mother.'

Perdita's heart sank. Her father was her staunchest ally. He, at least, might have taken her part in what she guessed would be a humiliating confrontation.

'The man's a monster!' she ground out. 'He hasn't wasted much time in coming to claim his pound of flesh...'

Ellen cackled aloud. 'He won't get much flesh from you, but you've done it now! I shouldn't be surprised if your ma and pa don't send you back to school with Miss Amy. I never heard of such a thing—setting yourself up against his lordship in the way you did.'

Perdita's eyes flashed. 'You know nothing about it, Ellen!'

'I've heard some—and I can guess the rest. We'd best get out our boxes. You'll be on your way to Bath next week.'

'No, I won't!' Perdita stamped her foot. 'I'll run away before I go back to that awful place.'

Ellen's smile broadened. 'And how will you earn your living, Miss Perdita? You won't do as a lady's maid, seeing that you've never yet set a straight stitch in your sewing, and young gels ain't popular as governesses. They ain't yet taking women in the army or the navy, though I make no doubt you'd fire a gun with the best of them. It's a pity that the war is over. You might have won it on your own.'

'Ellen, you may go,' Perdita snapped. 'You may keep your spiteful remarks to yourself.'

'I don't doubt that you'll hear worse this day,' the old woman forecast with some satisfaction. Nodding to herself, she left her charges to their lamentations.

'Did you see Rushmore?' Perdita asked.

'Yes, I peeped at him through the banisters. He...he's very grand, isn't he?'

'Grand, and proud, and arrogant, and hateful! Did... did he seem very angry?'

'I couldn't tell,' Amy said honestly. 'He seemed to cross the hall in a couple of strides. I didn't see his face. Knox showed him through to Mother in the study.'

Both girls were silent. Then Amy sighed. 'I wish we could be a couple of flies upon the wall,' she said. 'I'd like to know what he is saying.'

'Well, I can guess,' Perdita announced. 'His precious feathers have been ruffled. Most probably he's insisting that I grovel on my knees before him. Well, I won't do it. Mother can lock me in my room and make me live upon bread and water, but I won't give in.'

Amy laughed. 'Mother won't do that, and well you know it.'

'I know.' Perdita hung her head. 'But I'd rather she did that than look so disappointed in me. I wish I were more like you. You don't fly out as I do. You've even managed to charm Miss Bedlington, which must be the wonder of the age. Don't you mind that awful school?'

'I can stand it for another year,' Amy reassured her.

'Miss Bedlington doesn't bother with me. I'll never be a beauty, which is all that seems to worry her. Besides, I have my friends. They miss you, love.'

'I miss them too. It will be fun when you make your come-out with the others.' Perdita stirred uneasily. Her expression belied her words. It was clear that fun was the last thing on her mind.

'I wish that Mother would send for me,' she said at last. 'I'd rather get my scolding over with, whatever the result.'

'It may not be so bad,' her sister comforted.

'I don't know.' Perdita shook her head. 'What can be taking the Earl so long? I thought that morning calls were to last no longer than a half-hour.'

'They may be speaking of Wellington's campaign,' Amy suggested.

'Some hopes!' her sister cried. 'Mother is being given a blow-by-blow account of what took place at Almack's. It's sackcloth and ashes for me, I fear.'

Chapter Two

Perdita was mistaken. She would have been astonished to find that her mother was, at that moment, engaged in a battle of wills with the redoubtable Earl of Rushmore.

In the absence of the head of the Wentworth family from his home, Elizabeth had taken over the running of the household from the Countess. It had been a busy morning. She had managed to negotiate menus for the following week without offending the susceptibilities of the Earl of Brandon's treasured chef. She had also studied the household accounts. Now she turned to a pile of correspondence. There were invitations to so many functions, some to accept and some to refuse. Always at the back of her mind was the problem of Perdita.

Even so, she was startled when her visitor was announced. When she'd issued the invitation she had not expected him to call. Now, it seemed the Earl was intent upon an apology. Petty-minded, she thought scornfully. Perdita had been wrong, of course, but no man worth his salt would think it incumbent on him to pursue the matter. It was in no charitable frame of mind that she greeted her morning caller, but she offered at once to summon Perdita.

The Earl regarded her with a quizzical expression. ''I beg that you will not do so,'' he remarked.

'But, my lord, she must apologise to you. You are generous to waive the need, but it is necessary.'

'Do you think so, ma'am? You must do as you think best, of course. Certainly it will give me the opportunity to explain to the young lady that the fault was mine alone.'

Elizabeth stared at him. 'Sir, this will not do. Perdita is at fault and cannot be excused.'

'But nor can I, ma'am, nor can I. My remarks were not such as might be tolerated by any woman of spirit.'

'Perdita is overly endowed with that particular characteristic,' her mother observed drily. 'I fear it will not serve her well in present-day society.'

'You think not?' The hooded eyes rested with interest upon his companion's lovely face. Elizabeth was a famous beauty, but there was character in the set of that delicious mouth and her steady gaze. The girl had inherited more than her mother's looks. The Earl began to smile and that smile transformed his somewhat saturnine countenance.

Elizabeth was surprised. For the first time she was aware of Rushmore's famous charm as his blue eyes twinkled at her. He was deeply tanned and as he threw back his head to laugh, she caught a glimpse of strong white teeth.

She shook her head at him, and was about to speak when he lifted a hand to stay her.

'I don't mean to interfere in family matters,' he assured her. 'Perhaps you will allow me to explain. I am ashamed of my behaviour. I was bored and somewhat at odds with the world last evening. Life seems somewhat tame at present in the time of peace. For these past few years we have lived so close to the edge of existence. God knows, I had no wish for the war with France to continue, but we were not concerned with petty undertakings. Can you understand?'

'I do indeed, my lord. I had the same experience many years ago. It takes some time to settle into a more staid way of life.'

Rushmore smiled again. There would never be anything staid about this woman or her family. 'Then, ma'am, may I beg that your daughter be excused from making a totally unnecessary apology? She is very young, and I would not humiliate her. Summon her if you must. I will assure her of my regrets and ask her pardon.'

Elizabeth threw up her hands. She knew when she was beaten, but she frowned in mock annoyance. Then she caught Rushmore's laughing eyes, and her own lips curved in a smile. The more she knew of this man the better she liked him for his refusal to attempt to crush Perdita's spirit.

'That would be going too far, my lord. You are most generous, but Perdita may not be so lucky on the next occasion. Let us leave matters as they are. It will do my daughter no harm to reflect upon the wisdom of keeping a still tongue in her head, for a time, at least.'

'And will it last, ma'am?' Rushmore grinned at her.

'I think it highly unlikely, sir.' Elizabeth regarded her visitor for a long moment. 'Will you tell me something?' she asked at last.

Rushmore bowed. 'Most certainly, if I can.'

'Why are you here, my lord? It cannot be to enquire about Perdita's health. You know quite well that she did not turn her ankle. Nor have you come for an apology. Is there something else?'

Rushmore was silent for a time, and Elizabeth did not speak. She guessed that he was attempting to come to some decision. Then he looked up at her.

'I'd like your advice,' he told her bluntly. 'I find myself in something of a quandary.'

Elizabeth's face did not betray her astonishment, though she could think of no possible subject upon which she could advise this powerful man.

'Go on!' she encouraged.

'Well, ma'am, I seem to have acquired a ward—a girl of the same age as your daughter, and I don't know what to do with her.'

Elizabeth hid a smile. 'A serious problem, I agree. How do you find yourself in this position, sir?'

'Her father was my closest friend. He was killed at Waterloo. The girl has no other relatives, I believe, so I promised to look out for her.' Rushmore's face grew sombre. 'I could not refuse a dying man.'

'Of course not, but must this be a problem for you? Perhaps your own female relatives might take an interest in her?'

'They won't be given the chance,' Rushmore told her grimly. 'The girl is a considerable heiress. I won't leave her to their tender mercies. They'd have her wed to some impecunious younger son before she could draw breath.'

Elizabeth felt it wiser not to comment upon this remark.

'Have you met the young lady?' she asked.

'Not yet, ma'am. I've written, of course, and had some duty letters in return, but it is most important that I see her without delay. The child must have suf-

fered in her loss. She and her father were very close.
I understand that her mother died in childbed.'

'That is a tragic story,' Elizabeth said quietly.
'Where is your ward now?'

'She is at school in Bath, but I can't leave her there.'
Rushmore ran his fingers through his hair. 'What am
I to do with her?'

Elizabeth smiled at him. He was clearly at a loss
and there was something endearing about his air of
distraction. This was a problem well outside his previous experience.

'Then you have no plans for her?'

'I'll have to bring her out, of course—give her a
Season, I suppose. I'd like her to marry well. That is
why I went to Almack's. It wasn't very encouraging.'

'May I ask why you have come to me? Perdita can
have given you no good impression as to how I raise
my daughters.'

'Miss Wentworth is no milk-and-water creature,
simpering and swooning, and making sheep's eyes at
the men.'

It was Elizabeth's turn to laugh. 'And that is a recommendation in your eyes? Such girlish nonsense is
thought to be attractive?'

'Not to any man of sense. Your daughter, ma'am,
is the first intelligent girl I've met since my return
from the Low Countries.'

'For heaven's sake, don't tell her so,' Elizabeth exclaimed with feeling. 'Between you and her father
there will be no controlling her. Now, sir, what are we
to do about your ward? I'll help you in any way I
can.'

Rushmore rose, walked over to Elizabeth and kissed
her hand with courtly grace. 'I felt that you would not

fail me,' he said more cheerfully. 'I'll go to Bath and make myself known to her. If she'll agree to stay at school until next year, it will give me time to look about me. You have the entrée to Almack's, ma'am, so if I could persuade you to use your influence with the patronesses?'

'I'll do so gladly, but the girl must have a sponsor. My younger girl comes out next year. I wonder...? Would you care to have me present the girls together?'

Rushmore's harsh face lit up. 'Ma'am, I can think of nothing more suitable. You are too good. I should be at a loss myself. I suppose there must be gowns to consider and bonnets? Faced with such decisions I'd consider the provisioning of an army much less onerous. You will not find it tedious? I'm aware that I'm placing an extra burden on your shoulders...'

'It will be a pleasure,' Elizabeth told him truthfully. 'There is little enough we can do to serve the dependents of those men who gave their lives for us. It will be a privilege to be allowed to help in some small way.'

'Then we are agreed?' Rushmore's smile transformed his face. 'I am much in your debt, my dear ma'am. Naturally, expense will not be a consideration... You will not hesitate to let me know how I can help? There must be something I can do.'

Elizabeth returned his smile. 'Not for the moment, my lord. We have many months ahead of us before your ward leaves school. You say she is in Bath?'

'Yes! At Miss Bedlington's Academy. I do not know of it, do you?' He was surprised by Elizabeth's startled look. 'What is it, ma'am? Is something wrong? If the place is unsuitable she must leave at once.'

'It is a respectable establishment,' Elizabeth said

with some reluctance. 'I know it well. My younger girl is there.'

'Miss Wentworth also attended the school? That gives me an excellent opinion of the place. Clearly there was no attempt to crush her spirit.'

'Er...no! At least, the attempt did not succeed.' Elizabeth's tone was hollow. She had no wish to supply the Earl with details of Perdita's stay at the Academy, nor to inform him that her daughter had been expelled.

Then she heard a laugh of pure delight. Rushmore had understood her perfectly. Now he rose to take his leave of her.

'I'll go to Bath at once,' he promised. 'I must get to know my ward and tell her of your kindness. There will be many details to discuss. When may I call on you again?'

'Not for some months, I fear. My husband is ordered to his Mediterranean station. We sail for Gibraltar in ten days' time.'

Rushmore nodded. 'You will be glad to escape the English winter, I make no doubt. Then, ma'am, I shall look for your return.' He handed her his card. 'Letters to this address will find me if you have need of my assistance, or if you change your mind.'

'I won't do that,' she told him simply. 'We have one great advantage, sir.'

'And what is that, may I ask?'

'I imagine that the girls already know each other. My Amy is a friendly little creature. She will be glad to have her schoolfriend stay with us throughout the Season. Then neither girl will find it quite so daunting.'

Rushmore kissed her hand again. 'You have lifted

a great weight from my mind. I am deeply in your debt, ma'am. I hope you will not hesitate to command me in any way you wish.'

He did not wait for her to summon a servant to show him out. 'I have taken up far too much of your time,' he said. He bowed again and strode into the hall.

Knox stepped forward at once with his hat and cane. It was unfortunate that the Earl should have chosen that particular moment to glance at the ceiling, at the exquisite work of Robert Adam. On this occasion his eye was drawn to a movement on the first floor. Two faces were gazing down at him.

Perdita drew back at once, but not before she had become the recipient of a ravishing smile and an extravagant salute. Then the Earl was gone.

'Insolent creature!' she muttered. 'I suppose that he is well pleased with himself after treating Mother to a diatribe about my behaviour.'

'Well, at least he's gone,' Amy pointed out. 'And you weren't asked to apologise… That's something!'

'I don't trust him,' Perdita remarked in a gloomy tone. 'He'll have thought of something much much worse.'

'Oh, don't be such a goose! What could be worse?'

Perdita soon found out. Summoned to the study without delay, she could not believe her ears.

'You mean I am not to sail with you and Papa?' she cried. 'Oh, Mother, you promised…'

'That was before I realised that you have learned nothing in these past few months, Perdita. It was much against my judgment that we agreed to give you a Season after your expulsion from the Academy. It was a mistake. You are not yet ready to take your place in society.'

'But, Mother, I would have apologised to the Earl. Indeed I would! Anything but this.'

'His Lordship did not wish for an apology—'

'No, I expect he wouldn't,' Perdita cried bitterly. 'He'd prefer to ruin my life with his demands.'

'Nonsense! You are quite mistaken. For reasons which I find it difficult to fathom, his lordship did not take offence at your behaviour. You don't deserve such charity—'

'And I don't want it from him!'

'Perhaps not. You will not find *me* so charitable. For reasons which are known to you, I can't send you back to school, so you will go to Aunt Beatrice for the winter.'

'To Bath? Oh, Mother, please! It is a dreary place. I'd rather die!'

'That option is not open to you,' Elizabeth said austerely. 'Now let us have an end to these dramatics. We are not condemning you to a life of solitary confinement.'

'It will be almost as bad!'

'Don't put me more out of patience with you than I am already, Perdita. Aunt Beatrice is the kindest of women. She may not care to attend the Assembles, but there is still the Pump Room...'

Perdita threw her eyes to heaven, and Elizabeth was hard put to disguise a smile.

'No one insists that you drink the waters, my dear.'

'But, Mother, they are all decrepit. One cannot walk about the place for fear of falling over bath-chairs...'

'The Pump Room is not the only place to visit. You may go to the Sydney Gardens—'

'Almost as bad!' Perdita announced in dismal tones. 'Papa had promised to show me the Barbary apes, and to take me into Spain. Besides, you can see Africa across the Straits.' Her look at her mother was beseeching. 'Don't punish me like this!' she begged. 'I will be good! I will!'

Elizabeth was torn, but she had resolved that she would not weaken. 'Then show us that you mean it, my dear. Go to your aunt and spend the winter with her. You will be close to Amy and your friends, and the libraries and shops in Milsom Street will save you from a living death. Perdita, your Aunt Beatrice loves you dearly. She has been hoping for this age to have you stay with her. Can you not be generous with your time?'

Perdita was too distraught to speak, but she managed a brief nod. Open attack would have brought a sharp response from her, but an appeal to her better nature was something else.

'Very well, then,' her mother continued. 'You will travel with Amy when she returns to school, and Ellen shall go with you.' Her raised hand quelled the expected objection from Perdita. 'I am sending Ellen to help out. Your aunt's staff must not feel that you are an added burden.'

Perdita was reduced to silence.

'There is one other thing I have to say to you.' Her mother's tone was inexorable. 'You will not, I hope, attempt to persuade your father into altering this decision. Have I your word on that?'

Perdita nodded again. She was close to tears, but her own pride made her blink them back.

'I won't ask him,' she choked out. Then she fled to her room.

* * *

Amy found her huddled in the window-seat, weeping as if her heart would break.

Amy was dismayed. Her strong-willed sister seldom gave way to tears. 'What is it, love?' she cried. 'Mother can't be thinking of sending you back to school?'

'I'm sure she would, if Miss Bedlington would have me, but you know she won't. Still, I am to be sent to Bath, to stay with Aunt Trixie.'

'That isn't so very dreadful,' Amy comforted. 'Our aunt is such a dear.'

'But I wanted to sail with Father. Both he and Mother promised. It was to be my treat, and I've thought of nothing else for these past weeks.'

'You could speak to him,' Amy suggested.

'No, I can't. Mother made me promise...'

'Well, *I* could speak to him.'

'No, that would be almost the same thing. Oh, Amy, this is all the doing of that hateful creature, Rushmore. I can't think what he told Mama, but it was probably some heavily embroidered tale about our conversation.'

'He is a swine!' Amy agreed. 'Imagine a man like that attempting to damage your reputation! What a cur!'

'He is all of those things. I would have apologised, you know, in spite of what I said, but it wasn't enough for him. He wants to ruin my life!'

'He can't do that, for we shan't allow it.' Amy slipped an arm about her sister's waist. 'Cheer up, love! I know that you are disappointed, but selfishly, I am not. We shall be together in Bath, which will make all the difference to me at least.'

'I shan't be able to call on you. Miss Bedlington

will not allow it. I am forbidden to cross the threshold.'

'She won't refuse Aunt Trixie.'

'You think not? Our aunt is such a gentle soul.'

'You haven't seen her in action, dearest. That sweet manner hides a will of iron. Aunt has an astonishing ability to get her way when it suits her to do so. You don't know her as well as I. We were thrown much together after you left Bath.'

'Oh, pray don't think that I shall find her company a trial. She is the kindest of women. It is just that…well…I think my punishment is unjust. At least I can be in no doubt as to who is to blame.'

'Don't worry about Rushmore,' Amy advised. 'He isn't worth a second thought. Let us save our pity for his wife. What must it be like to be married to that monster?'

'I can't imagine!' This wasn't strictly true. Young as she was, Perdita had been well aware of the latent strength in the powerful arms which had swept her off her feet and carried her from the ballroom floor. Crushed against that brawny chest, she had felt a curious frisson of excitement behind her outward rage. If nothing else, it had given her a taste for battle. It was a pity that she was unlikely ever to meet the Earl again. A longing for revenge swept over her. It was so strong that she could almost taste it. God help him if he crossed her path again.

She wiped away the traces of her tears. 'I'm sorry, Amy,' she whispered. 'I've been thinking only of myself. You didn't complain when Mother and Father promised to take me to Gibraltar, though you couldn't go yourself.'

'I thought there would be another time,' Amy said

cheerfully. 'Besides, I'm always seasick. Apart from that, the life on a naval station is too stiff for me—all those disapproving matrons, and more etiquette than one is likely to find in London.'

Perdita smiled at last. 'Amy, you are a jewel!' she announced. 'You have reconciled me to my fate!'

'Oh, it won't be so bad!' Ever practical, Amy was ready with words of reassurance. 'Think of the shops in Milsom Street! Papa is sure to make you a handsome allowance... And then there are the libraries. Confess it, Perdita, you haven't enjoyed your first Season here in London...it can only be better in Bath.'

'It will be quieter.' Perdita grimaced. 'I doubt if there will be a gentleman under the age of sixty-five...'

'And shall you mind that?' Amy gave her sister a sly look. 'You've given me a scathing report on the younger men you've met.'

Perdita frowned. 'There must be something wrong with me. I can't find a single man I care to talk to. With one eye on my dowry, they mutter platitudes, and if I try to speak of things which interest me they look quite shocked. I won't be patted on the head and consigned to the nursery to rear a passel of children.'

'You make them uncomfortable!' Amy told her. 'Your sympathy for the Luddites hasn't gone down too well, nor have your views on the slave trade.'

'I won't change them!' her sister retorted fiercely. 'No civilised person can condone the trafficking in human lives.'

'Love, you are preaching to the converted, as you well know.'

'You keep your opinions to yourself far better than I do,' Perdita said ruefully.

'It doesn't stop me making up my mind to do something about it, as soon as I have the chance.'

'A blue-stocking, Amy?'

'Something like that!' her sister agreed cheerfully. 'I'm saving my ammunition until I can hit the target.'

Perdita was intrigued. 'And does Miss Bedlington know of your views?'

'She has not the slightest notion.' Amy's eyes were sparkling with amusement. 'As far as she is concerned, I am the unfortunate ugly duckling of the Wentworth family, and much to be pitied. My ravishing elder sister gets all the limelight, in spite of her scandalous behaviour. It is much to be deplored.'

Perdita smiled in spite of herself. 'You are like to give her a dreadful shock. My own exploits will pale into insignificance.'

'But not just yet, Perdita. You must give me time.' Amy leaned back in her chair. Her coltish figure gave little promise of the woman she would become. 'Is that the door?' she asked. 'Papa must be home. Shall we go down to nuncheon?'

Perdita straightened her shoulders. 'Do I look a wreck?' she asked anxiously. 'I don't wish to upset Papa, or Mother either.'

'I'd be glad to look as much of a wreck as you do at this moment,' Amy reassured her with a laugh. 'Come on! Just think of the hateful Earl of Rushmore. That will stiffen your resolve not to give way to a fit of the dismals.'

Perdita determined to heed this excellent advice. She managed a smile for her Mama, and was greeted with a loving bear-hug by her father. No comment was made about her reddened eyes, but Perry was stricken to the heart.

'What do you say to a drive in the park this afternoon?' he suggested. 'I'm promised that it will not rain, and I haven't yet seen your latest toilettes. From the size of the account, they must be something special indeed!'

'They are, Papa.' Amy grinned at him. 'Mother didn't insist upon my choosing white this time, so mine is a heavenly shade of blue and my bonnet has delicious feathers.'

'Perdita?'

His elder daughter looked up at his troubled face and forced an enthusiastic response. 'Mine is a primrose colour, Father. I like it above anything, and my bonnet too. Shall we need to bring a calash, do you suppose?'

'Great heavens, no!' Perry said with feeling. 'I draw the line at that. I won't be taken for a bee-keeper by my friends. Those frightful bonnet-protectors resemble nothing so much as hives.'

Even Perdita giggled at that, and the slight air of tension eased. Elizabeth gave her daughter an approving look. At least the child wasn't sulking in disappointment. Had she been too harsh? She thought not. What Perdita needed for the next few months was time to come to terms with the adult world.

Elizabeth was under no illusions as to the nature of the society in which she and her family lived. Allow the least breath of scandal to attach itself to either of her daughters and they would be ostracised.

Perry might claim that he didn't care if neither of the girls were to wed. She doubted if he had given serious thought to the alternatives. She and her beloved husband would not always be there to care for Amy and Perdita. What would happen to them then?

Did Perry consider what a lonely spinsterhood might mean to them?

Women had no rights. In the eyes of the law they did not exist. She'd had some little experience of these matters herself. Even a visit to her bank to enquire about a point concerning her inheritance had brought a pained smile of sympathy and the suggestion that perhaps her husband, her brother, or some male relative would be better fitted to understand the legalities.

With Perry's blessing, Elizabeth had moved her account at once. Dear Perry, he understood her fiery nature perfectly. She looked across the dining-table and gave him a loving smile. If only her girls could meet men who were happy in their own skins, who didn't feel threatened by allowing the female sex some modicum of freedom. Perry understood the need for women's suffrage, but she doubted if it would come in his lifetime, or even that of her daughters.

The light nuncheon of cold meats, sallets and fruit was soon disposed of. Then Perry consulted his watch.

'Well, girls,' he teased. 'How long will it take for you to beautify yourselves? Shall I have time to answer all my letters? You must give me fair warning before I summon the carriage. We cannot have the horses standing.'

'You are making game of us, Papa!' Perdita dropped a kiss upon his brow. 'When have we ever kept you waiting?'

'Not often.' Perry twinkled. 'The thought of an outing speeds you up amazingly.' He waited until the door had closed upon them. Then he turned to his wife.

'Perdita is behaving well,' he said. 'You must be proud of her.'

'I am. Perry, I need not tell you of her disappointment, but believe me, it is for the best...'

Perry let that pass. 'I hear that Rushmore called this morning,' he observed grimly.

'Now don't fly into the boughs, my dear. As far as Perdita is concerned he is as foolish as you are yourself. He would not hear of an apology—'

'I thought you were determined on it.'

A faint tinge of pink coloured Elizabeth's cheeks. 'The Earl announced that he alone was at fault. If I had summoned Perdita, he was determined upon assuring her of that fact. I could not allow it. She was at fault herself.'

Perry regarded his wife with interest. 'You crossed swords with him?'

'Well, not exactly! Rushmore did not call upon us for an apology. He came to make a request of us.'

'The plot thickens!' Perry teased. 'From your guilty expression, my love, I take it that you have agreed to the request?'

'Only if you have no objection, Perry. It seems he has a ward, through no fault of his own. He doesn't know what to do with her. I thought perhaps that we might help?'

'Indeed! And what made you agree?'

'Oh, I don't know. I liked him very much. I found him generous-minded. He would not hear that Perdita was at fault.'

Perry was not yet ready to forgive the author of Perdita's fall from grace. 'Overlooked, perhaps, because he needed a favour?'

'No, I don't think that of him. When you meet him, Perry, you will like him as I do.'

'And this girl?'

'The daughter of his friend who was killed at Waterloo. The girl has no other relations, or so I understand. Rushmore has promised to take care of her. She is at school in Bath.'

'Miss Bedlington's?'

Elizabeth nodded. 'Our girls must know of her. Sadly, I forgot to ask her name. Shall you object if I bring her out next year with Amy?'

'Of course not, my love! When did anything you decided ever come amiss with me?'

'Not recently!' Elizabeth teased. 'Though when we first met you found me something of a trial.'

'I never heard a truer word,' Perry said solemnly. 'When compared with you as a girl, Perdita is an angel!'

'You are biased in her favour.' Elizabeth gave him a mock frown. 'I'm glad you thought of driving in the Park, my dear. Perdita must not hide herself away today. That would give rise to gossip about the scene at Almack's.'

'She could always contrive to limp a little.' Perry was unrepentant about his daughter's behaviour. 'But even that will not be necessary if she is seated in the barouche. I must remind her to groan a little every now and then...'

'You are as bad as she is,' his wife told him severely.

'But you love me still?' Perry took his wife into his arms and kissed her soundly.

As Perry had predicted, the fine weather held for the rest of the day, so the collapsible roof of the family barouche stayed down, allowing the ladies both to see and be seen by the crowds in Rotten Row.

They were soon surrounded as friends pushed towards them through the press of gigs, tilburies and curricles. Perry cast a longing glance at several dashing phaetons, but his attention was soon diverted as three of his nephews rode towards him. There was no mistaking the family resemblance. Sebastian's boys bore a striking likeness to both his brother and himself, tall, dark, and blessed with a massive breadth of shoulder.

'Out to make your fortunes, lads?' he joked. 'Have you thrown your handkerchiefs to any of the heiresses?'

This sally was greeted by chuckles of amusement. 'We ain't ready to be handfasted yet, sir. Besides, which of them can compare with our own family?' Thomas beamed upon his cousins and his aunt.

Elizabeth shook her head at him. 'Are you just come from Ireland, then? You must have kissed the Blarney Stone, my dear. Your mother must be in despair. Is she never to be rid of you?'

'She hasn't said…' Thomas paused and cocked his head. 'What on earth is that noise? Surely it can't be rioting?'

'Sounds more like cheering to me,' his brother observed. 'Some bigwig must have decided to take the air today.'

As the noise increased a rumour rippled through the crowd. 'Wellington! It's Wellington! The Duke himself…!'

At Perry's order their coachman drew the barouche to the side of the main concourse in the Row. In the distance he could see a party of horsemen making their way towards him. They were well mounted and splendidly attired, but for the figure in the centre of the group.

Perdita craned her neck to study this man who was dressed in the plainest of riding garb without a star, a riband, or a decoration of any kind. Even had she not glimpsed the famous profile she would have known at once that this was the saviour of her country. There was no mistaking that air of authority and assurance.

Then her eye fell upon the man beside him and her pleasure vanished in an instant. Praying that Rushmore would not see them, she turned her head away.

Amy had noticed nothing amiss. 'Do look, Perdita,' she begged. 'The Duke is riding Copenhagen—the most famous horse in the world.'

Perdita stole another look at the group of riders. By now they were abreast of the barouche, and as she raised her head her eyes met those of Rushmore. With a word to his superior officer he left his companions and cantered over towards her.

His greeting was, however, for her mother. 'Ma'am, I am glad to see you here today and to have the opportunity of making the acquaintance of your husband.'

Elizabeth made the necessary introductions and the two men shook hands.

'I understand that you are about to leave for Gibraltar, sir. Do you know Spain at all?'

'No, my lord, at least, not nearly as well as you do yourself. You were at Salamanca, I believe?'

Before the Earl could reply, a hand descended upon his shoulder. 'Rushmore, you are the slyest of dogs,' a jovial voice remarked. 'Now I understand why you were so anxious to return to England...' A pair of bright blue eyes smiled down on the ladies.

'Your Grace, allow me to make the Wentworth family known to you.' Clearly, Rushmore was unfazed by the presence of the Great Man, though his voice and manner told of his respect.

'Ha! A naval man!' The Duke seized Perry's hand and pumped it with enthusiasm. 'Between our navy and our army we made short work of England's enemies, did we not?'

It was impossible to resist this easy camaraderie and soon Perry was deep in conversation with the Duke.

Both Perdita and Amy stared at Wellington as if they couldn't believe their eyes. For the moment Perdita had forgotten Rushmore. Then he addressed her directly.

'I trust I find you in good health today, Miss Wentworth? The foot is not giving you much pain, I hope?'

Perdita affected not to have heard him, but Elizabeth intervened.

'My love, the Earl is speaking to you,' she said sternly.

'Oh, I beg your pardon, sir, I was looking at the Duke.' Perdita avoided her mother's eye. Part of that statement was true, but she had heard the Earl quite clearly, and she had determined to ignore him.

'Deafness is a terrible affliction,' he whispered in a low voice. 'A tragedy in one so young. I'm told that an ear-trumpet helps to remedy the condition.'

Perdita would not be drawn. She kept her eyes fixed firmly upon the Duke, so Rushmore turned to Amy. 'And how do you go on, Miss Amy?' he asked. 'I hear that you are at school in Bath.'

'Yes, sir!' Amy's tone was uncompromising. 'I am to return next week.'

'And Miss Wentworth? Are you to travel to Gibraltar with your family?'

It was the most unfortunate of questions, and Rushmore was surprised to see Perdita's knuckles whiten as she clenched her hands. The enquiry had seemed to him to be innocuous, just part of the trivia which passed for conversation in polite society.

She looked at him then, and he was startled to see the enmity in her eyes. It was unmistakable.

'No!' she hissed. 'I am to stay with my great-aunt.'

Amy moved closer to her sister as if for comfort and both girls looked away. Rushmore was no fool. It was clear to him that the younger members of the Wentworth family had decided to close their ranks against him.

He shrugged. He'd been mistaken in Perdita. She was a silly, mannerless child, no better than the brainless females he had scorned at Almack's. He turned away and engaged Elizabeth in conversation.

Chapter Three

Always an admirer of feminine charms, Wellington was quick to join in their conversation. He eyed Elizabeth with fresh admiration.

'Ma'am, I trust you will be able to persuade your husband to bring you to my next reception?'

'You honour us, your Grace. Alas, we leave for the Mediterranean in ten days' time. I am so sorry...'

'The loss is mine, I assure you. Perhaps when you return?' He turned to Perry. 'My dear sir, you are a fortunate man. I envy you this bevy of beauties.' Doffing his hat to them, he turned to canter back to his waiting entourage. Then he noticed Thomas and nodded an acknowledgment.

'Good day to you, my boy! I hope I see you well?'

Thomas flushed with pleasure at this sign of recognition for one of his most junior officers from a man he regarded as almost a god. He bowed and muttered a reply.

The Duke laughed as he addressed Elizabeth again. 'This young man is also a credit to your family...a warrior who is an excellent dancer.' Still laughing, he rode away with Rushmore at his side.

Elizabeth was aware that her family party was the cynosure of all eyes. There could be no question now of Perdita's behaviour giving cause for censure. The Duke of Wellington himself had honoured them with his notice. She hid her pleasure in this fact as the carriage was besieged by curious members of the *ton*.

Perdita beckoned to Thomas to come close.

'The Duke is not in the least as I expected,' she whispered. 'He is quite charming… I had thought he would be hard and cold.'

'He's a dear!' Amy informed her cousin. 'He even said that I was a beauty. Do you think he meant it?'

Thomas grinned at her. 'Not for a minute!' he teased. 'Such ugly creatures as you are. How could he possibly mean it?'

'Now you are making game of us,' Amy announced with dignity. 'I can't think why he should imagine that you are a good dancer. You always tread upon my feet!'

'That's because they are always in the way.' Thomas was unrepentent.

As the usual banter between the two of them threatened to become heated, Perdita intervened.

'The Duke still puzzles me,' she said thoughtfully. 'One cannot doubt his habit of command, of course, but I can't believe some of the stories I have heard about him.'

'Which stories are those?'

'It is said…that he hanged some of his own men and flogged some others.'

'That's true, Perdita, but you do not know the circumstances. The men were hanged for ra—'' Thomas caught his aunt's eye and hastily amended his words. 'I mean that they showed no respect for the women in the Spanish towns we took. Others ignored his orders not to loot those towns. They were flogged for disobedience.'

'It seems harsh. Did he really refer to his army as "the scum of the earth"?'

'He did, but that same army is always fed and housed with the best that he can find for them. I've only seen him lose his temper once. That was when he arrived in a village to find that certain of his officers were comfortably installed in the best billets in the place, leaving their men without shelter or provisions. He turned them into the street. They weren't flogged, but his tongue was flaying enough.'

'I suppose that Rushmore was among them?'

'Good Lord, no!' Thomas stared at his cousin. 'What on earth gave you that idea? Do you suppose that his Grace would make such a close friend of the Earl if they were not of the same mind? Rushmore is as much a stickler for the comfort of his men as the Duke himself.'

'You sound as if you like him,' Amy ventured.

'I do. He is a great gun. Some find his wit a little trying, but he makes me laugh.'

A silence greeted these words, and Thomas grinned again. 'Has he been teasing you, my dears? You must give him as good as you get. That is what appeals to him.'

'Perdita has already done so,' Amy replied.

'Yes, and I don't care if it appealed to him or not. I find him hateful, Thomas. You are welcome to your own opinion. No doubt he is a marvel upon the battlefield. I could wish that he would go back there.'

'Difficult, Perdita! There are not more battles to be

fought, unless you care to provide him with one of your own?'

'I hope never to be in his company again.' Perdita turned to the gentleman by her side. It was the young man who had been cut out by the Earl. Now Perdita gave him a brilliant smile, raising hopes within his breast which were destined to remain unfulfilled.

Thomas was puzzled. It was unlike the normally sunny-natured Perdita to be so dismissive of one of her country's heroes. He raised an eyebrow in enquiry as he looked at Amy.

A quick glance at her mother told Amy that her mother was deep in conversation with Lady Castlereagh.

'I'll tell you about it later,' she whispered. 'Do you dine with us tonight?'

'I believe so. My aunt has asked the three of us. Do you go to the play with Perdita and your parents?'

Amy grimaced. 'No, alas! I'm not yet out, you know.'

'Never mind! We don't go either. We'll keep you company.'

Amy eyed him with interest. 'Will you teach me some card games? I'll need to understand about loo and faro if I'm not to become a flat next year.'

'I doubt that, you monstrous child. I trust you ain't planning to become a gambler? And where do you pick up these expressions? You ain't supposed to know them.'

'Don't preach, Tom!' Amy was unrepentant. 'Shall you go on later to a den of vice?'

A fit of coughing brought Thomas to the notice of his aunt. 'You must not stand about, my dears,' she said kindly. A glance at Perry caused him to give his coachman the office, and they continued their slow progress through the Park.

'The boys looked well, I thought,' Elizabeth observed to her husband. 'Though Thomas has a nasty cough...'

'I think he had a frog in his throat, Mama.' Amy was hard put to keep her countenance. She knew well enough that Thomas had almost choked upon her own outrageous question.

His scarlet face had aroused her curiosity. Tonight she would ask him to explain exactly what went on in a den of vice.

But Thomas was unforthcoming on the subject. 'Blest if you and your sister ain't the world's worst for asking questions,' he complained when his host and hostess had left with Perdita for the play. 'And you are worse than she is. What ails her, Amy? She wasn't her usual self tonight.'

'She's in disgrace...at least, she was... Did you not know what happened at Almack's?'

'Never go near the place,' Thomas said with feeling. 'I ain't ready to be handfasted yet. Those old biddies frighten me to death. Dance more than once with any of the girls and the announcement will be in the *Gazette* next morning.'

Amy laughed. 'You are allowed two dances, so I hear. Besides, who'd have you, Tom?'

This cheerful insult left her cousin unmoved. 'What happened?' he asked. 'I don't care to see Perdita looking so...well...subdued.'

'She's disappointed,' Amy told him. 'Now she is to go to Bath, instead of to Gibraltar,'

'As bad as that?' Thomas whistled. 'What has she done? It must be murder, at the very least.'

'Don't be stupid!' Amy snapped. She felt Perdita's disappointment almost as keenly as if it had been her own. 'If you must know, it is all the fault of that creature you admire so much…'

'Wellington? That cannot be! She hadn't met him before today.'

'Of course it isn't the Duke of Wellington. It's that…that Rushmore!'

'Good Lord! Has he offered for her? Don't tell me she has refused him?'

Amy was aware that all three of her cousins were staring at her open-mouthed. 'Are you mad?' she asked. 'That puffed-up creature would not dream of offering for Perdita. He made that all too clear.'

'Has he insulted her?' The young men caught each other's eyes. Much as they admired Rushmore, they were ready to defend their cousin's honour.

'Not exactly!' Amy said hastily. 'It sounded as if…well…as if mutual insults were exchanged. Rushmore doesn't care for Almack's, and Perdita overheard his comments.'

'But she don't like the place herself,' Henry objected. 'She can't complain if others feel the same.'

'It wasn't just that. It was unfortunate that Mother had just sat down when Rushmore made a reference to harpies. It was the outside of enough. He had just been holding forth about the ninnies and schoolroom misses.'

Crispin chuckled. 'Perdita wouldn't like that!'

'She didn't. She stepped back and stamped upon his foot.'

Amy heard a ripple of amusement. 'That ain't so

bad, Amy. Most probably he thought it was an accident.'

'No, he didn't. He thought that Perdita was attempting to attract his attention. His comments to his friend were…well…unkind. He said that she was hoping to make herself a countess.'

'And she heard him?' Crispin closed his eyes. He was the youngest and the gentlest of the brothers. He could well imagine the furore which ensued.

Thomas gave a shout of laughter. He had a lively appreciation of Perdita's fiery nature. 'Go on,' he begged. 'This is better than the play. What did she do?'

'She…er…told him that he was a popinjay who fancied himself the catch of the Season.'

For some strange reason this reduced her three companions to fits of helpless laughter.

'It isn't funny!' she told him with dignity. 'Everyone was staring! You know what gossips people are. Then Rushmore led Perdita into the dance. Mama says that it was to stave off comment.'

With eyes streaming, her cousins begged for more.

'Well…naturally, Perdita didn't care to dance with him. She tried to walk away, but he pushed her into a stumble. Then, if you please, he pretended that she had turned her ankle and carried her off the floor.'

'And to think we missed it!' Thomas mourned. 'I'd have given a month's pay to see Perdita's face.'

'And the Earl's, too.' Henry went off into fresh paroxysms of laughter. 'Rushmore must have been startled, to say the least, to be tackled by a bantamweight.'

Amy looked at the circle of grinning faces. 'I thought you all admired the Earl,' she told them stiffly. 'He is not the gentleman you think him to be. He came to see Mama, and now Perdita is to be punished for behaving so badly. He is a petty creature. I have no time for him.'

Thomas frowned at her. 'You are mistaken, coz. There is nothing petty about Rushmore...rather the opposite.'

Henry was quick to agree with his brother. 'You can't know that he came to complain about Perdita,' he pointed out reasonably. 'That is, unless you were party to the conversation?'

'I wasn't.' Amy would not be convinced. 'But why else should he call upon us? It was only after his visit that Mama told Perdita that she was to go to Bath, rather than Gibraltar.'

'It could have been coincidence.' Crispin, always the peacemaker, decided to intervene. 'Aunt Elizabeth reaches her own decisions. I doubt if even Rushmore could influence her. Is it not possible that she'd made up her mind to punish Perdita before he came to call? I imagine she was none too pleased to see her daughter in a public quarrel with one of the most powerful men in the kingdom.'

Amy looked at her cousin in disgust. 'Defend Rushmore if you must! You sound like a bunch of prosy old women. Since when are you on the side of caution and decorum?' She tossed her head. 'Perdita was right, in my opinion. I should have done exactly the same.'

'That don't make it right, Amy. The pair of you have never learned to fight your weight.' Thomas ruffled his cousin's hair. 'Bless me if you won't insist on taking on the heavyweights.'

Amy glared at him. 'You won't convince me,' she insisted. 'It is my fondest hope never to set eyes again upon the Earl of Rushmore, and Perdita feels the same.'

'Then you are in luck!' Henry announced. 'I understand that the Earl is to leave London as soon as Wellington can spare him. I doubt if he'll go to Bath. He don't look much in need of doctoring as far as I can see.'

This brought a smile, even from the irate Amy. 'Then let's forget him,' she begged. 'The cards are in the bureau, Crispin. Will you get them?'

Thomas threw up his eyes to heaven. Clearly, Amy had not forgotten her wish to be initiated into the mysteries of loo and faro. Shuddering at the likely reaction from his aunt, he was moved to suggest a game of spillikins, but Amy threatened to box his ears.

'Try it.' He grinned. 'I'll put you over my knee.'

Amy thought better of her threat. Perhaps it might be as well to use a little diplomacy. She laid a hand upon his arm and gave him a winning smile.

'You did promise,' she cooed.

'No, I didn't. How about a game of backgammon?'

'Backgammon is a game for two. Oh, don't be such a bore! We shan't be playing for money, because I haven't any. We can only play for counters. Of course, we could pretend that they have a certain value.'

'Well, be it upon your own head! We'll give you the thrashing of your life.' Thomas looked at his brothers and between them they settled down to trounce her.

This was not so easily accomplished. Amy had a head for cards and retentive memory, as they soon discovered. The counters mounted up before her and in less than a couple of hours her cousins found that their pockets were to let.

It was only when Ellen came in to claim her charge that Thomas admitted defeat.

'Remind me to warn Society at large,' he said darkly. 'Lord help all of our acquaintances when you are let loose upon the London scene.'

Amy was delighted. 'You owe me thousands,' she announced. 'But I'll cancel the debt if you'll call for me tomorrow. I want to see the wild beasts in the Tower.'

'I doubt if they are ready for you. When they see you coming they'll hide in the furthest corners of their cages.'

Amy giggled. 'Promise?'

'Very well, we promise. Tell Perdita, won't you? An outing will cheer her up.'

Amy beamed at him. It had been a pleasant evening, and best of all was the news that Rushmore would no longer trouble them. Perdita would be delighted. With any luck she would never see her enemy again.

Amy's hopes were premature. The Wentworth family had not been settled in their box at the theatre for above a minute or two when they heard the sound of cheering.

Perdita's heart sank. The new arrival could not be the Prince Regent. The London crowds were more likely to boo and hiss him rather than to cheer. One man alone could be the recipient of such an enthusiastic reception. She was not mistaken. The audience rose as the Duke of Wellington made his appearance.

As always, his dress was plainer than that of any man in his entourage, except for Rushmore. Though that gentleman was faultlessly attired in evening wear which was the pride of his tailor, it was Wellington who was the focus of all eyes. He wore no stars or decorations, and Perdita smiled to herself, realising that he had no need of them. The eagle profile was unmistakable, as was his erect carriage, and the clear air of authority.

Perdita sank down in her chair and grasped at the curtained drapes, intending to draw them slightly, so that she might hide herself from Rushmore's view. It was her mother who objected.

'Leave them, my love,' her mother asked. 'You won't be able to see the stage.'

To gain a clear view of the stage was not the object uppermost in Perdita's mind at that particular moment, but she did as she was bidden. Perhaps if she could move her chair back into the shadow she might escape Rushmore's notice? After all, he was in the middle of an excited throng, all milling about the Duke.

For a time she thought that she had succeeded, but in the end it was Wellington himself who spied the Wentworth party. Just as the curtain rose upon the play he bowed to her mother and father.

Perdita murmured a most unladylike expletive beneath her breath. She had no objection to the Duke; in fact, she admired him as did all his fellow-countrymen. But if he should take it into his head to pay her mother and father a visit during the interval, Rushmore would be certain to accompany him.

It was too much to bear. Wildly, she cast about for some excuse which would remove her from his presence. The headache, perhaps? No, that would not fool her mother for an instant. Perdita did not suffer from headaches. And neither could she lay claim to another twisted ankle. There was nothing for it but to sit demurely in the box and pray that the Duke had other claims upon his interest during the intervals.

It was a forlorn hope. The Duke had taken a fancy to both Perry and Elizabeth Wentworth, and their beautiful daughter was a pleasure to behold. He was quick to tell her so, when, as Perdita dreaded, he came to greet them. Rushmore merely smiled and bowed, but there was an ironic look upon his face.

Conscious that her mother's eyes were upon her, Perdita made her curtsy to both gentlemen, with a shy word of thanks to Wellington for his graceful compliments.

How fortunate that upon this particular evening she had chosen to wear her newest and most expensive gown. It was a creation of pure silk chiffon in a dark rose colour, worn over a white satin slip and trimmed at the hem with a band of appliqued flowers in toning shades of pink and cerise. A narrow trimming of the same fabric edged both neck and sleeves.

'You are in famous looks tonight, Miss Wentworth,' a low voice whispered in her ear. 'How well that toilette becomes you!'

Perdita was tempted to give the Earl a dagger-look. A dozen sharp retorts rose to her lips, but she uttered none of them. She had not worn the gown to impress him, nor was her appearance any concern of his. She managed a distant smile and turned away to listen to Wellington's comments upon the play.

Rushmore's lips twitched. Evidently he was not to be forgiven so easily, but the chit could not be allowed to continue to regard him as her enemy. If his ward was to join the Wentworth family for the coming Season, he was determined that the girl would be welcomed and made to feel comfortable. The loss of her father had been tragedy enough for her. It was his hope that a change of scene and the friendship of the Wentworth girls would go some way towards lessening her grief.

He studied Perdita's face in silence, marvelling at the wonderful bone structure and the fine carriage of her head. This was no simpering miss. She had accepted Wellington's compliments gracefully, but in a curiously detached way, as if her beauty was of no concern to her. He was intrigued.

'Are you aware that you are quite the loveliest creature here tonight?' he whispered.

Perdita turned to look at him. She could do no other, as he had addressed her directly.

'That is a matter of opinion,' she told him coolly. 'I can claim no credit, my lord. I did not design my face.'

Rushmore smiled at her. 'Well said, Miss Wentworth! I agree that it is a gift from God.'

Perdita was not listening. She had turned away to look at Wellington once more. The Earl saw her intent expression and was inspired. The girl had no time for compliments, but he had another ace to play.

'How do you find the Duke?' he asked. 'Is he all that you imagined?'

He had her attention then. Perdita forgot her private vow not to speak to him more than was absolutely necessary.

'He is all that I imagined and more,' she said. 'When I look at him I realise that he has hidden depths. Meeting him socially as we have done, it is hard to imagine that this one man held the fate of Europe in his hands. Yet always there is the sense that behind that affable exterior lies a will of iron.'

Rushmore smiled. 'He is already known as the Iron Duke,' he agreed. 'Yet I have seen him in tears, Miss Wentworth. The loss of life at Waterloo was a grievous trial to him. So many of his friends were gone, but he mourned the common soldier just as much.'

'The slaughter must have been appalling,' Perdita said simply. 'It is such a hideous waste of good men's lives.'

'In one way, perhaps, but they did not die in vain. Had Napoleon not been defeated we should have been living beneath a tyrant's heel… Would you have wanted that?'

'No, of course not.' Perdita grew thoughtful. 'What will the Duke do now, do you suppose? With his concern for the common people, perhaps he will enter politics.'

Rushmore stared at her. Clearly, there was more to Perdita than a lovely face. He had not expected to find her ready to discuss the political scene. Well, he would not talk down to her. Instead, he paid her the compliment of taking her question seriously.

'The Duke is no democrat,' he told her with a wry smile. 'I suspect that you have liberal views, Miss Wentworth. Wellington does not share them. He is against any extension of the franchise, believing as he does in the status quo. In his eyes this country is well governed by the aristocracy. He would not have the system changed.'

'But surely change must come? There are other worthy men who must have much to offer. They pay their taxes. Are they not entitled to have some say in how the country is run?'

Rushmore rose to his feet as the bell sounded to

warn that the second act of the play was about to begin.

'An interesting topic, is it not? We must discuss it further.' Bending to kiss her hand he followed his superior officer from the box.

He left Perdita wondering. It went much against the grain to admit that she had enjoyed their conversation, but it was true. Rushmore had not been patronising. Other men had patted her upon the head, figuratively speaking, and had indicated that subjects beyond fashion, gossip and thoughts of marriage were far beyond the grasp of the female mind.

Next time she saw him she would quiz him upon the rights of women in this male-dominated society. If he didn't agree that they were treated as non-citizens, at least he might discuss it with her.

Then she caught her mother's eye. 'Well done, my dear!' Elizabeth said. 'I am glad to see that you do not bear a grudge. The Earl is interesting, is he not?'

'I suppose so.' Perdita was not yet ready to forgive her enemy so easily. 'He was telling me about the Duke of Wellington.'

Elizabeth smiled to herself. It had not taken Rushmore long to find a way of undermining her daughter's resistance to him. 'You must tell me about it later, Perdita. We cannot hear enough about the Great Man, and I must suppose that Rushmore knows him as well as anyone.'

The Earl himself heard little of the rest of the play. Perdita had astonished him. How old could she be? Possibly eighteen? It had come as a shock to find that the girl had a head upon her shoulders and was capable of thinking for herself. He'd found her fiery and quick-tempered, but now he realised that there was far more to her than he had suspected.

Thoughtfully, he saluted her parents. It was clear that Perdita had been encouraged to read and to take part in discussions upon the topics of the day. Now he looked forward to their next encounter.

She hadn't mentioned Bath again. He'd surprise her there, guessing that Elizabeth had not yet mentioned her offer to sponsor his ward for the coming Season.

His thoughts turned again to Louise. Too much to hope, perhaps, that she would have Perdita's sparkle and quick intelligence, but he'd do his best by her, whatever her character. Again he blessed Elizabeth Wentworth for her understanding. Without her help he would have been hard put to launch the girl upon Society.

Now it was important that he visit Bath without delay. The Duke, he knew, was anxious to visit the property bestowed upon him by a grateful nation. With any luck he would release some members of his entourage to go about their own affairs.

Rushmore frowned. He need not stay too long in Bath. He'd been out of England for many years. His vast estates had claims upon his own attention, though they were well administered by his men of business.

Suddenly he longed to get away from London. Fastidious to a degree, the smell of death was still in his nostrils, and the stench in the capital was little better, compounded as it was of horse droppings, inadequate drainage, and streets which resembled open sewers.

And then there was the noise. The sounds of battle were bad enough, but they were over quickly. Here in London there was a constant cacophony of sound.

Rushmore grimaced. For a battle-hardened warrior

who had fought his way across half of Europe, he was becoming much too nice in his requirements. What did the constant assault upon his eardrums matter? The cries of the muffin-men, the flower-sellers, the rattle of carriage wheels and the non-stop bustle were of small matter, surely?

Yet he longed for the peace of the countryside, and knew his longing for what it was…a simple case of battle fatigue. In time he would come about, and take up the threads of his life again. But to what end? He was unwed, and but sparsely provided with relatives, most of whom he hadn't seen for years. If he died tomorrow, who would mourn him? It was a sobering thought.

Perhaps he needed a family of his own. Unless he provided an heir his line would wither and die. To date he had had no opportunity to look about him…to drop his handkerchief in any direction. Such females as he had encountered had not moved him, unless it was to a sense that breeding was the only way in which they could deal together. The thought repelled him.

Then, unbidden, a vision of Perdita floated across his mind. Ridiculous, he told himself sternly. The child was half his age. She disliked him intensely. That much, at least, was clear. Aside from that, she'd had no chance to look about her. Her parents, he surmised correctly, would examine her choice of husband with great care, vetoing anyone to whom her heart was not given fully.

Rushmore shrugged. What was he thinking of? A lovely face, a spirited temperament, and the exchange of a few words. It was no basis for marriage, and he knew it. Aside from anything else, the lady would not have him. It was a sombre thought.

Even so, he was forced to admit that both of his encounters with Perdita had raised his spirits, lifting for a time that cloud of boredom and lassitude which seemed to have enveloped him since his return to England.

Half his age she might be, but already there were signs of the woman she would become—an independent soul who was fully capable of thinking for herself. Had he found a kindred spirit? He dismissed the idea before it was half-formed. The notion was ridiculous. His lips curved in a grimace of self-mockery.

The trouble was that he had been celibate for too long. Now he was indulging in fantasy, seduced by his own imagination. The ideal creature of his dreams had no existence in reality.

The long years spent in Spain and Portugal during the Peninsular War had offered little chance of feminine company. The menfolk of those countries guarded their women closely, even from Wellington's senior officers. Some beauty might be glimpsed from behind an iron grille, or peeping from a closed carriage, but they made no public appearances.

He could not blame their protectors. The sight of an army on the march, followed by a motley rabble of camp-followers, would be quite enough to persuade fathers, husbands and brothers to keep their female relatives well hidden.

Some soldiers' wives had followed the drum, but for the most part the women were blowsy creatures, drawn from the poorest of the poor, and ready to sell themselves for what pickings they could glean from the men they tramped behind.

Rushmore didn't despise them. No one who had seen them in the aftermath of battle could possible do that. He'd watched them bind up sickening wounds, and carry water to the dying without regard for their own safety, but they were no more of a temptation to him than the cloistered Spanish beauties.

Later, as Wellington's army waited for Napoleon in the Low Countries, there had been opportunity enough for dalliance. In the hectic atmosphere of Brussels before Waterloo even the normally respectable had snatched at the chance of one last fling at life before it was snuffed out for ever. No one had expected Wellington to win. Napoleon's armies were considered invincible.

Rushmore had resisted the lures thrown out to him, uninfluenced by the general hysteria. He knew his commander well, and was quietly confident of victory. His lip curled in disgust. During those final days he had learned much about the female sex, confirming his belief in the fragility of feminine virtue.

He would not cuckold a friend, though on more than one occasion he had been offered the opportunity to do so. The camp-followers were more honest, he'd decided, though the high-born ladies who smiled their invitations at him would have been shocked to hear him say so.

Well, there were other remedies now that he was back in England. He had means enough to offer *carte blanche* even to the most expensive of the fair Cyprians who frequented the London scene. Years ago he'd set up one or two of them in charming little houses, placing no limits upon their expenses and making sure that their carriages and bloodstock were of the finest money could buy.

It was strange that the idea should hold so little

attraction for him now. He gave an involuntary sigh, and Wellington turned to him at once.

'I can only agree!' his superior officer told him with a smile. 'The play is poor. Thank heavens it is almost time for the second interval.'

This time they were summoned to the box of the Princess Esterhazy. Rushmore knew her to be one of the Lady Patronesses who ruled the roost at Almack's, but he was surprised to hear her scolding Wellington for his late arrival there in the previous week.

'We make no exceptions, your Grace. No one is admitted after eleven in the evening.' Her smile robbed the words of all offence.

'Quite right, ma'am!' the Duke agreed. 'Rules are rules and must be obeyed. Turn one away, and you must treat everyone alike.'

Rushmore warmed to the Great Man as he had done so often in the past. Wellington never stood upon his consequence. Clearly he had not taken offence at the refusal to admit him through Almack's hallowed portals, though a lesser man might have done so.

The Earl's eyes strayed to the opposite box to find it filled with friends and acquaintances of Perry and Elizabeth Wentworth. Perdita was invisible, surrounded by a crowd of hopeful suitors. The child would be certain to find a husband soon. That was only too clear. He didn't care to examine too closely the reason why he found the thought depressing.

He didn't see her again that evening. At the end of the play the Duke and his party were surrounded by well-wishers and the Wentworth box was empty by the time they were able to take their leave.

Refusing the suggestion of a visit to Watier's, Rushmore made his way back to his huge establishment in Grosvenor Square. Tonight, for some obscure reason, he found it little more cheerful than a mausoleum. He picked up a book and settled himself by the fire in the library, with a glass of brandy in his hand, to while away the hours before he went to bed. As he read, his black mood lifted, and he retired in a more contented frame of mind.

Perdita too had thrown off her depression. She'd enjoyed the evening, although the play had been dull and the acting indifferent. As always, Amy was still awake and anxious to hear the latest gossip about the world she was so soon to enter.

'Who was at the theatre?' she demanded eagerly. 'Did Wellington attend?'

'He did! Don't you ever tire of asking about your hero?' Perdita teased. 'He came to speak to us in the interval.'

'Really?' Amy's eyes were sparkling. 'I wish I had been there. Did you learn any more about his triumphs?'

'Yes.' Perdita grew thoughtful. 'The Earl of Rushmore told me something of them.'

'Rushmore? You mean you had a conversation with him?' Amy's astonishment knew no bounds.

'I couldn't ignore him, Amy, without disgracing myself further. And what he had to say was interesting.'

'Good Lord! Tell me all!'

For the next few minutes Amy hung on every word. Then she laughed. 'Rushmore has his uses, after all,' she announced. 'Have you quite forgiven him?'

'The man does not enter my thoughts,' Perdita said

with dignity. 'Now I have no feelings about him one way or the other.'

'Fibber! I think you dislike him as much as ever.' Amy was undeceived. 'Don't worry, love. He will not stay in London. Thomas tells me that he is to leave as soon as the Duke releases him. I doubt if we shall see him again. Surely that is welcome news?'

Oddly, Perdita did not find it so. She could think of no suitable reply, so she summoned her maid and retired to her own room.

Chapter Four

Amy was disposed to tease her cousins on the following day.

'Up before noon?' she cried. 'What happened? Were you turned away from the gambling halls?'

Thomas appealed to Perdita. 'Where does your sister get these notions?' he asked. 'It ain't ladylike even to be aware of such places.'

Both the girls laughed at him. 'Are we supposed to be blind and deaf?' Perdita said. 'Thomas, it is time that you grew up.'

'I ain't the only one. Are you ready for our outing, or must we wait for you to primp and preen before we set out?' He looked at his brothers and raised his eyes to heaven.

'We are quite ready.' Perdita picked up her reticule. 'Amy, where do we go first?'

'The Tower, I think. Then on to the Exeter Exchange to see the lions and tigers and the water spectacle. After that we might visit the waxwork effigies at Madame Tussaud's.'

Thomas groaned as he saw the list in Amy's hand. 'Anything else? Have you forgot the Peerless Pool and

Astley's Amphitheatre? It shouldn't take more than a
month to see them all.'

'Don't be such a misery! We haven't asked you to
take us to see the Elgin Marbles, Thomas, or the rest
of the sights at the British Museum.'

'Thank the Lord for that. You'd be wasting your
time, my girl. Headless statues ain't the thing for me.
Well, come on! Let's get on with it. Then we can take
you for an ice at Gunter's.'

Though Thomas affected to despise his cousin's
choice of entertainment he enjoyed it. The beasts in
both the Tower and the Exeter Exchange were savage
enough to still his criticism and the water spectacle
was well staged.

At Madame Tussaud's he made an effort to dissuade
Amy and Perdita from entering the Special Room, but
they would have none of it.

'Well, inspect the horrors if you must,' he said. 'But
don't expect me to catch you if you faint. It's all ex-
ecutions and the like.'

'I've never fainted in my life,' Perdita told him.
'Don't be such a milksop!'

Even so, both girls were looking rather pale when
they emerged from the chamber.

'I told you so,' Thomas said triumphantly. 'You
both look sick as parrots.'

'I'm glad we've seen it,' Perdita told him coolly.
'We don't wish to be sheltered from the uglier side of
life.'

Thomas whistled. 'Perdita, you ain't turning into a
blue-stocking, I hope? That will scupper your chances
of making a good match.'

Perdita fixed him with a basilisk look. 'What makes
you think that I am seeking a ''good match'' as you

are pleased to call it. Let me tell you, cousin, from what I've seen of men, I shall be happier on my own.'

This remark brought shouts of glee from all three cousins. 'So will they!' cried Henry. 'That is, unless you choose a bare-knuckle fighter.'

Perdita treated this remark with the disdain which it deserved. It was only when they reached Gunter's that she looked upon her irrepressible cousins with any degree of favour.

She sank into a chair with a sigh of relief. Three hours of sight-seeing had caused her new half-boots to nip her toes cruelly. It was Amy who noticed that the pale blue fabric uppers were becoming discoloured by a spreading stain.

'Dita, have you cut your foot?' she asked. 'That looks like blood to me.'

'It's nothing,' Perdita told her hastily. 'Though my boots do hurt after all this walking. Will you wait here for me whilst I go and change them?'

'I'll go with you,' Amy said at once.

'No, Jenkins shall take me in the coach and bring me back again. It won't take half an hour...'

'But shall you wish to go on walking, love?'

'Oh, Amy, we haven't done one half of what we planned for today, and we haven't much time before we leave for Bath.' With that Perdita rose to her feet, and hobbled out to the entrance, feeling as if she trod on knives.

By the time the coach reached Grosvenor Square she was in agony. Jenkins helped her down with a look of concern, but it was as much as she could do to mount the steps to the front door without crying out in pain.

'More trouble with your ankle, Miss Wentworth?'

a deep voice enquired. 'Who is the unfortunate gentleman this time?'

Perdita turned her head and looked into the grinning face of the Earl of Rushmore.

'What are you doing here?' she demanded abruptly.

'Well now, I had supposed that I might make morning calls as well as any other man in London. If you will have the truth of it, I came to see your Mama.'

'Again?' Perdita tried to review her behaviour at her last meeting with the Earl, but she could think of nothing but the excruciating pain as she took another step towards the door. A muffled shriek escaped her lips.

'What's wrong?' Rushmore swung her round to face him. 'Are you ill?'

'No…it's just that…well…I think I've hurt my foot.'

His glance travelled to the little half-boots.

'I think we might say that,' he told her grimly. 'Your boots are soaked in blood.' Without more ado he picked her up and strode past the butler into the hall.

'Fetch Miss Wentworth's maid,' he ordered as he passed the startled man to walk into the salon. He laid Perdita down upon a sofa and dropped to his knees beside her, unlacing her boots with deft fingers.

'Good God!' he said with feeling. 'You've taken the skin off most of your toes and damaged your heels as well. What have you been doing?'

'We were sight-seeing,' she told him faintly.

'Well, you won't see an uglier sight than this. Had you no comfortable shoes?'

'They didn't match my toilette,' she said lamely. 'My boots are new…'

'Women!' Rushmore threw his eyes to heaven.

Then he tossed the offending boots aside. 'You won't be wearing these again.' He looked up as Ellen entered the room, startled to see her charge with bare and bleeding feet, and being tended by a gentleman unknown to her.

'Good morning.' Rushmore said briefly. 'Miss Wentworth needs your help. Her feet are in sad case, I fear. Will you send for bandages and hot water? Then you may direct me to her room.'

A protest died on Ellen's lips. She knew quality when she saw it and this, she recognised at once, was a gentleman accustomed to being obeyed without question. She picked up Perdita's blood-stained stockings and rang the bell in reply to his request.

Ignoring Perdita's angry refusal to be helped, he took her into his arms once more and carried her up the staircase in Ellen's wake.

'I'll see to her now, my lord.' Ellen had been apprised of the gentleman's identity by the footman who came to do her bidding.

'Well, do please hurry, Ellen,' Perdita said. 'The others are waiting for me at Gunter's. I said that I should not be above half an hour.'

She heard a snort of disbelief from Rushmore. 'Are you quite mad?' he asked. 'You won't be walking on those feet again today.'

'Oh, yes, I shall.' Perdita winced as she dipped them into the bowl of water. 'They look worse than they are. I shall go on quite well if they are bandaged.'

'You can try, of course. Perhaps you hope to emulate the Indian fakirs who walk upon beds of nails or burning coals?'

'I shall manage!' Perdita glared at him as she waved away Ellen's attempt to coax her into lying upon her day-bed. 'I can't wear those,' she protested as Ellen produced a pair of her oldest and most comfortable slippers. 'Bring me my walking shoes.'

'Now, Miss Perdita, you'll never get them on over they bandages. You should listen to his lordship.'

'Why? This has nothing to do with him!' Perdita ignored the scandalised gasp and thrust the slippers aside.

'Miss Perdita, please...'

'Oh, let her try!' Rushmore was growing impatient. 'Some stupid human beings insist on learning the hard way.'

He was right, of course. Struggle as she might, Perdita was unable to force her bandaged feet into her walking shoes.

Scarlet with frustration, she looked up at her tormentor. 'Can't you go away?' she cried. 'You are quite without a sense of decorum. You should not be in a lady's bedchamber.'

'I hadn't realised that I was,' he said rudely. 'I had the impression that I was in the room of a foolish child, who will have her way if it kills her.'

Perdita was on the verge of tears. 'The others are expecting me back,' she stormed. 'My sister will wonder what has happened.'

'That is easily remedied. Ellen, will you ring the bell? Jenkins will return to Gunter's with a message for your sister. She must be reassured that you are resting quietly. Under no circumstances is she to interrupt her plans for the day. There is not the slightest necessity for her to do so.'

Perdita heard a snort of amusement from her old nurse and it angered her further. 'You take too much upon yourself, my lord. I could have sent that message myself.'

'Then why didn't you do so?'

This was unanswerable. To make matters worse, Rushmore was gazing down at the battered slippers which Ellen had succeeded in slipping upon Perdita's feet.

'Charming!' he murmured smoothly. 'Tell me, did you embroider these dear little rabbits yourself?'

Perdita did not answer him.

'I must study some further examples of your skill...a sampler, perhaps?' With a maddening air of interest he strolled about the room, examining the framed work upon the walls. 'These homilies are most uplifting,' he announced brightly. 'Did you choose them yourself? How suitable they are. I like this one in particular: ''Pride goeth before a fall''. I could not have imagined a better had I tried.'

'They are not mine,' Perdita ground out.

'Indeed not, my lord! Miss Perdita has never been able to set a stitch to save herself.' Ellen smiled at the forthright gentleman who seemed to have the measure of her troublesome charge.

Perdita closed her eyes. With Rushmore and Ellen in league against her there was nothing more to say. She gave a theatrical groan.

'I believe that I shall rest, after all,' she told them in a faint voice. 'Leave me now. I may be able to sleep.'

Rushmore laughed aloud. 'Never try for the stage, my dear Miss Wentworth. You would find yourself the target of rotten eggs. You are not the least convincing. Come now, can't you stand a little teasing? I had sus-

pected you of having a sense of humour. I should be
sorry to find that I was wrong.'

This brought Perdita upright. She glared at him, but
she did not speak.

'That's better!' he encouraged. 'Now, what are we
to do with you? You will not wish to stay in your
room all day. Shall you care for a drive in the Park?'

Ellen spoke up before Perdita could answer him.
'My Lord, that will not do,' she said quietly. 'It would
give rise to gossip if you took Perdita up in your curricle.'

'Quite right, Ellen. There is no room for a chaperon.
Suppose I carry her down to the salon whilst we await
the return of her parents? You might sit with us whilst
we enjoy a hand or two of cards, or discuss the latest
affairs of the nation.'

Perdita was about to refuse his offer, but the thought
of the alternative was a strong deterrent. She had finished her book and had found no opportunity to visit
Hatchards in Piccadilly for the purpose of changing it.
Possibly one or other of her many admirers might call,
but the offending slippers would give rise to anxious
enquiries and the need for explanations which she had
no desire to give.

Rushmore watched her in some amusement, guessing that she was torn between accepting his offer, and
giving him a sharp set-down. He was banking on the
hope that common-sense would reassert itself, and he
was not disappointed.

'You are too kind!' she said stiffly.

'Am I to take it, then, that you agree?'

Perdita nodded.

'Very well, then.' Rushmore bent down towards

her. 'If you will slip your arms about my neck I shall be able to carry you in perfect safety.'

Perdita glanced at Ellen, expecting further protests from her old nurse. She was somewhat disconcerted to note the look of approval upon Ellen's ruddy face.

Not for the first time it occurred to her that Rushmore had the most irritating habit of ingratiating himself with her nearest and dearest. Ellen might at least have insisted that two of the footmen carried her young mistress. The reason for her complaisance was not far to seek. She believed that Rushmore saw Perdita as a wilful child.

Perdita was given no further opportunity for reflection. Rushmore gripped her wrists and put her arms about his neck, lifting her as if she were the child that Ellen thought her. Then he made his way towards the head of the staircase.

He was but halfway down the second flight when a commotion in the hallway heralded the return of Perry and Elizabeth. For just a moment her parents stood transfixed.

Perdita's sense of humour got the better of her, and it was only with the greatest difficulty that she kept her countenance. How would Rushmore explain the fact that he was descending from Perdita's bedchamber with that lady in his arms? She could not blame her mother and father if they wondered at it.

Rushmore was, as always, equal to the occasion. He bowed and addressed Elizabeth directly.

'Ma'am, your daughter has met with a slight accident. Nothing to worry about, I assure you, but her feet are very painful and she finds some difficulty in walking.' He saw the look of alarm in Elizabeth's eyes. 'New shoes, ma'am,' he announced with a twinkle. 'They can be the very devil. Now, if you will show me where I might set her down?'

Elizabeth gave a sigh of relief. Then she led the way into the salon and waited until Rushmore had settled Perdita upon a sofa.

'How came you to rescue Perdita a second time, my lord?' she said at last.

'Pure chance, ma'am. I was at your door when she arrived from Gunter's.'

'Perdita, where are the others?' Perry came over to take his daughter's hand.

'I had to leave them, Papa, but his lordship has sent a message to them saying that they are not to give up the rest of the day as I am quite all right.'

'I am in your debt, my lord.' Perry spoke with some reserve. He was not best pleased by the scene he had just witnessed, much as he admired the Earl of Rushmore. He turned back to Perdita. 'How are your feet, my darling? Do they need attention? Perhaps we should send for Doctor Forbes?'

Perdita blushed. 'Really, Papa! All I have done is skin my toes. It was my own stupid fault. I should have known better than to walk for so long in my new boots.' She gave her father a loving smile. 'They will be better by tomorrow.'

Rushmore gazed down at the enchanting little face, and his heart turned over. When Perdita smiled the room lit up. He would have given much to have won such a smile from her on his own behalf. He turned to Elizabeth.

'I was on my way to speak to your husband and yourself, ma'am. The Duke has not yet released me from my duties, so I cannot get away. It occurred to me that some further discussion of our plans might be useful.'

Perdita pricked up her ears. Plans? What plans? She could think of no possible connection between her parents and this arrogant creature who stood before her, clearly perfectly at ease.

Elizabeth nodded and her lips twitched. 'I agree, my lord. One omission, at least, has been troubling me. Perry, will you show his lordship into the study? Just give me a moment to remove my cloak and bonnet before I join you.'

She waited until the men had left the room before she spoke again.

'Well, Perdita?'

'It is just as his lordship said, Mama. There was nothing amiss. Ellen was with us at all times.'

'Great heavens, Perdita! Do you think me a complete fool? The Earl would scarce attempt to ravish you in your own home and attended by a houseful of servants. I must hope that you were polite to him.'

'I did as he asked...eventually...' Perdita admitted. 'I wanted to rejoin Amy, but he wouldn't hear of it.'

'You'll agree that it would have been difficult, since you cannot walk?'

'Yes, he was right. It seems to be a habit of his.'

Elizabeth glanced at her daughter's face, but she made no further comment, though she was much amused. She had guessed correctly that Perdita found Lord Rushmore's attitude infuriating. He simply would not take her seriously. Well, it would do the child no harm, but peace must be restored if her girls and Rushmore's ward were to deal amicably together.

That thought was foremost in her mind as she entered the study.

'The omission, ma'am?' For once, Rushmore was not quite at ease.

'Why, my lord, you have not given me the name of your ward. I had intended to speak of her to both my girls, but I couldn't do so. Doubtless they will know her. Miss Bedlington's is not a large establishment.'

'I beg your pardon. Her name is Louise Bryant. As I understand it she has not been long at the school. The plan was that she should join her father at Brussels, but naturally, after Waterloo she was deprived of any such opportunity.'

'Poor child! She is Amy's age, is she not?'

'A little older, I believe. She must be seventeen or so by now.'

'And what would you have us do?' Perry was ready to throw himself wholeheartedly into any plan which might ease the suffering of a hero's orphan.

'My hands are tied for the moment. I must wait upon the Duke's pleasure. Hopefully, it won't be long before he will release me. I have written to Louise, of course, telling her of your kindness. I wonder...will the Misses Wentworth make themselves known to her? If she could feel that she had at least two friends to support her in the coming Season...? Her father felt that she was very shy, so it is certain to loom as an ordeal.'

Perry cast aside all his reservations about the Earl of Rushmore. The man was sensitive, after all.

'Pray, my lord, don't trouble yourself further,' he said warmly. 'Put it down to partiality if you will, but I don't know of two better-hearted girls than Amy and Perdita. They will be only too happy to befriend your ward.'

Elizabeth was not so sure. Rushmore had ruffled the

feathers of both her daughters, and she had quickly become aware that they were in league against him. Even so, she felt that they would not continue that vendetta against a lonely girl who had been so cruelly deprived of her sole remaining parent.

Her belief was confirmed later that day when she called the girls to her boudoir.

'Do you know a girl called Louise Bryant?' she asked without preamble.

Perdita shook her head, but Amy nodded.

'You left before she arrived,' she told her sister. 'And I don't know her well. She is the quietest creature in the world, always hanging back. Why do you ask, Mama?''

'I want you to befriend her. It is a tragic story. Her father died at Waterloo. She has no other relatives.'

Perdita clenched her fists until the knuckles whitened. She could not imagine life without her beloved father.

'Mother, you need not ask,' she said quietly. 'We'll do all we can to help her.'

'I hope so, my dear, especially when you hear the rest of the story. Louise's father was the Earl of Rushmore's closest friend...Louise is now his ward...'

A silence followed this startling piece of information, but Perdita spoke at last.

'All the more reason to befriend her,' she cried. Then she caught her mother's eye. 'I mean...unless she knows his lordship well, she may find him difficult to understand,' she amended hastily. 'He is not in the least conciliating.'

'As far as I know she has not yet met the Earl,' her mother replied. 'But why, may I ask, should he trouble to be conciliating? The opinion of a schoolgirl cannot possibly be of interest to him.'

Perdita was silenced. She was, she understood only too well, included in that particular group of people to whose opinion Rushmore need pay no attention. It was of little comfort to realise that had she been the most powerful woman in the land her views upon his conduct would have influenced him just as little. The man behaved as if he were a law unto himself. It was an accusation which had been levelled in the past at Perdita herself. Now she was beginning to see just how uncomfortable such behaviour could be to others.

'Perdita, are you paying attention? You seem to me to be woolgathering again.'

'Sorry, Mama! I was just thinking...when is Louise to come to stay with us?'

'At the first opportunity, my dear. It is unfortunate that your father and I must be out of the country for the next few months, but once we return I shall invite Louise. Meantime, I trust that you will both do your best to befriend her. I shudder to think of how she must have suffered in these past few months, without a soul to turn to. Miss Bedlington, I fear, is not the most tender-hearted of women.'

Perdita gave her the ghost of a smile. 'I won't argue with that, Mama.'

Little though she relished the idea of being connected in any way with the Earl of Rushmore, she was conscious of a feeling of relief. He had not, after all, found further reason to object to her behaviour and had sought out her parents on quite another errand.

Honesty compelled her to admit that few people could be more in need of friends than the unfortunate Louise. She was willing to play her part, and a mo-

ment's reflection convinced her that the girl was unlikely to be favoured with many visits from her guardian during her stay in Bath. She doubted if he would
trouble to seek out the company of the schoolroom
misses he had dismissed so casually at Almack's.

He had been quick to hand over the care of his ward
to her own mama. Naturally, he could not have refused
the last request of a dying man, but she could not think
that he would take a serious interest in Louise, other
than to see her married as soon as may be, and off his
hands.

Possibly he was already casting about him for a suitable candidate. Her mother's next words did nothing
to dispel that notion.

'I'm sorry that I shan't be able to meet Louise just
yet,' Elizabeth said quietly. 'But you girls must be my
proxy. I want her to feel comfortable with the idea of
coming to stay with us. Rushmore tells me that she is
a considerable heiress, and there are those who make
it their business to find out about such matters. You
must be her watchdogs. She must not form any unsuitable attachments.'

'At Miss Bedlington's?' Amy was incredulous. 'No
gentleman is ever allowed across her doorstep unless
he is a relative and even then Miss Bedlington is not
at ease. From her expression one would think that all
members of the male sex should be confined behind
bars.'

Elizabeth smiled. 'I did not imagine that anyone
would force an entry into your schoolroom, Amy, but
sometimes a stranger will attempt to strike up an acquaintance at a concert, or the play. You will guard
against that, I hope.'

'Mama, there are *no* young men in Bath. You

should see Aunt Trixie's beaux. They are carried to
see her in sedan-chairs and to climb the steps they
need two sticks. All they talk about is that filthy, dis-
gusting water, and the wonders it does for all their
ailments. Her bosom-bows are just as bad. To hear
Mrs Larwood, one must wonder that she is still alive.'

'Even the elderly have nephews, Amy, and grand-
sons too. I am sorry to say it, but sometimes they
cultivate their failing relatives for the worst of reasons.'

'Oh, Mama, you won't forbid us to go about at all?'
Perdita asked anxiously. 'I could not bear it.'

'Of course not, my dear. It is just that I would advise you to be cautious in your choice of friends.'

Amy threw an arm about her mother's neck. 'You
don't need to worry about Perdita,' she said solemnly.
'No gentleman has suited her to date, and as for me,
I don't intend to marry within the next six months.'

Elizabeth chuckled. 'I'm glad to hear it, but do pray
heed my words, No harm must come to Louise.'

'We'll look out for her,' Amy promised. 'I had intended to ask you if I might be a day girl for this last
term and stay with Perdita at Aunt Trixie's, but I shall
become better acquainted with Louise if I continue to
board.' She dropped a kiss upon her mother's cheek.
'I wish you will not worry so,' she said cheerfully.
'As I recall, Louise is so shy that she would flee if a
stranger tried to speak to her.'

Elizabeth smiled at both her girls. 'I would not have
you think me a fuss-pot, my dears, but I am conscious
of the responsibility for Louise.'

Perdita felt rebellious. 'Mama, you have not taken
her in charge just yet. Surely it is the Earl of Rushmore
who should be concerned.'

'He is, Perdita. That is why he applied to me. He is aware that an unwed military man can have no notion as to how to go on in bringing out a young girl. I wish you will forget your dislike of him, my love. It is Louise who needs our help at present.'

She expressed the same sentiments to her husband when he and she were alone.

'You look troubled, Lizzie.' Perry slid an arm about her waist. 'What is it, my love?'

'Oh, I don't know… I am wondering if we have done the right thing, I suppose, though I don't see how we could have refused to help Rushmore's ward.'

'Out of the question!' Perry replied firmly. 'But do you fear that she will be a trouble to you?'

'No…it isn't that. From all I hear she is a quiet and biddable girl, but both Amy and Perdita have taken the Earl in such dislike…'

'Need that concern you? If I am not mistaken, his lordship will not visit Bath more than is strictly necessary. To me he does not look like a man in need of healing waters.'

Elizabeth smiled at that, but then she gave him a reproachful look. 'I wish you will be serious, Perry. The very sight of him is enough to light Perdita's fuse.'

'I can't say that I blame her overmuch. I was taken aback myself to find her in Rushmore's arms today. Perdita looked as if she could have killed him.'

'Their encounters have been unfortunate, my dear. He is inclined to ride roughshod, you know. Perdita is more accustomed to being placed upon a pedestal by her hopeful swains.'

Perry's face darkened. 'You can't mean that Rushmore thinks of throwing his handkerchief in Perdita's direction? If I thought that, he would not enter this house again.'

'I thought you admired him.'

'I do…but he isn't for Perdita. She's just a child and he is old enough to be her father.'

'Nonsense! He can't have reached the age of thirty, and Perdita is no longer a child, my dear. It can't have escaped your notice that she has grown into an exceptionally beautiful woman.'

'She's still very young,' he growled.

'Now don't get upon your high ropes,' his wife advised. 'We are all aware that there isn't a man alive whom you would consider good enough for her. I can only put it down to a father's partiality.' She twinkled at him. 'What a pity that my own father didn't share your views. He couldn't wait to hand me over to you.'

Perry grinned at her. 'He recognised my sterling worth.'

'And also the fact that you sailed aboard an English warship and were able to spirit me out of a war-torn Italy.'

'Not so!' Perry told her stoutly. 'He'd already offered me your hand before then—'

'And for the same reason. Sadly, you refused that offer. I confess that it has always been the most lowering thought.'

'Minx!' Perry slipped a finger beneath her chin and raised her face to his. 'Tell me that you regret it, and I'll release you from your vows at once.'

'Never! You shan't escape so easily!' Confident in her love, Elizabeth offered him her lips. Then she slid her arms about his neck. 'Do you suppose that all will be well?' she whispered. 'If only I could be certain that Perdita will not come to dagger-drawing with the Earl if they should chance to meet in Bath.'

'Don't trouble your head about it, Lizzie. Dagger-drawing I can tolerate, but I won't have Rushmore throwing out lures to Perdita. I thank heaven that she *does* dislike him. She will find a dozen ways of hinting him away. Should you mention it to Aunt Beatrice?'

'No...I believe not,' Elizabeth said slowly. 'I don't even wish to put the notion into her head that Rushmore is to be considered a prospect for Perdita. Aunt Trixie is so romantical.'

Perry had the grace to blush, but he stuck to his argument. 'Did you not assure me that they are at odds whenever they meet? You can't have it both ways, Lizzie. If they quarrel so, neither can have a *tendre* for the other.'

To her credit, Elizabeth did not challenge this statement, though memories of her own wooing rose at once to mind. She and Perry had crossed swords from the very moment of their meeting. It had not stopped them from falling in love.

'You may be right,' she said without conviction. Under the circumstances she found herself wishing that her proposed voyage to Gibraltar might have been postponed. She didn't suggest it. Her decision to leave without Perdita had been a disappointment to her husband. She would not add to it by staying behind herself.

Even so, she could not repress a niggling presentiment of disaster. Then she shrugged. She was becoming fanciful. It was high time that she concentrated on everyday matters, rather than worrying about problems before they existed. What was it that Perry always said? 'Don't worry, it may never happen.' How she wished she might believe it.

Chapter Five

Elizabeth was given little time to indulge in further speculation. Within the next few days she and Perry were to leave for Portsmouth, where he was due to rejoin his ship.

Before then the girls must be sent off to Bath, with Ellen in attendance. Thankfully, the Earl of Rushmore did not appear, so she was able to draw up her lists and supervise the family packing without interruption.

Amy had cajoled her cousins into taking her on further expeditions about the capital, but Perdita did not go. Her feet were improving though they were not quite healed, and on the day before their departure she was glad of the excuse to join her father in his study for a companionable chat.

Perry settled her comfortably by the fire. Then he walked over to his strongbox and unlocked it, taking out a thick bundle of notes.

'Here, my dear!' He pressed the money into her hands. 'You must take this roll of soft... Doubtless, you will find a use for it.'

'But it is far too much, Papa!' Perdita stared in awe

at the roll of notes. She had never handled so much money in her life.

'I think you will not find it so,' Perry assured her. 'You must pay subscriptions in the Pump and the Assembly Rooms. There will be tickets for the concerts too...' He looked at her a little anxiously.

Perdita caught his hand and held it lovingly against her cheek. 'You must not worry that I shan't enjoy myself, Papa. Aunt Trixie is such a dear, and I shall have Amy close at hand. We shall be able to walk and ride and visit with our friends.'

'That's my girl! My darling, I am proud of you. I should have been disappointed had you fallen into a fit of the sullens.'

Perdita managed a wavering smile, which did not deceive him in the least.

'We shall miss you quite dreadfully,' she said in a low voice. 'These next few months will seem like an age.'

Perry's hand ruffled the fashionably short crop of curls. 'We shall miss you too,' he told her lightly. 'But you will be kept busy, especially in trying to keep Amy out of the shops in Milsom Street. Your mother and I rely on you to prevent her from buying bonnets and other fol-de-rols more suitable for a dowager than a schoolgirl.'

Perdita laughed at that. Amy's longing to be considered an adult had led her to experiment with headgear of terrifying dimensions, none of which she had been allowed to buy. Fortunately her own sense of humour had persuaded her in the end that an excess of cherries, apples and other fruits draped about the brims of some of the latest creations left her open to charges of running a market stall.

'Of course, I don't intend you to stint yourselves,' Perry continued. 'Doubtless you will see items in the shops without which a happy life cannot be sustained.' He had intended only to tease a little, but the effect on his daughter was unexpected.

'Papa, you are much too good to us,' she said in a muffled voice. Then she hurried away before her feelings overcame her.

Elizabeth expressed the same sentiments on the following day as the family's private chaise, accompanied by postilions, set out to take the girls to Bath. Their parents waved it out of sight. Then Elizabeth turned to her husband.

'Well, my dear, how much did you give them?' she asked with a twinkle.

'Oh, just a trifle,' he replied vaguely. 'I have sent Beatrice a draft upon my bank. The girls may apply to her if they find themselves at a standstill.'

'That, I suppose, is why Perdita is clutching her largest reticule as if she expects to be set upon by footpads before they have travelled a mile?'

Perry hugged his wife. 'Why can I never manage to deceive you, Lizzie? She has been very good. You'll agree that she deserves to be rewarded?'

Laughing, Elizabeth looked at him in mock despair. 'What am I to do with you?' she asked.

'I can think of a number of things...' Perry leered at her and twirled an imaginary moustache. 'Beware, my proud beauty! You will rue the day that you defy me!'

'You are impossible!' Elizabeth slipped past him. 'Behave yourself, monster! I have far too much to do to listen to your nonsense.'

'Now give me credit for something, Lizzie! Amy, you know, was determined to travel to Bath in the Mail Coach. Did I not dissuade her?'

'Perhaps we should have allowed it. I fancy she wouldn't care to repeat the experience.'

Amy did not share that belief. As she glanced at the passers-by she began to giggle.

'Our state procession is creating a stir,' she answered. 'That man has taken off his hat and bowed. I think I'll give him a gracious wave. It must be the postilions. He thinks that we are of the first importance...most probably princesses at the very least.'

Ellen gave a scandalised gasp. 'You will do no such thing, Miss Amy. Don't you dare smile at him. Such airs, I do declare! And with your family crest upon this carriage too.'

'No one would have noticed us if we had taken the Mail Coach.' Amy was unrepentent. 'Think of the fun we should have had, travelling with a group of strangers!'

Ellen snorted in disgust. 'Fun, indeed! You'd soon have changed your tune, squashed up as you would have been with a crowd of nasty, smelly folk from the Lord knows where.'

Amy grinned at her old nurse. 'Ellen, you are a snob!' she accused.

'I hope I know what is due to your father's consequence,' came the swift reply. 'Behave yourself, Miss Amy, and come away from that window, else you'll sit between your sister and myself. Then you'll see nothing.'

This dread threat caused Amy to offer an olive

branch. 'Have you ever travelled by the mail coach, Ellen? You seem to know a lot about it.'

'Indeed I have, and I may tell you that if you had ever done the same you wouldn't care to do so again. I thought my last hour had come!'

'Were you set upon by highwaymen?' Amy's eyes were sparkling.

'We were not! The guard was armed. He would have seen them off. It was much worse than that...'

'Oh, do tell us about it! It must have been a real adventure.'

'Some adventure!' Ellen sniffed. 'The driver had but one good eye, and his horses were in like case. Had he been sober he might have managed them—'

'He was disguised?' Perdita looked startled.

'Blind drunk is what I'd call it myself. He took a fresh noggin or two at every halt. When we reached Lunnon he fell off the box.'

Both girls shouted with laughter.

''Tweren't funny, I can tell you,' Ellen said darkly. 'I thought we must be overturned. The Lord knows how we came out of it with a whole skin.'

'Well, you did!' Amy patted the old woman's hand. 'Now you have got your wish and can travel without fear.'

'That's as maybe! 'Tis a long way to Bath, and we must stop along the road...'

'But Father sent a man ahead to bespeak a private parlour at the inns. I doubt if anyone will try to abduct us, Ellen, although, of course, they may have designs on you.' Perdita could not resist a little gentle teasing.

She was rewarded with a grim smile. 'Get on with you, miss. You know what I think about men.'

'We do indeed! Ellen, I believe you have some dark

and sinister secret in your past. Tell us of the dastardly deed.'

'Miss Amy, you are a complete hand! Now, give over with your teasing, the pair of you! Young ladies should not be speaking of abduction and the like.'

Amy was tempted to suggest that perhaps they should sing hymns. Instead, she turned to the safer subject of Ellen's nephews and nieces. As always, Ellen waxed voluble upon the doings of the younger members of her family, and it was not until they reached the first halt that she felt obliged to offer yet another word of caution.

'Now remember!' she warned. 'You are not to speak to strangers, or acknowledge them.'

'Not even if they drop dead at our feet?' Perdita enquired with a smile.

'There wouldn't be much point if they were dead!' Ellen felt that she had scored a point as she motioned her charges to follow the landlord to their private dining-room.

She did not allow them to waste much time. A long journey still lay ahead of them and she was anxious to reach Bath before nightfall.

In the event it was mid-evening before they arrived at Laura Place, to be greeted with huge delight by Miss Beatrice Langrishe. Two of that lady's most faithful beaux and one of her women friends had joined her in a game of cards, but at the sight of Amy and Perdita she came towards them with outstretched arms.

'Welcome!' she cried. 'My dears, you must be exhausted! Let me ring for some refreshment for you, unless you care to go to your rooms at once. Did you have a pleasant journey? And how are your mama and papa? I can't wait to hear your news.'

Both girls disclaimed the notion that they might be tired, or that they were in need of refreshment.

'Nonsense! You'll take a glass of wine at least!'

To Amy's gratification she was included in this invitation. Miss Langrishe, it was clear, had no high opinion on the restorative properties of a glass of milk or a hot posset. Nor did she feel that it was in the nature of human beings to deprive themselves of the best cuisine that money could buy, and that at frequent intervals. Her chef was a legend in Bath. Now he sent in a tray of appetising morsels including hot oyster patties and tiny vol au vent cases, some filled with creamed mushrooms, others with curried eggs and yet more with shredded ham in a Cumberland sauce.

Perdita noted with amusement that at the sight of food her aunt's companions made no attempt to take their leave and Miss Langrishe beamed upon the assembled company as they took full advantage of her hospitality. An evening spent in the company of her friends represented, to her, the height of civilised living. She nodded her encouragement as Amy helped herself to a second devilled chicken leg.

'That's right, my love. With your slender figure you need have no worries about increasing embonpoint. How I wish that I could say the same.'

This brought immediate protests from her two admirers. The goddesses of antiquity, so they claimed, could present no finer appearance than in Miss Langrishe in the full bloom of her maturity.

The lady chided them for blatant flattery, but she was not displeased, though she accused them of pandering to her vanity.

'I'm a silly old woman,' she said without a trace of affectation when her friends had left. 'The Captain cannot know that certain of his remarks were passed on to me. He described me as gliding across the floor of the Assembly Rooms like a galleon under sail... Well, perhaps I am no sylph, but neither, I hope, do I look like a warship.'

'Dear Aunt, I am sure he meant it as a compliment. Is it not obvious that ships and the sea were his life for many years?' Perdita smiled at her aunt. 'How could he honour you more than by comparing you with what he loves best in the world?'

'That, I fancy, is his stomach!' Miss Langrishe signalled to the footman to pour the girls another glass of wine. 'It will do you no harm at all for just this once,' she said in reply to Perdita's warning glance at Amy. 'You will sleep well this night, and tomorrow you shall tell me all your news.' She had noted the drooping eyelids of her guests and dismissed them to their rooms as soon as they had drained their glasses.

'Ellen will think that we are as drunk as her coachman.' Amy giggled as they climbed the staircase. 'Aunt Trixie is a dear, isn't she? She never makes me feel as if I'm still in the nursery.'

'Well, don't let Ellen know that we had a second glass of wine, or we shall never hear the end of it,' Perdita warned.

Miss Langrishe had foreseen the difficulty. At her express request, Ellen had retired to recover from the rigours of the journey, and it was her own personal maid who attended to the girls.

'Back to the prison-camp tomorrow,' Amy groaned as she climbed into bed. 'How shall I bear it for these next few months?'

'It may not be so bad,' Perdita comforted. 'Let us speak to Aunt tomorrow. We can explain about Louise and she may have some ideas as to how we can win her friendship. She may not be too happy with the idea of being ordered to live with a family of strangers.'

'Ordered?' Amy said blankly.

'Oh, yes! I don't suppose that the Earl has used much tact. Most probably he sent her a couple of lines making his wishes clear. As far as I know he hasn't even met her yet.'

'That's hardly his fault,' Amy protested. 'The Duke would not release him—'

'Stuff! He might have asked for leave of absence upon compassionate grounds.'

Amy sighed. 'Oh dear! Let's hope that Louise does not take him in the same dislike as you do.'

'He may be sent away again,' Perdita said hopefully. 'There must be trouble somewhere in the world where his obnoxious character would be useful.'

Privately, Amy thought it unlikely, but Perdita was asleep before she could pursue the subject.

Miss Langrishe was not an early riser. She was in the habit of receiving favoured guests in the comfort of her bedchamber as she sipped her morning chocolate.

There, resplendent in an embroidered silk robe and a matching cap of fetching design, she smiled at the girls as they came to wish her a good morning.

'Now, my dears, how do you go on? You slept well, I trust? I confess that I can't wait to hear your news of London and the family.'

She was an excellent listener, with the rare gift of

giving each speaker her full attention without feeling the need to interrupt with comments of her own.

Perdita realised that this was part of the secret of her great-aunt's charm. She brought out the best in her companions, making them feel that their own opinions were of value and worthy of serious consideration. In her presence even the most stupid of creatures felt themselves cleverer and wittier than in fact they were.

She and Amy related all the family gossip, and as much as they knew of the topics uppermost in the minds of polite society during the Season. Miss Langrishe knew of all the latest scandals, thanks to her very efficient grapevine, but she didn't betray that fact. She exclaimed over the meeting with the Duke of Wellington, and teased Amy over her evident devotion to her hero, wondering as she did so if her nieces would trust her enough to discuss a matter that was clearly troubling them.

When they hesitated, she decided to offer a little encouragement. Her approach was gentle.

'Perdita, I won't insult you by pretending that I don't know why you are here,' she said. 'Your mother explained matters when she wrote to me. She mentioned the Earl of Rushmore... Now, my love, may I beg you never to look back? We cannot change the past, but we can look to the future. You must put that episode behind you.'

Perdita was silent. It was Amy who spoke.

'We should like nothing better, Aunt. If only we might be sure that we should never see him again. He's a hateful creature.'

Miss Langrishe looked at the mutinous faces. 'I know the name,' she observed. 'I think I met his father long ago. An arrogant rakehell, if I ever saw one…killed on the hunting field, I believe, but with more charm than any man I ever met.'

'His son has not inherited that quality,' Perdita said stiffly.

'But why let it worry you, my dear? I doubt if you will see him again. From all I hear, it is highly unlikely that he will come to Bath for the waters.'

'He will come for another reason, Aunt. His ward is at school with me. She is to come to live with us next year to share my Season.' Amy was unenthusiastic.

'But why? Has she no relatives?'

Both girls began to explain the situation.

'Of course, we are sorry for her, Aunt. We can't begin to imagine the pain of losing her father, but if only someone else had been her guardian!'

'Don't dwell upon it, my dears. Louise must be our first concern. Amy, do you know her well?'

'No! That is another worry. She is so very quiet…not exactly unfriendly, but not the life and soul of any gathering.'

'Would there be room for two of you, Amy?' Her aunt's lips twitched. 'We must all get to know her better, I think. Now, what do you say to bringing her to see me? I shall procure tickets for the next concert at the Assembly Rooms. I believe we shall all enjoy it.'

'Miss Bedlington may not approve, Aunt Trixie.'

'You may safely leave Miss Bedlington to me. Perdita and I will accompany you when you return to school this afternoon. I shall speak to the lady then.'

'But, Aunt, I can't! She said that I was never to darken her doors again.' Perdita had the grace to blush.

Miss Langrishe gave her a grim smile. 'How dra-

matic! That sounds like a remark from a bad play.
There will be no difficulty, I assure you.'

She spoke no more than the truth. When she walked
into the Academy later that afternoon Perdita was reminded forcibly of the description of her aunt as a
galleon under full sail.

Miss Langrishe had chosen her toilette with care.
Her flowing garments owed nothing to the present
fashions, but they became her imposing figure well.
The most casual observer would have been aware of
the cost of the fabulous silk brocade of her voluminous
cloak and of the jewels nestling in her towering turban.

She winked at the girls. 'Nothing like full fig for
intimidating the opposition,' she announced. 'I believe
we shall have no problems with Miss Bedlington.'

She was right. Beside the tall figure of their aunt,
Miss Bedlington looked insignificant, and the girls
were surprised to see that she looked a little nervous.
Amy she welcomed with as much warmth as it was in
her nature to show and even Perdita was greeted with
a stiff bow. However, it was the formidable Miss Langrishe for whom the owner of the Academy reserved
her most fulsome welcome.

Miss Bedlington was no fool, and in the imposing
figure of the woman before her she could see unlimited
opportunities. Her Academy was her livelihood, and
Miss Langrishe had the entrée to the highest circles in
Bath. Her elderly friends might not have daughters of
their own, but they had granddaughters and nieces, and
a word of recommendation would go far.

She exerted herself to be accommodating, agreeing
that young ladies on the verge of their come-out must

be exposed by degrees to the pleasures of the adult world.

Miss Langrishe settled herself in the largest chair in the room. To Perdita it seemed as if she were seated upon a throne, graciously accepting a glass of ratafia.

'I have never believed it wise to take young girls from the schoolroom and throw them into Society untrained,' Miss Langrishe announced. 'They must appear gauche. It can do their prospects no service.'

'Quite, ma'am, quite...although they do receive some training here.'

'I'm sure you do your best, Miss Bedlington.' Miss Langrishe was at her grandest. 'I cannot fault your academic standards, but among the *ton*, you know...?'

Miss Bedlington understood her visitor perfectly. Miss Langrishe intended to have her way. If it wasn't blackmail, it came close.

'What do you suggest, ma'am?' she asked politely.

'Why, with your permission, of course, I think that the girls must be allowed to come to me as much as possible. Louise Bryant, I understand, is to share her Season with my niece. I plan a programme of concerts for them...nothing too extreme, of course.'

'A splendid idea!' Miss Bedlington's voice lacked conviction, but Beatrice Langrishe did not appear to notice.

'Then, of course, there will be small dinner-parties... I plan one for tomorrow evening. Shall we say that the carriage will collect the girls at six?'

Miss Bedlington felt unable to disagree, and Perdita looked at her aunt with awe as she left the Academy for Laura Place.

'How do you do it, Aunt?' she asked. 'Miss Bedlington agreed to everything.'

Her aunt looked a little conscious. 'Perhaps I should not tell you this, but I look for the Achilles' heel, my dear. Miss Bedlington is aware that my recommendation can help her. She won't set up her will against me.'

Perdita smiled. 'What a dangerous creature you are, Aunt Trixie! I am not tempted to enter the lists against you.'

'Why should you, my love? After all, I am on your side.'

Perdita felt comforted. It was such a boon to be surrounded by uncritical affection. Her parents loved her dearly, but the relationship with her aunt was different. With Beatrice Langrishe she could speak of things which she could never mention to them. She wondered why that was. Possibly because they were not so closely bound by ties of blood? Possibly not. She was unable to decide, but in the meantime she could bask in the loving affection of the older woman.

She had had to confess that she was curious about Louise, and when the two girls arrived on the following evening, she realised that Amy's assessment of the girl's character had been correct.

Tall and fair, Louise was no beauty, but there was intelligence in the fine grey eyes and a pleasing regularity in her features. Her manners were beyond reproach, but there was an air of reserve...a barrier...which discouraged intimacy.

Miss Langrishe appeared to be unaware of it. Before the arrival of her guests she appealed to the girls for help.

'My guests are new arrivals here,' she told them innocently. 'I wonder... They are bound to feel a little ill-at-ease. Could you possibly help them out…ask them about themselves…their families…their interests? It is so daunting to be forced to dine with strangers, and Miss Murray, in particular, is very shy.'

It was enough to enlist their help and even Louise felt enabled to play her part. In thinking of others, she had forgotten her own shyness. Miss Langrishe had nothing but praise for her co-hostesses.

'Well done!' she smiled. 'We shall have you leading your own salons before next year is out… It isn't difficult, is it, if one remembers that a favourite topic of conversation with most people is themselves?'

Three beaming faces agreed with her. The girls had done well, encouraged by the compliments and the old-fashioned courtesies which they had received from the other guests. Elderly shoulders had been straightened and moustaches twirled at the sight of these fresh young creatures.

Miss Langrishe too came in for her share of praise.

'Well, m'dear, I can't say when I've enjoyed an evening more,' Captain Merton told his hostess. Then he turned to his friends, but recently arrived in Bath. 'Did I not say that you would find the town far from dull?' he said. 'All this nonsense about it being a dead-and-alive hole! How can that be so when we are invited to enjoy the company of such charming ladies?'

They were quick to agree with him, and departed expressing the hope that they might be allowed to return such delightful hospitality, and enquiring if Miss Langrishe meant to bring her party to the next concert in the Assembly Rooms.

'Indeed! We should not miss it for the world,' she smiled.

It was enough to send Amy and Louise back to the

Academy quite reconciled to another week of study before their next outing.

Miss Langrishe rang for her tea-tray before she and Perdita retired for the night.

'No need to ask if you enjoyed your evening, my dear,' she said warmly. 'I was proud of you. You made my guests feel welcome.'

'They were interesting people, Aunt. It was a pleasure to speak to them.'

'Most people are, if one takes the trouble to draw them out. Shall you be able to make a friend of Louise, do you suppose?'

'I hope so, though it may be difficult to get to know her…she is so quiet and shy.'

'She is more reserved than shy, I fancy, though she did well enough tonight.'

'She must be feeling the loss of her father, Aunt. I'd like to have spoken of him to her, but it is difficult to know what to say that could possibly be of any comfort. Don't you find it so?'

Miss Langrishe considered for several moments. 'We human beings have a curious attitude to death,' she said at last. 'I have never understood why it should be found embarrassing. I suppose it is thought an unwelcome reminder of one's own mortality, but the subject should not be avoided with the bereaved. Above anything, they need to be encouraged to remember their loved ones and to speak of them.'

'But surely that is distressing?'

'It helps, my dear, and as to words of comfort, well, I have my own philosophy.'

'Which is?'

'A simple one, Perdita. I believe that our loved ones

never die as long as we remember them. They live on in our hearts.'

'That is beautiful!' Perdita raised her aunt's hand and held it against her cheek. 'I shall remember it all my life.'

Beatrice Langrishe patted the dark curls. 'Have you any plans for this week?' she asked.

'I am at your disposal, Aunt. Shall you wish me to attend you to the Pump Room?'

Miss Langrishe gave a hearty laugh. 'Never think that I take the waters, my love! Nasty-tasting stuff! In my opinion a good burgundy is much better for one's health.'

Perdita was tempted to giggle. 'So you don't visit the Pump Room? I thought that everyone did so.'

'They do, my dear. I would not miss the morning gathering for the world. How else would one learn the latest gossip?' Miss Langrishe gave Perdita a sly look. 'The waters have their uses. They encourage the potted plants to flourish.'

Perdita could not keep her countenance. The thought of her aunt disposing of the medicinal offerings into the nearest plant pot was too much for her, and her shoulders shook with laughter. Her stay with aunt Trixie promised to be much more entertaining than she had at first imagined.

That lady's dry sense of humour was a source of great joy to her, and she had the ready ability to convulse Perdita at unexpected moments. It was difficult to keep a straight face on the following morning when Miss Langrishe surveyed the decrepit occupants of the Pump Room. 'As you see, Perdita, we are gay to dissipation!' she announced, as she turned to greet an aged gentleman who came to them with all the speed he could muster.

Miss Langrishe engaged him in conversation, using him as a shield as she tossed the contents of her glass over the roots of the nearest plant. In spite of her ironic remarks, she enquired most kindly about his health and appeared to be enthralled as he related the most intimate details of his digestive processes. It was enough to put Perdita off her nuncheon until she managed to thrust the conversation from her mind.

'Aunt, will you tell me something?' she asked as she helped herself to a plate of cold meats and sallets.

'Certainly, my dear, if I can. What is it you wish to know?'

'Don't think me forward, but, well…I wondered why you choose to live here…in Bath, I mean?'

'You think it unsuitable for me?'

'Not exactly, I suppose, but there are so many old people.'

Miss Langrishe smiled at her. 'What a delightful compliment, my love. You forget that I am not in the first bloom of youth myself.'

'But you don't behave like an older person, and you don't think in an elderly way… Would you not prefer to live in London?'

'Not in the least, Perdita. I have always loved this city and the surrounding countryside. For me there is as much to interest here as in the capital. It is possible to study a smaller canvas with as much enjoyment as a larger one.'

'You mean the people?'

'I do. It is the most absorbing subject in the world.

One learns as much about oneself as one does of others.'

'I wish I could feel the same,' Perdita said slowly.

'Look outwards, my love! That way it is possible to forget oneself and one's own troubles.'

'I haven't any troubles, Aunt,' Perdita said impulsively. 'I am so happy here with you.'

'That's my girl!' Miss Langrishe patted her head. 'Now, what do you say to some shopping in Milsom Street? I must not disgrace you at the concert.'

Perdita thought this highly unlikely, and that opinion was confirmed as the days passed and her aunt added to her already vast collection of jewels, scarves and headgear. She also bought gifts for the girls, dismissing their protests with a smile.

'Now you won't rob me of the pleasure of giving you these trifles?' she asked. 'I have no children of my own, so this is an unexpected joy for me.'

It was as they were preparing for the concert in the Assembly Rooms that Amy took Perdita aside.

'Can we talk?' she asked.

'Now? We haven't much time, you know.'

'This is important!' Amy looked troubled.

'Then tell me...'

'It's Louise. I don't want to betray a confidence, but...well...she has an admirer.'

'What!'

'Oh, don't fly into the boughs, Perdita. She hopes to marry him.'

'She must be mad!' Perdita said with conviction. 'How on earth did she meet him? She's still at school.'

'It was after she heard the news about her father.

She was sitting in the park and, well…she was distressed. He asked if he could be of service to her.'

'Oh, Amy, does she know anything about him? It can't be right that he would offer for her in this way. Rushmore will go mad!'

'He isn't here!' Amy said stubbornly. 'I, for one, don't blame her. Who else has offered her sympathy and comfort?'

'I'm sure he meant it kindly, but this can't be right. Does Miss Bedlington know?'

'Of course she doesn't.'

'Then how did Louise…? I mean, how did she come to be allowed out on her own?'

'She just walked off. She's so quiet that Miss Bedlington didn't miss her.'

'But this man? Who is he, and where does he come from?'

'He lives in Bath. He has connections here.'

'Well, I think he might have waited before proposing to Louise. She could have been in no condition to consider.'

'Oh, don't be so prosy! He didn't offer on that day, you goose. She has known him for some weeks.'

'That will please Rushmore.' Perdita's ironic tone was not lost upon Amy.

'Why should he not be pleased? He wants her to marry, doesn't he? After all, she'll be off his hands.'

'I think you'll find that he doesn't take his responsibilities so lightly.' Perdita left it there, but her sister's news had cast a cloud upon her spirits. Rushmore's appearance in Bath could not now be long delayed. She shuddered to think of his reaction.

His arrival was unexpected, but she sensed his presence halfway through a concert. She glanced round and her heart sank. That thunderous expression boded ill for both Louise and her admirer. Perdita was in no doubt that the connection was already known to him.

Chapter Six

Under the cover of a particularly spirited passage in the music Perdita nudged her sister.

'Rushmore is here,' she whispered. 'He is standing by the door. Don't turn your head! I believe he has seen us already.'

Amy waited for a moment or two. Then she stole a glance in his lordship's direction.

'Oh, Lord, just look at his expression! He must have murder on his mind... shall I tell Louise?'

'Wait until the interval,' Perdita hissed. 'I doubt if he will approach us in the middle of the recital, but I think we should warn Aunt Trixie.'

Very little escaped that lady's notice. 'Yes, I have seen the Earl,' she announced. 'It is impossible to mistake him. He is the image of his father, and sadly he wears the same unfortunate look. Don't allow it to worry you, my dears. His ill humour can have nothing to do with you.'

Minutes later the music stopped and the players retired for refreshments. To Perdita's relief, Miss Langrishe and her party were surrounded at once by a group of her friends. With any luck they would stay throughout the interval, making it impossible for Rushmore to approach them.

She was mistaken. The crowd parted as if by magic to allow his lordship through. His bow to Miss Langrishe was stiff in the extreme.

'My name is Rushmore, ma'am. I am sorry to break in upon your party in this way, but—'

'No need for formality, Adam. My dear boy, I knew you when you were in leading strings. What a pleasure to see you again! Come, sit by me and tell me all your news. I was sorry to hear about your father.'

His lordship was nonplussed. Whatever reception he had expected, it was most certainly not to be greeted by this affable smiling elderly lady as if he were barely out of the nursery.

'Thank you, ma'am!' He bowed again to acknowledge the expression of sympathy. 'You are very kind. However, if you will forgive me, I have come to find my ward. Miss Bedlington assured me that I should find her here.'

He bent his gaze upon Louise with such a stern expression that she quailed and shrank closer to Perdita.

'You have not met, I think,' Miss Langrishe said in an equable tone. 'Louise, my dear, you must make your curtsy to your guardian.'

Louise rose to her feet, curtsied, and resumed her seat.

'I think we must go before the music starts again,' Rushmore said sharply. 'I have much to say to you—'

'But not at this particular moment, I must hope.' Miss Langrishe was in full command of the situation. 'My dear boy, I can't allow you to steal my guest away in this hurly-burly manner. Louise does not know you. I cannot allow her to leave here with a man who is a stranger to her.'

'Must I remind you that she is my ward, madam?'

'You have already done so.' Miss Langrishe beckoned Colonel Waters to her side. 'Here is Rushmore's boy,' she said. 'Is he not the living image of his father?'

The Colonel agreed. Privately he considered that the likeness was astonishing, even down to the ugly look upon his lordship's face.

Miss Langrishe appeared to be unaware of it. She knew quite well that Rushmore was at a standstill. He could hardly drag Louise from the Assembly Rooms by main force.

'Do sit down, my dear,' she begged. 'You know both Amy and Perdita, I believe. They must be happy to see you here in Bath.'

Perdita's gasp of disbelief at this astonishing statement apparently went unnoticed by her aunt, but it brought a grim smile to his lordship's lips. He did not argue further as he took a seat beside her. She could not resist the opportunity to taunt him further.

'Are you fond of music, sir?' she asked. 'I hear that it is said to soothe the savage breast.'

'At this moment I feel savage,' he told her coldly. 'I might have known that I should find you somewhere in this plot.'

'Which plot is that, my lord?' Perdita gave him her sweetest smile. 'Does someone plan to assassinate you?'

'Don't raise your hopes, Miss Wentworth. You won't be rid of me so easily. I am speaking of this unfortunate attachment. You must have known that Louise is embroiled in an unsuitable affair.'

'You are well informed, sir, especially as you have not met Louise before this evening.

'I am well informed because she wrote to me herself. Good lord, she even thought that I'd be pleased to give my permission as it would take her off my hands!'

'Pray moderate your language, sir! You shock me!' Perdita raised her fan, revealing nothing of her face except a pair of sparkling eyes. She was enjoying herself hugely.

'I'll do more than shock you! I'd like to put you across my knee!'

'Great heavens, my lord...such violence! It can only recommend you to the female sex. We are said to prefer the company of undesirables, you know.'

'It's God help the man who takes you on,' he snarled.

'The feeling is mutual, sir.'

Rushmore was about to reply when the musicians returned. A request for silence was met with a hush from the audience and he was forced to listen with all the patience at his command until the concert ended.

He was on his feet at once, and he addressed Miss Langrishe direct.

'Ma'am, I believe you can have no knowledge of what has been taking place in secret, as far as my ward is concerned. I must insist—'

'You may insist to your heart's content, my dear Adam, but this is hardly the place. Louise and my nieces stay with me this evening. I would suggest that you return to Laura Place with us. Then you may explain yourself.'

Perdita hid a smile. Miss Langrishe had wrong-footed this angry young man. Now he was to be asked to account for his own behaviour, rather than criticising that of others. It did not improve his temper.

Her aunt swept into her salon and ordered tea. 'Wine for you, my lord?' she asked.

'No, I thank you, ma'am. Now, if I might explain the reason why I am here in Bath?'

'Yes, I think you should do that.' Miss Langrishe sat back in her chair, prepared to give him her full attention. She had known from the first that something was sadly wrong. Even Rushmore's son would not have appeared with a face like thunder, prepared to remove his ward without a by-your-leave. None of this showed in her expression.

'May I not speak to Louise in private?' Rushmore said stiffly.

'Oh, we are all friends here, my dear. We have no secrets from each other.'

'Ma'am, I think you will find that that may not be the truth of it. This morning I received a letter from Louise, in which she expressed her intention to be married.'

Miss Langrishe was unable to hide her astonishment. She turned to the shrinking girl. 'Is this true?' she asked.

'Ma'am, there was nothing underhand,' Louise whispered. 'I wrote to my guardian at once, asking his permission for me to wed. I thought he would be pleased.'

'Did you, indeed?' Rushmore was barely in control of his temper. 'How old are you, miss? Not yet seventeen, I fancy. What age is that to make a decision for life?' He stood over the girl until she cowered away from him.

'You are being unfair,' Perdita told him. 'Have you met the man to whom Louise is betrothed?'

'Louise is not betrothed,' he said darkly. 'Nor will she become so, for the next year or more.'

'You haven't answered my question.'

'With all respect to your aunt, Miss Wentworth, this matter need not concern you—'

'But it *does* concern us,' Perdita flashed back. 'Louise is a dear friend of ours.'

'You surprise me! Since the welfare of our friends must be of importance to us I had imagined that you would advise her of the folly of her action, rather than supporting her against me—'

'They have not done so,' Louise told him in a faint voice. She was on the verge of tears. 'Miss Langrishe and Perdita know nothing of this, and I told Amy only yesterday.' A sob escaped her lips.

'Perdita, I suggest that you and Amy take Louise to her room. The Earl and I will discuss this matter further...' Miss Langrishe waited until the door had closed behind the girls. Then she turned to Rushmore.

'Well, Adam, have you taken leave of your senses? This is no way to go on. You have frightened Louise half out of her wits. Take care or you may push her into an elopement.'

'I think not, ma'am.' His lordship's voice was cold. 'She will leave Bath with me tomorrow. From now on I don't intend to let her out of my sight.'

'That may be difficult for you. Where will you take her? To your London house to be locked in her room? It seems a somewhat Gothic course of action and it won't enhance her reputation, or your own, unless of course, you intend to wed her yourself.'

'What!' The Earl's roar of anger could be heard

throughout the house. 'Allow me to inform you, ma'am, that nothing could be further from my mind.'

'I'm glad to hear it. In any case, I doubt if she would take you. Now, do sit down, my dear, instead of behaving like a nincompoop. It may surprise you to hear that I am entirely of your opinion in this matter, but it is always a mistake to indulge in dagger-drawing with the young. Nothing is more likely to harden their opposition to your wishes, especially when a supposed grand passion is involved.'

Rushmore was strongly tempted to swear aloud, but he restrained himself from doing so. 'Grand passion, indeed! Louise is a schoolgirl, ma'am. I am at a loss to understand how she came to be allowed the freedom to become acquainted with this fellow. Miss Bedlington has much to answer for.'

'Have you thought of this from Louise's point of view?'

'I have not, Miss Langrishe.' Rushmore threw himself into a chair. 'An understanding of young girls is quite beyond me.'

Miss Langrishe reflected privately that this statement most probably included his lordship's understanding of women in general, but she did not say so.

'Louise must have been very lonely,' she said gently. 'Not even her schoolfriends were at hand to comfort her, and Miss Bedlington, though an excellent teacher, is not the warmest of creatures... I lay no blame on you, my dear boy. I know that your time is not your own, but can you wonder that Louise would be affected by an offer of affection?'

'I suppose not,' Rushmore admitted grudgingly. 'But what am I to do? Your nieces already regard me as an ogre, as I'm sure they have informed you. I can expect no help from them.'

Miss Langrishe regarded him thoughtfully. 'I think you may be mistaken in that belief. The girls are not as gullible as you might suppose. Naturally they will defend their friend, but it won't have escaped their notice that this young man, whoever he may be, has done Louise no service in attempting to attach her affections in such an underhand way.'

Rushmore said nothing, though clearly he was unconvinced.

'They will know, of course, that he should have sought a proper introduction to her, through her connections, and asked her guardian for permission to address her.'

'Well, at least we are agreed in that respect,' the Earl said heavily. 'Louise is an heiress, ma'am, and a tempting target for any gazetted fortune-hunter, especially as she is so young. I blame myself, you know. I promised her father that I would take good care of her.'

'And you will do so, Adam. You shall not think that you have let her down. Now, we must consider what is to be done. A fresh start is needed, I believe. Why not call upon us tomorrow when we may have a sensible discussion with Louise?'

'I still think it would be best to take her back to London—'

'Nonsense! Will you make a martyr of her? We must consider a more subtle approach. Let us speak to her about the young man. Then, at least, you will be in a position to make enquiries about him. And do try not to scowl at her, my dear. More flies were caught with honey than with a blunderbuss.'

She was rewarded with a reluctant smile.

'That's better!' she approved. 'Use your charm, my dear. Louise is an intelligent girl. If you reason with her sensibly, she will understand your concerns.'

His lordship looked at her and his gloomy expression lifted. On an impulse he kissed her hand. 'What a diplomat you are!' he said admiringly. 'You should be in government, ma'am.'

Miss Langrishe laughed at that. 'Not all of my views would be welcomed in political circles,' she said cheerfully. 'Where are you staying, Adam?'

'I am at the York House, ma'am.'

'For several days, I hope?' Her look was full of meaning.

He threw up his hands in surrender. 'It shall be as you wish. I promise not to drag my unwilling charge back to London tomorrow.'

'How sensible! Believe me, all will be well, if you allow a little time to straighten out this muddle.'

He left her then, but he had barely gained the street before Perdita returned to her aunt's side. She was clearly ill at ease.

'Was I wrong to speak out as I did?' she asked anxiously. 'The Earl seemed about to threaten to beat Louise…'

'His lordship had had a shock, my dear, as had we all.'

'I know, but he might have spoken more gently instead of flying into the boughs as usual.'

'It was understandable, my love. Even your father, tolerant though he is, would have found such behaviour unacceptable. Don't you agree?'

Perdita nodded. 'I know that it was wrong,' she admitted. 'But, Aunt, she felt so sad and lonely…'

Miss Langrishe patted her hand. 'Has she told you anything about this man? I have been wondering why he did not approach her guardian first.'

'He is a visitor to Bath, Aunt Trixie. He knew no one who might have provided him with an introduction to Louise. He spoke to her on impulse, I believe, when he found her weeping in the park. That was kind, you will agree.'

'It was, my dear, and might have been forgiven if matters had gone no further, but you will not tell me that he proposed on that occasion. There must have been clandestine meetings. Why did Louise agree to that?'

'She knew that Miss Bedlington would forbid her to see him.'

'In this instance, Miss Bedlington would have been right. Louise was in her care. How could she countenance a friendship with a stranger of whom she knew nothing?'

Perdita was silent for several moments. 'What does the Earl intend to do?' she asked at last. 'I suppose he will punish Louise by sending her to Yorkshire, or some such place.'

'Not at all,' her aunt said mildly. 'Naturally, his lordship wishes to have a sensible discussion with Louise. That would be wise, I think, don't you?'

Perdita grimaced. 'Do you think him capable of a sensible discussion, Aunt? For my part, I do not. He is too accustomed to issuing orders and having them obeyed. Doubtless he will storm and rave, or try to crush Louise with his unpleasant sarcasm.'

'Shall we wait and see what happens before we condemn him out of hand? And, my dear, do try to persuade Louise not to be a watering-pot. Few gentlemen can cope with tears, and when they are at a loss they become irritable. If Louise will exercise a little self-control…?'

'I don't expect it would make much difference if she were as calm as the Sphinx,' Perdita told her bitterly. 'The Earl regards Louise as a tiresome schoolgirl, which she is not. She is my own age, after all, and will make her come-out next year. Girls of seventeen are often wed at the end of their first Season.'

'And a great mistake it is, for the most part. Is it not wiser to gain a little experience of the world before making such a serious decision? You must have thought it so. I know you have had offers, my dear.'

Perdita smiled. 'I can lay claim to no great wisdom, Aunt. It's just that I was never tempted to accept, and Mother and Father would not force me.'

Miss Langrishe was satisfied. As she had long suspected, Perdita, although impulsive by nature, had great strength of character. If Rushmore could win her to his side, she would bring her influence to bear upon Louise.

With this in mind, she was at pains to leave Rushmore and Perdita alone together on the following day.

'Am I too early for Miss Langrishe?' his lordship asked as he was shown into the salon 'Perhaps I mistook the time.'

'My aunt will not be long, sir. She felt it best to visit Miss Bedlington with Amy and Louise to ask that the girls be allowed to extend their stay here.'

'An excellent idea,' he said stiffly. 'Your aunt, at least, will keep an eye upon my ward.'

Perdita was silent, ignoring him as he took a turn about the room. Finally he swung round to face her.

'You are very quiet, Miss Wentworth. Have you nothing to say to me? No comments upon my brutal manner, or my monstrous behaviour yesterday?'

'You frightened Louise,' she said defiantly. 'That is no way to persuade her to confide in you.'

To her astonishment he smiled at her, and that smile transformed his face.

'I lost my temper,' he admitted. 'But for the most part I was angry with myself. I felt that I had failed in my promise to Louise's father. I had not provided the care which she was entitled to expect.'

Perdita's eyes widened. Rushmore's explanation came very close to an apology, and she had not expected it.

'You could not have known what was happening,' she said carefully. 'But I hope that you can understand it.'

Rushmore sat down beside her. 'I can, but I am sorry that she felt the need to seek affection elsewhere. Believe me, I have her best interests at heart. I want to see her happy.'

'Then will you not tell her so, my lord? She is a gentle soul, and will not set her will against yours if it can be avoided.'

'That will be difficult,' he mused. 'She fancies herself in the throes of a great passion, I suppose. I have no experience of such matters. I can't think what is to be done.'

This was another surprise. It sounded like an appeal for help.

'Are you asking for my advice, my lord?' she asked in astonishment.

'I am, my dear.' His eyes were twinkling. 'Even ogres are not infallible. You think highly of your friend, but I do not know her in the least. Won't you help me to win her round to my way of thinking?'

Perdita hesitated. 'What have you in mind? You don't intend to spirit her away and lock her up, I hope?'

'On a diet of bread and water? No, that would be too Gothic, and it would serve no purpose. I'd like her to regard me as her friend. How best shall I persuade her?'

Perdita was in no doubt of his sincerity, but if she agreed to help him it would be a strange alliance. She would be in league with her enemy. Rushmore sensed her indecision.

'We have not been the best of friends, Miss Wentworth, but this is more important than personal antipathy. Louise's whole life may be at stake. Do you agree that we should put her future first?'

Perdita found it impossible to refuse. 'I agree!' She held out her hand and Rushmore took it in his own. Then he raised it to his lips.

'Thank you!' he said simply. 'I knew I could rely on you.'

Perdita blushed and drew her hand away as if she had been stung. There was something disturbing about the touch of that warm mouth against her own flesh. To cover her confusion she spoke sharply.

'There are certain conditions, sir.'

'And they are?'

'You will *not* browbeat Louise, my lord, nor shall you seek to harm her friend, whoever he may be.'

'I had not planned to have him knocked on the head, my dear. As yet I do not even know his name.'

'You agree to my conditions?'

'I do. Now, what is our next move?'

'Sir, I believe that you should speak to Louise, telling her of your wish to be her friend. She is an intelligent person, and will understand your concerns. She will know that you are quite within your rights to make enquiries about her admirer and to seek an interview with him. She cannot object to that.'

'I'd like to wring his neck!' Rushmore said with feeling. 'I wonder how he learned that she was heiress to a fortune?'

'You can't be sure of that,' Perdita scolded. 'Now you are jumping to conclusions.'

'Am I?' Rushmore was unconvinced. 'This has been a havey-cavey game—a chance meeting with a vulnerable girl, a whirlwind romance, with no attempt to contact those who have her interests at heart? No, Perdita, there is something smokey here.'

Perdita did not take her companion to task for using her given name. The force of his argument had confirmed her own suspicions. Now it was important to unmask this fellow, if he was indeed a fortune-hunter.

'It seems a little difficult to believe,' she whispered. 'Are there really men who prey on defenceless women?'

Rushmore took her hand again, holding it firmly in his own. 'For some it is a way of life,' he said. 'But I am determined that Louise shall not fall victim to such a creature.'

Perdita did not draw her hand away this time. It was oddly comforting to be in such complete accord with the complex creature who sat beside her. Had she misjudged him from the first? It would not be the first time she had been mistaken in her assessment of character.

Her mother's words came back to her. Elizabeth

advised always to judge by actions rather than words. Well, she would see if the Earl of Rushmore's actions matched his words.

She had not long to wait. A bustle in the hall announced the return of her aunt together with Amy and Louise. At the sight of her formidable guardian Louise shrank back, but he advanced towards her, holding out his hand.

'I hope I see you well,' he said kindly. Then he turned to Beatrice Langrishe. 'I'd like a private word with Louise,' he said. 'May I have your permission, ma'am?'

It was given at once, but it was a cowed Louise who was led into the study.

'Oh, Lord!' Amy pulled a face. 'Will he use his riding crop, do you suppose?'

'He will not,' Perdita said firmly. 'The Earl has promised to listen to Louise. He will not lose his temper. He has given me his word.'

Amy's mouth fell open. 'Given *you* his word? I thought you were at dagger-drawing with him.'

'We were thinking of Louise,' Perdita said with dignity. 'All other considerations must be set aside...for the moment.'

The private interview was short, and when Louise was returned to her friends she had lost the somewhat haunted look which had bedevilled her.

His lordship made no reference to the matter uppermost in his mind. Instead, he promised himself the pleasure of seeing the ladies at a ball in the Assembly Rooms on the following evening.

'Oh, are we to be invited too?' Amy was in transports of delight.

'Why not, my love?' Miss Langrishe smiled benignly upon her companions. 'It is high time that you and Louise were put in the way of things.' She turned to Rushmore. 'Such a mistake to throw these girls straight from the schoolroom into society. Don't you agree, my lord? And this, after all, is Bath…not quite so formal as the London Season.'

'Ma'am, I cannot disagree if I have the choice of three such charming partners.' Rushmore's bow was faultless.

Perdita caught his eye, and was strongly tempted to laugh.

'His lordship is an enthusiastic dancer,' she observed slyly. 'I doubt if he will ever lack for partners. He has a most persuasive way of leading a lady out.'

He gave her an appreciative grin. 'No hard feelings?' he asked in a low voice.

Perdita affected not to hear him. It was too soon to forgive him for her present situation. But for Rushmore, she would now be aboard her father's ship, sailing for Gibraltar and all the delights of a visit to the Mediterranean.

Yet honesty compelled her to admit that he was not the unfeeling creature she had thought him. His concern for Louise was genuine enough. This enforced visit to Bath might be a blessing in disguise. She was now in a position to help Louise out of what might prove to be a dangerous situation. With Rushmore as her ally all might yet be well.

She waited until Amy and Louise were deep in discussion with Miss Langrishe about the coming ball. Then she drew Rushmore aside on the pretext of consulting him about the purchase of a riding mare.

'Have you come to some agreement?' she asked quietly.

'Yes. Louise had given me the young man's name and his direction. I have promised to speak to him.'

'So you did not forbid the marriage outright?'

'No, Miss Wentworth, but let me assure you that it will not take place.'

Perdita did not argue. 'But you will make enquiries about him? That is only fair, I think.'

'Consider it done. Louise has admitted the necessity. I was at some pains to point out to her the difficulties she might face if she has been deceived in him. Her faith in this fellow is absolute, so she has no fear that I shall find anything untoward.'

'You don't share the belief, I know.'

'I don't, but I shall go on slowly. Love is blind, so they say. Proof of his perfidy must be overwhelming before she is convinced.'

'And you will let me know what you discover?'

'Of course. Are you not my ally? Now, smile at me as if I have made some splendid joke. Louise must not think that we are plotting against her.'

Perdita's low laugh sounded false to her own ears, but Amy looked up in astonishment.

It was not until later that day, when the two girls were alone, that she challenged her sister.

'What was his lordship saying to you?' she demanded. 'Suddenly you seem much in charity with him. Never say that you will take his side against Louise?'

'Of course not, but in some ways he is right. It may sound prosy, but you will agree that Mother and Father would not countenance such behaviour from either of us.'

'I know it.' Amy hung her head. 'But Louise is our friend. We must support her, even though we think that…well…the clandestine meetings were wrong.'

'It could be more serious than an offence against propriety,' Perdita told her. 'The Earl has pointed out to me that Louise is a considerable heiress. Suppose this man should be a fortune-hunter?'

Amy's eyes widened. 'I don't see how he could have known,' she objected. 'She does not mention it.'

'Rushmore says that there are certain men who make it their business to discover these things. They live by preying on wealthy women.'

'It can't be true,' Amy said decidedly. 'Matthew Verreker loves Louise for herself alone. He is so tender with her and he sends her such wonderful letters filled with poetry.'

'Letters too?' Perdita looked at her sister. 'How does she receive them? They cannot go to the Academy.'

'No!' Amy coloured a little. 'They have a hiding place. It is a hole in an old tree near the park. Oh, Dita, you won't tell his lordship?'

'No, since from now on everything must be above board. Rushmore is to arrange a meeting with Mr Verreker.'

Amy gasped. 'Oh, Lord! Does Rushmore intend to call him out?'

'Of course not, goose! But he would like to know more about this man. That is not unreasonable, is it?'

'He didn't sound reasonable yesterday,' Amy said darkly. 'I wonder what has changed his mind. Did you manage to persuade him?'

'He has been speaking to Aunt Trixie, I believe.'

Amy's face cleared. 'He did seem calmer today,' she admitted. 'I hope this new mood lasts until Matthew returns from London.'

'Mr Verreker is not in Bath at present?'

'No, he was called away at short notice yesterday…some private family business, so he told Louise.'

Perdita caught her sister's eye. 'It could not be that he had heard of the Earl's arrival in Bath?'

'There you go, believing the worst of him before you know the facts!' Amy was still unwilling to admit that Louise might have been the victim of a confidence trick. 'You sound exactly like the Earl, and I thought you hated him. What has he said to make you change your mind?'

'He told me that he wished to be Louise's friend, and I believe him.'

'Hmm! More likely that he has his eye on her fortune for himself. At his age he must be thinking of taking a wife.'

'Now who is jumping to conclusions?' Perdita felt a sudden spurt of anger. 'Amy, you must not let your affection for Louise lead you into folly. You won't be a party to arranging meetings, or collecting letters, will you?'

'No, I won't do that, but pray don't preach at me! You ain't a model of discretion yourself, you know.'

Perdita laughed at that. 'There's no need to remind me, Amy.' She took her sister's hand. 'We must not quarrel, you and I. Now tell me, are you not excited by the thought of attending your first ball?'

This delightful prospect raised Amy's spirits at once. The details of a possible toilette were discussed at length, though Miss Langrishe had insisted that both the younger girls were to wear simple white gowns.

On the following evening she looked at Perdita enviously, admiring her sister's overdress of pale yellow silk worn over a satin slip. It became the older girl's dark beauty to perfection, set off as it was by the yellow riband which confined her raven curls.

'No one will look at us,' she mourned. 'Louise and I are likely to spend the evening sitting with the chaperons.'

'Nonsense! Rushmore has promised you at least one dance, you know.'

Amy grimaced. 'He'll probably march up and down as if he's on parade.'

'Sourpuss! His lordship is an excellent dancer. Besides, there will be other young men, I promise you… Aunt has taken pains to make sure of it.'

In the event Miss Langrishe might have spared herself the effort. As her party entered the Assembly Rooms they were accosted by a familiar figure.

'Why, it's Thomas!' Amy's face was wreathed in smiles as she held out both her hands to her cousin. 'Oh, I am so glad to see you. Are the boys here too?'

'Large as life, and twice as ugly…' Grinning, Thomas motioned his brothers forward to greet the ladies.

Chapter Seven

Miss Langrishe welcomed her young relatives with open arms. 'With so many young people about me I shall be the envy of Bath,' she cried happily. 'Thomas, where are you staying? There is plenty of room for you in Laura Place.'

'Wouldn't dream of it, Aunt!' Thomas gave her a smacking kiss. 'You've trouble enough with the girls, I fancy. We are putting up at the York House. Can't fault it, I must say.'

Perdita pricked up her ears. The Earl of Rushmore was also a resident of the most exclusive, and expensive, hostelry in Bath. She drew her cousin to one side.

'What made you come to visit us?' she asked. 'I had not thought to see you here. Bath is hardly the most exciting place for a young man on furlough...'

'Promised your father we'd look in on you,' Thomas told her in a tone so casual that it aroused her suspicions at once.

'Then Aunt Trixie did not send for you?'

'Good Lord! Why would she do that?' Thomas did not disguise his look of relief and Perdita knew at once that she had asked the wrong question.

'I see. How fortunate that you should find us here on this particular evening. We might have been at the theatre.'

'Oh, no! Rushmore said—' Thomas clapped his hand to his mouth.

'Dammit, Perdita, must you trick a fellow in this way? You weren't supposed to know.'

'So it was the Earl who summoned you here?' Perdita's colour rose as her anger mounted. 'I wonder why he imagines that he has the right to do so? What was his excuse?'

'Now, coz, don't get upon your high ropes! Bless me, if you don't fly off before you give a fellow a chance to explain.'

'I'm listening,' said Perdita coldly. 'And your explanation had better be good.'

'Spitfire! Don't try your tricks on me! I ain't one of these mooncalves who swoons when you look at him. You'd best change your tune, or I shan't explain at all.'

Perdita gave him a conciliatory smile. 'I'm sorry!' she said meekly. 'But I do want to know.'

'Very well, then! Rushmore sent me a note. He thought that if we came to Bath you might cool down a bit.'

Perdita drew herself up to her full height. 'I can't think what he meant by that!' she answered.

'Come off it, Dita! You've been at odds with him ever since you met.'

'Not without reason!' Perdita told him bitterly.

'Well, that's just it, you ninny! It troubled him. Blest if you females don't take a fellow in dislike without a word of explanation. How was he to know that you'd been sent to Bath because of him?'

Perdita looked at Thomas in dismay. 'Oh, you did not tell him, did you? I would not give him that satisfaction.'

'It wasn't of much satisfaction to him. In fact, he looked...er...nonplussed. He had asked Aunt Elizabeth to overlook that scene at Almack's—'

'And you believed him? Well, he can be plausible, I suppose.' Perdita frowned. She was lost in thought for several moments. 'Thomas, do you understand him?' she asked directly. 'Why should it matter to him if I think well of him or not?'

'It don't!' her cousin told her bluntly. 'His ward is his concern, and you and Amy are her friends. He felt that you might set her against him.'

Perdita's colour rose. 'I hope I should not be so foolish, Thomas. On one point at least the Earl and I are in agreement. We wish her a happy future.'

'Yes, I can understand it! There is something about her, isn't there? Some quality? I can't think what it is, but it sets her apart from other girls.'

Perdita was startled. She had never seen Louise in quite that light, but there was a look in her cousin's eye which she could not mistake.

'Louise is a schoolgirl,' she told him slowly and deliberately. 'This is the first occasion on which she and Amy have been allowed to attend a ball. Dance with her if you will, but pray don't try to turn her head.'

'I doubt if I could. Look at those eyes! She looks as though she can see into a person's heart.' With a charming smile he invited Louise to dance.

'They make a handsome couple, don't they?'

Perdita spun round to find the Earl of Rushmore standing by her side. She nodded briefly, still annoyed by his lordship's temerity in summoning certain members of her family to Bath.

His eyes rested for a moment on her profile. 'Thomas, I take it, has been unable to hold his tongue? Well, ma'am, I expected it. Are you at odds with me once more?'

'Naturally, I am delighted to see my cousins.' Perdita gave him a steady look.

'Yes, I thought you would be. Do you care to dance, Miss Wentworth? On this occasion I'm sure that you won't turn your ankle.' His smile was intended to rob his words of all offence, but Perdita's colour rose.

'I have no wish to dance with you,' she told him coldly.

'A wise decision! It will be difficult for us to talk in such a crowd.' He looked at her with twinkling eyes. 'But perhaps you have no wish for conversation either?'

'We have nothing more to say to each other, my lord. I am sorry if you thought that I should set Louise against you. Unlike yourself, I don't propose to interfere in matters which are none of my concern.'

Rushmore grasped her firmly by the elbow and led her to a secluded alcove. 'Dear me! Was it not only yesterday that you assured me that your friendship for Louise made her welfare your concern?'

'I wasn't referring to that!'

'I know it, you prickly creature! Come now, let us be honest with each other. You hoped to keep the reason for your visit to Bath a secret from me, isn't that it?'

'I see no reason why it should interest you.'

'But it does, my dear, since I am to blame for it. It

was not intended, I assure you. Do you still regret the loss of your visit to Gibraltar?'

Perdita did not answer him for a time. She was never less than truthful, and now she was struggling with conflicting thoughts.

'I wanted to go,' she said at last. 'But now, I can't think it important. Tell me, sir, have you learned anything of this Matthew Verreker?'

Rushmore's face darkened. 'I'd hoped to meet him today, but the fellow is nowhere to be found.'

'He is gone to London, I believe. Louise told Amy that he'd been called away on family business.'

'How convenient! When did he leave, I wonder?'

Perdita gave him a demure look. 'He left on the day that you arrived, my lord.'

Rushmore caught her eye, and they both began to laugh.

'We are on the right track, I think. Give me a few days, Perdita. I have made *some* enquiries about this man of mystery. He's unknown at any of the hostelries in Bath, so he must be in private lodgings. He isn't a subscriber here at the Assembly Rooms, and neither the Master of Ceremonies nor such of the visitors I have spoken to know him by name.'

'Verreker is a visitor to Bath himself, so Louise told Amy. He has no connections here who might give him an introduction into Bath society.'

'Poor fellow! A worthy object of compassion to Louise, I must suppose.' He looked up as she approached, accompanied by Thomas.

Anxious to intervene in what he suspected might develop into an awkward confrontation, Thomas handed Louise to a seat beside her guardian. Then he turned to Perdita. 'You promised me a dance,' he said. 'I've come to claim it.'

As she reached out a hand to him, her companion rose to his feet. 'Miss Wentworth is promised to me,' he told the young man with a smile. He took the outstretched hand in his own, and tucked it beneath his arm.

Perdita was tempted to giggle at the look of astonishment on her cousin's face. Then, to her consternation, she heard the first notes of the waltz.

'What is it?' Rushmore sensed her hesitation. 'You *do* waltz, Miss Wentworth, don't you?'

She nodded, but it was with the greatest reluctance that she allowed him to take her in his arms. His hands were gloved, as were her own, but she could sense the pressure of the powerful arms about her waist as he swung her into the dance.

All her misgivings vanished as she surrendered to the movement and the music, and Rushmore smiled down at her.

'Aren't you glad that I persuaded you?' he whispered.

'You did not *persuade* me, sir. You brushed aside my offer from another partner, as usual, and dragged me on to the floor. If you go on like this I shall become a wallflower. No one will dare to approach me.'

'You? A wallflower?' He threw back his head and laughed. 'I dare not leave your side, Miss Wentworth. I shall not see you for the rest of the evening.'

She smiled, but she did not answer him. Then, as she looked about her, she realised that many of the other couples had stopped dancing and were grouped by the side of the floor, even though the music had continued.

'My lord,' she whispered, 'we are the only couple left. Pray let us sit down.'

'Are you tired?' he teased.

'No, but...we are making an exhibition of ourselves.'

'We are giving a demonstration, Perdita. It is all thanks to you. You are an excellent dancer.'

She coloured and shook her head, but she was too embarrassed to continue, and after another turn about the room, Rushmore led her to a seat beside her aunt.

'That gave us all such pleasure, my dears!' Miss Langrishe beamed upon them. 'What it is to have such grace and energy!'

'But not less than your own, I'm sure, ma'am.' Rushmore bowed to her. 'May I engage you for the next waltz?'

'Good gracious! A woman of my age? Go on with you, my boy... It is a kind thought, but—'

'Miss Langrishe, were you not the belle of the London Season? Your graceful dancing is still a legend. You cannot have forgotten it.'

'Well, no, but...it is so many years since.'

'But you have not lost your interest? Confess it, ma'am, you have given in to temptation. You may not have waltzed in public, but I suspect that you have learned in private.'

'Wicked creature! How did you guess? Have you been speaking to the Colonel?'

'No, Miss Langrishe, but once a dancer, always a dancer. Now, do I have your promise?'

His request was supported by the girls. 'Dear Aunt, we wish to see you enjoying the ball,' said Amy. 'Your toes are tapping when the music starts, and his lordship is an excellent partner, as Perdita will assure you.' She gave her sister a look which was filled with meaning.

Miss Langrishe needed no further persuasion, and when she and Rushmore took the floor the girls were startled into silence.

Like many large people, Miss Beatrice Langrishe was light upon her feet. Somehow her massive bulk was forgotten as she floated across the floor in perfect time with her partner.

Amy leaned towards her sister. 'Rushmore is making himself agreeable this evening,' she observed. 'He looks like the cat that has found the cream. Has he unmasked Verreker? That is his intention, surely?'

'He hasn't yet met Mr Verreker, as you know. You told me yourself that he is gone from Bath.'

'Well then, why is he so pleased with life this evening?'

'Must he have your permission to enjoy himself?' Perdita's tone was cooler than she had intended.

'Oh, hoity-toity! Here's a change! Are you defending him, Dita? I tell you what! You have spent too much time in his arms. First at Almack's, then when you blistered your feet, and now tonight. Take care, or I shall think that you have a *tendre* for him.'

Perdita glared at her. 'If this were not a public place I'd pull your hair, you little monster! The Earl is worried, though he does not show it. No one seems to know the name of Verreker. What has he told Louise about his family...his parents?'

'They were killed in a carriage accident.'

'And other relatives...aunts, uncles, brothers, sisters, cousins?'

'He has none.' Amy looked at her sister. 'I didn't mean to snip at you, but don't you see? I know that it sounds strange, but he and Louise have so much in common, being orphaned as they are… It is another bond between them.'

'But curious, Amy. How many people do we know who have not a relative in the world?'

'Not many,' Amy admitted cheerfully. 'Though some would be glad to have it so. I can think of a few myself.'

'So can I, and one of them is sitting beside me!'

'You don't mean it, Dita. Now confess it…you ain't quite so set against the Earl as you once were.'

'No, I'm not, but I cannot like his assumption that he may do exactly as he wishes.'

'Well, it takes one to know one,' Amy teased. 'How many times have I heard Mama accuse you of the same thing?'

'This is different,' Perdita said with dignity. 'I, at least, do not attempt to order other people's lives, but, well, he has convinced me that he wishes to protect Louise.'

'And he has chosen you for his ally?'

'You too, Amy. He knows that we are fond of her. Has she no idea when Mr Verreker will return?'

'I don't think so. I'll admit that it is a little odd that he should go away just now, leaving her to face the Earl alone.'

'It was the action of a coward.'

'Well, you know, he may have hoped that the news of her betrothal would be less surprising if she explained it to Rushmore herself.'

'Then he's either a fool or a scoundrel!' Perdita cried hotly. 'It would have been more honourable to seek out the Earl and ask permission before addressing himself to an innocent girl.'

'Keep your voice down, Dita! You may be mis-judging Mr Verreker. Louise is convinced that he will make himself known to his lordship as soon as he returns from London.' She grimaced. 'I wish that I may not be there. The Earl of Rushmore is not the man to cross, I fancy.' She looked up as her cousin Henry came to claim her for the next dance.

'It's a cotillion,' he said a little doubtfully, 'and with complicated steps, as I recall. Would you prefer to wait for a country dance?'

'Not in the least,' Amy told him grandly. 'I know the steps of the cotillion as well as you do. Of course, I should have preferred to waltz.'

'No chance!' her cousin grinned. 'I don't want Aunt Trixie on my case. You ain't out yet, so you can forget the waltz.'

'A stickler for the proprieties, are you, Henry?' Rushmore's deep voice broke into the conversation. 'I must say that I hadn't noticed it before this evening.'

Henry blushed and looked an appeal at Miss Lan-grishe. 'I don't mean to be a spoilsport,' he said in an injured tone. 'But—'

'You are quite right to consider your cousin's rep-utation,' she assured him. 'But you must not tease her.'

Henry's sunny smile returned. 'Old Amy don't mind, do you, coz? Blest if she don't look as fine as a fivepence tonight.' He held out his hand to lead her into the dance, and, mollified by the compliment, she took it.

As she passed him, Rushmore bent to whisper in her ear, 'What do you say to a turn about the anteroom later, Miss Amy? No one will see us there, and you may waltz to your heart's content.'

Amy was startled, but after a quick glance at her aunt to seek the lady's approval, she smiled and nodded.

'Amy will be your slave for life,' Perdita teased. Rushmore's whisper had been loud enough for all to hear. 'Is this your way of making her your ally too?'

Rushmore slipped into a seat beside her. 'I had no ulterior motives,' he said quietly. 'It is just that... well...she looked so disappointed.'

'It was good of you to wish to please her.' Perdita gave him a long look. He had surprised her once again. She was beginning to suspect that beneath his autocratic manner he had a kind heart.

'You are the person I wish most to please,' he remarked in a conversational tone. He had half-turned to look at her and saw at once that he had gone too far. Her colour rose and the easy camaraderie which he was beginning to enjoy so much vanished at once. He changed the subject swiftly.

'I need your advice,' he said. 'If Matthew Verreker is indeed a fortune-hunter, it may not be enough simply to discredit him. Where their affections are engaged I find that women are prepared to forgive even the most villainous behaviour. Do you agree?'

'I cannot help you, sir. I have not met a villain, and my own affections have never been engaged.' Perdita's tone was cool, and her manner was stiff, as she sought to hide her confusion. Why should Rushmore announce so calmly that he wished to please her? It had been said in a casual way, but she had sensed at once that it marked a change in their relationship. Amy's words came back to her. Was she indeed developing a *tendre* for this arrogant creature who sought her companionship at every opportunity? She pushed the thought aside as Rushmore continued.

'I have thought about this matter carefully. Louise was an easy target as she was so much alone. She has had so little pleasure. Perhaps if we were to show her a little more of life beyond the Academy?'

'My aunt agrees with you. That is why she allowed both Amy and Louise to attend the ball this evening.'

'It is a start,' he mused. 'Louise has made some friends and your cousins have been more than gallant. What I hope is that she will realise that her happiness does not depend on Verreker alone.'

'What do you have in mind?' Perdita asked cautiously.

'I wondered if we might undertake an expedition into the countryside. The weather is holding well, and a picnic is always popular.'

Perdita was undeceived. 'A picnic, sir? Is that something you enjoy?'

He gave her a rueful smile. 'No, it isn't! I don't care to share my food with insects. I had enough of that in the Peninsular War, but I am prepared to suffer in a good cause.'

'Very noble of you!' Perdita had recovered her composure. 'The girls would delight in it, and my cousins too.'

'And you?' Again there was something in the question beyond polite enquiry.

'Of course, but there may be difficulties. You must ask my aunt's approval. She may not care to allow it.'

Perdita was mistaken. Miss Langrishe was happy to agree to the expedition, although she begged to be excused from joining the party.

'Picnics are for the young,' she announced. 'I am

too advanced in years to think of dining other than at a table. Bless me, if I sat down upon the ground, I might never get up again!'

'You could sit in your carriage, Aunt.'

'No, no! You shall not persuade me, Perdita.' Miss Langrishe turned to Rushmore. 'You understand, my lord?'

The Earl bowed. 'I can't accept your reference to advancing years, ma'am,' he said gallantly. 'But as to the rest, I have already explained to Miss Wentworth that alfresco dining is vastly overrated and only to be undertaken upon special occasions.'

'And this is a special occasion, Adam?' The old lady's eyes rested briefly on his face.

'Yes, ma'am, I think so. If possible, I'd like to change the direction of Louise's thoughts...to show her that Verreker need not be the centre of her world. She needs young friends, and laughter, and other occupations for her mind.'

'You are right, of course. Have you seen Miss Bedlington? If Louise is to spend more time away from the Academy, you should speak to her.'

Rushmore's face darkened. 'I have not paid her a visit yet. I could not trust myself to speak in any civil way about her lack of supervision. Such neglect is monstrous! Bath has its share of villains, I imagine. I can't believe that she allowed my ward to wander unattended, at risk of insult or the attentions of some cutpurse, aside from striking up a friendship with a stranger.'

Perdita was alarmed. 'Oh, please!' she whispered as her aunt's attention was distracted by the arrival of the Colonel. 'I beg that you will say nothing of that friendship to Miss Bedlington. She does not know of it, and

it will only stir up trouble. She hates men and…
well…I think her a vicious creature.'

'Because she hates men? I thought you hated them
yourself!' Rushmore's eyes were twinkling as he
looked down at her, and she was relieved to see that
his angry expression had disappeared.

Perdita knew that he was teasing her, but she would
not be drawn. 'I can't imagine how you came by that
idea, my lord,' she said sedately. 'I have the highest
regard for my father and my uncles and my cousins.'

'That wasn't quite what I meant, Perdita. You told
me earlier that your affections had never been engaged
in any particular way. Why is that, I wonder?'

She was spared the need to reply to this impertinent
question by the arrival of Amy, who was bursting with
excitement. She addressed Rushmore direct.

'Sir, the next dance upon my card is a waltz, and
you did promise, if you recall…'

'So I did!' His lordship rose to his feet. 'Come, Miss
Amy, let us remove ourselves from the public gaze.'
He tucked her hand within his arm and led her into an
adjoining salon.

Thomas stared after them in astonishment. Then he
spoke to Perdita. 'Should Amy be wandering off like
that, alone with Rushmore? That ain't the refreshment
room, you know.'

'Don't make a cake of yourself!' Perdita replied
with some asperity. 'Amy longs to waltz, and she can't
do so in public. His lordship offered to give her a turn
about the salon.'

Thomas grinned at her. 'He's putting himself out
for you ladies tonight. I've never seen him quite as
affable. What have you done to him, Perdita?'

'This is merely an example of his good manners,'

she replied in a lofty tone. 'You might study them yourself.'

'Ouch! I'll hold my tongue in future.' Thomas turned to Miss Langrishe. 'Aunt, do you care for a glass of wine? I've promised to find a table for Louise and the rest of our party.'

'Well, do you go on, my boy. I expect that you are starving. It is a common complaint with the young men of my acquaintance. Your brothers will bring us along to join you.' Miss Langrishe eyed him fondly as he ushered Louise away.

'Such a dear creature, isn't he, Perdita? Will you think me a meddlesome match-maker if I say that Louise could do much worse?'

'Than Thomas, Aunt?' Perdita was startled. 'Why, he's just a boy.'

'He's five years older than you are yourself, my dear, and he is not a boy. Have you not noticed how he looks at her?'

'Calf-love!' Perdita announced scornfully. 'Oh, I know that he was with Wellington's army, but he has no thought of marriage. If you could but hear him on the subject!'

'Opinions can change…sometimes overnight. However, let us say no more of it. When do you plan to go upon this picnic?'

'Quite soon, I think. Rushmore believes that the weather will hold for the next day or two. You see no objection?'

'Oh, no, my love! Your cousin will take good care of you, and Rushmore will accompany his ward. The carriage is at your disposal, naturally, but I imagine you will prefer to ride?'

'Oh, yes, I've missed it so. We were out each day

in London, riding in Rotten Row. Shall we be able to hire good mounts in Bath?'

'Most certainly, Miss Wentworth.' Rushmore was standing by Perdita's side. 'Will you leave it to my discretion?'

'Only if you promise not to mount me upon a slug,' she said mischievously.

He laughed at that. 'I should not dare,' he replied as he offered Miss Langrishe his arm. 'Shall we join the others?'

Rather to Perdita's surprise, Thomas had managed to secure the best table in the refreshment room. Now he was awaiting their pleasure with the offer of small savouries, a selection of patties, ices, and beverages ranging from tea and coffee to lemonade, orgeat, and wine.

Miss Langrishe accepted only a glass of wine. 'Lord preserve us from the efforts of the cook here,' she whispered to Perdita. 'All his offerings taste like sawdust.'

Perdita smiled. 'You have high standards, Aunt. Will you not try a pastry boat? The filling is delicious.'

Her aunt shuddered. 'I have too much regard for my digestion, Perdita. Your cousins must be blessed with stomachs of cast-iron. Look at their plates, my dear.'

Perdita giggled. 'Perhaps it's time that we discussed the picnic…otherwise, between the three of them, they are likely to clear the tables.' She turned to Rushmore. 'Sir, I wonder if you will explain what we have in mind.'

The Earl kept his suggestions brief, but they were received with undisguised pleasure. Only Louise looked a little hesitant.

'What is it, my dear?' Miss Langrishe was all concern.

'It is just that...well...I am not the most experienced rider in the world,' Louise confessed. 'I could not manage a spirited mount.'

'But there is not the least need for you to do so,' Thomas assured her quickly. 'We shall choose a steady mare for you and you may ride at your own pace. Henry and I will be beside you in case you feel a little nervous.'

He could not have made his feelings more obvious if he had shouted them aloud. Perdita frowned at him, but then she caught Rushmore's eye. Noticing his bland expression she was strongly tempted to give him a sharp set-down. He shook his head at her.

'Never interfere with the blossoming of young love,' he whispered sententiously. 'It is a fragile thing.'

Perdita felt a little spurt of anger. 'I fancy this is all a game to you,' she said furiously.

'No, Perdita, you are quite mistaken. This is not a game to me. I have my objectives, certainly, but I don't propose to tell you of them here and now.'

'More mysteries?' she said scornfully. 'What an exciting life you lead, my lord!'

'I hope to make it even more exciting in the future, my dear. However, at the moment we are discussing our expedition to the countryside. To date, I am required to find three horses for you ladies, one of which, I am warned, must not be a slug.'

'Make that two!' Perdita told him crisply. 'Amy will not thank you for finding her some ancient nag incapable of breaking into a trot.'

'It may surprise you to hear that I had not thought

of doing so.' Rushmore refilled his glass in a graceful toast to her. 'What an astonishing family you are! I had thought your sister merely a jolly schoolgirl.'

'And now?'

'Now I find that she has a head upon her shoulders. It is a refreshing change.'

'Pray don't attempt to patronise her, sir.' Perdita was furious.

'I had no intention of doing so. It was meant as a compliment. You are both a credit to your parents, Perdita, as I told your mother.'

'She did not say so,' Perdita answered doubtfully.

'No, she was cross with you at the time.'

'And you were not?' she challenged.

'No, I had a curious mixture of emotions.'

'Of which amusement was uppermost, I must suppose?'

'No, it was not. I was surprised, I will admit. I had expected to encounter yet another simpering miss. You disabused me of that idea.'

'I...I have a hasty temper, sir, and your remarks—'

'Were unforgivable, I agree. You were right to give me a set-down. I deserved it.' Rushmore smiled down at her. 'We began at odds with each other, my dear. Since then I have been trying to recover my character in your eyes.'

'My opinions can be of no great interest to you, my lord.' Perdita felt once again that they were reaching dangerous ground. She rose and gave her hand to Crispin, the youngest of her cousins, overriding his objection that he was the worst dancer in the world.

'Then you must learn,' she assured him. 'You won't improve by standing about like a statue. It takes practice, that is all.'

'A strong-minded lady!' Rushmore observed as the young couple walked away. 'With that face one might expect her to trade upon her looks alone, but she does not.'

'She is very dear to me,' Miss Langrishe replied quietly. 'It is Perdita's passion for justice which gets her into scrapes. Appeal to that and you will always have her by your side. Like her father, I cannot see it as a fault.'

'They are a delightful family, are they not, ma'am?'

'They have great charm. Partly it is their openness and their interest in other people. One can always be sure that the girls will tell the truth, however painful it may be for them.'

'I don't doubt it.' Rushmore's eyes had never left Perdita as she and Crispin circled the floor. 'You will think me foolish, Miss Langrishe, but I would describe her as "lion-hearted".'

'I don't think you foolish, Adam. I won't insult your intelligence by pretending that I have not understood you, but are you quite sure?'

'I was never more certain of anything in my life. I love Perdita. I think I've done so from the moment I set eyes on her. I want to ask her to be my wife, but there may be obstacles in the way.'

'Such as?'

'The gap in age…her parents may not like it. Unlike some others, they are sure to consider her happiness before all else.'

'As you will do, if you love her, but this is non-sense, my dear. There cannot be ten years between you. She would not be marrying a greybeard.' Miss Langrishe studied his face. 'Is Perdita aware of your feelings for her?'

'No, ma'am. Unlike Mr Verreker, I shall not make her an offer without her father's permission.'

'I expected nothing less of you, but you will have a lengthy wait, I fear, before Perdita's parents return to this country.'

'It is no matter, ma'am.' Rushmore's smile transformed his face. 'It will give me time to plan my campaign.' He gave his companion a rueful look. 'What do you suppose would be her answer if I were in a position to offer for her now?'

'She would think you had run mad,' Miss Langrishe told him bluntly. 'Go slowly, Adam! Perdita's pride will be offended if she believes that you are making game of her. First persuade her to be your friend before asking more of her. Her love may come unbidden.'

Rushmore took her hand and raised it to his lips. 'I must hope that she will be as good a friend as you are, Miss Langrishe. At least you do not frown upon my hopes.'

'Of course not! You will make a vastly entertaining couple, sir, though I have no doubt that battle will be joined at regular intervals. You have my blessing, but I warn you. Perdita must not be hurt. I make as strong an enemy as a friend, you know.' Her look was filled with meaning.

He laughed at that. 'Another strong-minded lady? I don't doubt that either.' Then he grew serious. 'You need have no fears on that account. I would defend Perdita with my life.'

Chapter Eight

As Rushmore had predicted, the weather continued to hold fair and two days later the party assembled at Laura Place for their expedition.

Perdita inspected her mount with unaffected pleasure. As he had promised, the Earl had chosen the best of what the local livery stable had to offer, both for herself and for Amy. Blaze was a mettlesome chestnut and his half-brother slightly darker in colour except that he lacked the distinctive white flash which had given Blaze his name.

'Well, Miss Wentworth, will they do?' The Earl was smiling down at her.

'We could not wish for better,' she announced warmly. 'May I take Blaze? He seems so friendly.' For an instant she rested her cheek against the horse's massive head, and he made no move to pull away. 'Amy, shall you be happy with his brother?'

'Will I not!' Amy was already in the saddle. 'Is this not the best scheme in the world? How I've missed our rides in London.' She bent to pat her horse's neck. 'Lancer is so fresh…he's longing for a gallop.'

'But not through the town, I beg of you, Miss

Amy!' Rushmore's smile robbed his words of all offence. 'Let us take it slowly until we reach the open
country.'

Amy laughed. 'It shall be as you say, my lord. Our
cavalcade will proceed with all decorum.' She glanced
behind her. 'Lord, what a crowd we are! Do we need
quite so many grooms?'

The Earl regarded her gravely. 'Miss Langrishe's
chef is on his mettle,' he announced. 'Though he dis-
approves in general of eating out of doors he intends
to prove the haute cuisine is not beyond his powers
even there...'

Amy giggled. 'So we have a full staff for our alfresco picnic? I wonder if he has sent along the family
silver?'

'I should not be the least surprised. I suggested that
the White Hart could well provide sufficient for our
needs in the way of food and drink, but I was turned
down out of hand.'

'A new experience for you, my lord?' Perdita observed mischievously.

'On the contrary, Miss Wentworth. It has happened
all too frequently in recent weeks.' He was laughing
down at her and she blushed, turning away quickly
before he could offer to help her to mount, and accepting the assistance of one of the grooms.

Amy led the way, accompanied by Henry. She knew
Bath well, and took the road to the north-west, out of
the town. The gradient was steep, but they rode at a
leisurely pace until they reached the heights above.
There Amy stopped and threw out her arm in an extravagant gesture.

'I love this place,' she cried. 'Is it not a perfect
jewel, set in the bowl of the hills? It was so clever of

the Romans to discover the warm springs. Did you know that they called it Aqua Sulis?'

Her enthusiasm brought a smile from the rest of the party, though Henry could not resist the opportunity to tease her. He grimaced.

'Are we to have a history lesson?' he cried. 'Lord, Amy, I hope you ain't got your heart set on going to see the ruins.'

She gave him a disarming grin. 'Not today, you Philistine! Come on, I'll race you to that far copse of trees!'

Henry needed no second challenge and they set off at a speed which made Louise turn pale. With Thomas on one side of her and Crispin on the other she was minding instructions from the two young men as to how best to control her horse. From that height it seemed a long way to the ground. She longed to close her eyes to shut out the distance she might fall, but determination won the day and her fears soon lessened as the mare walked on at a steady gait.

'Well done, Miss Bryant! You are a natural, I believe.' Thomas voiced his encouragement.

Louise managed a rueful smile. 'You flatter me, Mr. Wentworth. I fear I am a nervous rider. I had a bad fall as a child and would not try again. I am not so brave, you see.'

'I don't agree!' Thomas said stoutly. 'You didn't refuse to join our party, though you had every reason for doing so. It takes courage to do the thing you fear.'

'I'm told it is the only way to conquer those fears,' she said quietly. 'I'm glad I came. It is so pleasant to be out of the town and in the fresh air, enjoying this lovely countryside.'

'And also the company of your friends, I hope?'

She coloured a little. 'Of course! I do not need to tell you that. Amy and Perdita have been so kind to me, and I cannot speak too highly of Miss Langrishe.'

'I'm glad of it,' Thomas said simply. He caught his brother's eye and saw that Crispin was longing to join his cousins in their gallop. 'Miss Bryant, do you feel confident enough to ride with me alone if Crispin leaves us?'

'Oh, yes!' Her warm look caused his heart to skip a beat. 'I feel quite safe with you.'

Crispin kept a commendably straight face, though he winked slyly at his brother and ignored the answering frown. A jerk of Thomas's head sent him off at a gallop to the distant wood to join Amy and Henry.

'We are losing our party one by one,' Rushmore observed. 'Do you long to try out Blaze, Miss Wentworth?' He and Perdita were bringing up the rear of the party. 'I have sent the grooms ahead to our destination, but at this pace it will take some time for us to reach them. Please don't feel that you must stay behind to keep me company.'

Perdita gave him a suspicious look. Was he teasing her? 'I don't!' she announced in withering tones. 'I am thinking of Louise. She must not be made to feel that she is the only female who cannot ride her horse at speed.'

'Very commendable, my dear!' Rushmore's eyes were twinkling. 'May I hope that your charitable intentions will extend to me today?'

'Certainly, my lord! I should not dream of urging you to venture more than a trot. The consequences of a fall must be uppermost in your mind!' She was baiting him deliberately. The Earl was a noted horseman, as she well knew.

'True! It would be disastrous, especially in view of my advancing years. I will try to keep my seat, but there are other ways of suffering a heavy fall, Miss Wentworth. I fear that your advice has come too late.'

Again Perdita was aware of some hidden meaning behind his words, but she refused to acknowledge it. Was Rushmore attempting to flirt with her? She would have none of it.

She changed the subject hastily. 'Has Mr Verreker returned to Bath?' she asked. 'I had hoped that he might have been to see you.'

'I have heard nothing yet. Louise cannot give me his direction. She does not know it. I have been wondering how she and this creature keep in touch, if she cannot send to his lodgings.' Rushmore frowned. 'Surely she cannot be receiving letters at the Academy? Miss Bedlington would know of it.' He glanced at Perdita's face and was suddenly enlightened. 'Won't you trust me?' he asked gently. 'I believe I have the right to know.'

Perdita flushed with embarrassment. 'Oh, it's all such nonsense, sir! It sounds like the plot of some Gothic novel...'

'Well?'

'Well, I'm afraid that they leave letters for each other within a hole in some tree-trunk in the park.' Perdita looked away, expecting an explosion of rage. Instead, she heard a shout of laughter.

'Oh, no! And she takes this mountebank seriously? That is the outside of enough! Gothic indeed! How right you are to think it nonsensical!'

'I expect she felt that she had no choice,' Perdita told him quietly.

'There is always a choice, Perdita.' Rushmore's face

grew serious. 'She might have insisted that Verreker spoke to me before allowing matters to go so far. This underhand way of going on merely confirms my opinion of him.'

'But you don't know what pressures have been brought to bear on her. He sounds a plausible rogue. Doubtless he convinced her by an appeal to her affections.'

'So you are coming round to my way of thinking?'

'Yes, my lord. I cannot think it right to behave as he has done. If he has used Louise's love for him to persuade her into folly, it is a shameful thing.'

'I doubt if he knows the meaning of the word, my dear.' He was silent for a time, and then Perdita broke into his thoughts.

'Is there nothing we can do?' she asked.

'We can wait. If Verreker is the type of man I think him, his return will not be long delayed. His absence might cause Louise to think more carefully, or to seek the advice of her friends. If Verreker is to win his heiress he must not lose influence over her. He may also have another consideration in mind.'

'And that is…?'

'These charming rogues spend most of their time in dun territory. I should not be surprised to learn that he is penniless and deep in debt. His need for a rich wife may be of the utmost urgency.'

Perdita considered his words. 'Then, sir, why not ask Louise to leave a note for him? She could explain that you have agreed to see him, and it might… er…flush him out.'

'An excellent idea! My worry has been that he would persuade her into further folly, such as an elopement.'

'Oh, no!' Perdita stared at him in horror. 'That would ruin her in the eyes of all her friends. She would not be received...'

'It could happen, especially if he believes that I shall oppose his suit. You know her better now, Perdita. Tell me, would she agree to such a course of action?'

'Oh, no!' Perdita said decidedly. 'Louise is a gentle soul, but she has a stubborn streak, and she does know right from wrong. She is already a little ashamed of what has happened...not of falling in love, of course...but of not informing you about Verreker from the first. I think she was overtaken by events. Everything happened so fast.'

'A whirlwind romance, in fact?' The Earl's tone was dry. 'I am not surprised. Speed is of the essence with these fortune-hunters. They can't afford anyone the time for close scrutiny of their lives.'

'We may still be wrong about him,' Perdita said cautiously.

'I don't believe that, and nor do you, I think?'

'No!' she admitted. 'The more I hear, the more convinced I am that you are right.'

She was rewarded with a brilliant smile. 'Am I to believe my ears?' he teased. 'The redoubtable Miss Wentworth offering an olive branch?'

'I hope I am not so foolish to disagree with you for the sake of disagreement, sir. In this case I believe that you are right.' Without waiting for his reply, she spurred her horse ahead to ride alongside Louise.

They were almost at their destination, and in the distance they could see the well-known vantage point which had been chosen as their picnic site. The snowy cloths were already laid upon the ground, with rugs beside them. As they watched, the grooms began to unpack the hampers.

'No tables or chairs?' Amy exclaimed. 'I confess, I feel deprived. All that is offered is food and wine, and none too much of that.'

These facetious remarks were treated with the contempt which they deserved. The grooms withdrew to a respectful distance, leaving the rest of the party to enjoy their meal.

As a picnic it went far towards restoring the status of alfresco dining. Guided by Miss Langrishe, her chef had taken the comfort of the assembled party much to heart. Devilled legs of chicken were surrounded by paper collars to avoid the danger of greasy fingers. Tiny pastry cases held an assortment of delicious fillings. Paper-thin slices of fine York ham were rolled around asparagus spears and stout containers held salads of every kind.

'May I?' Rushmore advanced towards Perdita, bearing a bottle of the finest Burgundy.

'Take care, my lord! On the return journey I have no wish to fall from my horse.' Perdita smiled at him as she held out her glass.

'Fall? Not you!' Rushmore served the rest of the company and then he returned to stretch out on the grass beside her with a sigh of satisfaction.

'Well, sir, do you still tell me that you have no time for picnics?' Perdita said in a rallying tone.

'Allow me to assure you, ma'am, that this is not in the least like a bivouac in the Peninsula.'

'Tell me about Spain,' she said suddenly. 'Was it very dreadful?'

'It is always hard to lose one's friends,' he told her slowly. 'You will have heard of the famous battles—

butchery for the most part…but there were other trials for our Commander. His allies let him down… promised supplies of both materials and men did not arrive…' Rushmore lapsed into silence. When he spoke again it was with admiration in his voice. 'We were fortunate in the Duke. He is a consummate diplomat.'

'Amy would love to hear you say so,' Perdita told him. 'He can not have a more fervent admirer.'

'There are those who would disagree with you,' he told her with a smile. Then he looked about him. 'Dear me!' he said. 'We are deserted once again. It must be our venture into politics, Miss Wentworth. The subject is inclined to cause the eyes of most young people to glaze. Where are they going, do you suppose?' His eyes rested briefly on the departing figures in the distance.

'I think they intend to climb to the top of yonder hill. Do you care to join them, sir?'

'Not in the least, my dear. I can imagine nothing more comfortable than to be exactly where I am at this particular moment.'

Perdita blushed. He had made his meaning all too clear. She stole a glance at his face and froze. His expression had changed completely.

'What is it?' she asked.

When he spoke his words seemed to come with difficulty.

'Stay where you are!' he ordered in a low voice. 'Don't move a muscle!'

Perdita gazed at him in astonishment. 'What on earth…?' she began. Then her eyes followed the direction of his gaze and the words died in her throat. An adder was sliding through the heathland within inches of her foot. There was no mistaking the distinctive pattern on its skin. Sheer terror held her rooted to the spot. Her heart was pounding in her breast and her mouth was dry.

Then Rushmore's hand closed about his riding crop. He struck just once and killed the snake outright.

'I…I…' Perdita swayed. Then she found herself in Rushmore's arms, clutching his coat and shaking uncontrollably.

'There!' he soothed as he stroked her hair. 'You are quite unharmed, my dear.'

Perdita found that she was babbling. 'I thought it was going to strike! I was never so frightened in my life. Oh, let us go away from here…there may be more of the creatures in the undergrowth!' For the moment it had escaped her notice that she was gathered to his lordship's brawny chest, and in spite of his reassurances he had shown no disposition to release her.

Instead he shook her gently. 'The snake would not have killed you,' he observed mildly. 'You are a healthy young woman and well able to survive a bite. Besides, for all we know, it could have been a grass snake.'

'It was not, and well you know it, sir. I can recognise an adder when I see one, and they are venomous.'

She heard a chuckle. 'You are well informed, Perdita. Now where, I wonder, have you seen such a reptile before? Are they to be found at Almack's?'

'No!' she retorted sharply as she began to recover her composure. 'The only snakes at Almack's walk about on their own two feet.' She managed a wavering smile. 'If you must know it, I have seen an adder at the zoo.' She shuddered. 'I had to turn away. The mere sight of the creature reduced me to a jelly. It was so...so silent and so slithering.'

'It hadn't any option but to crawl, my dear.' Rushmore rested his head against her hair. 'Adders have no legs. Now tell me, how many people do you know who have died of snakebite?' Purposefully, he kept his tone light, but in truth he was keeping his own emotions on a tight rein.

He hadn't lied to Perdita. It was unlikely that an adder bite would have killed her, but certainly it would have made her very ill. He dared not think of those few heart-stopping moments when she had been in serious danger. He could only be thankful that she had obeyed his order to keep still. That had taken courage of a high order. If she had screamed and run towards him or fainted upon the spot the reptile, feeling itself threatened, must certainly have struck. His blood ran cold at the thought of it and his arms tightened about her.

Perdita made no attempt to release herself for a moment or two. She was still trembling, and it was a comfort to be held so closely to his lordship's breast. No harm could come to her within that strong embrace. Then distant voices recalled her to the impropriety of her situation. She looked up to see the rest of the party returning from the summit of the hill, and Amy, in particular, looked dumbfounded to find her sister in Rushmore's arms once more.

Perdita struggled to free herself, and began to offer a halting explanation when the Earl forestalled her. He gave a brief account of the incident in the most casual of tones, sending the three young men in search of the snake, which he had tossed into a nearby patch of scrub. They could not wait to see it.

'Oh, Mr Wentworth, pray take care!' Louise begged faintly. 'The creature may not be dead.'

'No doubt about it,' Thomas cried in triumph. He found a stick and lifted the lifeless snake on to the path. 'I ain't seen one so close before. I didn't know they were so small. Look at the markings! The thing is beautiful in its own way.'

'You are right!' Amy had joined him and was regarding the snake with interest. 'I wonder if there are any more around this place?''

This artless question was enough to bring a low cry from Louise, who had grown pale. Even Perdita glanced about her nervously. It was enough to bring a sharp remark from Rushmore.

'Thomas, you are frightening the ladies,' he reproved. With a lifted arm he signalled to the grooms. 'Let us mount up and be on our way. The men will follow us, but I'll send Dent ahead to the nearest inn to bespeak a private parlour.'

'Oh, do we need…?' Thomas caught his lordship's eye and lapsed into silence. It had not occurred to him that the female members of the party might wish to attend to their toilettes and to use certain other facilities which only an inn might offer.

Rushmore's thoughtfulness was not lost upon Perdita. What a spectacle she must present, she thought ruefully. The fashionable shako which matched her dark-green riding habit was still lying upon the ground. She had removed it before the picnic. Fashionable it might be, but the day was over-warm to be wearing a hat for hours.

Now she regretted removing it. Her hair had become disarranged in the Earl's embrace, and her clothing was sadly crushed. She looked across at him and saw that he had read her mind.

'I am in like case,' he whispered. 'My lapels have suffered...'

Perdita flushed with mortification as she examined the ruined coat. In her terror she had clung to the Earl with such force that she had almost destroyed the loving efforts of his fashionable tailor.

'Don't worry!' he chuckled. 'I have another coat, and consider that I lost this one in a good cause.'

'You are too kind!'' she said stiffly. The warmth in his voice was raising eyebrows, and Amy, in particular, was giving her a look that was full of meaning. Perdita ignored it, but when she was in the saddle again she took care to remove herself as far as possible from Rushmore's side, leaving him to ride with Thomas and Louise.

'Come on, Dita, you ain't given your mount his head today!' Henry and Crispin were ready to offer her a challenge, but she shook her head. 'Amy will go with you,' she said.

'No, I won't! Off you go!' Amy waved her cousins on ahead. Then she turned to her sister. 'Did you arrange that encounter with the snake on purpose?' she demanded mischievously.

'Of course not!' Perdita did not pretend to misunderstand her meaning. 'I...I did not mean to... er...find myself in his lordship's arms, but I was frightened. You would have felt the same yourself.'

'I doubt if I'd have clung to him as if my very life depended on it,' Amy replied drily. 'He'd killed the adder by then. There was no further danger... I can only think that you enjoyed it. After all, you must by now be getting accustomed to his embrace.'

'Now you are being stupid!' Perdita did not trouble to hide her annoyance, which was all the sharper because it was dangerously close to the truth.

'Am I? You have no *tendre* for him, then?'

'Amy, you know my feelings about the Earl. We are allies for the moment, but only to help Louise. Beyond that we do not have a single thing in common.'

'I doubt if his lordship would agree with you. Are you blind, Perdita? Did you not see his face when you were in his arms? When we came up to you I thought he must have made you an offer upon the spot!'

'That proves how little you know about him,' Perdita said sharply. 'He thought me a fool to be so frightened, and he laughed about it.'

'It did not prevent him taking you in his arms... unless, of course, you hurled yourself at him?'

'I don't know why I listen to you, Amy. I had forgotten that you are just a silly schoolgirl with a vivid imagination.' Perdita spurred her mount into a fast trot. Then she allowed him to lengthen his stride until she was galloping fast towards her cousins in the distance.

Amy was about to follow when she realised that Rushmore had come up beside her. His eyes were fixed upon Perdita's disappearing figure, and he was chuckling.

'Well, Amy, what have you said to send her off riding like the very Devil?' he asked.

'Oh, did you not overhear our conversation, sir? How did you know that she was cross?'

'Intuition, my dear, and a certain familiarity with the set of her head when she finds herself in a serious disagreement.'

'You are growing to know my sister well, my lord.' Amy smiled at him, but she did not answer his question.

'I hope so, Amy.' Rushmore gave his companion a steady look, and she could not mistake his meaning.

Greatly daring, she ventured a little further. 'You think highly of her, sir, I believe.'

A smile touched the corners of his mouth. 'Is it so obvious? I had thought to have kept my feelings hidden for the time being. It is too soon…and I have no wish to drive Perdita away.'

'She has not noticed, I assure you.' Amy grinned at him. 'Whenever I broach the subject, she flies into alt.'

'I see. She feels that you are giving rein to your imagination?'

'That's it!' Amy told him candidly. 'But I see more than she does. No one takes much notice of a schoolgirl.'

'A formidable schoolgirl, if I may say so, Miss Amy. Have you nothing more to tell me?'

'Well, yes, I have, my lord. Have you noticed that we are being followed?'

'The gentleman silhouetted against the skyline? Yes, I spotted him some time ago.'

'And do you recognise him?'

'No, but I can make a guess that Mr Verreker has returned to Bath.'

'Then why does not he come up to us and make himself known to you?'

'That is a mystery we have yet to solve. Perhaps he fancies himself invisible. He cannot be a military man. He would make a perfect target for a sniper, out in the open and without cover.'

'Are you tempted?' she asked slyly.

'Strongly tempted, you minx! Unfortunately, I am unarmed. Ah, I see that we are coming to the inn. I wonder if the gentleman will join us?'

'I thought we were to have a private parlour?'

'That's true. It need not stop him sending up his name.'

The mysterious stranger did not satisfy their curiosity, but later they saw him in the stable-yard chatting to the ostlers. A glance at Louise told Amy all she needed to know. Her friend went red and white by turns. She seemed about to stop as she passed the man, but he turned aside and walked into the inn without a sign of recognition.

Amy eyed him closely. Then she nudged Perdita. 'That is Matthew Verreker, I'm sure of it,' she whispered. 'If you doubt me, look at Louise.'

Their friend was having difficulty in controlling her emotions. The tears welled up as she followed Matthew with a despairing glance.

Amy seized her hand. 'That's Matthew, isn't it?' she said without hesitation. 'Louise, you can't go on like this. He *must* speak to your guardian.'

'Of course...I know it...and he will do so...but this is neither the time nor the place. I know that well enough.'

Perdita made her way to Rushmore's side. She was having the utmost difficulty in hiding her disgust. 'When will he come into the open, my lord? To put Louise in this position is the outside of enough.'

'We shall not have long to wait, I think,' he told her quietly. 'Louise is a gentle soul, but even she is beginning to see that matters have gone far enough. She must get in touch with Verreker and insist upon his meeting me.'

'I shall tell her so without delay.' Perdita was incensed. It was one thing to offer to help Louise, but another to support her in what appeared to be blind folly.

Whatever was said, it served to stiffen Louise's resolve. She was quieter than ever as the party returned to Bath.

On the following evening a message was brought up to Rushmore's apartments at the York House.

'A gentleman, you say?' Rushmore paused in the act of tying his stock.

'Well, sir, I do not know him, but he claims to have business with you.'

Rushmore smiled. Trust a servant to place his unexpected visitor at his true place in society. 'You had best send him up,' he said as he put the final touches to the arrangement of his neckcloth. Then he allowed his valet to help him into his coat, dismissing the man with the assurance that he must not wait up. His lordship might be late to retire that evening.

Now he eyed his visitor with interest. At the inn on the previous day a single glance had told him much of what he needed to know. Clearly, Matthew Verreker's looks were his stock-in-trade. Tall and fair, his features were cast in a classic mode. Dark blue eyes showed to advantage against his tanned skin, as did his perfect teeth, glimpsed when the generous mouth curved into a smile.

He was smiling now, as he held out a hand to Rushmore.

His lordship's eyesight seemed to be failing. For some reason, he appeared not to see the proffered hand.

'I beg you will sit down, Mr Verreker,' he said with the utmost courtesy. 'What may I do for you?'

'You may grant me my heart's desire!' the gentleman cried in ringing tones. 'My life is in your hands, my lord.'

'Quite a responsibility!' the Earl observed mildly. 'Tell me…upon what does your survival depend?'

Verreker gave him a wounded look. 'Pray, sir, do not torture me. Louise…Miss Bryant…must have told you of our strong attachment. She promised that she would do so.'

'She kept her word. And now…?'

Verreker was nonplussed. He had been dreading this interview with Louise's guardian, but his lordship's manner was unexpected. He knew of Rushmore's reputation. He had made it his business to find out, and had expected a stormy scene, and invitation to a duel, or, at the very least, to be refused admittance to the Earl's presence. On the contrary, this quiet gentleman seemed prepared to be reasonable. True, he had refused an offer to shake hands, but that might be the way of these haughty aristocrats.

Possibly Louise was right in thinking that Rushmore would welcome the opportunity to be rid of all responsibility for her. He'd doubted her, of course. In his experience, no sane person would refuse control of a handsome fortune, especially if its owner was little more than a child. He gave the Earl a solemn look.

'Now, sir, I am come to beg for your indulgence. Give me leave to pay my addresses to your ward.'

Rushmore leaned back in his chair and regarded Verreker with half-closed eyes. 'I thought you had already done so.'

There was a hint of menace behind the quiet words

and his companion picked it up at once. He hung his head, but when he looked up at last his blue eyes were filled with guileless innocence.

'That was ill done of me,' he admitted simply. 'But if I might explain the circumstances? When I met your ward she was alone, bereft of friends, and visibly distressed. I felt obliged to offer her my help.'

'Quite the Good Samaritan, in fact! Naturally, you had no idea who she was?'

'Of course not!'' Verreker bridled at the thought. 'She was just a young girl, quite unprotected, and possibly at the risk of unwelcome attentions—'

'Including your own?'

'Miss Bryant was grateful for my help,' Verreker assured him. 'I saw her safely back to the Academy.'

'For that, at least, I must be grateful, sir. What I cannot accept is your behaviour from then on... clandestine meetings, the exchange of letters, and finally this suggestion of a betrothal.'

'It is not a suggestion, my lord. We are betrothed.'

'Let me assure you that you are not, and nor are you likely to become so—' Rushmore caught himself in time. He must not refuse this creature out of hand. Nothing would be more likely to drive Louise into his arms. 'You will understand my position,' he continued. 'I cannot countenance an attachment undertaken in this underhand way.'

'I have no excuse except that our love struck like a bolt of lightning.'

'Then let me advise you not to get burned.' There was something in Rushmore's eyes which struck terror to the heart of his companion, but the look was swiftly veiled.

Verreker was at a loss. He was beginning to understand the Earl, and he knew in his soul that this man was his enemy. Rushmore would never allow Louise to marry him.

He was tempted to cut and run, but he had too much at stake. His pockets were to let, and his creditors were gathering like sharks about a wounded fish. Within weeks, or possibly even days, they would close in on him and consign him to a debtors' prison. Only the certain prospect of a marriage to a wealthy bride would hold them off.

He made a last despairing appeal to Rushmore. 'Sir, would you break Louise's heart?' he asked in a low voice.

'My ward is seventeen years old. Better a little unhappiness now than to suffer a lifetime of misery.'

'But I would make her happy...I swear it.'

'How? I know nothing about you, Mr Verreker. You have not mentioned your past life. Where do you come from? Who are your parents? What are your prospects? You have said nothing of these things.'

'I come from the north of England, sir. Sadly, my parents are dead. They cannot speak for me. As to prospects, well...I have influential friends...I think of entering politics.'

'Do you, indeed? And what settlements would you make upon my ward?'

Verreker glared at him. Then his eyes fell. 'I...I have nothing to offer her but my love...but surely that is beyond the price of rubies?'

'Possibly, but it will not put a roof above your head, nor fill your larder. Louise cannot help you. The control of her fortune is in my hands.'

'Her fortune?' Wide-eyed and innocent, Verreker stared at him. 'My lord, I had no idea! Do you tell me that she is an heiress? Well, I suppose that that must be the end of me.' Apparently crushed, he rose from his chair and prepared to take his leave. 'I see now why you are against me. You think me a fortune-hunter.'

Rushmore gave him a lazy smile, but his knuckles whitened. He was strongly tempted to thrash Verreker within an inch of his life. The man must think him a fool!

'And I am wrong, of course?' he mocked. 'Now, sir, let me warn you. There will be no more clandestine meetings, nor an exchange of letters. You may see Miss Bryant for one last meeting. Miss Langrishe, I am sure, will allow you to present yourself at Laura Place. I shall speak to Louise myself.'

'She will defy you,' Verreker cried hotly. 'We are tied together by the bonds of love.'

'Oh, spare me your histrionics!' Rushmore eyed his companion with distaste. 'You should consider a career upon the boards, sir. I shall tell Louise that she must wait...at least until she has enjoyed her London Season.'

'I see!' Verreker looked at him with undisguised hostility. 'You hope that someone more suitable will offer for her?'

'She is unlikely to be approached by anyone *less* suitable,' his lordship suggested with a pleasant smile. 'In a year's time, who knows? If she is still of the same mind...well...we'll see.'

Silently, Verreker cursed him to perdition. He could not afford to wait a year and he suspected that Rushmore knew it.

Chapter Nine

After ridding himself of his unwelcome visitor, Rushmore strolled round to Laura Place. The walk gave him time to think. A shrewd judge of men himself, he had seen Verreker for what he was...a handsome fly-by-night, living on the fringe of society, and always with an eye to the main chance.

Doubtless the fellow had a pack of creditors after him. That had been all too clear when the Earl had insisted upon a delay. With any luck he would be thrown into a debtors' prison before he could carry his plans much further.

The Earl frowned. That would not do, he decided. He must not make a martyr of Matthew Verreker. Louise would feel obliged to stand by him out of loyalty, if for nothing else. Could she really be so naive as to take the fellow at face value? With a sigh, his lordship realised that she had done so. Perhaps he could expect little else from a seventeen-year-old.

As always, his thoughts strayed to Perdita. Would she have been so gullible? A smile curved his lips. Perdita was all woman...capricious and sometimes unreasonable in his eyes. Fondly he recalled how she had clung to him after he had killed the adder. It was a very feminine reaction, but in his heart he knew that behind that lovely face lay a strong reserve of common sense.

He was assured of it when she greeted him in the salon at Laura Place. Perdita looked at him intently.

'Something has happened,' she insisted. 'Won't you tell me what it was?'

'Verreker has been to see me,' he told her as he drew her towards the window-seat.

'And what did you make of him?'

'I thought him false in every respect, Perdita. All he could offer me by way of recommendation were high-flown sentiments.'

Perdita chuckled. 'Those will carry no weight with you, I think.'

'You think me impervious to the softer feelings. I assure you that I am not, my dear, but in this case I found it impossible to believe him. He claimed not to know that Louise had any expectations.'

'That could be true,' Perdita said slowly. 'She does not flaunt her prospects...'

'I think she had no need to do so. If I am not mistaken, this fellow knows her worth down to the last penny.'

'But what can you do, my lord? You can't force her to give him up.'

'I hope I should not be so foolish as to consider it. I have asked Verreker to wait for a year. If Louise is still of the same mind after her London Season, then we'll see.'

Perdita looked at him. 'Remind me not to take up any cause against you, sir. Verreker durst not wait a year, if your suspicions are correct.'

'Louise does not know that. It is my hope that she will see my views as sensible.'

'She will...as long as you don't fly into alt, my lord.'

'Now, would I do that, Perdita? I am the most reasonable of men. If she will but listen to my arguments, all may yet be well. Don't you agree?'

Perdita was tempted to argue the point. Did Rushmore truly believe himself to be the most reasonable of men? The notion made her want to laugh. Then a glance at his face told her that he was deeply worried. The interview with Matthew Verreker had confirmed his worst suspicions.

Now he was in a quandary. Outright condemnation of the man would persuade Louise to fly to his defence, but he could not pretend to give his blessing to the match. The situation needed careful handling.

'My lord, it is not for me to give advice,' she told him slowly.

'But I have asked for it, my dear. I'd welcome your thoughts on how I should proceed. I have no wish to drive Louise away.'

'Then speak to her of her father. Tell her how happy you are to fulfil his wishes in becoming her guardian and that you will never regard it as an unwelcome burden upon you.'

'Do you think I should? I have avoided the subject of her father's death, fearing that it would cause her pain.'

'Perhaps it will, but it may also bring relief. My own feeling is that we need to speak of those we have lost. It keeps their memory alive and somehow it brings them closer to us.'

Rushmore took her hands in his. 'You have wisdom

beyond your years, Perdita.' Something in his tone brought the hot colour rushing to her cheeks.

'My lord, we should rejoin the others. This private conversation must give rise to comment and I would not have Louise believe that we are plotting against her.'

He released her hands at that and strolled over to Miss Langrishe, who was deep in conversation with the girls.

'Your pardon, ma'am, but may I steal my ward away from you for a few moments? I have something to discuss with her in private.'

Louise paled and threw a hunted look at Thomas. This was the moment she had dreaded. Matthew must have been to see his lordship. Now she had to learn her fate.

'Use the study, Adam.' Miss Langrishe nodded encouragement to the shrinking girl. 'Go along, my dear!'

Louise walked to the door with lagging footsteps, and Thomas watched her with a frown. He made as if to rise to his feet, but a look from Miss Langrishe stopped him.

'Leave it, Thomas!' she ordered. 'You must not interfere. The Earl has every right to speak to his ward alone.'

A silence fell upon the assembled company. Only Crispin and Henry were unaware that momentous decisions were being made in the other room. Perdita and Amy fell prey to speculation, and Thomas wore a thunderous expression.

Miss Langrishe called him to her. 'Don't make a cake of yourself, my boy,' she advised. 'Rushmore will not eat Louise, nor threaten to beat her.'

'He had best not do so,' Thomas muttered darkly. 'Else he'll have me to deal with. She is afraid of him, you know.'

'Then she is a very foolish girl, and you are not much better. You know the Earl...you have served with him...I thought that you admired him.'

'I do, ma'am. He is the best of men, but Louise don't know it, you see. Have you not noticed how she quakes whenever he appears?'

'Thomas, you could change all that. In your company Louise seems perfectly at ease. I think she sees you as a friend. Why not speak to her about the Earl? She may trust your judgement.'

Thomas brightened. 'Do you think I should?'

'I am convinced of it, my dear boy. It is of great importance that Louise learns to have faith in her guardian.'

Thomas glanced towards the door. 'What can be taking them so long?' he asked impatiently. 'I hope he ain't laying down the law as if Louise is one of his captains.'

Miss Langrishe laughed. 'I doubt if he'll do that. Now, are we in agreement, Thomas? You will try to persuade Louise to feel more in charity with the Earl?'

'It depends...I don't know what he's said to her. If she is in tears again he will have lost my good opinion of him.'

Fortunately his lordship was spared this dreadful fate. Louise looked perfectly composed when he led her back into the room and the sigh of relief from all her friends was almost audible.

Normal conversation was resumed at once, but the subject of the interview was carefully avoided.

* * *

It was not until the gentlemen had departed and the young ladies retired to their rooms that their curiosity was satisfied.

A tap at the door brought Louise to join her friends in their bedchamber.

'Well, what happened?' Amy could not contain her excitement. 'Did Matthew go to see his lordship?'

'Yes. I believe they spoke together for some time…'

'And did Rushmore call him out? Is there to be a duel?'

'Of course not, Amy… What a ghoul you are!'

'No, I'm not, but I've never seen a duel. It always happens at dawn, you know. I thought if we could find out where it was to be held we might rise early and go to watch. We could have hidden behind a tree.'

'Be quiet, you wretched little monster!' Perdita glared at her sister. 'You can't wish to see a man get killed.'

'That doesn't always happen,' Amy told her stoutly. 'Sometimes they delope…that is, they fire into the ground or up in the air. I don't see the point myself.'

'Shut up!' Perdita cried. 'Don't you see? You are upsetting Louise—'

'No, she isn't. There is to be no duel. His lordship was not too hard on Matthew about the way we met, nor of our assignations and the letters. He was more concerned as to Matthew's background and his prospects.'

'Well, that sounds reasonable enough,' Perdita announced. 'After all, he takes his promise to your father very seriously. Your papa would have done the same, I'm sure.'

'The Earl reminded me of that. He spoke so kindly of my father. They were the best of friends and he feels the loss…' For a moment her lip quivered. 'Now he wants me to go on as my father would have wished.'

Perdita threw an arm about her shoulders. 'You would agree to that, I'm sure. And in caring for you, your guardian must feel that he has not lost his friend completely.'

Louise smiled at her through misty eyes. 'That is almost exactly what he said. I think I have misjudged him. He has a generous heart.'

'So, are you to be allowed to go ahead with your betrothal?' Amy was all impatience.

'Not for the moment, though the Earl did not dismiss it out of hand. He pointed out that your own mama has kindly promised to sponsor me for the coming Season. All he asks is that I wait until I have made my come-out with you, Amy.'

'And you don't mind waiting?' Amy was bewildered. 'It will be almost a year.'

Louise managed a faint smile. 'His lordship admitted that at seventeen a year can seem a lifetime, but he told me too that true devotion would stand up to the test.'

'So you have agreed?'

'Yes, I have.'

'But what will Matthew say?'

'I expect he will be disappointed, but I am to be allowed to see him and to explain. That is, if Miss Langrishe will allow me to receive him here. He is to call tomorrow… Certainly he cannot object to the Earl's suggestion.'

Louise was mistaken. When Matthew Verreker was shown into the study at Laura Place, it took him less than a minute to learn that all his plans had been foiled. His soulful expression disappeared to be replaced by one of fury as he listened to her.

'My darling, you can't have agreed to this!' he cried. 'Oh, cruel…cruel! How are we to bear it?'

'I believe it is what my father would have wished, my dearest. I am not yet out, you know…and, well…his lordship is convinced that true devotion will stand the test of time.'

'He's a liar!' Verreker shouted. 'He hopes that you will forget me…I know his thinking…he made it clear enough.'

Louise laid a placating hand upon his arm. 'Will you not wait for me?' she begged. 'We have pledged our troth for a lifetime…is a year so long?'

It was only with the greatest difficulty that Verreker managed to control his rage. He looked in disgust at the innocent face of the girl beside him. What a vapid creature she was…swayed by the latest argument to reach her ears. Once he'd welcome the compliant nature…now it had turned against him. He assumed a mournful expression.

'I told the Earl that I was unworthy of you,' he muttered. 'I should never have attempted to attract your interest, but this is a bitter pill to swallow. I see it all now. I was mistaken. You do not care for me with the passion which I have for you.'

Louise's face was twisted in pain. 'Don't say that!' she pleaded. 'I have risked everything for you. I knew quite well that we were wrong in behaving as we did.'

'Ah, is our love to be measured by convention? I had thought better of you.'

Gentle though she was, Louise was growing impatient. For the first time it occurred to her that her lover had a tendency to declaim as if he were acting in a third-rate play. She turned away and that slight movement sounded a warning.

Verreker pulled himself together quickly. At this stage in his affairs he could not afford to lose her. She was his last hope. Without her there would be no time or opportunity to restore his fortunes before the duns moved in. Tenderly he slipped an arm about her waist.

'Forgive me, my dear one!' he murmured. 'You are my life, my only love. We have been so close these last few weeks. I have learned to look for you each day, to offer you my heart, and to bask in the warmth of your affection. Have we not been everything to each other? We have laughed and cried together, sharing our troubles like good friends. Is that not so?'

'I won't deny it, Matthew.'

'Then listen to me, dearest. Rushmore is my enemy. I don't know why, but he has other plans for you. For all we know he may intend to wed you himself.' As Louise gasped he stopped her with a lifted hand. 'Don't discount it, I beg of you—'

'But this is nonsense,' she protested. 'He was my father's friend.'

'So he claims, but what do you know of him? Did he come to see you as soon as he returned to England from the continent of Europe? Has he shown you any affection? No! It was not until you announce your intention to be wed that he arrived in Bath. I think you should beware of him. The Earl is not all he seems.'

'I think you are misjudging him. I did so myself at first, but he has spoken so kindly of my father. All that concerns him now is that I shall be happy.'

She heard a snort of disbelief.

'He has a curious way of showing it. Don't you care that he has ruined all our plans?'

'He has asked us to wait, that is all.'

'That is all?' Verreker's face was ashen. 'He has broken my heart. Tell me, are we to be allowed to meet during this waiting time?'

Louise was silent.

'Just so!' Verreker cried in triumph. 'And letters are forbidden too?'

'All he said was that we should not meet in secret. If you write to me I must show the letters to Miss Langrishe.'

'Splendid! What pleasure she will derive from reading private correspondence! No, thank you! You had best make up your mind, Louise. We are to be parted for ever. Rushmore is a heartless brute!'

'I don't think so,' Louise said quietly. 'All he asks of me is to do as my father would have wished.'

Verreker cursed beneath his breath. Rushmore was a clever devil! He had seized upon the one argument which would sway this girl. He decided upon a final throw of the dice.

He took Louise's hand in his. 'He is right, of course,' he told her with a winning smile. 'And what would have been your father's first consideration? That must have been your happiness, my dear. Will you send me away like this? I won't believe that you have played me false. I believed your love to be as strong as mine. Did we not say that we were two halves of one whole?'

'I haven't played you false,' she whispered. 'But—'

'But you lack the courage to trust me?'

'Of course not.'

'Then listen to me carefully. Rushmore intends to part us, but there is a way to force his hand.'

'I don't know what you mean.'

'We must elope, my love. Once we are wed he can do nothing. Even he cannot come between husband and wife.'

Louise snatched her hands away. She was deeply shocked. 'You must be mad!' she cried.

Verreker threw his arms about her. 'Of course I'm mad…mad with love for you… Believe me, this is the only way if we are ever to make our dreams come true.'

'I can't do it…and I won't!' Her face was set.

Matthew Verreker knew when he was beaten, and now he too was shocked. Who would have suspected that this gentle girl had such a streak of stubbornness in her nature? Now disaster loomed before him. His creditors would not wait, and money he must have before the month was out.

The idea of abduction crossed his mind. One night alone with this stupid creature would still all objections to their marriage. She would be damaged goods, especially if he took care to let the circumstances be known to all her friends and acquaintance.

He was unaware that his expression had changed, but Louise glanced up at his face and was afraid.

'I must go,' she said. 'I'm sorry, Matthew, but I could never agree to such a plan. Will you not trust *me* to wait for you?'

'You must do as you think best,' he told her coldly. 'I shall not contact you again. If you change your mind, a letter will find me.' He looked at her bent head, and knew then that the letter would not come. He bowed and left her.

Pale with fury, he strode off into the town contemplating the ruin of all his hopes. His careful plans had come to naught, but she'd seemed such an easy target, and finding her alone in the park had been a heaven-sent opportunity. He'd seen at a glance that she was gentry. It had been so easy to offer her his sympathy, and later, when he had made enquiries as to her background, his love.

Fatherless and vulnerable, she'd fallen into his hands like a ripe plum until the arrival of the Earl of Rushmore. Slow-burning hatred for his enemy consumed him as he walked along. The Earl was a powerful man, but he would learn that he had met his match in Matthew Verreker. There were other ways of gaining possession of the funds he needed.

Abduction? It might be worth a try, but Louise no longer walked in the park alone. And Rushmore? Matthew did not underestimate his enemy. If he made Louise his wife, it was more than likely that she would soon become a widow. Rushmore had killed in battle. If he was given just cause, it was more than likely that he would kill again.

But there was another way. In the past he had always made contingency plans in case certain of his schemes fell through. This time he hadn't thought it necessary, but an idea crossed his fertile mind and he began to chuckle.

The scheme was not his own. He had heard of it some years ago. It had been tried in this very place. True, it had not met with much success, but the intended victims had been an elderly couple. Now, in the case of a young girl...? As he considered all the possibilities he knew that it could not fail.

Unaware of the plans being made for her, Louise had sought the company of her friends. Amy was bursting to know the outcome of her interview with Matthew Verreker, but, cautioned by Perdita, she held her tongue until Louise should choose to speak of it.

'I expect you want to know,' Louise said at once. 'I have explained to Matthew that we must wait.'

'What did he say to that?' Perdita asked. She suspected that she knew the answer to the question before her friend could reply.

'He was disappointed,' Louise told her in a low voice. 'He thinks the Earl a monster...and...well... I'm afraid we quarrelled about it.'

'He will come round,' Amy assured her cheerfully. 'When gentlemen are crossed they fly into the boughs, but they get over it and then forget what they have been quarrelling about.'

Louise gave her a sad little smile. 'This was not quite the same as your differences with your cousins, Amy. Matthew says that he will not contact me again. If I change my mind, I am to write to him.'

'Change your mind?' About what? Perdita was seized with a feeling of dread. 'Surely he does not expect you to go on meeting him in secret and hiding letters in the park?'

'No, he doesn't, but he is convinced that his lordship means to part us for ever.'

Amy took her hand. 'Are you very unhappy about it?' she asked. 'Perhaps if we spoke to the Earl he might agree to you meeting Matthew in company.'

'I said as much, but Matthew will not have it. It is not enough for him...' She turned her head away and gazed through the window, fighting back her tears.

Perdita moved to sit beside her. 'Is there something more?' she asked. 'I hate to see you so distressed. You say that Mr Verreker wishes you to change your mind? What has he suggested to you?'

Louise began to sob. 'He…he wishes me to agree to an elopement,' she gasped. 'I can't! I can't!'

'Of course you can't!' Perdita's anger threatened to overwhelm her. 'What kind of man is he even to suggest such a thing?'

'He must be mad! Doesn't he realise that the Earl would follow you? I believe that I shall offer to go with him, Louise. You will need a friend when he catches up with Mr Verreker.' Amy's eyes were gleaming with excitement.

'Amy, if you can't be sensible you may leave the room. Louise has no intention of eloping with Mr Verreker.' Perdita turned to her friend. 'How have you left things with him?'

'It is as I told you. I must make the decision whether or not to see him again.'

'Let him suffer for a while,' Amy advised. 'That is, if you truly wish to see him again.'

'Do you, Louise?' Perdita cast a searching glance at her friend's face. 'I think you cannot have suspected that he would stoop so low.'

'I don't know! I'm so confused. Matthew seemed different somehow. He's always been so kind, but today I saw another side to his character.'

'Well, now you have plenty of time to consider how you should go on.' It was with a feeling of relief that Perdita heard a bustle in the hall which heralded the arrival of all three of her cousins, together with the Earl of Rushmore.

'Girls, I beg you will not speak of this to his lordship,' Louise begged anxiously. 'It can only give him a poor opinion of Matthew.'

Amy and Perdita nodded. A horse-whipping would

be the likely outcome and that would serve no purpose except to relieve the Earl's feelings.

Rushmore was too circumspect to question Louise directly. Her dead father's wishes would be uppermost in her mind, he knew. Now he felt he could trust her to follow his own advice.

Miss Langrishe beamed at him, and made no objection when he suggested that the young people might enjoy a stroll in the park. She had turned down his invitation that she join them.

'Bless you, my dear boy, I can think of nothing more exhausting. Why do you think I live here in Laura Place, rather than in the Royal Crescent? I am all for convenience, you know, and here I need struggle only a few yards to the shops.' She chuckled. 'My feet do very well as long as I don't punish them too much.'

'Then you might prefer to drive in a barouche, ma'am?'

'Not this morning, Adam, I thank you. I have much to do, and the Colonel intends to call upon me with tickets for a subscription ball. Now, off you go…the girls will enjoy the outing.'

Her charges needed no further encouragement. Both Amy and Louise knew that their return to the Academy could not be long delayed, and they intended to enjoy their freedom to the full.

They hurried ahead with Thomas and his brothers, leaving Perdita and the Earl to follow at a slower pace. Perdita gave her sister a suspicious look. It seemed almost as if Amy was at pains to throw her together with his lordship.

Then she dismissed the idea. Amy was merely giving her the opportunity to discuss Rushmore's plans for Louise.

He did not leave her long in doubt.

'Verreker has been to see Louise?' he asked.

'He came this morning, my lord.'

'Oh, I wondered...' He looked ahead to the party of young people strolling happily in the sunshine. 'She does not seem to be overly distressed...I must hope that she made my wishes known to him.'

'She did.'

'And what was his reaction?'

Perdita considered her next words carefully. She had promised not to speak of Verreker's plans for an elopement, but there could be no harm in mentioning his anger.

'He was not best pleased,' she admitted.

She heard a suppressed laugh. 'Perdita, I shall regard those words as a masterpiece of understatement. Confess it now—he was furious?'

'Well, yes, he was, but he could not sway Louise. You may not think it, but she *was* distressed. They had a serious quarrel, and he went off in a rage, saying that they must part unless she changed her mind.'

'Really! This is good news indeed, except that you are keeping something back from me, I think. What was she to change her mind about?''

Perdita was silent.

'Well?'

'Sir, I cannot betray a confidence. Louise insisted that she must do as her father might have wished.'

'I see. And it was enough to cause him to withdraw his suit? You surprise me! I had not thought that he would give her up so easily.'

Perdita felt that she was on dangerous ground. She

tried to hurry ahead towards the others, but a large hand closed about her wrist and Rushmore drew her arm through his.

'Don't run away, my dear!' he said. 'I won't ask you to break your word, but we are speaking of a dangerous man. He is at *point non plus* and he cannot afford to let Louise escape. As I see it, he has few choices open to him.'

Perdita averted her face. In seconds her shrewd companion would have the secret out of her, and that might lead to disaster.

Rushmore strolled on, apparently unaware of any tension.

'Yes,' he continued, 'few choices. One, I fancy, might be to suggest an elopement.'

Perdita gasped and tried to withdraw her arm from his, but he would not release her.

'Louise, I fancy, would not agree to that,' he mused. He looked down at the lovely girl beside him, and then he smiled. 'Don't worry, my dear, I shall neither call him out nor horse-whip him. Perdita, has anyone ever told you that your face is the mirror of your thoughts?'

She coloured deeply and turned her head away.

'No, I shall not make a martyr of this creature,' he continued. 'He is safe enough for the moment. Louise herself must see him for what he is, and she may not have long to wait.'

'Sir, what can you mean?'

'Verreker is facing ruin, I believe. I should not put it past him to have considered abduction—'

'Oh, no!' Perdita's hand flew to her mouth. 'He could not be so wicked.'

'Needs must when the devil drives...' Rushmore

considered for some moments. 'I have no wish to frighten her, but she must not be left alone.'

'But if you set a guard on her she will think that you don't trust her.'

'She won't suspect my guard.' Rushmore chuckled.

'But who?'

'I was thinking of your sister, Amy. Shall we take her into our confidence?'

Perdita sighed with relief. 'Sir, you could have thought of nothing better. Amy will guard Louise and consider it an adventure. Why, she was planning to attend the duel if you had challenged Verreker.'

'She has much to learn,' he said softly. 'Verreker is not a gentleman. I could not have challenged him.'

There was something in his tone which caused Perdita to look up at him. She was startled. This was not the laughing, teasing man she knew. There was murder in his eyes. She shrank away from him.

Rushmore sensed it at once and when he spoke again it was in a rallying tone. 'Your sister is a jewel.' He laughed. 'She was prepared to rise at dawn to attend us on some blasted heath or other? Where was she to hide?'

'Behind a tree, I think. Her greatest worry was that you would delope, or miss each other in the fray.'

'Good heavens! I see that I am unlikely to be lucky in my ally. Remind me not to offer her a pistol. We shall have bodies everywhere.'

'Pray be serious, sir.' Perdita returned to the matter in hand. 'Matthew Verreker would be foolish in the extreme to attempt to abduct Louise. He must surely know that you would follow him?'

'He won't have forgotten that possibility. He may hope to ruin Louise before we catch him.'

Perdita blushed, but she did not pretend to misunderstand him.

'Of course, it will avail him nothing.'

Again, she saw the bleak look in his eyes.

'It won't happen,' she assured him earnestly. 'Let us speak to Amy and to Aunt Trixie. Louise must not be left alone. Shall we tell Thomas and the boys?'

The suggestion brought a reluctant smile from Rushmore. 'I think not. If Thomas were to learn the facts, Amy might get her duel after all. It could serve no purpose, except to cause a scandal in which Louise might be named, and rouse sympathy for Verreker if he should be wounded.'

'I'd shoot him myself!' Perdita said fiercely.

'Yes, my love, I know you would, but there are other ways to bring him down. I have set matters in train...enquiries are being made here and in London. The man must have a past. This cannot be his first attempt to secure an easy living for himself.'

If Perdita was startled by the endearment she gave no sign of it. She walked along sedately with her companion.

'And how do you find Bath?' he asked with an easy grin. 'Not quite as boring as you had at first imagined?'

'Not in the least,' Perdita shuddered. 'This will teach me not to yearn for excitement. I have had enough to last a lifetime.'

'Oh, I hope not, my dear.' Rushmore twined her fingers in his own. 'You have your life ahead of you. I hope...I mean, I am certain that you will find it interesting and fulfilling.'

Perdita allowed her hand to rest in his. 'It's difficult,

isn't it?' she said frankly. 'I mean, one does not know what lies ahead.'

'But that is the beauty of it. Imagine if some seer told you! Would you wish to know? There would be no surprises.'

'Most of my surprises have turned out to be unpleasant recently,' she told him with a rueful smile.

'Ah, yes, but you must not give up hope! All this will change—' Rushmore caught himself in time. He must not speak of love just yet, or even attempt to attach Perdita to him. Let her grow to know him as a trusted friend. That must be enough for now.

Chapter Ten

Amy made an excellent co-conspirator. Once taken into the Earl's confidence she was even able to face the dismal prospect of returning to the Academy as a boarder with a certain degree of equanimity.

Her eyes sparkled at the thought of becoming Louise's bodyguard, though she objected when Rushmore refused to lend her a pistol.

'But suppose we are attacked?' she cried. 'We should fight, of course, but we'd be no match for a group of ruffians.'

'An attack is highly unlikely if you stay together,' Rushmore told her. 'All I'm asking is that you make quite sure that Louise does not go out alone. You girls are allowed to walk in Bath, I believe?'

'Only in a stupid crocodile! We look like a group of schoolgirls.'

With commendable restraint the Earl refrained from mentioning that that was exactly what they were.

'But you are able to go into the shops to make small purchases?'

'Only in company with each other.'

'Good! I may be imagining danger where none exists, but it would be foolish to take a risk. Take care that you don't get separated and, whatever the temptation, don't stray into alleyways or lonely streets.'

Amy's eyes widened. 'Then you do fear an attempt at an abduction, sir?'

'Only if an opportunity were to present itself. I am certain that Louise will be watched, but once it is seen that she is never left alone such plans would be abandoned.'

'But I thought you said that Verreker was desperate?'

'He is. I don't underestimate him, but it is difficult to arrange an abduction in a crowded street. He would need help…a closed carriage…and the knowledge that he could spirit Louise away without detection.'

'You are well informed, my lord. Have you ever considered abduction yourself?' Amy gave him a teasing look.

'I have been tempted, my dear.' The Earl's eyes strayed to Perdita. 'To date I have managed to resist that temptation… Now, let us change the subject. You will attend the subscription ball?'

Perdita threw him a look of gratitude. Amy, she knew, would be alert for danger. Pray heaven she would not take her new responsibilities to extremes. She was capable of challenging Verreker herself.

Later she said as much to Rushmore, but he persuaded her to set aside her fears.

'Amy has a good head upon her shoulders,' he assured her. 'She sees the need to follow my instructions to the letter. I have pointed out that everything she does must be low-key. Louise must not become aware that we are worried about her safety…' For a few moments he was lost in thought. 'Verreker has not returned?'

'No…and it is the strangest thing, but Louise is not as crushed as I had expected. After all, she fancied herself in love with him, else she would not have agreed to the betrothal.'

'She was vulnerable,' Rushmore said slowly. 'At the time she would have fancied herself in love with anyone who showed her kindness.'

'Then you think it was merely infatuation?'

'Possibly not even that. Of course she may have believed herself to be in the grip of some grand passion…'

Perdita gave him a curious look. 'You sound as if you have no time for sentiment, my lord. Do you believe all love to be an illusion?'

Perdita had caught him unawares. He swung round to face her with an expression that made her catch her breath. His eyes had an inner glow. Then he turned away and walked over to the window, staring across the busy expanse of Laura Place as he fought to control his voice.

Then he turned and smiled at her. 'No!' he said 'I believe in love…as I'm sure you do yourself. It is not the same thing as infatuation.'

'It must be very difficult to know the difference, sir.'

'You have experienced neither feeling?'

'No…have you?'

'Not infatuation, certainly.'

'And love?'

'You ask too many questions, my dear. Gentlemen are shy in speaking their innermost thoughts. Had you not noticed?'

'Oh, I beg your pardon, my lord. I had not intended…I mean, I have no wish to pry.'

'I know that, Perdita. And I am wrong in fighting shy of your questioning. These matters should be discussed among friends.' Even so, he did not pursue the subject.

'Have you heard from your parents?' he asked.

'Mother wrote from Portsmouth before they sailed. Now I expect that we shall have a lengthy wait before the next letter.'

'You must miss them sorely.'

'We do, but Aunt Trixie has been the solution.' Perdita twinkled at him. 'Letter writing is her passion. She will have no dealings with crossings and recrossings in the interest of economy. She is happy to pay the cost of her outpourings and of ours. We write a little each day, with details of how we spend our time. Then at the end of the week the letters are sent off. I had thought that the news must be stale by the time they reached their destination, but the Colonel has the matter in hand.'

'Carrier pigeon?' Rushmore teased.

'Not exactly, but the Colonel has connections with a number of naval men. It is his boast that no service is more expeditious than that to Gibraltar through his friends.'

Neither of them knew it, but Miss Langrishe had been taking full advantage of this service. Since Perdita was in her care she had felt obliged to write to Perry and Elizabeth with her views upon the appearance of the Earl of Rushmore. As yet she had had no reply.

Now she resolved to tell the Earl about the content of her letter.

'Was I wrong?' she asked. 'I feel as if I am *in loco parentis* to Perdita. I thought it best to tell Perry and Elizabeth what is happening here.'

'Nothing is happening,' Rushmore assured her firmly.

'But that is nonsense, my dear boy. Any fool can see that you are falling deeper in love each day.'

'Perdita does not see it, and I have done nothing to persuade her.'

'Adam, I respect you for your honourable behaviour, but there may come a time when your feelings overcome you. Can you wait until her parents return? Is it not best to let them know of your desire to wed Perdita?'

'I have written to them myself. Perhaps I was a little premature. Perdita has given me no encouragement—'

'Give her time!' Miss Langrishe begged. 'You have gained much ground with her. I noticed how she listened carefully when you spoke to Amy of your plans.'

'A military man is expected to be in command of strategy,' he said lightly. 'I still have far to go, ma'am.'

She nodded and did not argue the point. 'Amy will obey your wishes?' she asked.

Rushmore nodded.

'I cannot say that I like the situation, Adam. I had hoped to take the girls out shopping into Milsom Street when next they come to visit me.'

'Then you must do so, Miss Langrishe. As I explained to Amy, you cannot possibly be in danger in the centre of the town.'

Later he was to recall those words, and so did his companion. For the moment they had no idea of the perils which lay ahead.

'There is one other matter,' he said at last. 'May I ask you to undertake a commission for me?'

'Gladly, my dear boy! What do you have in mind?'

'It is Louise's birthday next week. I should like to give her some token...a brooch...a bracelet possibly. Had her father been alive he would not have let the occasion pass unnoticed.'

'You will not accompany her to the jeweller yourself?'

'No!'' For once he looked a little ill at ease. 'I would not have her think that I am trying to buy her friendship.'

Miss Langrishe shook her head. 'I shan't deny that the gift has come from you, my dear, but you misjudge Louise. Have you not noticed? She is gaining in confidence by the day. She no longer sees you as an ogre.'

'I have Thomas to thank for that, I believe.' He cocked an inquisitive eye at the old lady. 'Do you see a match there, ma'am?'

'Should you have any objection, Adam?'

'Not in the least. Louise could not do better. That young man is sound to his backbone.'

Miss Langrishe smiled. 'You must not make it too easy for them.'

'That is unlikely to happen. Thomas must soon be recalled to his duties, and I want her to have her Season before taking such an important step. She has seen nothing of the world.'

'A wise decision!' Miss Langrishe frowned. 'I wish we could be certain that Matthew Verreker has given up all hope of her.'

'So do I, but Louise is well protected now. I must return to London soon myself. The Duke will wish to see me...' He was lost in thought for several minutes.

'What is it, Adam? You are still not easy in your mind?'

'No!' he told her frankly. 'I don't trust Verreker to lose his prize without a struggle. I need to know more about him. This cannot be his first attempt to capture a wealthy wife. That in itself is not a crime, but he struck me as a confidence trickster. If only we had some evidence against him he could be given in charge and prosecuted. It would put an end to his activities.'

'But you have already made enquiries and found nothing, so you tell me.'

'He's expert at covering his tracks. I hear no word of him in Bath. That leaves London. He must seek the company of the wealthy, so possibly my men will have some news for me.'

'When will you leave?' she asked.

'Within a day or two. It won't be easy.' He gave her a rueful smile. 'I shall leave my heart behind.'

'But not for long, I fancy. We shall miss you, Adam.'

'I wonder!' Rushmore was seized with doubt. Perdita might welcome his absence with a sigh of relief. At worst she would not give him another thought.

He was mistaken. Rather to his surprise, the news of his imminent departure brought a chorus of protest from Amy and her cousins. Even Louise asked to know when he would return.

Perdita said nothing. Her face was in shadow, so it was difficult for him to read expression. Had she welcomed the news? He looked at her, praying that he would not see triumph in her eyes. From the first she had seen him as her enemy, though of late she had become his unwilling ally.

He joined her on the window-seat. 'Have you nothing to say to me?' he asked in a low voice.

Perdita kept her eyes fixed on her folded hands. She had been badly shaken by his decision to return to London.

'I had not thought that you would leave us at this time, my lord.' Her tone was cool. He must not guess that she wanted him to stay. 'There may still be danger to Louise.'

'I think we have done all we can, Perdita.'

She made no reply.

'Besides, I think you have forgot. I am a serving soldier, my dear. My time is not my own. The Duke gave me leave to come and see my ward, but I cannot extend my stay by much longer.'

'Of course not!' Perdita rose as if to leave him, but he caught her hand.

'Are you concerned only with Louise?' he asked. 'We have been friends, I think. I shall miss our conversation. Will you not say the same?'

Perdita was very close to tears. She dared not attempt to answer him. It was ridiculous. Why should she be upset by his departure? And why should the prospect of a future without him appear so bleak?

It was Miss Langrishe who came to her rescue. She called Perdita to her with an innocent enquiry about a proposed shopping trip.

'It is Louise's birthday soon,' she whispered. 'We are to choose a brooch or a bracelet for her from the Earl.'

'Is he unable to choose the gift himself?' Perdita snapped. Her nerves were at breaking point.

'He does not know what would please her.' Miss Langrishe wore an imperturbable expression. She had noticed the interchange between Perdita and his lordship, and knew that it had ended in a difference of opinion. Well, it would be no bad thing if Rushmore went away for a time. Perdita might then realise how much she had grown to enjoy his company.

Louise's birthday fell on the same day as the subscription ball towards the end of that week. There was no time to be lost if a suitable gift was to be chosen and engraved for her, so the following morning Perdita and Miss Langrishe set out for the jewellers.

Rushmore had not mentioned price. He would have considered it an irrelevance, so the ladies were free to make their choice from the treasure trove on offer. It did not take them long. They settled upon a slim gold bracelet of classical design, instructing that it should be engraved on the inside simply with Louise's name and the date.

They had intended to go on to visit the largest haberdasher in the town, but as they gained the street again Miss Langrishe stumbled. Perdita was quick to catch her elbow, thinking that her aunt had merely tripped. Then she heard a gasp.

'What is it?' she cried in alarm. 'Aunt Trixie, are you ill?'

'Not really, my dear. It is just a touch of gout, but the pain is severe. Shall you mind if we go back to Laura Place? I need some lace and some gloves, but at this present time I cannot think…'

'Of course we must go back. Aunt, you should have told me. Have you anything to ease the pain?'

Miss Langrishe nodded, but it was not until she was safely back at home and had taken the draught prescribed by her own doctor that she felt herself again. She even managed a chuckle.

'My chickens are come home to roost!' she admitted. 'This complaint is the result of a surfeit of good living.'

'Have you had it before?'

'Just a touch of it in a single finger. This time it has affected my right hand.'

Perdita looked down at the swollen knuckles beneath the reddened skin. 'It looks extremely painful, Aunt. Will the draught make you sleepy? Perhaps if you were to rest?'

Miss Langrishe nodded. 'I shall feel better later in the day. Then we shall finish our shopping.'

'You must not think of it. The girls will be here this afternoon. You shall commission us to buy whatever you need.'

'I don't know, Perdita. His lordship warned of possible danger in the town.'

'But not if we stay together, and, if you wish it, Ellen shall go with us.'

'I wish you would ask Rushmore or the boys.'

Perdita laughed. 'Gentlemen hate shopping, Aunt, as well you know. Now you shall not worry about us. Bath is crowded, and we shall not stray from the main street.'

Miss Langrishe was still doubtful, but at last she gave a sleepy consent and was persuaded to retire to her bedchamber.

* * *

Released from their studies, both Amy and Louise were happy to fall in with her plan later that afternoon. Mindful of her aunt's wishes, Perdita allowed a grumpy Ellen to accompany them.

Their purchases took longer than she had expected. Both Amy and Louise were in need of new white gloves for the ball. Then they became distracted by a display of artificial flowers and gaily coloured ribbons.

Perdita called them to her. 'Help me to choose,' she begged. 'Aunt is in need of several yards of lace for trimming. It is so very expensive and I don't want to make a mistake.'

'We could change it if she doesn't like it,' Amy pointed out.

Louise was fingering the lace. 'It is truly beautiful,' she said wistfully. 'Miss Langrishe could not fail to like this cobweb pattern.'

'But it is white and she wanted black. I wonder if they have it…' Perdita called an assistant to her, and the girl went into the rear of the shop.

They were unprepared for the scene which followed. As the assistant returned she was confronted by the furious owner of the store.

'How dare you leave your post?' he shouted. 'Idling your time away and leaving customers unattended. I should dismiss you on the spot.'

Perdita looked at the shrinking girl, who grew red and white by turns. There was nothing of her. She looked badly undernourished, and clearly it was fear of losing her post which brought the first few stammered words.

'Sir, I did not mean to—'

'Silence! Get your things and go—'

'One moment, please!' Perdita was at her most imperious. 'At my request, this lady went to make enquiries about some lace for me.'

The man swung round and stared at her. Then he too went red. 'I beg your pardon, madam. I did not know.'

'And you didn't trouble to find out, did you, before behaving in this disgraceful way?'

By this time they had an interested audience, and the man was aware of it. He glared at the rest of his staff who had drawn near. Then he turned back to Perdita, containing his anger only with great difficulty. He was unaccustomed to being taken to task, especially by a chit of a girl.

Perdita saw his sneering expression and knew that it was only the presence of other customers in the shop which kept him from insulting her.

'May we not discuss this matter in private, miss?' he asked.

'No, we may not. You made your comments in public. They shall be answered in public. Allow me to inform you that I do not expect to be treated to such a display of ill temper when I bring my custom to a shop.'

'It was not directed at you,' he muttered.

'Kindly go away,' Perdita told him coldly. 'This young lady will serve me. She, at least, is courteous.'

He had no option but to slink away, but all the pleasure had vanished from their shopping expedition. Perdita was tempted to cancel all her purchases and stalk out of the shop. It was concern for the assistant which caused her to change her mind. In the event she bought far more than she had intended.

'Will you be all right?' she asked the girl.

'Yes, miss, thanks to you.'

'Come then, girls!' With her head held high, Perdita swept out into the street.

Beside her, Ellen sniffed. 'There you go again!' she muttered. 'Behaving like a duchess.'

Perdita stopped and turned to face her. 'And was I wrong?' she demanded. To her astonishment the old woman smiled.

'Not this time, my pet. That poor critter was ready to faint clean away when she was dismissed.'

'I hope we have prevented that, Ellen.' Perdita looked ahead to see that Amy and Louise had stopped. To her alarm they seemed to have been accosted by a young man. There was something familiar about him.

Perdita hurried towards the little group. Then she realised with a sigh of relief that the young man had served her in the haberdasher's store on a previous occasion. He was the son of the owner.

'Is something wrong?' she asked.

'I don't think so, madam, but we are missing a length of lace. It may have fallen into this young lady's reticule by mistake...' His eyes rested on Louise.

'Oh, do you think so?' Louise was untroubled. 'I did leave my reticule open on the counter. I was not paying attention, I'm afraid.'

'Then, Miss Bryant, if I might ask you to look?'

Louise was perfectly willing to do so. The packet of lace was there, and she handed it over with a puzzled look.

'And if I might have your direction, miss?'

'You have our direction,' Perdita said coolly. 'We live in Laura Place. Our packages are to be sent there.'

It was a curious incident, but no member of the party gave it another thought. It was not until later that day that Perdita found herself wondering how the young man knew Louise by name. It did not matter. The incident might have happened to anyone. She did not trouble to mention it, either to Rushmore or Miss Langrishe.

They had other news to occupy their minds. Thomas had been recalled to London, and his brothers had decided to accompany him.

Their imminent departure cast a cloud over preparations for the ball, although they were not to leave beforehand.

And Rushmore too was soon to leave them, Perdita thought in despair. He must have convinced himself that the danger to Louise had passed. Verreker had not been seen in Bath, and he had neither written to Louise nor been to see her. Possibly he was pursuing some other wealthy prospect.

Perdita took herself to task. Her fears for Louise's safety had been groundless. Why, then, was she still a prey to doubt? It was dispiriting and she vowed to pull herself together. Her lowered spirits might be due to the fact that her cousins were to leave them short of dancing partners and young company. As for Rushmore...well...it must be a relief to be spared that sardonic presence for the next few months. In her heart she knew that she was being unfair. The Earl did not sneer at her, nor was he mocking or bitter. Sardonic was not a description which might be applied to him.

It was not until the evening of the ball that she realised the truth. That night she was looking at her best in a gown of creamy spider gauze over a matching satin slip. Her only ornament was a string of river pearls.

Rushmore had engaged her for the waltz. This time she had no reservations so she gave herself to the pleasure of the dance. Her enjoyment communicated itself to him.

'Happy?' he asked quietly.

'Of course, my lord!' Perdita gave him a brilliant smile.

'I'm glad of it! In these last few days I have found you a little...er...preoccupied.'

'I know. It's just that...well...this resolution of Louise's problem seems too easy. Do you not agree?'

'I've been surprised,' he admitted. 'But you have noticed nothing untoward?'

For a moment Perdita considered telling him of the curious incident when the lace was found in Louise's reticule, but she dismissed the notion. That could have nothing to do with Matthew Verreker. She shook her head.

'Then put these worries out of your mind. You are in famous looks tonight, my dear. I am the envy of every man in the room.'

Perdita blushed. 'Sir, I wish that you would not...'

He gave her a tender look. 'You must be the only woman in the world who does not care to be complimented upon her appearance.'

'It is not the most important thing,' she told him in a low voice. 'I can think of worthier reasons for a compliment.'

'So can I!' Suddenly the Earl forgot his promise to himself. After all, he had written to Perdita's father, stating his intentions, and Miss Langrishe knew of his feelings for her. He was doing nothing underhand. Before he left for London he must tell Perdita of his love.

'Do you not find it warm in here?' he asked. 'Let us find a place where we can talk.'

'But this waltz is not over,' she protested.

'We can waltz again later,' he told her firmly. 'This is important, my dear.'

Unsuspecting, she allowed him to lead her to a sofa in the adjoining anteroom. He took a seat beside her, but he was silent for so long that she was seized with dread.

'What is it?' she cried. 'Are you keeping something from me? Does this concern Louise?'

Rushmore took both her hands in his. 'I have been keeping something from you, but it does not concern Louise. Can you not guess, Perdita?'

She drew her hands away. 'You are speaking in riddles, sir. I cannot read your mind.'

'How I wish that I could read yours. Tell me, shall you miss me when I leave for London?'

To her horror, Perdita felt her colour rising. She tried to smile. 'You are certain to be missed, my lord. When you and my cousins leave, we shall be bereft of half of our company.'

'Don't torment me, my dear one. That was not what I asked you.'

Perdita tried to rise, but he slipped his arm about her waist, and held her to him.

'Don't be afraid,' he whispered, 'I love you. I want you to become my wife... I have written to your father asking his permission to address you.'

Perdita was too shocked to answer him. His offer had been totally unexpected and it startled her.

'You have written to my father?' she asked in disbelief. 'How dare you, sir? Are my own wishes not to be considered?'

'They are of the first importance, but your parents must be consulted, as you know.'

'Kindly remove your arm,' she said stiffly. 'You said once that I planned to become a Countess. Let me assure you that nothing is further from my mind.'

Rushmore released her at once. 'So nothing I have done or said since that unfortunate evening has changed your opinion of me?'

'I won't lie to you, my lord. I was wrong in thinking of you as I did. We have been allies, you and I, but only in regard to Louise. You have been kind to her…but that does not make us friends.'

'I see! You have not learned to trust me?'

'I have, but I will not be your wife.'

'Won't you reconsider? You might offer me some hope. I can wait, Perdita. Only say that you will think about my offer.'

'Sir, it would be useless,' she told him firmly. 'I have no wish to wed you, and that must be an end of it.'

Rushmore dropped his head in his hands, but at that moment another couple entered the room. Their curious look brought Perdita to her feet.

'Please take me back to my aunt,' she said in a low voice. 'We are giving rise to speculation.'

On their return to the ballroom Rushmore surrendered her to her cousin Henry. Then he took a seat beside Miss Langrishe.

'Well, my boy? You look as if Napoleon has escaped.'

'I've ruined any chance I might have had, ma'am. I hadn't meant to speak so soon, but tonight I couldn't hide my feelings…'

'So Perdita has refused you?'

'Yes, she offers me no hope. She will not even think about my offer.'

'You moved too fast. She is still so young, my dear.'

'In some ways…I agree…but not in others. Sometimes she surprises me.'

Miss Langrishe smiled to herself. Perdita had not planned it so, but it would do the Earl of Rushmore no harm to be forced to struggle for her affections.

'Go away!' she advised. 'When you return, Perdita may have changed her mind.'

Rushmore shook his head, convinced that he had lost his only love, but Miss Langrishe had her own beliefs confirmed.

For the next few days Perdita was subdued. Rushmore's offer had come as a surprise and must, of course, be refused, but she could not be easy in her mind. Had she been unkind? The look on his face returned to haunt her. His lordship had looked stricken to the heart. How unworthy it had been to remind him of the casual remark he'd made at Almack's. After all, he had offered her his heart and she could not doubt his sincerity. At last she told her great-aunt.

'Don't worry about it, Perdita!' that lady advised. 'After all, gentlemen cannot always have their way. You did not wish to marry him, and you told him so. That is fair dealing, so it seems to me.'

'I suppose so,' Perdita said reluctantly. 'It is just that…well…I might have been more tactful, but he caught me unawares.'

'The Earl is a man grown. This is a disappointment for him, but in my experience gentlemen do not suffer overlong. All the fond mamas in London will regard him as a catch. He won't be deprived of female company. When next we hear of him it is likely to be in the society pages of the *Gazette* with news of his betrothal.'

For some strange reason this did nothing to reassure Perdita. As the days went by she found herself wondering how the Earl was spending his time. He did not care for Almack's, that she knew, but there were other diversions, such as military reviews and balloon ascents, to say nothing of the daily parade of beauties in Rotten Row.

He was welcome to them, of course. It was just that she seemed unable to rid herself of the habit of looking for his tall figure everywhere she went and searching other faces for that same quizzical smile. There seemed to be a curious flatness in the conversation of those about her. She had grown to enjoy the Earl's challenging banter, but even that could not account for the fact she felt so lost without him.

'I knew it!' Amy announced. 'It has turned out as I thought it would. You are in love with Rushmore!'

'Don't be stupid, Amy! What on earth gave you that ridiculous idea?'

'Only the fact that you've been mooning about like a love-sick calf ever since he went away. I tell you, Dita, I long to find a place where *no one* is in love. Between Louise, who quotes Thomas and his perfections until I tire of hearing her, and you, who have not a word to say to anyone, I find the whole thing overrated, especially for a bystander.'

'I'm sorry! I have been finding Bath a little dull of late. It was much more interesting when the boys were here.'

'But not, of course, the Earl of Rushmore?' Amy's

tone was teasing, but then she saw Perdita's face crumple. 'Oh, love, I didn't mean to distress you. I thought he must have spoken before he went to London.'

'He did,' Perdita whispered in a broken voice. 'But I refused him…'

'Well, that is not so very dreadful,' her sister soothed. 'He will come back. I can't think why you did it, though. You deal so very well together, and he is besotted with you.'

'He won't come back. I told him that he must not hope. I was unkind, and now I am regretting it. It was just that… Oh, Amy, I did not know just how much I cared for him. I wouldn't admit it, even to myself. Now I have lost him and I don't know how to bear it.' A little sob escaped her lips.

'Cheer up!' Amy advised. 'Don't forget that the Earl is a military man. Even now he is planning his campaign to win you.'

'Or to win someone else.' Perdita would not be comforted.

'Don't be such a watering-pot!' Amy's reply was scathing. 'You are suffering from boredom as much as anything. Let us ask Aunt if we may hire the horses for another ride into the country. The grooms could escort us. We must do something or we shall fall into melancholy.'

'Would that be wise? We promised the Earl that we would stay in town.'

'The men could be armed in case of an attack upon Louise. *That* would provide a diversion for you.' Amy's eyes were sparkling.

'It isn't one that I should welcome. I believe that

we should stay in Bath for the present. We know that Louise is safe here.'

Perdita was wrong, but she did not know it at the time.

Chapter Eleven

Miss Langrishe was not an early riser, so Perdita was startled to receive an urgent summons to her room whilst she was still abed the following morning.

Throwing on her robe, Perdita hurried along the corridor, expecting to hear that her aunt's attack of gout was worse.

'Are you ill, ma'am?' she asked anxiously. 'Must I send for the physician?' The old lady's pallor was alarming.

Miss Langrishe shook her head. 'He can do nothing in this instance.' With a shaking hand she held out a letter to Perdita. 'This was delivered at first light.'

The letter was addressed to Louise.

'You have not opened it?'

'No, my dear. Clearly it is a private correspondence. Oh dear, it must be from that dreadful creature, Ver reker!'

'It could be from his lordship.' Perdita scrutinised the writing. 'It is not a woman's hand.'

'Adam would have sent a letter by the post and franked it in the usual way. It would have borne his seal. He would not have sent some urchin to the door to hand it in.'

'Then Thomas?'

'Your cousins have returned to London, as you know. And Thomas would not write without asking permission first. Oh, my dear, I hoped that we had heard the last of Verreker.'

'It could be a letter of farewell,' Perdita comforted. 'He may have given up all hope of Louise. Possibly he has found another target.'

'I hope you may be right.' Miss Langrishe was unconvinced. 'I shall not rest until I know the contents.'

'Louise will show it to you, Aunt. She knows that she must do so. The Earl was most insistent on that point.' Perdita handed back the letter, disturbed by the older woman's agitation. 'The girls will be here this afternoon, so do try not to worry. Louise has changed, you know. She is no longer quite so gullible, and she does not speak of Verreker as she was used to do.'

'You are right, my dear. She does not go about as if she is wearing the willow, but who knows what that creature has in mind?'

'It may not even be from him.' Perdita managed a brief smile.

'Who else would write to her? It *is* from him, I know it.'

'Even so, you do not need to fear for her. She will do nothing foolish. Adam…his lordship…has persuaded her that she must behave as her late father would have wished.'

'How sensible you are, my dear! I am a foolish old woman, seeing danger behind every bush.' The colour was returning to her cheeks. 'Even so, I shan't be easy

in my mind until we know the contents of this letter.'
She pushed the offending missive away from her.

Perdita left her then, but her thoughts were troubled.
Her words of encouragement had sounded unconvincing even to her own ears. Verreker was not the man to write a noble letter of farewell. He must have some other plan in mind.

She was unprepared for the magnitude of the shock which awaited her that afternoon.

'I have no secrets from you, ma'am.' Louise blushed a little when Miss Langrishe handed the letter to her. 'Please open it yourself.'

'No, no, my dear, though I must admit that we are mighty curious. The letter did not come by the post, you see. Now, pray don't keep us in suspense...'

She waited expectantly as Louise tore the missive open and scanned the contents. Then she heard a gasp. Louise was swaying and would have fallen if Amy had not slipped an arm about her waist.

'What is it, my dear? Oh, do sit down! Perdita, will you ring the bell? Bates must bring some brandy—'

'No, please! I am all right. It is just that I did not expect...' With a trembling hand Louise held the letter out to the old lady.

It was brief, but Miss Langrishe paled as she read it aloud. 'Your friends and acquaintances will wish to know how you came by the piece of lace stolen in Bath some days ago. This unpleasantness may be easily avoided, for a certain consideration. You may signal your compliance by visiting the cathedral tomorrow at eleven...alone. Failure to do so will result in charges being laid with the magistrates. There were several witnesses to this theft.'

Miss Langrishe was as white as the ribbons which trimmed her gown. 'What is all this, Louise?' she asked. 'I have heard nothing of it.'

'It didn't seem important enough to tell you, ma'am. It was all a mistake. We bought your lace, and then the man came running after us in the street. He said some lace was missing.'

Amy looked confused. She was still trying to grasp the enormity of what was being suggested.

'But that could have nothing to do with you,' Miss Langrishe protested.

'He found the missing lace in Louise's reticule,' Perdita told her slowly. 'We wondered why he should ask for Louise's name and her direction. Then we thought nothing more about it.' Anger threatened to consume her. 'This is nothing more than a cheap attempt at blackmail. Verreker must be behind it.'

'No! You are mistaken!' Louise went red and white by turns. 'He was not there. How could he know of the missing lace?'

'I don't know, but it all sounds very smoky to me. An assignation in the cathedral? He mentions consideration, but he must know that you are much too young to be in control of your own fortune.'

'But he has threatened to lay charges with the magistrates.' Louise was close to tears. 'I must keep the appointment, if only to enquire—'

'You will do no such thing,' Perdita told her sternly. 'Nothing can be proved against you. You had best ignore the letter. Throw it in the fire!'

'No! I believe that we should keep it.' Miss Langrishe was insistent on the point. 'How I wish that Rushmore had not left us. He would know exactly what to do.'

'I will go back to the shop,' Perdita told her. 'There is some mystery here. Why ask for a secret meeting? The owner might have come to see you here.'

She thought she knew the answer. The letter bore all the signs of Verreker's hand.

At eleven in the morning the cathedral would be deserted. There were several entrances. What could be easier than to throw a veil over Louise's head and hurry her away by a side door?

'I will go with you,' Miss Langrishe said at once. Her gout was no better, but she was determined to accompany Perdita.

It came as no surprise to Perdita to discover that the owner and his son were absent from the shop in Milsom Street that day. An obsequious male assistant announced that they had been summoned to the funeral of a distant relative.

'I don't believe it for a moment,' Perdita fumed. 'They must be in league with Verreker.'

'Is that likely, Perdita? I detest the man as much as you do yourself, but such a notion seems far-fetched.'

'Perhaps! But once he has Louise and her fortune he could offer them a share of it.'

'They have not reckoned with Adam.'

'No, Aunt, but he isn't here. How clever they were to wait until he'd left for London! They may hope to spirit her away tomorrow. By the time he found them it would be too late.'

It was her aunt's turn to offer comfort. 'That won't happen, my dear. Louise must not keep the appointment.'

'He may lay charges purely out of spite—'

'Let him do so. My name is good enough, I think, to counter any accusations.'

Miss Langrishe was mistaken. It was an apologetic officer of the law who arrived at Laura Place the following week, but he could not be persuaded from his duty.

'My apologies, ma'am!' The young man was all deference. 'But I am afraid there is no help for it. The young lady must be taken in charge.'

'I wish to see the magistrate,' Miss Langrishe announced in awful tones. 'He is well known to me.'

'As you wish, madam.' The young man was prepared to wait. The charge was clear, and he doubted if this formidable lady would away the decision of his superior. He was right.

'Beatrice, I am very sorry,' that gentleman informed his friend. 'The law is clear in this respect. Miss Bryant must be taken into custody. Naturally, she will not be lodged in the common gaol. The gaol-keeper will take her into his own house.'

'Frederick, she is a child. This is a trumped-up charge.'

'She will be given an opportunity to defend herself, but the law is clear. This is a serious accusation. If proved as Grand Larceny, the penalty could be death.'

'For a scrap of lace?' The old lady's face was ashen.

'It depends on the value. If the value is more than one shilling, which, in this case, it is, the law is severe.'

Miss Langrishe seemed to be breathing with difficulty and her companions became alarmed.

Perdita addressed the magistrate. 'This has come as

a grave shock to my aunt. As you see, she is not well. As for me, I cannot believe that you would allow an innocent girl to suffer such a fate.'

'Miss Wentworth, I have the highest regard for your aunt, but the law is clear. Miss Bryant must appear at Taunton Assizes to answer the charges laid against her. I can assure you that, in practice, the sentence is rarely death if the accused is found guilty.'

'What then?'

'A reprieve means transportation to Botany Bay for a period of fourteen years.'

'Merciful indeed!' Perdita faced the guardian of the law with flashing eyes. She was about to say more when a low moan from her aunt brought her to that lady's side.

'Don't worry, Aunt!' she comforted. 'The Earl will know what to do.'

Miss Langrishe was beyond comfort. 'He isn't here,' she whispered. 'Frederick, must you take Louise in charge at once? May she not stay here? I will guarantee that she does not leave Bath.'

'I'm sorry, my dear, but that is not possible. It would set a bad precedent. We should be charged at once with operating one law for the rich and another for the poor.'

'You do that anyway!' Perdita told him rudely.

'Not if we can help it, Miss Wentworth. We are not all corrupt.'

Perdita was ashamed of her outburst. Clearly, the magistrate was uncomfortable in exercising his duty, but he would not be dissuaded. She thought him an honest man.

'Where will you take her?' she asked.

'To Ilchester, Miss.'

'To the Somerset County Gaol?' Perdita was horrified. 'My dear, sir, you would not expose her to those conditions...the company of thieves and murderers and women who are no better than they should be?'

'Of course not!' The magistrate was growing impatient. 'She will be lodged in the gaol-keeper's own house, as I have explained. Now, if you will forgive me, we are wasting time. If the young lady will collect such things as she may require?'

He looked at Louise, but she made no move to follow his instructions. Perdita doubted if she had heard him. Frozen to the spot in shock, she seemed incapable of movement.

Perdita turned to Amy. 'Pack her things,' she whispered. 'For the moment we can do nothing more to help her.'

'I could go with her,' Amy offered. 'With the two of us together, it might be easier.'

This suggestion was turned down by the magistrate, though he tried to soften the blow. 'Naturally, you may come to see your friend as often as you wish,' he announced. Then he turned to Miss Langrishe. 'Beatrice, Miss Bryant will suffer little more than to be deprived of the company of her friends for the time being.'

'Rubbish!' Perdita told him shortly. 'Bath is a positive hive of gossip. How long do you suppose it will be before this sorry tale gets out? Louise is innocent, but tongues will wag. What will this do to her reputation? If nothing is proved against her, there will still be those who believe that there is no smoke without fire.'

'That cannot be helped,' the magistrate said firmly. He was no coward, but he offered a private prayer of thanks that his prisoner was the meek Miss Bryant, rather than this fiery little beauty who refused to be overawed by the power of his office.

Perdita was furious, but anger gave way to pity as a mute Louise was led away. Then she pulled herself together.

'The first thing to do is to write to Rushmore,' she cried as the sound of the carriage wheels died away. 'Aunt, will you do it, or shall I?'

Miss Langrishe seemed to have aged by a full ten years. 'I would do it gladly,' she whispered. 'But I cannot use my hands...' She looked at her red and swollen fingers.

'Then I will write.' Perdita sat down at the escritoire. Her note was brief and pithy, setting out the facts, but it was only when it had been dispatched to London that she felt easier in her mind.

'I hope that the Earl will come at once, don't you?' The normally ebullient Amy was subdued. 'Louise looked as though she was being led to execution.'

'Oh, don't say that!' Perdita shuddered. 'She will be safe enough until the date of the Assizes. I can't believe all this. What can Verreker hope to gain?'

'You think he is behind it?'

'Nothing is more certain,' Perdita told her. 'Perhaps he hopes that the Earl will buy him off if he agrees to drop the charges.'

'But, Dita, we know they are not true. We were there. We saw what happened. If we speak out in court?'

'We may not be believed. We are Louise's friends. We must be expected to support her.'

'But we would not lie on oath,' Amy said stoutly.

'It has been known. Oh, Amy, this is all so horrible! I cannot wait for Rushmore to arrive.'

Perdita tried to curb her impatience for the next few days, but there was no word from London, nor did the Earl appear in Bath.

'Where is he?' she cried in anguish. 'I won't believe that he has abandoned us.'

'He could be away from London,' Amy suggested. 'He'll get your letter when he returns. Meantime, shall we go to see Louise?'

'Oh, yes!' Perdita seized on the suggestion with relief. 'It will ease Aunt Trixie's mind if we are able to assure her that Louise is well. Possibly, she may come with us.'

That hope was quickly dashed. The attack of gout had flared alarmingly, and now it was impossible for Miss Langrishe to set her feet to the ground.

Her spirit was undaunted. 'Take what you can to make Louise comfortable,' she said. 'Chef shall provide some hampers of food. Perdita, you must ask the child if there is anything she needs...anything at all.' Her eyes grew sad. 'I feel that I have failed sadly in caring for her. Who could have imagined that it would come to this?'

'No one, Aunt, and you must not blame yourself.' Perdita frowned. 'How could you have guarded against such wickedness?' She sighed to herself in desperation. Where was Rushmore? Surely there had been time enough for him to return to Bath.

It was with heavy hearts that she and Amy set off for Ilchester. Miss Langrishe had not opposed the plan, though she had insisted that they took Ellen with them.

'Thank heavens that Father insisted that we kept our own carriage here in Bath,' Perdita told her aunt. 'I thought it an extravagance at the time, believing that we should have no use for it, but he said that the horses might as well be stabled here as in London.'

Miss Langrishe looked troubled. 'I won't forbid you to go to Ilchester, my dears, but I shall not rest until you are safely back again. You will have no gentlemen with you for protection.'

'We shall have our own driver and the groom. Besides, we shall have Ellen too. She would make a formidable foe should anyone attempt to offer us an insult.'

'And no one offers insult to Perdita, Aunt Trixie. She has a way of looking down her nose which is guaranteed to freeze the daffodils.' Amy's cheerful attempt at a joke succeeded in lightening the atmosphere, though Miss Langrishe was careful to point out that daffodils were not to be found in early autumn.

'She'll find something to freeze,' Amy assured her. 'Pray don't worry, Aunt. We shall not be gone for many hours. It is not as if we were planning a stay at any of the inns along our route. We shall stop only to bait the horses.'

'That's true...and if you carry provisions with you there will be no need for you to dine among strangers.' Miss Langrishe rang the bell to summon her chef. 'We must make up a basket for Louise. Heaven knows what the sheriff is giving her to eat.' She began to discuss a lengthy list.

'Dear Lord...Aunt is sending enough food to cover the fourteen years of transportation,' Amy whispered to her sister.

'That remark is in the worst possible taste.' Perdita

frowned. 'It has given Aunt Trixie something to do.
She longs to help Louise, but for the moment there is
nothing we can suggest, other than to make her imprisonment more comfortable. Aunt feels that she has
failed in her care of Louise.'

'She did try,' Amy pointed out reasonably. 'At one
time I felt that she might strike the magistrate when
he refused to leave Louise with us. For heaven's sake,
did he expect that we should spirit her away?'

Perdita grew thoughtful. 'It might have been the answer. We could have taken her to London, to Aunt
Prudence...'

'With the officers of the law hot upon our heels?'

'You are right. It would not have served. In fact, it
would have made matters worse. Perhaps it's as well
that the opportunity did not arise. It's just that I can't
bear to think of Louise in that hateful place. She must
be in despair, deprived of her friends and with such
charges hanging over her.'

'We must take what we can.' Ever practical, Amy
turned to the matter in hand. 'Must I fetch her things
from the Academy? She will need a change of clothing. I'll think of some story for Miss Bedlington.'

'Will you do that, love? Perhaps if you mentioned
that she wasn't well?'

Amy tried, but the scandal was common knowledge
in Bath. Miss Bedlington saw it as a personal affront.
The news that one of her pupils was held in a common
gaol threatened to ruin her reputation and deprive her
of her livelihood. She made no secret of her disgust.

Amy lost her temper. 'May I remind you that in this
country a person is presumed to be innocent until they

are proved guilty,' she cried. 'Are you judge and jury?'

'Hold your tongue, miss! Such impertinence! It does not surprise me. You and your sister are a disgrace to the name of womanhood.'

'And you are its ornament? My sister is worth a dozen such as you!'

'Get out, you little viper! You may take your own possessions as well as those of your thieving friend. If you return I'll have the law on you.'

'That won't be necessary, ma'am. If I never see you again it will be too soon.' With this parting shot Amy stalked away.

'That seems to be the end of my schooldays,' she told Perdita. 'Must I tell Aunt Trixie?'

'You can't avoid it. Oh, Amy, did you have to fly at Miss Bedlington? Aunt has enough to worry about at present.'

Amy chuckled. 'Do I hear the pot calling the kettle black? She insulted you, and she called Louise a thief. I couldn't let it pass. You'd have done the same yourself.'

'I suppose so. Well, we had best get it over with. Let us hope that Aunt won't be too distressed.'

Miss Langrishe surprised them. She listened with relish to the story of Amy's confrontation with Miss Bedlington.

'Quite right!' she said at last. 'I never liked the woman. She's such a crawling, encroaching creature. Let her keep her precious respectability. She'll get no more recommendations from me.' Then she beamed at Amy. 'No harm done, I think,' she announced. 'The loss of a few weeks' schooling cannot harm you.'

'Aunt, you are a treasure!' Amy kissed the papery cheek. Then she looked at the list beside the old woman's hand, and she began to laugh. 'We are taking just the one coach to Ilchester,' she teased. 'I fear the horses will have a struggle to get us there.'

She was rewarded with an answering smile. 'Louise may have need of all these things, my dear. Far better to be on the generous side than to skimp our help.'

She was proved right. The girls made an early start on the following day and the journey passed without incident.

Perdita was unusually silent, and Amy guessed that she was dreading what they might find.

'Cheer up!' she comforted. 'We may be pleasantly surprised. Louise may be quite comfortable.'

Her optimism proved to be ill-founded. On arrival at the gaol they were directed to a dark and dismal dwelling built inside the prison walls.

'This can't be right!' Perdita cried in dismay. 'The sheriff is said to have six children. This house is much too small to house a family.'

Amy signalled to the groom, telling him to knock at the door and ask directions. When he returned he was accompanied by a stout individual who was clearly a stranger to the benefits of soap and water. The man opened the carriage door with a flourish.

'Welcome, ladies! You are the Misses Wentworth, I believe. Pray step down. Miss Bryant will be glad to see you.'

'You are the sheriff?' Perdita asked in disbelief.

'At your service, ma'am!' The man bowed, releasing noxious odours from his unwashed clothing. Combined with the powerful smell of gin, this was enough to send Perdita searching for her handkerchief. On the pretext of blowing her nose, she held it to her face.

Amy was made of sterner stuff. She jumped down with a smile, and offered the man her hand. The look she gave Perdita was filled with meaning. The sheriff must be treated with respect if he were to be persuaded to become their ally.

Perdita gave an imperceptible nod. Then she ordered the unloading of the coach. The number of large hampers brought a smile to the sheriff's face, and to the faces of the round-eyed children who poured out of the open doorway. Their numbers seemed to be endless.

Perdita's heart sank. The children seemed to be healthy enough, but there were so many of them. What must conditions be like indoors? She was soon to find out.

Pressed by the sheriff to step inside his home, Perdita felt a tug at her sleeve.

'Lord, Miss Perdita, I don't like this. Must you go inside? Miss Bryant could come out to you. I don't doubt that the place is full of lice, and the Lord knows what else besides.'

'Hush, Ellen! You need not come indoors, but Amy and I must not offend the sheriff. Wait here! We shall not come to harm.'

She spoke with a confidence she was far from feeling, but she stepped indoors to be greeted by a fat and blowsy woman with a new baby in her arms. Her clothing was stiff with grease and beer stains, but she smiled happily at her visitors, apparently oblivious of the dirty conditions in which she lived and the appalling noise. Dogs and cats roamed freely about her kitchen, and Perdita shuddered as she saw the state of her pot cloths. Possibly they had once been white. Now they were almost black.

'Miss Bryant is in her room,' the woman told them. 'Will you go up, ladies? It's small, but it is all we have to offer her.'

Perdita and Amy left the chaos behind and climbed the stairs. There were but two bedrooms, and they averted their eyes from the squalor visible through the open door of the chamber on their right. The other door was closed.

Perdita tapped gently, but there was no reply. Cautiously, she tried the doorknob and peered into the room.

Louise was sitting on a trestle bed, apparently in a stupor.

'Oh, my dear!' Perdita hurried towards her and gathered the girl into her arms. 'We had no idea! Can this possibly be worse than the gaol itself?''

Recognition dawned slowly in Louise's eyes. Then the tears came and she wept for several minutes against Perdita's shoulder.

'Forgive me!' she said at last. 'I meant to be brave, you know, but I cannot sleep for the noise and I am always hungry.'

'You cannot mean that they are starving you?' Amy was indignant.

'They give me what they can, but they are very poor and there are many mouths to feed. The sheriff's wife means well, but...but...I cannot eat what she prepares.'

'Why is that? Is she a poor cook?'

'I don't know. I haven't touched the food since I saw her licking her cooking utensils clean...'

Perdita closed her eyes in horror. Then she pulled

herself together. 'There will be no need for you to do so. Aunt has sent supplies…enough to feed you and the sheriff's family for several weeks.'

Amy leaned out of the window and called to the groom to fetch a hamper to her. 'You must eat,' she insisted. 'You will need all your strength if we are to get through this.'

Louise gave her a pitiful look. 'I had hoped to see my guardian,' she whispered. 'Has he washed his hands of me?'

'Of course not!' Perdita was firm in her denial. 'We wrote to him at once, but he must be out of London. He has estates in Cheshire and in Derbyshire, you know.'

'But when will he be back?' Louise was fast losing her composure. 'The Taunton Assizes are not for some weeks. Must I stay here until then? I'd rather die—'

'No, you wouldn't!' Amy said firmly. 'Is the common gaol worse than this? Perhaps you could be moved?'

'Oh, never say so! You can have no idea. I can see the prisoners from my window…wretched creatures, most of them. They fight for food. It goes to those who can afford it. The others beg through the outer bars from passers-by.'

Amy and Perdita stared at her in silence.

'Then there are the women. I did not know such creatures existed. They sell themselves quite openly for favours and for money.' Louise's eyes grew sad. 'I cannot say that I blame them. How else can they survive?' She gazed at her friends in despair.

It was then that Perdita came to a decision. She would go to London herself. There, at least, she might learn something of Rushmore's whereabouts. She was convinced that her letter hadn't reached him.

If that plan failed she would seek the help of Thomas's parents, her uncle Sebastian and aunt Prudence. This would be a last resort. Thomas had inherited a fiery temper. Feeling as he did about Louise, Perdita would not put it past him to attempt to rescue her by main force. She knew how quickly gossip travelled in polite society. Now she prayed that the news had not yet reached him.

Once her decision was made she was impatient to put her plan into action, but she kept her thoughts to herself on the journey back to Bath.

Ellen looked at her averted face. 'Now, Miss Perdita, don't take on!' she begged. 'You have done all you can, giving that sheriff creature extra money and all that food.'

'And we promised him more if he could make Louise more comfortable,' Amy added.

'I know it, but what can he do? The place is a shambles.'

'It could be worse,' Amy told her quietly. 'Louise understands that they are not cruel people. They mean to be kind.'

'But she is suffering so. It is hard indeed when she is innocent.'

'Take heart, Perdita. For all we know, his lordship may have returned to Bath. He may be with Aunt Trixie even now. He will know what to do.'

'Oh, yes!' Perdita cried with feeling. 'All else aside, he must be told what has happened.'

That fond hope was to be disappointed. Only Miss Langrishe awaited their return. She had not seen the Earl.

'How is Louise?' she asked at once. 'Tell me how you found her! Is she well in health?'

'I think so, but she is very low in spirits.'

'Well, that is to be expected, my dears. She has her own room?'

'Yes, Aunt.' Perdita saw no point in explaining that it was little larger than a cupboard. Nor did she feel the need to mention the noise or the filthy conditions in the sheriff's home. 'Your gift of food was welcomed,' she added. 'The sheriff and his wife are very poor.'

'You left money with them? It is the best incentive to take good care of a prisoner.'

Perdita hesitated, but Amy suffered no such inhibitions. 'Perdita gave them all we had,' she admitted.

Miss Langrishe reached into her reticule and found a key. 'Unlock my desk, Perdita, and bring me one of the leather bags you find there.'

Perdita was about to hand it to her, but Miss Langrishe waved the bag aside. 'Keep it!' she said. 'You will find enough in there to pay the gaoler when you go to Ilchester again.'

Perdita guessed that the bag was filled with golden guineas. 'It is too much,' she protested. 'Aunt, it will worry me to be in charge of so much money.'

'Then lock a part of it in your room. Won't you let me salve my conscience in this small way? At this present time I feel distraught...I did not tell you earlier, as I had no wish to distress you, but this has happened before.'

Both girls stared at her. 'You mean that another innocent person was accused?' Perdita exclaimed.

'It happened some years ago, to an elderly friend of

mine. She too was accused of shoplifting here in Bath, and in the same way.'

'The theft of lace? Why should that be, I wonder?'

'Lace is expensive, Amy, and it is soft enough to be slipped quite easily into a lady's reticule.'

'Then this is just a copy of that crime?'

'In a different shop, but clearly the story has not been forgotten.'

'What happened to your friend?'

'She was found to be innocent, but the months in custody had a sad effect upon her health. It took her years to recover.' Miss Langrishe wiped away a tear.

Perdita took her hand. 'My dear Aunt, don't distress yourself. Louise is young. She will not suffer as an older person might. Let me write to the Earl again. My letter can't have reached him.'

'Will you do that, my dear?' It was with a heavy heart that Miss Langrishe sought her bed that night. She had grown sadly aged in the past few days.

'This isn't helping Aunt Trixie.' Amy commented. 'I wish we could do more to help her. Another letter to the Earl must take some time to reach him.'

'I don't intend to wait,' Perdita said decisively. 'Amy, I must go to London.'

Amy brightened. 'Yes, that is the answer. I'll go with you. Aunt must see the sense of it.'

'She is not to know in advance,' Perdita warned. 'She will either forbid it out of hand. Or insist that I take Ellen.'

'But if we are together?'

'I want you to stay here.' She stilled Amy's protest with a look. 'Have you not noticed? Aunt's gout is getting worse. Do stay with her, I beg of you. You can explain...'

'But what do you intend to do?'

'I'll try to find the Earl. He lives in Berkeley Square, so I understand.'

'But he may not be there. You can't roam the streets of London unattended.'

'I won't do so. If all else fails, I shall go to Uncle Sebastian. He and Aunt Prudence will help us.'

'But there is Thomas,' Amy objected. 'He can be a firebrand. He won't hesitate to go to Ilchester and confront the sheriff. He'll get himself arrested.'

'I know that, goose, but Thomas may not be there. There was some talk of his regiment being sent to Manchester.'

'I hope you are right, but what will you do if you can't find Rushmore and our aunt and uncle have left for Cheshire, as they do at the end of each Season?'

'Don't be such a pessimist! I'll come back to Bath, of course.' Perdita smiled. 'At least I won't be short of money.'

'No, but Aunt would have a fit it she knew that you were putting it to such use.'

'That can't be helped. It is in a good cause, and I'm sure that the Earl will repay her.' At the thought of taking action Perdita felt as if a great burden had been lifted from her shoulders. She looked at her sister's downcast face. 'I wish that you could come with me, love, but you must handle matters here. We don't know what may transpire in these next few days. Verreker may reappear and some further attempt be made at blackmail.'

'Oh, do you think so?' Amy's eyes began to sparkle. 'Let them try! They will have me to reckon with. When will you go, Perdita?'

'As soon as may be. Tomorrow we must walk to

the offices of the mail coach. I'll buy a ticket and find out the times of departure. Now remember, no one must suspect.'

'Ellen will be the greatest danger,' Amy said slowly. 'She knows us both so well.'

'Then she must be diverted. I'll send her to Aunt when we go out. Doubtless she will have a sovereign remedy for gout.'

The plan worked as Perdita hoped it would, and by noon on the following day she returned to Laura Place with a ticket for the London Mail Coach hidden in her reticule.

Chapter Twelve

Perdita left the house before first light on the following day, easing open her aunt's front door with the
utmost care.

She had taken the precaution of wearing her oldest
cloak and bonnet, and as she hurried through the darkened streets she attracted no attention.

Now she blessed her aunt's decision to live in Laura
Place. It was but a short distant to the courtyard of the
inn where the Mail Coach awaited passengers. Perdita
was the first to arrive, so she chose to take a corner
seat facing the front of the coach. The air was chill
and she shivered as she awaited her fellow-travellers.

Hopefully, none of them would recognise her. A
journey by public conveyance was not the most favoured method of transport for Miss Langrishe's
friends and acquaintances. Even so, she felt relieved
when all the seats were taken by strangers.

It was still dark when the driver climbed aboard and
gave his horses the office. They moved out slowly
over the cobble-stones until they reached the outskirts
of the city, where he urged them to greater speed.

Perdita was happy to discover that none of her companions felt disposed to talk at such an early hour. A young woman travelling alone must be sure to arouse unwelcome curiousity, and she had no wish to answer questions, however well meant. The driver already viewed her with suspicion. She had no luggage worthy of the name, and carried only a soft bag which held her night attire. She guessed correctly that he had no wish to be pursued by an irate father or brother, intent on removing the young lady from the coach.

Perdita shrugged. That would not happen. With luck it would be many hours before her absence was discovered, and far too late for her aunt to send anyone in pursuit.

She tried to suppress a pang of conscience. Would Miss Langrishe realise that she was acting for the best? The thought of adding to her aunt's worries was distressing, but the need to find the Earl of Rushmore must outweigh all other considerations.

She fell into a reverie, remembering that well-known smile and the twinkle in the dark eyes when he was amused. She sighed inwardly. His lordship would find little to amuse him in her news. He had promised to make enquiries about the loathsome Matthew Verreker. If only he had managed to discover some information which might be laid with the authorities, so that the creature might be prosecuted. With any luck the man could be transported to Australia or some such place, where he would be incapable of doing further harm.

Lost in thought, she was unaware that the growing light of day had revealed the faces of all the other occupants of the carriage. At last she realised that she was under scrutiny from a burly man who sat immediately opposite. He leaned forward to address the woman beside her.

'Do you care to travel forward, ma'am?' he asked. 'You may take my seat if you prefer to ride with your back to the horses.'

The woman favoured him with a long look. Then she transferred her gaze to Perdita. 'No, thank you, sir,' she said with an ironic smile. 'I am quite comfortable in this seat.'

The man nodded, but he continued to stare at Perdita. The pretty little chit was quite an armful, and she seemed to have no male protector with her. His curiosity aroused, he began to wonder about her. Was she seeking a position in London? There might be some opportunity for him there. On the other hand, her manner and her clothing suggested that she was a lady. Perhaps she was running away. He could still offer to be of service to her.

Perdita stirred uncomfortably. He was making her nervous. She was tempted to give him a downing stare. Instead she closed her eyes and leaned back in her seat, wishing that she had chosen a bonnet with a larger brim, which would have hidden more of her face.

Thank heavens the woman beside her had refused to give up her seat. How hateful it would have been to have the man in close proximity, doubtless with his legs and arms pressed against her own.

Her suspicions were confirmed at the first halt. She was the last to descend from the coach, and she found him waiting beside the steps.

He bowed. 'May I offer you some refreshment against the morning chill, miss?'

Before she could reply, the older woman stepped in front of her. 'This young lady is with me,' she said without preamble. 'She does not speak to strangers.'

The man backed away with a muttered apology, and as he walked off Perdita was amused to see that the backs of his ears were red with embarrassment.

The woman shared her enjoyment. 'There are some as never misses a chance to make a nuisance of themselves,' she announced.

'I have to thank you, ma'am. I must hope he will take you at your word. He was making me uncomfortable.'

'Ignore him, miss. He won't come near you again, else he'll feel the weight of my arm.' The woman chuckled as she hefted a well-filled basket as if it were a feather. 'I've seen the likes of him before, especially on this run. Sometimes I think they makes the journey just to pick up solitary maids. Shall you be wanting refreshment, my dear?'

'No, thank you, but—'

'I know. You'll be wanting to make yourself comfortable. Come along with me. I'll show you where to go.'

When they returned to board the coach, Perdita was glad to find that her tormentor had exchanged his seat inside the coach for one upon the roof.

'There now, that's better!' her rescuer announced. 'The cold wind will chill his ardour.' She laughed heartily.

Perdita thanked her once again. 'Do you make this journey often, ma'am?' she asked.

'As often as I can, miss. I visit my son in London town. 'Tis hard to live so far away when I have grandchildren waiting to see their Nan, but we are farming folk. 'Tis difficult to leave the work.'

'How old are the children and what are their names?' Perdita's question was enough to set her companion off upon what was clearly a favourite topic. In the next few hours she learned all there was to know about the little family in London.

'There now, I'm rattling on as usual,' the woman said at last. 'It's my besetting sin. Your ears must be ringing with my chatter.'

'It's a pleasure to hear of such a happy family,' Perdita said with conviction. 'I miss my parents so much. My father is a naval man, and they are away at sea.'

'So you are alone?'

'Oh, no, I have an aunt in Bath, and my sister is staying with her.' For a moment Perdita wondered if she were saying too much, but instinct told her that the farmer's wife was to be trusted. 'I also have relatives in London.'

'You are going to them?'

'Well, yes...but not at first, perhaps.' Perdita spoke with a confidence she was far from feeling, and after a brief glance at her face, her companion changed the subject, and lifted the heavy basket onto her knee.

'We had best eat now,' she said. 'Will you join me, miss?'

Perdita hesitated. 'Ma'am, I would not rob you of your vittles.'

This brought a chuckle from her companion. 'Bless you, there's enough to feed an army,' she announced. 'I make nothing of going short.'

When she opened her basket, Perdita realised that her friend had not exaggerated. Home-made crusty bread nestled alongside a fat cheese. A cold cooked chicken helped to fill the basket, as did part of a ham, and hard-boiled eggs were tucked into any available space. The woman handed Perdita a snowy napkin.

'Eat hearty!' she advised. 'There's nothing like good food for keeping up your strength.'

Perdita needed no further encouragement. The sight of the food made her realise that she was very hungry. Not a bite had passed her lips since dinner on the previous day. She removed her gloves, picked up the napkin and set about a piece of chicken with relish.

'I should have thought of this myself,' she admitted. 'I suppose I imagined that we'd be fed at the wayside inns where we stop to bait the horses.'

Her companion sniffed. 'There's no telling what you'd get. Sometimes the food is poor and pricey with it. Then, if the coach is running late, the driver don't give you time to eat.' She cut a generous slice of ham and handed it to Perdita on a slice of bread.

'You are very kind, ma'am. After all, you do not know me. My name is Perdita Wentworth. May I know yours?'

'I'm Bessie Griffin, miss. Aside from all else, my dear, it would not do for you to eat alone in a public dining-room. You've seen what can happen...' She jerked her head upwards to remind Perdita of the passenger outside.

Perdita looked away. 'You must think it strange for me to be travelling on my own,' she said at last. 'Believe me, the matter is urgent, else I should not have done so. I *must* find Rushmore.'

'Now, miss, don't cross your bridges before you come to them. For all you know, you may be in the gentleman's company before the day is out.'

'Oh, I *do* hope so,' Perdita said with feeling. 'He will make everything right again, I know it.'

Something in her tone brought the older woman's eyes back to her face and she smiled to herself. She knew the signs of a woman in love. She hoped with all her heart that the gentleman felt the same.

Their arrival in London was greeted with sighs of relief from all the occupants of the coach. The outside passengers were cold and windswept, whilst those inside were suffering from stiff limbs after their lengthy journey.

Perdita helped her companion down the steps. Then she stepped aside as the woman was greeted by a stocky young man who was the living image of his mother.

'No, miss, don't you wander off now!' Mrs Griffin extricated herself from her son's embrace. 'You'll be needing a hackney cab. Be quick and see to it, Ned.'

Ned was quick to obey his mother's wishes, but Mrs Griffin was not satisfied. 'Where to?' she asked Perdita.

The address brought a smile of satisfaction to the jarvey's lips. Only the quality lived in Berkeley Square, and it appeared that the young lady was to be his only passenger. His plans to charge her at least double the usual fare were soon destroyed.

'How much?' Mrs Griffin demanded.

The martial light in her eyes caused him to revise his estimate, but she brushed it aside with scorn.

'Highway robbery!' she announced. 'Ned, go and find another cab—'

'Nay, ma'am, don't take up a man so fast. Seeing

that the young lady is alone, I'll make a special price for her.'

He tried to hold out for his price, but he was no match for Mrs Griffin and found himself agreeing to a fare which he considered an insult. Damn these country bumpkins. Sometimes their cunning could outwit his own.

Ned handed Perdita into the cab.

'Now don't you go paying this thief a penny more,' Mrs Griffin advised. 'I know his face. I'll have the law on him.'

Perdita was strongly tempted to giggle at the dejected appearance of her driver. How Amy would have enjoyed meeting Mrs Griffin. She leaned from the window of the cab, holding out her hand.

'May I call to see you, ma'am, when I return to Bath?'

'No call for that, Miss Wentworth. Still and all, I shall be glad to see you. You'll find us at Bluebell Farm.'

She waited until Perdita's cab had disappeared from sight. Then she took her son's arm and walked away.

Suddenly Perdita's confidence deserted her. She felt very much alone. Suppose his lordship should be away from home? It was with a sigh of relief that she saw the knocker still on the door. Rushmore must be in residence.

She paid off her dispirited driver, walked up the steps, and lifted the knocker. The door opened almost at once, and she was confronted by a stately individual in full livery.

'Yes, madam? May I help you?' the man asked politely.

Perdita summoned up her courage. 'I must see the Earl of Rushmore,' she announced. 'Is he at home?'

'His Lordship dines out this evening, ma'am. If you would care to leave a message…?'

'No…I must see him at once. Pray give me his direction. Is he at White's or Watier's?'

Gorton, the butler, knew better that to continue this discussion in the open street. 'Will you not step inside, ma'am? I should like to be of service to you.'

'Well, you can be!' Perdita told him bluntly. 'I'll find his lordship if you will tell me where he is to dine.'

Gorton led the young lady through into the salon, pausing to order ratafia from one of his underlings.

'With respect, miss, I should not advise it. The gentlemen's clubs are mostly to be found in St James's Street.'

'And so?' Perdita's chin went up.

Gorton looked hard at her. His ability to assess the position of his fellow human beings was legendary. He had no difficulty in coming to the conclusion that this was a Lady of Quality. Perdita was also a beauty. It was not his place to speculate upon her relationship with his master, although he had heard some talk of an orphaned ward. Perhaps this was the girl.

'Ma'am, the area is not used by members of the female sex,' he explained.

'I can't help that,' Perdita cried. 'Oh, don't you understand? I have come from Bath to see His Lordship, and this matter will not wait.' She rose to her feet. 'Will you call me a cab, if you please?'

It was clear to Gorton that her likely destination was St James's Street. If this was indeed the Earl of Rushmore's ward, he shuddered to think of his master's reaction if he allowed the young lady to destroy her reputation.

'That would mean an unnecessary delay,' he said carefully. 'No lady may gain admittance to the clubs. They may not even agree to take a message for you. Allow me to send out footmen, madam. That will be the quickest way.'

Perdita tried to hide her impatience, but a moment's reflection convinced her that he was right. She nodded, and he disappeared to give his orders.

When he returned he was bearing a tray. 'May I take your cloak, miss—?'

'I am Perdita Wentworth. Yes, thank you!' Perdita looked at the clock, and was shocked to find that it was almost midnight.

The difficulties of her present situation struck her for the first time. She had made no plans beyond finding Rushmore, but unless his lordship left at once for Bath she would have no place to lay her head that night unless she took a chance upon finding her aunt and uncle still in residence at their London home.

Now she bemoaned her own stupidity. She should have asked the jarvey to drive her past their house on the way to Berkeley Square. A glance at the knocker would have told her if they were at home.

Gorton looked at her troubled face and poured her a glass of ratafia. The young lady appeared to be exhausted. She sipped gratefully at the wine, but refused his offer of food.

'I am too tired to eat,' she told him simply. 'Will...will they be long, do you suppose?'

'It's hard to tell, miss, though I've warned them of the need for haste.' Gorton poked at the fire, stirring the logs to flame. 'Perhaps if you closed your eyes,

Miss Wentworth, and tried to rest, the time would pass more quickly.'

He knew now who she was. The elder Miss Wentworth was a famous beauty, and extremely well connected. Most certainly she was not his master's ward, but she was a lady of some spirit. This was no time for speculation, but he could not help wondering at the reason for her errand. To present herself at Berkeley Square, alone, and at this late hour, meant trouble, he was sure of it.

Should he have sent for Rushmore? It might have been wiser to have denied his master, but Gorton knew determination when he saw it. This young lady was perfectly capable of sitting upon the doorstep until the Earl returned.

He looked down at her and saw that she was growing sleepy. The wine and the warmth of the fire had done their work. He waited until the sound of her regular breathing told him that she had drifted off. Then he slipped into the hall, prepared for a lengthy wait before the Earl returned.

It was minutes only before he heard the sound of running feet.

'Where is she?' Rushmore burst into the hall, all his famous composure vanished.

'Miss Wentworth is in the small salon, my lord. I believe she has fallen asleep.'

Rushmore brushed past him though he slowed his pace. He opened the door to the salon gently, and walked towards Perdita on silent feet.

She was sleeping like a child, long lashes hiding the lustrous eyes and resting softly upon her cheeks. As Rushmore looked at her, a wave of tenderness engulfed him. He took an unresisting hand and raised it to his lips.

She stirred then and looked up at him. Her smile made his heart turn over.

'Oh, Adam, I am so *very* glad to see you.' She held out her hands to him with a gesture that could not be mistaken.

'My darling!' Rushmore gathered her into his arms. 'Let me hold you to my heart! What is it, my dear one? The men assured me that not a moment was to be lost...'

Perdita rested her head against his shoulder. 'Didn't you get my letter? I had to come. I could not think what else to do,' she said. 'Oh, my dear, I don't know how to tell you.'

'No, I didn't receive any letter! Tell me what's wrong!'

Perdita responded to the urgency of his tone. Best to speak and be done with it. 'Louise has been arrested,' she said.

Perdita sensed his shock before he spoke. 'Tell me what happened,' he suggested quietly.

She kept the tale short. It was only when she spoke of the conditions under which Louise was living that her voice faltered. 'We cannot leave her there,' she said in broken tones. 'Oh, Adam, I am sure that Verreker is behind this wicked charge. Have you learned nothing of him?'

'I have!' Rushmore's face might have been carved in stone. 'He is known by other names. In Tunbridge Wells he attempted to elope with an heiress. There he was known as Martin Vincent. He left a trail in London too. This time his target was a wealthy widow. She knew him as Michael Vardy.'

'And it is the same man? How can you be sure?''

'The description is exact. And the Bow Street Runners are no fools. They tell me that in planning an alias a man will almost always use the same initials.'

'And is there evidence against him...enough to prosecute?'

'Sadly, there is not. That is why he was able to appear in Bath.'

'But what can we do? There must be something...?'

'I don't know, my dear one, but we shall beat him, rest assured.' Rushmore rested his cheek upon Perdita's hair. 'Your father has written to me, my love. I am permitted to address you, but only after he has learned of your wishes. I must confess that my hopes were dashed by that condition.'

'Really, my lord?' Perdita gave him a demure look. 'I wrote to my parents quite recently.'

Rushmore held her away from him, searching her face for confirmation of his dearest wishes. 'Then am I allowed to hope...?' he said in disbelief.

Perdita was no dissembler. 'Yes,' she told him shyly. 'Oh, Adam, I love you with all my heart. I did not know it until you went away. Then I thought I'd lost you.' Her lips quivered.

'Never in this life!' His glowing expression banished the last trace of doubt. He tilted her face to his and kissed her with a gentleness that stole her heart away. She clung to him, not wanting the kiss to end, but at last he put her from him with a rueful smile.

'Have mercy on me!' he begged. 'I am not made of stone.'

Perdita did not stir. She felt so safe within the shelter of his arms.

'I must send you to your bed,' he said at last.

'Oh, I am to stay with you?' The prospect filled her with delight, but his lordship knew where his duty lay.

'I planned to send you to your aunt and uncle, Perdita, but Gorton tells me that they have already left the city, and I would not have you return to Bath tonight. It would be too exhausting. We shall make an early start tomorrow.'

Perdita nestled closer to his breast. 'I never want to leave you again, Adam. These past few weeks have been a torment.'

His lordship kissed her again, this time with rising passion. She was happy to respond to the urgency of his caress, but he checked himself once more. Her innocence was touching. Clearly she did not realise that he was on the verge of losing all self-control.

'You would tempt a saint,' he told her thickly. He rose and rang the bell. 'My housekeeper will take care of you, my darling. Sleep well. You are safe beneath this roof.'

Perdita clung tightly to his hand. 'I shall always feel safe with you,' she whispered. 'Oh, Adam, is it wrong to feel so happy when Louise is in such trouble? You *will* save her, won't you?'

'All will be well, I promise.' Rushmore dropped the lightest kisses upon her brow and delivered her into the care of the fresh-faced woman who was smiling at both of them.

Alerted by Gorton, Mrs Derby now shared his belief that the young lady in her master's arms would soon become the next Countess of Rushmore. She had known the Earl since boyhood and, like the rest of his staff, she had been troubled by the recent change in his demeanour.

Always courteous to those who served him, he had seemed preoccupied and almost unaware of his surroundings. Now she knew the reason for it. A glance at his face told her that he was his old self again, merry and cheerful, but with an added glow.

'He's radiant,' she told Gorton later. 'That's the word I'd use...but there's something else upon his mind.'

Gorton nodded, but there was no time for a discussion. His master had ordered the carriage and his fastest team to be ready at first light. There was packing to be done, and a groom to be sent ahead along the route to Bath. Of recent weeks Rushmore had kept fresh teams in readiness at certain coaching inns on the way and Gorton had wondered at it at the time. Keeping teams along the Great North Road was one thing, but Bath? It now seemed likely that the Earl had been expecting trouble.

Perdita had fallen into a dreamless sleep, though it seemed only minutes before she was awakened by two smiling maids. One bore her breakfast tray, and the other carried her clothing, freshly washed and ironed.

'Is his lordship waiting?' she asked anxiously.

'You are not to hurry, ma'am. My master hopes that you will make a good breakfast before you leave.'

Perdita sipped obediently at her chocolate, and buttered two fresh rolls which she spread with raspberry jam and ate with relish. The bowl of fruit looked tempting, but she was eager to dress and hurry to her love again.

He was waiting in the hall below. He came towards her and took her hands in his, kissing them each in turn.

'Ready?' he asked.

Perdita nodded shyly, aware that she was under benevolent scrutiny from a surprisingly large number of servants. Everyone in the Earl's household seemed to have found some task to perform in the hall that morning.

Rushmore too was aware of it, but he made no comment as he led Perdita to the waiting coach.

'Shall you require the services of a maid, my love?' he asked anxiously. 'One of the girls is ready if you wish it.'

Perdita looked up at him and her heart was in her eyes. 'No!' she whispered. 'I'd rather be alone with you.' Then she gave him a mischievous smile. 'I got here on my own, you know.'

Rushmore winced. 'So you did, my darling. The thought of that journey makes me shudder. I trust that you were not offered insult.'

She did not mention the man who had approached her. 'I was befriended by a farmer's wife,' she told him. 'She couldn't have been kinder.'

Rushmore settled her comfortably within the crook of his arm as the driver gave his team the office.

She was silent for so long that he grew worried.

'What is it?' he asked. 'Are you regretting your promise to me?'

'Oh, no, Adam!' She gave him a look of perfect trust. 'It's just that…well…I can't believe that I'm not dreaming. Am I truly to become your wife?'

Rushmore chuckled. 'I must hope so, otherwise you are in a most compromising position for a well-bred young lady.'

'Oh, you mean that I should not have stayed with you last night?'

'You did not stay with *me* my darling. You stayed in my home, guarded by a bevy of servants and an extremely moral housekeeper. I was referring to our present situation.'

Perdita snuggled closer to his breast. 'It can't be wrong to feel so happy,' she announced. 'When did you first know…I mean, when did you change your mind about me?'

'It took some time,' he told her in solemn tones. 'At times I was in fear of my life…those dagger looks were enough to fell me to the ground.'

'Well, I thought I hated you, you see. I thought you bored and quite puffed up with pride.'

'And the temptation to prick the bubble was too much for you? You were quite right, my love. I must have been insufferable.'

'You were!' She could not resist the opportunity to tease him. 'I despised you so! I thought it unworthy of a gentleman to come to see my parents and insist that I be punished.'

'I did not do so, dearest.'

'Oh, I know that now, but at the time I did not know about Louise.'

Perdita's face grew sad. 'We should have taken better care of her,' she whispered. 'I wish that we had never entered that wretched shop.'

'You could not have known what was planned. Try not to worry so, Perdita. Louise is in no immediate danger.'

'Oh, how can you say so? The conditions at the gaoler's house are enough to kill her.'

'No, they aren't, uncomfortable though they may be. Louise is young and healthy. I doubt if she will take much harm as long as there is no infection in the house. I feared abduction more. If the Duke had not required my presence here in London I should not have left Bath.'

'And now?'

'I have an extended furlough. I shall not leave you again.'

Perdita lifted her face to his. 'I am so glad,' she whispered.

He kissed her then, gently but insistently. It was a kiss which banished all her worries. With Adam she would have no fears for the future. She responded warmly, pledging her love to him beyond all doubt.

He held her close. 'Now you shall tell me, my darling. When did you know you loved me? I had given up almost all hope, you know... You seemed determined never to forgive me.'

'I have been so foolish.' Perdita blushed and hid her face against his coat. 'More than anything, my pride was injured. I soon knew that I was wrong, but I would not admit it. I am sadly stubborn, I fear.'

'A shocking character, indeed!' The Earl laughed and dropped a kiss upon her hair. 'I thank heavens for your stubborn nature. You don't give up, my dearest, do you? How many girls, I wonder, would have travelled unprotected on the Mail Coach?'

'Amy would!' Perdita assured him. 'In fact, she cannot wait to do so.'

'I believe you! But then, the ladies of the Wentworth family are quite out of the common way, are they not? I consider myself the luckiest man in the world to have captured the heart of one of them.'

Perdita lifted her face to his. 'You sound like Papa,' she teased. 'He always blesses the day he met my mother. He loves her dearly, as you must have noticed.'

'Who could not?' he answered gallantly. 'Your mother is a most remarkable woman. Her elder daughter is likely to follow in her footsteps.'

'Thank you!' she said gravely. 'You could not have paid me a more handsome compliment.'

'You have not welcomed any others from me. You surprised me from the first, you know. I think it was your total lack of vanity about your beauty—'

'But I told you, Adam. My appearance is an accident of nature, and not of my own making.'

'That's true, but many lovely women think it enough to absolve them from the need to use their minds.'

Perdita laughed. 'I've seen it for myself, but it must be very dull to sit about looking decorative, and without an idea in one's head.'

'You won't suffer that fate!'

'Perhaps not, but I wish I had some ideas as to how we can help Louise. Is there nothing we can do?'

'There is a great deal, Perdita. I believe that Verreker is still in Bath.'

'In hiding?'

'I think so. He must be behind this plot to injure her. It cannot be coincidence that she has been accused so quickly after she refused all idea of an elopement.'

'It was a wicked plan,' Perdita cried.

'But not original. Your aunt will remember the first occasion. That time no charges were laid against the perpetrators.'

'So Verreker must have felt that he too would be immune from prosecution if he were caught?'

'Possibly. He is a desperate man. He must have thought it worth his while to attempt blackmail.'

'But if he is in Bath it must be possible to find him, and what of the owners of the shop? They must be party to this plot?'

'There must be a strong connection, and we shall find it, never fear. I took some action after you retired last evening.'

'What did you do?'

'I sent for the experts, Perdita. The Bow Street Runners are already on their way to Bath. They will keep a close watch on the shopkeeper. Verreker will be anxious to know how matters are proceeding. He cannot fail to contact his friends before too long.'

'I still don't understand,' Perdita told him. 'What benefit can it be to him to lay these charges against Louise and have her taken into custody? It can only be a longing for revenge.'

'Not necessarily. He knows that she has powerful friends. Will they allow her to stand trial? He must believe that they will go to any lengths to avoid that slur upon her character.'

'But if she is found to be innocent, as she must surely be, he can gain nothing.'

'Mud sticks, my dear. Verreker will know it well enough. There are always those who claim that there is no smoke without fire. The damage to Louise's reputation will be immense if she appears in court.' Rushmore's face grew grim.

'And if you find him, Adam? What then?' Perdita looked up at the Earl and caught her breath. This was a man she did not know. At that moment he looked capable of murder.

She gave a little cry of anguish. 'You will take care, my darling? You must not kill him. He isn't worth it.'

'I shall not kill him, but before I have finished with him, he may wish that I had done so. Now, let us leave this unpleasant subject for the moment. We are coming to the inn where we shall change our team.'

'So soon?' she asked in wonder. 'The time has gone so quickly.'

Rushmore smiled down at her. 'We have covered many miles, my love. Come, you must be in need of some refreshment!' He helped her down as the land-lord came bustling out to greet him. Bowing low, he led the Earl indoors.

Perdita's face showed her amusement as she was shown into a private parlour.

'Something amuses you, Perdita?' His lordship was puzzled.

'I was thinking of the contrast between this and my previous journey. It is all so…so comfortable.'

He caught her to him, then. 'That will always be my dearest wish, my dear. I promise to guard you from all harm. Now, try to eat. We have a long journey ahead of us.'

Perdita needed no further encouragement. As she looked at the table laden with viands she realised that she was very hungry. There were pies and pasties of every kind, flanking a massive joint of cold roast beef and a succulent ham.

Rushmore poured her a glass of wine.

'Is it not a little early?' she demurred.

'Drink it!' he said firmly. 'It will help you sleep. You have had a trying time, my love. Miss Langrishe is sure to be distressed if you arrive in Bath looking exhausted.' He waited until her glass was empty. Then he refilled it for her.

'I shall be tipsy,' she warned.

'Then I shall have you in my power,' he teased, twirling an imaginary moustache. 'Who knows, the evil Earl may have his way with you…?'

Perdita blushed, but she was laughing, much to his satisfaction. The look of strain had vanished from her face, and he was glad of it. She had borne enough in these past few days.

When they resumed their journey, he held her in his arms until she fell asleep. Then he looked down tenderly at the lovely flower-face. She would not suffer further if it lay in his power to prevent it.

This was not the time to tell her that he expected swift developments. Verreker needed money urgently. To obtain it he must act quickly. His most likely ploy would be to offer to drop the charges against Louise in return for a handsome settlement. It was fortunate that Perdita could not, at this moment, see the expression upon the Earl's face.

I'll see him in hell first! he vowed silently.

Chapter Thirteen

They arrived at Laura Place to find the family in a state of acute anxiety. Perdita had been dreading a confrontation with her aunt, but Miss Langrishe was too relieved to see her safely returned to Bath than to do more than to give her a reproachful look.

She took Perdita in her arms. 'Wilful child! Could you not have trusted me with your plans? Ellen or one of the grooms might have travelled with you—'

'Forgive me, ma'am. I had no wish to worry you, but it seemed to me that I must go to find the Earl without delay.'

'You were right!' Miss Langrishe turned to Rushmore. 'This is a pretty coil, is it not? What are we to do? I feel that I have failed Louise in every way.'

'Ma'am, that is not so, believe me!' His lordship looked grave. 'Louise may be living under wretched conditions, but at least she is safe. My fear was that she might be abducted. You took care to see that it did not happen.'

'We never left her alone,' Amy said quickly. 'But we did not expect this accusation. If you could but see her in the gaoler's house, you would not be so content.' She turned away to hide her tears.

'You think me content? Amy, you do me less than justice! I shall not rest until the charge is dropped.'

'But, Adam, what can we do? Perdita will have told you that she and Amy tried to see the owner of the shop, but he was nowhere to be found.'

'He cannot stay away for ever. The Runners are here in Bath. They will find him, and Verreker too.'

But in the event it was Perdita who saw Verreker first. As she and Amy crossed the Pulteney Bridge on the following morning, he strolled towards them, doffing his hat politely. When he made as if to pass them, Perdita stepped in front of him.

'You?' she cried in disbelief. 'I wonder that you dare to show your face in Bath.'

'And why should I not do so, Miss Wentworth? This is still a free country, I believe.'

'It should not be so for you. You should be behind bars—'

'Like your friend Miss Bryant? A sad business, that! I was taken in by her. It had not occurred to me that such a girl would take to thieving.'

Amy stepped towards him with an arm upraised, but Perdita held her back. 'No!'' she said firmly. 'This criminal will get his just deserts when the Earl of Rushmore catches up with him.'

'Ah, yes, the noble Earl! Such a warlike gentleman! Will you pass on a message from me, Miss Wentworth? If the Earl should offer me violence in any way, I'll have him charged with common assault.'

'You cur!' Perdita could contain herself no longer.

'Any man worthy of his salt would have found employment instead of preying on defenceless women.'

'Are you accusing me? That would leave you open to a charge of slander, my dear. You should take care to curb your tongue. After all, you have no shred of proof. I was deeply shocked to hear that your friend had been taken in charge.'

'Liar!' Amy hissed. 'You are behind this plot!'

'Miss Amy, I will make allowances for your youth, and your affection for your friend, but really I cannot allow you to make such statements without contradiction. What possible connection could I have with this haberdasher's store? I am not in the habit of buying lace and ribbons either for myself or my friends. You are quite mistaken, but may I give you ladies a word of advice?'

He waited, and smiled when he received no answer from either of the girls.

'You may not welcome it,' he continued. 'But there is a simple answer to the problem. In these cases I understand that a charge is often dropped if suitable recompense is offered.'

Perdita gave him a look of cool disdain. 'I thought it must come to this,' she said. 'We are now at the hub of it, are we not? Let me assure you, Mr Verreker, we shall not buy you off. You will not receive one penny for this attempt at blackmail.'

'Then, ma'am, though I can only refute these hysterical and unfounded accusations, I fear that your friend must stand her trial. Such a pity! It will quite destroy her reputation in Polite Society.' Verreker gave them an ironic smile. 'That, of course, must be the happiest outcome. If she is found guilty I doubt that she will be hanged, but I wonder how she will enjoy life as a convicted felon in Australia…' He brushed past them, and strolled unhurriedly across the bridge.

'I could kill him!' Amy was trembling with rage. 'I'd like to stab him through the heart, though I doubt if I could find it. Oh, Perdita, what are we to do?'

'Adam will know,' Perdita told her quietly. 'Don't worry! Verreker will not best him!'

'You seem very sure of that, but love has made you blind. You heard what Verreker said. He knows how to use the law. I'd hoped that Rushmore could force him into a confession with the use of a horsewhip, if necessary.'

'Adam won't do that, though he was tempted. To lay himself open to a charge of assault could serve no useful purpose.'

'What then?'

'He feels that we must not frighten away our quarry. Up to now Verreker has had the luck of the devil on his side. It cannot last. Sooner or later he will make a mistake and then we shall have him.'

'But what of Louise? We have no time to lose. It is but weeks to the Assizes. She must be out of her mind with fear at the thought of standing in the dock like a common felon.'

'Adam has gone to see the magistrate,' Perdita comforted. 'He may have better news for us.'

Amy shot a sharp look at her sister. 'Something has happened between you two, I think. I saw it at once when you returned last night. In spite of all, you both have a certain look…'

Perdita smiled. 'How quick you are!'

'Lord, it would be obvious to a babe in arms! Have you accepted him?'

'Yes. He knows now that I love him. Oh, Amy, I have no right to feel so happy in the midst of all our troubles.'

'I don't see why not,' Amy said stoutly. 'Thank heavens that we have something to celebrate at this awful time.'

'We cannot celebrate just yet, but you are happy for me?'

'Of course!' Shaken though she was by the encounter with Matthew Verreker, Amy managed a teasing grin. 'What a pair you are! You will deal together famously, though I expect that battle will be joined at frequent intervals. Never mind! It will remind his lordship of his fight against Napoleon.'

'It won't be in the least like that,' Perdita said with dignity. 'We shall be a sober married couple.'

Amy laughed aloud. 'I'll believe that when I see it. Oh, Dita, are you sure? You hated him so much at first.'

'I was a fool! It was not love that blinded me, but my own stupid pride. I am such a stiff-necked creature. I refused to see what was under my nose. Adam must be a saint. He loves me in spite of all my faults.'

Amy laughed again. 'He does not strike me as a saintly creature, which is probably as well. You could not live without a challenge, sister dear.'

'But you do like him, don't you? You forgave him long before I did myself.'

'I discovered that there was nothing to forgive. We misjudged him, but I believe that he loved you from the first moment he laid eyes on you.'

Perdita's eyes were shining. 'He told me that himself. Oh, Amy, I'm the luckiest person in the world. I can't believe that I'm to be his wife.'

'Have you told Aunt Trixie?'

'No, of course not. I wanted you to be the first to know, but we planned to keep our love secret until Louise is freed.'

'Then you must not go about looking starry-eyed,' Amy scolded. Then she smiled. 'Your news will come as no surprise to Aunt Trixie. She foretold this very outcome whilst you were in London.'

Perdita had the grace to blush. 'I haven't been very clever,' she admitted. 'I did not know that I had advertised my feelings.'

'Only to those who know and love you, Dita.'

'Thank heavens for that. Come, Amy, let us hurry back to Laura Place. Adam must have returned by now. He may have news for us.'

This was so, but the news was not encouraging. As Adam had expected, his rank availed him nothing in pleading Louise's cause. The magistrate had made it clear, if not in so many words, that in England no one was above the law.

'Then she must stand trial?' Miss Langrishe had aged visibly in the last few weeks. Her gout was worse, and now she could not move without pain. 'It seems so wicked that she must be humiliated in this way to answer a trumped-up charge.'

'It may not come to that,' Adam said quietly. 'Verreker is being watched. My men have found him here in Bath.'

'We spoke to him this morning,' Perdita said softly. 'He was crossing the Pulteney Bridge.'

Miss Langrishe gasped. 'And what had he to say to you? I wonder that he dared to show his face in public.'

'He is quite untroubled, Aunt. He denies all knowledge of any plot, claiming that he does not know the owners of the shop. He did suggest, however, that it might be as well for Louise's friends to pay what he termed ''compensation''.'

Miss Langrishe grimaced. 'I have been wondering... Adam, do you think perhaps it might be as well—?'

'Out of the question, ma'am!' he told her firmly. 'Pray do not give up hope that we shall come about. There is still time.'

'I hope you may be right, but if anything should go wrong? The child would not survive a voyage to Australia, penned in the hold of some prison ship with those who are treated as cattle.'

'Oh, Adam, you would pay before you let that happen to her, would you not?' Amy pleaded.

Adam took Perdita's hand. 'Am I to believe that there is only one among you who has faith in me?' he said.

Amy and Miss Langrishe were quick to reassure him, but they still had questions.

'I want to believe you, Adam,' the older woman said. 'But, if this case should come to trial, how is Louise to prove her innocence?'

Adam frowned. 'I'll admit that it won't be easy,' he said quietly. 'She may not give evidence on her own behalf, nor may her friends give evidence for her.'

'How unfair!' Perdita was incensed 'What of her counsel, then?'

'He, too, may not address the jury on her behalf.'

'And this is English justice?' Perdita was pale with anger.

'He is allowed to examine and cross-examine witnesses.'

'I see.' Perdita lost her temper then. 'I wonder that you can be so sanguine, my lord. It seems to me that Louise is to be condemned unheard.'

'Not so, my dear!' Rushmore took Perdita's hand in his. 'There have been developments.' He reached into the pocket of his coat. 'This letter was delivered to me this morning.'

'What is it?' Miss Langrishe eyed the missive as if it were some loathsome reptile. 'Not more bad news, I hope?'

'Not at all.' Adam unfolded the paper. 'The letter is anonymous, of course, but it contains some interesting information. Apparently the three plotters are disappointed that no effort has been made to buy them off. Each would like to propose a compromise, but they are afraid of the other two.'

'But what does this mean?' Perdita cried. 'It cannot help Louise.'

'It is the first glimmer of hope,' Adam assured her. 'I have never believed in honour among thieves. When these men are taken, each will attempt to save his own skin by revealing details of the plot.'

'But you will need evidence against them,' Perdita cried in despair. 'As yet we have nothing.'

'Don't give up hope, my love!' Oblivious of his companions, the Earl dropped a kiss upon her brow. 'This news is encouraging, believe me!'

Miss Langrishe recalled him to a sense of decorum. 'My dear Adam, you forget yourself!' she accused. 'That is, unless you have offered for Perdita.'

Adam did not hesitate. 'You knew of my intentions, ma'am. Perdita's father gave me permission to address her. Now I am happy to tell you that she has agreed to become my wife.'

'Oh, my dears! What joyful news! Perdita, come and kiss me! I wish you both happy, indeed I do, but bless me, there can be no doubting it. You are well matched and must have years of loving companionship ahead of you.' Suddenly, Miss Langrishe looked more her old self. The colour returned to her cheeks and her worn expression vanished.

Perdita was blushing furiously. 'Aunt Trixie, you don't seem surprised,' she whispered.

For the first time in weeks Miss Langrishe laughed. 'Your secret must have been obvious to a blind man,' she teased. 'The symptoms were all there, my dear, though it took you some time to recognise them for yourself.'

Perdita clung tightly to his lordship's hand. 'I didn't think it possible to feel so much in love. It is quite wonderful…' When she looked at Adam her heart was in her eyes. 'But, Aunt, we have agreed that this is not the time to celebrate our betrothal. We shall wait until Louise is cleared of this monstrous charge.'

'I hope that may be soon.' Amy began to pace about the room. 'How can she clear her name if she is not to be allowed to speak in her own defence?'

'I did not say that,' Adam assured her. 'If the worst should happen and she is brought to trial, she will be allowed to assure the court of her innocence. Her lawyers, I can tell you, will be the finest in the land, and there will be many witnesses to her good character.'

'It may not be enough.' Amy was close to tears. 'She must be terrified.'

'I intend to reassure her, my dear. Tomorrow I shall go to Ilchester—'

'How can you offer her any hope?' Amy would not be comforted. 'What can you say to reassure her?'

Adam looked at the anxious faces of his companions. 'I don't wish to raise unfounded hopes, but today I had a long talk with the magistrate and I told him the full story. He is a reasonable man and he accepts that Verreker, after failing in his first attempt to gain Louise's fortune, is probably behind this latest attempt. He is ready to proceed against the man with the full rigour of the law, but he must have proof.'

'And in that we are sadly lacking.' Amy was disconsolate. 'We need a miracle, and they are hard to come by.'

'Stranger things have happened. Now, Amy, what do you say? Will you go with me to see Louise?'

Perdita looked startled. 'Am I not to go to Ilchester too?'

'My love, I need you here. I believe that events will now move fast. My men have orders to report to you if they have any news.' He bowed to Miss Langrishe. 'Forgive me, ma'am! I would have asked that you be told, but I thought you not in the best of health.'

'Your news has cheered me, Adam. Perdita and I will see your men together should the need arise. There may be something we can do.'

'No!' he said firmly. 'I beg that you will take no action, however tempted you may be. I know my little hot-head here!' He slipped a loving arm about Perdita's waist. 'She is fully capable of entering the fray alone. It would be a mistake. The quarry shall not escape us, but he will flee if he suspects that we have any evidence against him.'

Miss Langrishe struggled to her feet. 'Come, Amy! Let us leave these love-birds to their billing and cooing. If you are to visit Louise we must find some more comforts for her. You will tell me what she will need most.'

Amy looked more cheerful as she followed the older woman from the room. She longed to see Louise again, and although the Earl had not been specific as to his future plans he had succeeded in lifting her spirits.

As the door closed behind them, Adam took Perdita in his arms. He slid a finger beneath her chin and looked deep into her eyes. 'It is a lifetime since I kissed you, my lovely bird of paradise.'

Perdita twinkled at him. 'I thought that term was reserved only for females of a certain profession,' she teased.

He smiled. 'You are well informed, my love. How do you come by these slang terms?'

'Amy is forever quizzing our cousins,' she admitted. 'Are you shocked?'

'Never, my darling, but in this instance my compliment comes from the heart. Your aunt described you as a love-bird, but to me you are something far more splendid. Have you any idea how much I love you? It is not your beauty alone, my dear one, though that is a joy to behold. I love your spirit, your courage, and your loyalty to your friends.'

He kissed her then, and Perdita returned his kiss with a passion which shook them both. All her inhibitions vanished as his warm mouth sought her own. She threw her arms about his neck and held him to her, murmuring inarticulate words of love.

'Ah, what a jewel you are!' he said softly. 'You are all I want in life.' He kissed her eyelids and then the corner of her mouth, straying from there to press his lips against the soft flesh of her neck. 'When shall we be married, Perdita? You will not keep me waiting? Already I dread to lose you to another.'

'That can never be,' she told him. 'I am yours and always will be.' She began to chuckle. 'You do not mention my faults, my lord, but they are legion. How are you to deal with a wife who has a hasty temper and is stubborn into the bargain?'

'I shall think of a way,' he promised with a wicked look. 'Ah, my love, where should we have been without your stubbornness? It carries you through against all manner of difficulties. You speak of faults, but I have plenty of my own.'

'Indeed you have!' She gave him a demure look. 'One, in particular, I find very hard to bear.'

'And what is that? Tell me, and I shall try to correct it.'

Perdita heard the note of anxiety in his voice. 'Why, sir, I doubt if you will manage it. You have an unnerving habit of always being right. It has infuriated me on more than one occasion.' She laughed happily, secure in the certainty of his love.

'Minx!' He drew her to him and kissed her soundly. 'You had me worried, dearest. More remarks like that and my hair will turn quite grey—'

'Nonsense!' Perdita reached up to stroke his cheek. 'Kiss me again!' she whispered. 'I could stay in your arms for ever.'

'Temptress!' He held her away from him and shook his head. 'This is more than flesh and blood can stand. Let us join your aunt before I forget myself completely. What do you say to a drive about the town this afternoon? Miss Langrishe might enjoy it.'

Swift colour rose to Perdita's cheeks. Innocent

though she was, she could not mistake his meaning. She jumped to her feet. 'That is an excellent idea,' she said hurriedly. 'I will go and speak to Aunt Trixie at once.'

Adam pressed a kiss into the palm of her hand and closed her fingers over it. 'Keep this, my love! It is a promise for the future.' He released her then and turned away, conscious that he had come close to giving his caresses an urgency which was far beyond the bounds of decorum. Yet he knew that he had not frightened her. Perdita would never behave in a missish way. She had given her love to him without reserve, in the open and honest way so natural to her.

He knew now that his passion was returned a hundredfold. He gave a rueful smile. That knowledge made it difficult to control his feelings, but he would do so. His lovely bride would be well worth waiting for.

He rang the bell and ordered his carriage for later that afternoon, hoping as he did so that Miss Langrishe would feel well enough to drive abroad.

She did not disappoint him. Though still in some pain she assured him that she was well enough to make the expedition.

'I feel so much better, Adam,' she told him. 'There is nothing like good news to give one's spirits a lift.'

'Then, ma'am, let us hope that we shall have more of it.' He rapped on the roof of the carriage and the horses made their way slowly through the crowded streets.

Miss Langrishe waved to her acquaintances. Clearly, she was delighted to be released from the confines of her home.

'Bath has changed so much since I first came to live here,' she observed. 'Adam, may we drive along the Royal Crescent? The houses there are very fine, and the view across the town is wonderful. How I should have liked to live there, but the climb to the heights is steep, and the Crescent was too far to be conveniently placed for the life I lead.'

Perdita could not agree with her, though she looked with pleasure at the graceful sweep of the Crescent. 'This must be the most beautiful city in England,' she cried warmly. 'I wonder that everyone does not come to live here.'

'Great heavens, Dita, don't say that!' Amy was laughing. 'The place would become impossible. Let us keep Bath a secret for as long as possible.'

Adam smiled at their enthusiasm. 'Do you care to drive out for a little way?' he asked Miss Langrishe. 'The view from the heights above the city is quite spectacular.'

He was right, and for a time his companions gazed with delight upon the scene below, with the city set like a golden jewel in a bowl of the Somerset hills.

'You have made a fortunate choice, ma'am,' Adam remarked. 'The place has so much to commend it.'

'And you must not regret the Crescent, Aunt.' Amy would have none of it. 'I, for one, am glad to be near the shops and the Pump Room and the Theatre.'

'Not the historic sights, Miss Amy?' Adam was disposed to tease her.

Amy chuckled. She was not in the least put out. 'They are well enough in their way,' she admitted 'But they are not so exciting.'

He laughed and let it go, but Amy quizzed her sister later.

* * *

'Does Adam think me a featherhead?' she asked as they prepared for bed.

'Of course not! What gave you that idea?'

'I don't know. I suppose it's because he laughs at me. Still, I like him in spite of it. Do you mind that you are not to go with us to see Louise?'

'No, I can understand his thinking. I trust his judgment, Amy. If he thinks it best for me to stay here, I will do so.'

Amy gave an unelegant whistle. 'There's a turn-up for the book! I thought I'd never live to see the day.'

Perdita frowned at her. 'Up to now he has been right. Now, what are you taking to Louise?'

Amy listed the clothing, the blankets, the food and the little luxuries which Miss Langrishe had insisted on providing.

On the following morning they were quickly stowed away inside the coach, and Perdita waved Adam and her sister off with no expectation that the day ahead of her would prove other than uneventful.

She was mistaken. As she was engaged in writing to her parents she was summoned to the salon. There she found her aunt in conversation with a burly man who introduced himself as a Bow Street Runner.

'Have you news for us?' she cried eagerly.

'Yes, ma'am. The subject is here in Bath.'

'We know that. We spoke to him yesterday. Have you discovered anything more about him?'

'He is known to us, Miss Wentworth, though under another name. We tracked him first in Lunnon town, where he's wanted for forgery, as well as theft and fraud.'

'Great heavens, is that not enough? Why is he not taken?'

'Proof, ma'am. We are building a case against him, but we must have proof. If he is charged and we have insufficient evidence, he will escape the law as he has done before.'

'Could you not search his rooms?'

'Aye, if we could but discover where he's staying. He's gone to ground, miss.'

'But he walks about the town quite freely—'

'And then he disappears. Oh, he has rooms at the Saracen's Head, but he ain't never there.'

'Perhaps he should be watched more closely,' Perdita's tone was icy.

'Quite, ma'am, but he's a slippery customer. We are doing our best.'

'Of course you are,' Miss Langrishe soothed. 'Be sure to let us know if you have further news…'

When the man had left she looked at Perdita's averted face.

'Don't lose heart, my love. I know that you had hoped…'

'I'm beginning to feel that any hope may be misplaced,' Perdita told her despairingly. 'The weeks are going on and the Assizes will soon be held. Oh, Aunt, this man is old in the ways of wickedness. Shall we ever be able to defeat him?'

'I thought that you had faith in Rushmore,' Miss Langrishe told her lightly. 'Will you give up on him because we have had no success as yet?'

'No, of course not!' Perdita's voice was shaking. 'It is just that…oh, Aunt, I can see no ray of hope on the horizon.'

'Take heart, my dear. Do you finish your letter to your parents. It will help you to feel closer to them.'

The advice was easier offered than taken. Perdita found herself unable to concentrate. It was as she was gazing endlessly into space that she was summoned for the second time.

'Miss Wentworth, there is a person here to see you.'

'I can see no one. Send him away.' Perdita could think of no one among her acquaintance who would be welcome at that time.

'The person is most insistent, ma'am. She says that it is most important that she speaks to you.'

'A woman?' Perdita was mystified. 'I can't think what...? However, you had best send her in.'

She did not recognise her visitor at first, but something about the thin figure seemed familiar.

'Good morning!' she said politely. 'Have we met, ma'am? I'm sorry, but I can't recall—'

'Yes, Miss Wentworth, we have met.' The woman stood just inside the doorway, clearly ill at ease in such opulent surroundings. 'You were kind enough to take my part at the haberdasher's shop when the owner threatened to dismiss me.'

'Oh, yes, I remember.' Perdita frowned at the recollection. 'A brute, if ever I saw one! I must hope that he didn't make good his threat when we had left.'

'No, ma'am, not immediately, but something happened the following week...' She was swaying where she stood and Perdita hurried to her.

'You are ill!' she cried. 'Will you not sit down?' She grasped the woman's arm and was startled to find that it was almost fleshless. Perdita rang the bell to summon Bates.

'Bring me some wine if you please,' she ordered swiftly. 'This lady is not well... She is in need of a restorative.'

But when the wine arrived her companion refused it.

'I need a clear head for all I have to tell you, madam. I did not know until last evening that your friend had been accused of stealing lace. It is untrue, of course. I saw it being slipped into her reticule.'

Perdita gasped. 'By whom?' she demanded.

'By the owner's son…the man who followed you out of the shop to ask if Miss Bryant had it about her person. He knew I'd seen him, but he passed it off as a practical joke, instigated by his friend.'

'And this friend? Did you know him, Mrs…?'

'My name is Margaret Tarrant, ma'am. I did not know him then. It was not until the following week that I heard a curious conversation. I was in the storeroom above the shop when one of the panels slid aside. I had not noticed it before. I could see into the room beyond quite clearly, and I was surprised to see that it was comfortably furnished…not like a storeroom in the least.'

'A hidden room?' Perdita was growing excited.

'Yes, Miss Wentworth. The two men within were quarrelling. There seemed to be some argument as to the speed with which they should proceed against Miss Louise. The stranger was all for haste, but the owner's son would not hear of it. He was all for caution.'

'Can you describe this man?'

'He was tall and fair…quite handsome in his way and dressed like a gentleman, though his language was not that of any gentleman I ever heard. His name seemed to be Virkir, or something like that.'

'Could it have been Verreker?' Perdita felt a sudden surge of hope.

'Yes, ma'am, that was it. I didn't mean to eavesdrop and I hoped they hadn't seen me. I was at the back of the store behind some boxes, but my cough gave me away. I was dismissed that same afternoon.'

'Oh, my dear, I am so sorry, but if only you had come to me before! So much unhappiness might have been avoided.'

'I have been ill, Miss Wentworth. I knew nothing of your friend's arrest until last evening when my friend gave me the news. I could think of nothing but my son, you see. I could not work, and I feared the child would starve.'

'That will not happen,' Perdita told her firmly. 'You must let me help you. You have done us a service far beyond anything that I might have hoped for. Now, ma'am, you shall come to meet my aunt. She takes some light refreshment at this time of day and will be glad of your company whilst you tell her what has happened.' Perdita had guessed that her companion was faint with both hunger and distress.

'I did not come to beg,' Miss Tarrant told her quietly.

'I know that, ma'am. You came to help us if you could.' Perdita gave her a smile of encouragement. 'Will you not trust me and set your pride aside for once? It is a difficult thing to do as I know to my own cost, but we owe you so much. It would make me happy if you would accept my help. Will you deny me that pleasure?'

A faint smile was her reward. 'You make it difficult to refuse you, Miss Wentworth…'

Perdita's heart was singing as she led her companion into the salon and Miss Langrishe saw the change in her at once.

'What has happened?' she asked quickly. 'And who is this lady, Perdita? We have not met before, I think.'

'Oh, Aunt, you will be happy to know her. Mrs

Tarrant has brought such news.' Perdita made the introductions quickly. 'She can prove that Louise is innocent.'

This was enough to bring Miss Langrishe upright in her chair. 'Pray sit down, ma'am, and tell me what you know.'

Perdita was on fire with plans, but she waited long enough to explain that Mrs Tarrant had come to Laura Place in haste, and without breaking her fast.

'My dear, you must be starving…' Miss Langrishe rang her bell and ordered substantial additions to her mid-morning tray. 'Now, Perdita, please be patient! Let me hear what Mrs Tarrant has to say…then we shall see what is to be done.'

Perdita was only half-attending as the story was repeated. Her head was filled with plans. First of all she must summon the Bow Street Runner back again. He had left her his direction. If Mrs Tarrant could be persuaded to wait until he returned, the man might act upon her information. She broke into the conversation to suggest this to her aunt, and received that lady's agreement.

Perdita gave her visitor an anxious look. 'What of your son, ma'am? Shall you be able to leave him for so long?'

'He is with my friend this morning. Pray do not worry, Miss Wentworth. Davy will take no harm for an hour or two.'

'Then, Aunt?' Perdita looked a question.

'Yes, send for the Runner, my dear. There is no time to lose.'

Chapter Fourteen

When the man returned he questioned their visitor for so long that Perdita grew alarmed.

'This lady is not well,' she protested. 'You are tiring her beyond endurance.'

Mrs Tarrant waved aside the protest. 'I feel much better, ma'am. Pray do not concern yourself. I'd like to help in any way I can.'

Perdita eyed her closely. The small amount of food she had eaten seemed to have revived her. Now she was able to answer the Runner's questions clearly and without prevarication.

The man's smile saluted her courage. 'Thank you, madam. You are a vital witness. May I ask if you are willing to give evidence on oath?'

Mrs Tarrant nodded. 'Yes, I shall tell the truth.'

'Then, ladies, I shall leave you for the moment. Matters must be set in train. We have already searched out quarry's rooms at the Saracen's Head without success.'

'Did you not need a warrant?' Perdita looked surprised.

The man closed one eye in an elaborate wink.

'Chambermaids can be obliging, miss, and if a certain door is left ajar it don't take above a few minutes for experienced men to look about them. Course, that won't apply to searching the shop premises. For that we'll need the magistrate's permission.'

'His lordship will see to that,' Perdita told him. 'Can you return this evening? The Earl will be back by then.'

'Yes, ma'am. Thanks to this lady we have some news for him at last.' He bowed himself out of the room.

Mrs Tarrant too was ready to leave.

'How shall we ever be able to thank you, ma'am?' Miss Langrishe wiped away a tear. 'I had almost given up hope of seeing any happy outcome to these wicked charges. Mrs Tarrant, I know that your life is hard. Will you not let us help you?' She reached into her reticule.

'Not money, ma'am, I beg of you.' Mrs Tarrant flushed.

'Why ever not? You have a son, I believe. You could make his life more comfortable.'

Their visitor shook her head again. Then Perdita intervened.

'Mrs Tarrant is right, Aunt Trixie. To offer money might be construed as bribery, but there can be no objection to sending Davy a few small luxuries.' She turned to the embarrassed woman again. 'Do say you will accept them,' she coaxed. 'Your son will enjoy them, will he not?'

Mrs Tarrant caught her hand. 'You are too good,' she said in a broken voice. 'My child has cried from hunger, and it broke my heart to be able to give him nothing.'

'Then come with me!' Perdita led her to the kitchens, and there she filled a basket to overflowing with cold fowl, a joint of beef, a piece of ham and a large fruit pie.

Mrs Tarrant raised a hand in smiling protest. 'No more, Miss Wentworth, if you please. This is enough food to feed us for a week, and I am grateful to you.'

'Don't speak of gratitude, ma'am. We shall be always in your debt. Now give me your direction. The Earl will wish to see you. You may be sure of it.'

Miss Langrishe was lost in thought when Perdita returned.

'I have been wondering if we should expedite matters,' she announced. 'Shall I invite the magistrate to dine with us this evening? It would not seem unusual. Frederick dines here often in the ordinary way.'

'With respect, Aunt Trixie, I believe that it would not be wise just now. He is involved in Louise's case. It might be seen as an attempt to influence him.

'I suppose so.' Miss Langrishe sighed. 'Oh dear, how I wish that Adam might have chosen another day to go to Ilchester. He will know what to do.'

'He will, and at least we have splendid news for him. I can't wait for his return. If only the hours would pass more quickly...'

As the day wore on, she ran to the window a dozen times to catch a first glimpse of his coach. When it arrived at last she flew down the stairs, and, regardless of the curious glances of passers-by, she seized his hand and almost dragged him into the hall.

His eyes began to twinkle. 'What a welcome!' he teased. 'Am I to believe that you have missed me?'

'Come into the salon,' she urged. 'And you, too, Amy. So much has happened whilst you've been away.'

'You do not ask about Louise.' Amy spoke in a low voice. 'Oh, Dita, she is so crushed in spirit. She has lost all hope.'

'But she must not do so! That is what I want to tell you!' Perdita hurried them through to greet her aunt. 'We have such a story for you. Aunt, will you tell it, or shall I?'

'You had best do so, my dear. You have been bursting with excitement since this morning and I fear you may explode.'

Perdita laughed. Then she rushed to give them an account of the day's events, speaking so quickly that a childhood stutter returned to trouble her.

Adam cast aside his cloak and slipped an arm about her waist, drawing her to sit beside him on the sofa.

'Slow down, my darling!' he advised. 'This is all good news indeed. Can there be more?'

'Oh, yes! The Runner is coming back tonight, but he must get a w-w-warrant from the magistrate.' Perdita looked at the faces of her companions and in their expressions she saw growing hope.

'Oh, Adam, they must release Louise,' she cried. 'Don't you agree?'

'We may have to wait for a time,' he said cautiously. 'We have only Mrs Tarrant's word that the lace was placed in Louise's reticule. It may be thought that she has made the accusation in revenge for being dismissed.'

'You would not say so if you had met her,' Perdita cried hotly. 'And what of Verreker? He told me that he had never visited the shop. Amy will bear witness to that. Why is he living in a secret room?'

'There is no law against it, dearest. You say that his room at the Saracen's Head holds nothing suspicious.'

'So the Bow Street Runner said.'

'Then the room above the shop is our best hope. When I have seen the man I will visit the magistrate. If the case against Verreker is promising we may get the warrant to search the premises.'

'Oh, Adam, I felt so sure...' Perdita could not hide her disappointment.

'Patience, my love! You are right in all respects, but we are dealing with a slippery customer. He will take advantage of a single loophole in the law and we must not lose him now.'

Perdita could only agree.

However, Perdita did not rest until Adam returned late that night with the promised warrant.

'Satisfied?' He showed her the document. 'Now we must hope that the Runners find evidence.'

'When will they search?'

'Tomorrow. Verreker is in the habit of visiting the Pump Room in a morning, doubtless searching for another gullible victim. They will seize the opportunity to surprise the owners of the shop.'

'He spoke of jewellery, too.' Perdita reminded him with an anxious look. 'He said it was too dangerous to sell it at present.'

'That is our best hope, my love. The Runners have a description of the pieces. They need only find a single stolen item if they are to charge him. I would stake a handsome bet that his ill-gotten gains are in that secret room.'

'I hope you may be right.' Perdita rested her head against his shoulder. 'I thought it would be so easy to get Louise released. Now, it seems, we are still beset with difficulties.'

Adam kissed her very gently. 'They will be overcome,' he assured her. 'I promise that by noon tomorrow you will be easier in your mind.'

Perdita raised her face to him. 'I believe you,' she said softly. 'Oh, my love, you are my rock. How should I ever live without you?'

'You need never do so, my dearest.' His mouth came down on hers and she was swept away on a dizzing tide of passion as his warm lips claimed her own. She was breathless when he released her but he continued to rain kisses on her eyes, her cheeks, the corners of her mouth and the tip of her nose.

'Go away, you temptress!' he exclaimed at last. 'You would seduce a saint, and I am no saint...'

'Why, sir, you shock me!'

Adam saw the laughter in her eyes and tried to grab her as she danced away from him, but Perdita was too quick. Still laughing, she fled for the safety of her room, though it went much against the grain to leave him.

An unknown longing seized her. Their love was incomplete, she knew that well enough, but it was hard to wait for true fulfilment. Now she prayed that the months would fly until her parents returned. Only then would she be able to wed her love.

Amy was waiting for her. 'Did Adam get the warrant?' she asked eagerly.

'Yes. The men will search tomorrow. I pray that they may be successful.'

'So do I. Louise is at the end of her tether. You

would not care to see her looking so…so resigned. She
seemed like a stranger to me.'

'That will change,' Perdita comforted her. 'Let us
see what tomorrow brings…'

It was better news than they had hoped. Verreker
had been taken as he left the Pump Room, charged
with the theft of a diamond necklace, sundry brooches,
and two valuable bracelets.

It was enough to persuade the magistrate to reconsider his decision to prosecute Louise.

He gave orders that the prisoner be returned to Bath,
under arrest, where he could re-examine the case
against her.

'There is no direct connection with the alleged theft
of the lace,' he explained to Adam. 'But I have heard
enough to have my doubts about the owners of the
shop. Will you present yourselves at a hearing in three
days' time?'

'And Miss Bryant?'

'Will be released into your custody, my lord. Remember, you are surety for her!'

Adam nodded his thanks. He had said nothing to
Perdita, but he too had been worried about Louise's
state of mind. The girl was a shadow of her former
self. She was silent, biddable, but seemingly with no
will of her own. She could not be persuaded to discuss
the case, even to proclaim her innocence.

'She looks as if she has gazed into the pit!' Amy
was in despair. 'Will the magistrate take her silence
as proof of guilt?' She tried to curb her growing anger.
'Louise should not have been sent to Ilchester. Why
could he not have left her in Adam's care before this?

The experience has scared her. I doubt that she will ever be the same…'

'He can do so now because we have new evidence,' Adam told her.

'And Louise will recover her spirits,' Miss Langrishe added. 'The young are resilient. Just give her time. Then she will think of this as a bad dream.'

'But only if we are successful.' Amy resumed her pacing of the room. Then she stopped in front of Adam and faced him squarely. 'What if aught should go wrong?' she demanded. 'Will you spirit her away? You cannot let her be transported.'

'She will not be transported,' he told her firmly. 'Don't cross your bridges before you come to them, my dear. Let us wait for the hearing.'

To everyone at Laura Place it seemed an age before that day arrived, but three days later those connected with her case met at the Magistrate's Court.

'This is not a trial,' he explained at once. 'But new evidence has come to hand, and I intend to make sure that there is no miscarriage of justice in this case before committing the prisoner to the Assizes.' He looked about his court until eye rested upon the owner of the shop who was sitting beside his son.

'Well, Joshua Keay, have you anything to add to your previous evidence against the prisoner?'

'I stand by every word of it,' Keay insisted. 'What I should like to know is why this person is present here today?' He pointed to where Verreker sat, flanked by a couple of Bow Street Runners. 'This case is no concern of his.'

'You seem very sure of that,' the magistrate told him smoothly. 'Perhaps he is well known to you?'

'I never set eyes on him before this day.' Keay glared at his quietly spoken questioner.

'Strange! The items which he is alleged to have stolen were found upon your premises, hidden beneath a floorboard in a private room.'

'That is naught to do with me, I've been away, sir. Bath is overcrowded, as you may know. Sometimes visitors beg us for accommodation as a favour. We have no way of knowing their past history.'

'And your son was equally unaware of the presence of this person upon your premises?'

'Speak up, Jem!' Keay glanced in irritation at his son.

'No, sir...I mean, yes, I did not know of it...I was with my father...' The young man went red and white by turns.

'So your staff are at liberty to let accommodation without your knowledge? You are very trusting, sir.'

The sneering tone was not lost on Keay. He shot a malignant look at the magistrate, but that gentleman was unaware of it. He was signalling to the usher.

The Keays stiffened as Mrs Tarrant was led into the room, and Perdita glanced at Matthew Verreker. He had been lolling back, apparently at ease and untroubled by the presence of the guards. Now his hands betrayed him. He clenched them until the knuckles went white.

Once Mrs Tarrant's identity had been established, the magistrate began to question her.

'I must ask you, madam, do you know anyone in this room?'

'Yes, sir. I know the Earl of Rushmore and the ladies. Mr Keay was until recently my employer. I know his son, of course, and the young man's friend, who is sitting over there.' She pointed to Matthew Verreker.

'It's a lie!' Jem Keay was on his feet. 'I do not know this man. He is no friend of mine.'

His father managed an ingratiating smile. 'Pay no attention to her, sir!' He addressed the magistrate direct. 'This woman was dismissed for theft and insolence. This is her way of taking her revenge—'

'Silence!' the magistrate thundered. 'I'll have no further interruptions!' He turned back to Mrs Tarrant. 'Now, ma'am, since it was your evidence which led to the recovery of certain stolen items, will you tell us how you came by this information?'

Mrs Tarrant was pale but composed as she began to speak. 'I had gone up to the storeroom at the shop, sir. I could hear voices, which surprised me as there seemed to be no one in the room apart from myself. Then a panel slid aside and I could see into the room beyond. Mr Jem Keay and his friend were quarrelling about a sale of jewellery—'

'All lies!' Jem Keay's voice rose to a shriek. 'What has this to do with the charges against the Bryant woman?'

'We shall come to that in time, young man.' The magistrate's expression was stern. 'You deny again that you know this man?' He pointed to Verreker.

'I do!' came the sullen reply.

'Then how could Mrs Tarrant have known about the items hidden in the room unless she had overheard your conversation? Your unknown lodger would not, I imagine, have been talking to himself.'

'She's a thief! She could have put them there herself.'

'But she did not know of this room. I believe the

entrance is so well concealed that the Runners had some difficulty in discovering it.'

'She's sly! Who is to know what she finds when she is poking about in secret?'

'What, indeed? Now we know that Matthew Verreker has been living upon your premises. You claim that this was without your knowledge?'

'I do.' Jem was at pains not to look in Verreker's direction. 'Mrs Tarrant must have let the room to him.'

'This sly creature had the authority to do so in your absence?' Everyone in the room was aware of the magistrate's disbelief. 'Indeed, you do surprise me!'

He began to shuffle his papers. 'Now we shall come to the charges against Miss Bryant. You have given us fresh evidence, Mrs Tarrant. Will you please repeat it to this court?'

'The young lady fell into a trap,' she said. 'She had left her reticule open upon the counter whilst she was purchasing some ribbons. I saw Jem Keay slip the lace inside. Later, he followed her into the street and asked if she would look for it. There were a number of witnesses... Then he asked for her direction.'

'Why do you listen to her?' Jem Keay shouted wildly. 'Will you take her word? Can't you see that she is trying to destroy us?'

Joshua Keay placed a restraining hand on his son's shoulder. Then he rounded upon the magistrate.

'It is one person's word against another,' he snarled. 'Have you proof which will stand up in a court of law?'

'Why, yes, I believe we have!' He looked at the Earl of Rushmore. 'My lord, will you tell us what happened next?'

'We received a letter,' Adam said. 'The writer offered to drop the charges against Miss Bryant in return for a settlement.'

'You did not pay?'

'No, sir. I regarded it as a cheap attempt at blackmail.'

'And you have this letter still?'

'I have it here.' Adam produced the letter from his pocket.

The magistrate smoothed it out with every appearance of satisfaction. 'And here we have some accounts made out to certain customers of the shop owned by Mr Keay.' He bent to examine the papers on the desk before him.

'Jem Keay, you will approach the bench,' he said as he held up a slip of paper. 'This is signed by you. Will you confirm it as your writing?'

'I don't know!' Jem's eyes darted about the room and settled upon his father as he begged for reassurance.

'You do not recognise your own hand? I must disbelieve you. Now, young man, cast your eyes upon this note! The likenesses in the characters are impossible to ignore, are they not?'

Jem cracked then. He swung round screaming as he looked at Matthew Verreker. 'You devil! You made me write it, didn't you, to keep your own hands clean?'

Then his father was beside him. 'Be quiet, you fool!' he hissed. 'Will you condemn yourself out of your own mouth?'

'I won't swing for him!' Jem was beyond control. 'He is the one who planned the whole. We were to share…he promised…'

One of the Runners was already out of his seat,

ready to restrain the hysterical figure, but no one was prepared for what happened next.

Verreker moved with the speed of a striking snake. In a single movement he caught the remaining Runner in a choking grip, seizing the man's pistol with his other hand.

'Stand back!' he ordered in a pleasant tone. 'I doubt if any of you will care to have this man's blood upon our hands, and I shall not hesitate to kill him if I must.'

Slowly he backed towards the door at the rear of the court, dragging his captive with him.

'He goes with me,' he continued lightly. 'Try to follow and you will find a corpse.'

'Give it up, man!' Adam began to move towards Verreker and his captive. 'You can't escape, and this will make things worse for you.'

Verreker's harsh laugh echoed around the room. 'Stay where you are, my lord, and spare us your heroics. Worse, you say? I think not. You, above anyone, have ruined all my plans. It would be a pleasure to kill you, and I am strongly tempted, but you shall not persuade me into wasting a shot.'

He paled as Adam continued to advance on him.

'Stand back!' he screamed. 'If you take another step, I'll put a shot into this fellow's brain.'

Adam smiled and shook his head, but he did not stop.

Verreker's face was a mask of indecision. As he had threatened, he could fire at the Runner, but Adam was likely to prove the greater danger. With a grunt of satisfaction he levelled the pistol and fired.

The shot took Adam in the shoulder, halting him in mid-stride. With a cry of horror Perdita flew to him, gazing in anguish at the spreading stain upon his sleeve. She looked up at Verreker.

'I'll kill you for this,' she promised.

'You may try, Miss Wentworth, though I doubt if you'll succeed.' Verreker was smiling as he looked at her. 'It is a flesh wound only, I believe. Such a pity! I was aiming for the heart!'

'You dog!' Perdita ground her teeth. 'You won't escape the law.'

'Always the warrior, my dear? What an accomplice you would have made, unlike these weaklings whom I took into my confidence.' Verreker cast a withering look upon Keay and his son. 'I should have known that they would crack at the first sign of pressure.'

'You can't get away,' Perdita insisted. 'Give up now, and your case may be reviewed more leniently.'

'I am for the hangman's noose. You may depend on it. Do you suppose that your noble lord here has any other plans for me? Now, Miss Wentworth, let us have no more heroics. Pray do not follow the example of your friend, I beg of you. Your face is quite extraordinary. It would be a pity to reduce so much beauty to a mass of pulp and a few slivers of bone.'

Perdita ignored him. She was looking at the flow of blood which poured steadily from Adam's wound.

'It isn't as bad as it looks,' he whispered quietly. 'Stand away from me, my love! That pistol holds but two shots and he has wasted one of them. If I could but persuade him to fire again...' His eyes told her that he was in mortal fear for her safety, but she rose and rounded on Verreker.

'I'll strike a bargain with you,' she announced. 'I can't allow his lordship to bleed to death. Give me your cravat to staunch the flow and I will help you.'

She was well aware that she must hold Verreker's attention, and if, possible, give Adam the opportunity to reach him. Her heart misgave her. Just how badly was Adam injured? He knew well enough that she might lose him, but the firm pressure of his hand stilled all her fears.

Verreker nodded in quick appreciation of her words. 'I have to hand it to you, madam. You are worth fifty of that milk-and-water miss I planned to wed. Here!' He snatched at the snowy linen about his throat and threw it to her.

It fell short and Perdita moved towards him, but he backed away, still holding his gun against the Runner's temple.

'No tricks!' he warned as he edged towards the door. 'I shall not hesitate to shoot, and my next shot will be fatal. Now, ma'am, how do you propose to help me?'

Perdita was trembling and her mouth was dust-dry, but her main emotion was one of fury. Verreker must not be allowed to get away, but she could not think of a plan to stop him. He was now too far away from her to give her the chance to stumble against him, but even if she had been able to do so she would have put the Runner's life at risk, to say nothing of her own.

She stared at him helplessly, hating the smirk of triumph on his lips. How many other lives would he go on to ruin, she wondered? Beside her Amy's face was the picture of outrage, and Louise had fainted. It was then that the door behind him opened, and Thomas burst into the room. For the moment he did not understand what was happening in the court.

'Where is she?' he shouted. 'What have you done with Louise?'

Startled by the intruder, Verreker dropped his guard for just an instant, but it was enough for Adam. Even with his left arm hanging useless, he moved with astonishing speed, knocking the pistol aside, and using a strong right hook to connect with Verreker's jaw. The man fell like a sack of coals.

Then pandemonium reigned as the Runners hurried to secure him and his two accomplices. Perdita saw nothing of it. She was on her knees beside Louise, trying, with Amy's help, to restore her friend to consciousness.

Thomas thrust them both aside and gathered Louise to him. She opened her eyes and gave him a loving look.

'Oh, Thomas, I have been so frightened,' she whispered.

'That is all over, my dearest. You will never be frightened again.' He picked her up and looked at Adam. 'Where is your carriage, my lord?' he asked stiffly.

'It is waiting. Do you go ahead to Laura Place with the ladies.' Adam was swaying on his feet. 'Perhaps you might request the services of a surgeon for me?'

'You are injured, sir?' Thomas softened his tone.

'Merely a scratch, I believe, but the ball should be removed…'

'I see. Well, sir, Louise must be my first concern, but I shall wish to speak to you later.'

'I'm sure you will!' Rushmore grimaced as he looked at Thomas's retreating back. The boy had a right to be furious with him. Louise might so easily have been killed. As a guardian he had fallen far short of his own high standards.

Then a soft hand slipped into his own. 'Don't blame yourself!' Perdita said. 'You saved her in the end.'

Adam took her in his arms. 'You should go back with the others, my love. This has been a terrible ordeal for you. I wonder that you did not faint when Verreker threatened you. I confess that I was terrified for you.'

Perdita lifted her face to his and her eyes were twinkling.

'Why, sir, I did not dare,' she told him. 'I recalled that you have no time for missish vapourings...'

'You are a wonder!' he said fervently. 'I don't know what I have done to deserve you. Come, my love, let us see the magistrate. I believe that the charges against Louise will be dismissed.'

He was right. Jem Keay was already babbling out his evidence faster than the Runner could record it, in an effort to save his own skin.

'And Verreker?' Perdita was anxious to know the fate of her adversary.

'He will either hang or be transported, Miss Wentworth. Either way he will no longer be a danger to society.'

'I am glad of it.' Perdita held out her hand. 'My aunt is hoping that you will dine with her at Laura Place, sir. Will that be possible, do you suppose?'

'It will be my pleasure, ma'am. This case will go to the Assizes. It is now out of my jurisdiction.'

'Come, Perdita!'' Adam took her arm. 'Your aunt will be awaiting you. Shall we walk back to Laura Place?'

The sun was shining when they reached the street, and as they strolled along in the balmy air the world seemed a better place. Perdita felt that a dreadful weight had been lifted from her shoulders.

'I can't believe that it is really over,' she said softly. 'Now we have nothing more to worry us...'

'Speak for yourself, my darling!' Adam gave a wry smile. 'I suspect that I am in for a most unpleasant interview with young Thomas.'

His suspicions were well founded. They saw Thomas sitting outside Louise's room, his head in his hands, and slipped away to wait for him.

'Well done, miss!' The physician patted her hand as he finished his task. 'You have been brave. I would guess you to be a soldier's daughter.'

Louise gave him a misty smile, but she was looking beyond him towards the door.

'I'll send the young man in,' the physician said. 'But you must rest, my dear. I have prescribed a sedative, but you must not let him tire you.'

'He won't do that.' Louise sighed with content as she rested her head against the pillow. 'He is always so gentle with me.'

She spoke no more than the truth. Thomas approached her as if she might shatter to fragments before his eyes. She lifted a hand to wipe a stray tear from his cheek.

'I am stronger than you think,' she whispered. 'You must not worry so.'

He bent his head and kissed her hands, but speech was beyond him. He sat motionless for several minutes until she drifted into sleep. Then he went to find the Earl.

He walked in upon a family gathering. Miss Langrishe was seated with the girls, whilst Adam explained that the charges against Louise had been dropped.

Thomas stalked over to him. 'Can you spare me a moment in private, sir?' he said.

'I can spare you all the time you need to give me a dressing-down, Thomas, but it need not be in private. I am well aware of my shortcomings. Whatever opinion you have of me, it cannot be worse than my own.'

'I am glad you think so, sir. Let me tell you that your role as a guardian leaves much to be desired. Louise has been neglected and today she was almost killed. Good God, sir! Imprisonment...humiliation...what else will you let her suffer?'

'Stop!' Perdita was on her feet at once. 'How dare you, Thomas? We have been dealing with a man who would stop at nothing to gain his ends. Adam saved our lives today. You might remember that!'

'Perdita is right, my boy!' Miss Langrishe said gently. 'No one could have known the depths to which this man would sink. We were all outwitted...but Adam did his best to ensure Louise's safety.'

'Without too much success, I fear!' Thomas was still smouldering with rage.

'Don't be such a gooby, coz!' Amy said inelegantly. 'Must we have a family feud? Adam is to wed Perdita, and you, no doubt, will offer for Louise. May we not be friends again?'

'Well, sir, may I offer for Louise?' Thomas gave the Earl a belligerent stare.

Adam's smile lit up the room. 'With my blessing, Thomas. Indeed, I hoped that you would do so.' He held out his hand.

Thomas was nonplussed. He had expected opposition...an argument...an outright refusal. Now his dearest wish was to be granted. A surge of happiness overwhelmed him.

'Well, that's all right then!' He took the proffered hand and beamed upon the assembled company. 'I must tell Louise. How long shall I wait? I must not wake her, I suppose.'

A chorus of protest answered him until abashed, he returned to sit by Louise's bed until his love should wake.

Perdita stole a look at her aunt's face. Miss Langrishe looked exhausted. The events of the morning had taken their toll, and now reaction was setting in.

Amy caught her sister's eye and nodded. 'Aunt, will you not rest for an hour or two?' she coaxed. 'Perhaps, when we dine tonight, we may allow ourselves a celebration. After all, we have much to celebrate today, and you will wish to enjoy it to the full.'

'You are right, my dear.' Miss Langrishe allowed herself to be helped from the room.

Adam turned to Perdita. 'And what of you, my darling? Do you also wish to rest?'

'Great heavens, no!' Perdita beamed at him. 'This has been an adventure! Just think! If I had gone to Gibraltar I should have missed it!'

'Fraud and lies and attempted murder, Perdita? In our future life together I shall be hard put to provide you with enough excitement, but I shall try.' He was laughing down at her.

She gave him a wicked look. 'I'm sure you will succeed, my lord, though I can't think how.'

'I shall have to prove it to you before too long. How soon may we be married?'

Perdita nestled happily against his chest. 'As soon as my parents return to England. It is late autumn now, and they return in early spring. Of course, by then I may have changed my mind...'

'About what?'

She heard the anxiety in his tone and chuckled to herself.

'Why, sir, about becoming a Countess. You cannot be surprised. After all, it was you who told me that I had no hope of doing so. An ape-leader was the term you used, I think.'

'Why, you little minx, am I never to live that evening down?'

'I hope you will remember it for all your life, my love.' Perdita's eyes were shining. 'It was the night we met. I, for one, will never forget it.'

'Nor I!' He kissed her then, and they were lost at once in a world which promised nothing but happiness for the future.

* * * * *

Look out for the next title from Meg Alexander,
The Matchmaker's Marriage, *available from*
The Regency Lords and Ladies Collection
in February 2009.

The Regency

LORDS & LADIES
COLLECTION

More Glittering Regency Love Affairs

VOLUME THIRTY

Dear Deceiver by Mary Nichols

Dominic could be certain Emma had been lying to him. He wasn't even sure that Emma Woodhill was her real name. So why was he so attracted to her when he was already engaged to someone else? Still, Dominic was determined to discover the truth and give Emma *all* the help she needed…

The Matchmaker's Marriage by Meg Alexander

Despite admonitions to be discreet, Amy Wentworth had never learned to hold her tongue! But it was her good nature which led Miss Charlotte to take Amy under her wing – and try to find her a husband. But could Charlotte convince her good friend Sir James Richmond that Amy was the one he wanted?

On sale 6th February 2009

www.millsandboon.co.uk

M&B

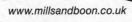

The Regency

LORDS & LADIES

COLLECTION

More Glittering Regency Love Affairs

Volume 17 – 4th January 2008
One Night with a Rake by Louise Allen
The Dutiful Rake by Elizabeth Rolls

Volume 18 – 1st February 2008
A Matter of Honour by Anne Herries
The Chivalrous Rake by Elizabeth Rolls

Volume 19 – 7th March 2008
Tavern Wench by Anne Ashley
The Incomparable Countess by Mary Nichols

Volume 20 – 4th April 2008
Prudence by Elizabeth Bailey
Lady Lavinia's Match by Mary Nichols

Volume 21 – 2nd May 2008
The Rebellious Bride by Francesca Shaw
The Duke's Mistress by Ann Elizabeth Cree

Volume 22 – 6th June 2008
Carnival of Love by Helen Dickson
The Viscount's Bride by Ann Elizabeth Cree

Volume 23 – 4th July 2008
One Night of Scandal & *The Rake's Mistress*
by Nicola Cornick

M&B

The Regency

LORDS & LADIES
COLLECTION

More Glittering Regency Love Affairs

Volume 24 – 1st August 2008
The Reluctant Marchioness by Anne Ashley
Nell by Elizabeth Bailey

Volume 25 – 5th September 2008
Kitty by Elizabeth Bailey
Major Chancellor's Mission by Paula Marshall

Volume 26 – 3rd October 2008
Lord Hadleigh's Rebellion by Paula Marshall
The Sweet Cheat by Meg Alexander

Volume 27 – 7th November 2008
Lady Sarah's Son by Gayle Wilson
Wedding Night Revenge by Mary Brendan

Volume 28 – 5th December 2008
Rake's Reward by Joanna Maitland
The Unknown Wife by Mary Brendan

Volume 29 – 2nd January 2009
Miss Verey's Proposal by Nicola Cornick
The Rebellious Débutante by Meg Alexander

Volume 30 – 6th February 2009
Dear Deceiver by Mary Nichols
The Matchmaker's Marriage by Meg Alexander

"To say that I met Nicholas Brisbane over my husband's dead body is not entirely accurate. Edward, it should be noted, was still twitching upon the floor…"

London, 1886

For Lady Julia Grey, her husband's sudden death at a dinner party is extremely inconvenient. However, things worsen when inscrutable private investigator Nicholas Brisbane reveals that the death was not due to natural causes.

Drawn away from her comfortable, conventional life, Julia is exposed to threatening notes, secret societies and gypsy curses, not to mention Nicholas's charismatic unpredictability.

"There is a dead man stinking in the game larder. I hardly think a few missing pearls will be the ruin of this house party."

England, 1887

Christmas festivities at Bellmont Abbey are brought to an abrupt halt by a murder in the chapel. Blood dripping from her hands, Lady Julia Grey's cousin claims the ancient right of sanctuary.

Forced to resume her deliciously intriguing partnership with the enigmatic detective Nicholas Brisbane, Lady Julia is intent on proving her cousin's innocence. Still, the truth is rarely pure and never simple…

Available 19th December 2008

www.mirabooks.co.uk

MIRA

Love is the most tempting betrayal of all…

Scotland, 1561

By trying to help the reckless, defiant Mary, Queen of Scots take her rightful place on the throne, Lady Gwenyth Macleod is at perilous odds with Rowan Graham, a laird accomplished in both passion and affairs of state.

The more Gwenyth challenges his intentions, the less he can resist the desire igniting between them. But will Gwenyth's last daring gamble lead her to the ultimate betrayal – or a destiny greater than she could ever imagine?

Available 16th January 2009

*Immerse yourself in the glitter of
Regency times through the lives
and romantic escapades of the
Lester family*

Jack Lester had every reason to hide the news of
his recently acquired fortune: he wanted an
attractive, capable bride who would accept him
for himself, not for his new-found riches.

But he had to make his choice before the society
matrons discovered the Lester family were no
longer as poor as church mice. He must convince
Sophie, the woman of his dreams, to
marry him as poor Jack Lester.

*Immerse yourself in the glitter of
Regency times through the lives
and romantic escapades of the
Lester family*

Now the news was out that the Lester family
fortunes had been repaired, Harry Lester knew the
society matrons would soon be in pursuit, so he
promptly left London for Newmarket.

Fate, however, proved more far-sighted, having
arranged for a distraction in the person of
Mrs Lucinda Babbacombe. Lucinda is a beautiful,
provocative but unwilling conquest – who
to Harry's irritation cannot be ignored.

MIRA

Immerse yourself in the glitter of Regency times through the lives and romantic escapades of the Lester family

Miss Antonia Mannering and Lord Philip Ruthven had been childhood friends who had not seen each other for years. And although considered a very eligible bachelor, Philip remained unmarried.

With Philip's close friend Harry Lester recently married, Antonia only hopes that she can convince Philip of the bliss marriage brings, that she can run his home and not disgrace him in Society. But is Philip ready to set up his nursery… with Antonia as his wife?

The much-anticipated finale to the
Moreland quartet!

London, 1879

Had Theo Moreland, the Marquess of Raine, killed
her brother? American journalist Megan Mulcahey
had to know. But to find out, she needed to
infiltrate the marquess's household.

The new American governess intrigued Theo. Miss
Mulcahey had come to Broughton House to teach
his young siblings. Now the strange pull of their
immediate desire both troubled and excited him.
But why was this delicious vision snooping around
his mansion like a common thief?